SOMETIMES ALL THAT
GLITTERS . . . IS LOVE

Allison looked up into Peter's dark, sensuous eyes and lifted her face to him, inviting his lips, sending a rich message of desire and welcome.

"Oh, Allison, I want you."

"I want you, too," she answered with quiet joy.

She laughed softly as he undressed her, peeling away the clinging silk and delicate lace until she was naked before him.

"You are so beautiful, Allison."

I am beautiful for you, Peter. You make me beautiful. She stood there unashamed, feeling his desire, feeling so special.

Then they were in bed, touching, whispering, exploring, breathless in their wonder and passion and need . . .

BOOK YOUR PLACE ON OUR WEBSITE AND MAKE THE READING CONNECTION!

We've created a customized website just for our very special readers, where you can get the inside scoop on everything that's going on with Zebra, Pinnacle and Kensington books.

When you come online, you'll have the exciting opportunity to:

- View covers of upcoming books
- Read sample chapters
- Learn about our future publishing schedule (listed by publication month *and author*)
- Find out when your favorite authors will be visiting a city near you
- Search for and order backlist books from our online catalog
- Check out author bios and background information
- Send e-mail to your favorite authors
- Meet the Kensington staff online
- Join us in weekly chats with authors, readers and other guests
- Get writing guidelines
- AND MUCH MORE!

**Visit our website at
http://www.zebrabooks.com**

BEL AIR

KATHERINE STONE

Zebra Books
Kensington Publishing Corp.

http://www.zebrabooks.com

ZEBRA BOOKS

are published by

Kensington Publishing Corp.
850 Third Avenue
New York, NY 10022

10 9 8

Printed in the United States of America

Part One

Chapter One

Los Angeles, California
June, 1984

"Allison! I'm so glad you haven't left yet!"

"Hello, Meg." Allison smiled at the familiar drama in her friend's breathless voice. Virtually everything in Meg Montgomery's life was an "event"; it had always been that way. Of course, today actually qualified. Today Meg was getting married. Allison guessed calmly, "Is there a problem?"

"Yes! Jerome Cole just called. Apparently he is deathly— no, not deathly—*incapacitatingly* ill. Food poisoning or something."

Allison frowned slightly, a begrudging acknowledgement that this was at least a bit of a "situation." Jerome Cole was *the* wedding photographer for Los Angeles's wealthiest brides—brides like Meg and Allison. For the heiresses of Bel Air and Beverly Hills, a gold leaf album filled with photographs by Jerome Cole was as much a wedding staple as Mendelssohn's March, pearl-studded satin gowns, five-tiered cakes, and fountains of champagne.

There certainly are other perfectly good photographers in Los Angeles, Allison mused. But on this day, the third Saturday in June, all other good photographers would be booked. Not that the pictures mattered, not *really*, Allison thought. But Meg was so excited, so much in love, so hope-

7

ful that every detail of her fairy-tale wedding would be perfect. The pictures didn't matter, but, still, it was too bad. . . .

"Jerome has an assistant," Meg continued while Allison was searching for a way to convince her friend that this was not, in fact, the end of the world. "And she is available."

"Oh! Good."

"Allison, I wondered if you could give her a ride? She doesn't have a car! And I don't want to worry about a cab getting lost."

"Of course I'll give her a ride, Meg."

"Great. Thanks. I think she lives quite near you. She has a basement apartment in a house on Montana and Twentieth in Santa Monica." Meg gave Allison the street address and asked, "Is that close?"

"Very. Only about five blocks away."

"Good. Her name is Emily Something-that-sounds-French. She doesn't sound French, though. I just talked to her. She'll be ready at three-twenty. Is that OK?"

"Absolutely. Meg, this is all going to be fine. It's such a perfect day for a wedding." Allison added, forcing enthusiasm, "I'm really looking forward to it."

I'm not really looking forward to it, Allison thought as she replaced the receiver.

Only a month ago, Allison had been planning her own wedding. Only a month ago, she had reconfirmed the Saturday afternoon date in September with Jerome, who would take the pictures; with Francois, who would provide the cut flowers, boutonniers, and corsages; with Wolfgang, who would prepare the rehearsal dinner at Spago; and with Martin, who promised that, as with Meg's wedding, the Bel Air Hunt Club would be Allison's for the entire day . . . the entire *night* if she wanted it.

Two weeks ago Allison had called them all, apologetically, to cancel. *Cancel,* not reschedule. The marriage of Allison Fitzgerald and Daniel Forester was not going to happen, not in September, not ever.

It was your decision, Allison reminded herself. *Your* decision. At the moment, the emotions and thoughts that had guided her with such apparent ease to the momentous decision were in hiding, taking with them the buoyant confidence Allison needed to counterbalance the sudden heavy weight of doubt.

Allison glanced at her watch. It was only three o'clock. She could leave at three-fifteen and still reach Emily's apartment before three-twenty. Allison could spend the next fifteen minutes thinking—stewing—about Dan, or she could call Winter, her best friend.

It was an easy choice.

"Meg must be in a tailspin!" Winter exclaimed after Allison told her about Jerome.

"Actually, she sounded surprisingly calm. This crisis probably distracted her from all the usual wedding day anxieties."

"There's still an hour left before the wedding. Plenty of time for a few more mini-dramas."

"True. I just hope everything goes all right."

"So do I. And it will. It should be a fabulous party, not to mention an interesting one." Winter elaborated merrily, "Connecticut's bluest-bloods and Wall Street's wiliest wizards mingling among the roses with Hollywood's glitziest and Rodeo's ultra-chic and—"

"Winter! I'm afraid the East Coast blue-bloods and financiers are going to be underrepresented, except for Cameron's family."

"*Daahling*," Winter whispered with mock horror and an elegant upper crust accent, "they don't approve of Meg Montgomery of Bel Air?"

"Of course they do, to the tune of many parties, galas, and receptions in honor of the newlyweds beginning the second they arrive in New York."

"Oh. So it will just be the usual group?" Winter sighed theatrically.

"I'm afraid so," Allison commiserated gaily. Just the usual group. Just four hundred of the richest and most famous men and women in Southern California.

"I've got to go," Winter said, suddenly realizing the time.

9

"I'm not quite ready and Mark should be here in five minutes."

"Mark?"

"Mark. He's a third year medical student at UCLA. I met him in the Sculpture Garden Thursday evening, during my sentimental stroll around campus."

"And you're taking him to Meg's wedding?" *At the Club?*

"Why not? You'll sit with us at the ceremony, won't you?"

"Yes. Of course."

Mark looked at the street address he had hastily written in the margin of his neuroanatomy class notes, memorized it, and left his apartment on Manning Avenue five minutes before he was to pick her up. Holman Avenue was quite close and quite familiar. During his first year of medical school, Mark had dated a law student who lived in an apartment on Holman.

Mark knew Holman Avenue existed and was a plausible address for a student. But what about Winter Carlyle? Did the remarkable woman with the implausible name actually exist? Winter Carlyle was not listed in the phone book, and directory assistance either couldn't or *wouldn't* provide a number.

Winter Carlyle was a mirage, pure and simple, a vision of violet and velvet and ivory that had danced in his memory for the past two days, ever since she had vanished as mysteriously as she had appeared.

"Are you a neurosurgeon?" she had asked, startling him with the question, the surprising interruption, and *her.*

"I beg your pardon?"

"Are you a neurosurgeon?" She gestured gracefully to the *Textbook of Neurosurgery* that lay beside him on the grass.

Mark was studying. He had chosen a patch of grass in the Sculpture Garden on the UCLA campus, preferring the warmth and light of the early evening sun over the shadowy heat of his small apartment or the air-conditioned chilliness of the Health Sciences Library. The campus was virtually deserted during the recess before Summer Quarter. Until that moment, Mark had been alone amidst the silent bronze statues.

"No, I'm not a neurosurgeon."

"May I look at your book?"

"Sure."

"Thank you."

Before Mark could stand, Winter had floated gracefully onto the grass. She took the heavy textbook he handed to her, turned it facedown on her lap, and opened to the index. She scanned the medical terms, frowning as she searched, then smiling slightly when she found what she sought. She turned eagerly to the text, carefully reading the words; then she frowned again, not satisfied with what she read, returned to the index, and began the process anew.

Mark watched in silent fascination, fascinated by her serious, purposeful search, but mostly fascinated by *her*.

She was stunningly beautiful. Shiny coal-black hair cascaded over her bare shoulders, a sensuous tumble of silky curls, and her skin was the color of rich cream. Her lovely eyes were black-lashed, hypnotic, *violet*, and even during her scholarly search her full, pink lips seduced.

Every movement—her slender arms, her tapered fingers, the thoughtful tilt of her head—was ballerina graceful, elegant, natural. If she was aware of Mark's appreciative gaze, it didn't bother her. Perhaps she expected it.

She is probably quite used to being admired, Mark decided.

So he simply admired her and waited. Finally, she closed the neurosurgery text, gave it a frown laced with disappointment, and sighed.

"Is there something I could help you with?" Mark offered quietly.

"Are you a doctor?"

"I'm a third year medical student. I'll get my degree in a year." Mark wondered if that credential would meet with ap-

11

proval or more disappointment.

"Are you taking a course in neurosurgery?"

"I'm doing a clerkship in Surgery. This month I'm on the Trauma Service. We see quite a bit of emergency neurosurgery, so—"

"So you *do* know about subdural hematomas?"

"Yes." Of course. Subdural hematomas were standard third year medical student fare. But how did she know about them? Why were they so important to the remarkable violet eyes? Who *was* she? "What would you like to know?"

Winter considered Mark's question and finally answered, "Everything, I guess. I have a friend . . ."

"Is he hospitalized at UCLA?" Mark interjected. If she wanted information about a patient, it would be best for her to speak directly with her friend's doctor. Mark could easily arrange that for her.

"He's a she, and she *was* hospitalized at UCLA three years ago. In fact, she was on the Trauma Service." Winter paused. She had very specific questions, but they didn't make sense out of context. "Could I tell you about her accident? Do you have time?"

"Sure."

"Thanks. Well, let's see. Her name is Allison. Until three years ago, what she did every moment she could was ride horses—ride and *jump*. She competed in show jumping—you know, six-foot-high brick walls, green and white railed fences covered with geraniums, that sort of thing. She was champion, really a champion. She was the youngest member of the 1980 U.S. Olympic Equestrian Team; but, of course, she didn't get to go to Moscow because of the boycott. This year was going to be her first chance to compete in the Olympics." Winter paused, sighed softly, and continued quietly, "Three years ago Allison had a terrible accident. It happened on the final fence during a jump-off. Something—a noise, a mouse, the wind, *something*—startled her horse when he was already in midair and she was hurled against the jump."

Winter shuddered at the memory. It should have been

such a triumph for Allison; she had been seconds away from winning the Grand Prix of Los Angeles. But, instead, it was the end of her dreams and the beginning of a nightmare. Winter had been in the grandstand at the Bel Air Hunt Club proudly watching her friend fly over jump after jump. Allison looked so small and delicate on Tuxedo, her elegant champion horse, but her slender arms and legs were very strong. She expertly, invisibly, controlled Tuxedo's immense power, perfectly timing the gait, guiding him over the obstacles swiftly, flawlessly, *happily.*

Allison looked so happy when she rode! Even when she was competing, even when her concentration was intense, her eyes sparkled and her lips curled in a soft smile.

Allison smiled and Allison won. She loved show jumping and she was the best.

"Her horse was uninjured, but Allison . . . She was like a rag doll—limp, lifeless, broken. They rushed her to UCLA, to the Trauma Service, and they did emergency neurosurgery to remove a subdural hematoma. The doctors told us— Allison's parents and me—that a subdural hematoma is a blood clot pressing on the brain."

"That's what it is."

"Could you show me?"

Mark leafed through the neurosurgery text, to pages she had found but hadn't understood, and to new pages that might help her. He started with a colorful drawing of the anatomy of the brain. Mark explained it briefly, then turned to a drawing she had looked at before, one that showed a subdural hematoma and various neurosurgical approaches to its removal.

"Can we go back to the anatomy of the brain?"

When Mark found the page, Winter studied it in thoughtful silence, carefully reading the tiny foreign words and delicately tracing pathways of nerves and veins and arteries with her graceful fingers.

"Different parts of the brain control different things, like memory and vision and movement. Is that right?" she asked after she found a path that connected the back of the brain with the eyes.

"Yes." Mark was impressed that she had deduced that so quickly. He retraced the path she had just discovered and elaborated, "For example, the occipital lobe controls . . ."

Over the next thirty minutes, Winter asked questions and Mark answered them, expanding detail with each answer, amazed at how swiftly she understood, how each question was more insightful and sophisticated than the last. He watched her eyes, serious, thoughtful, widening and narrowing with confusion, enlightenment, confusion again.

"The damage caused by the subdural hematoma would depend on which parts of the brain were compressed," she murmured.

Mark nodded solemnly.

"And on how promptly it was removed," he added, then hesitated, not wanting to ask. Over the last thirty minutes her sadness had vanished, replaced by wonder and curiosity. But now she was talking about damage, and they were back to specifics—the tragic story of her friend. "How is Allison?"

Mark's question didn't cause a cloud of sadness or a storm of pain; instead, it brought a surprised violet sparkle. She had forgotten he didn't know the story ended happily!

"She's *fine*," Winter answered emphatically. She qualified it a little, her voice softening sympathetically as she recalled her friend's shattered dreams, "She'll never jump again, of course. She'll never be an Olympic champion. It would be much too dangerous. Her depth perception is off, and she had other injuries—broken pelvic bones and crushed nerves—that make her less strong than she was."

Mark nodded solemnly. Allison was probably very lucky to be alive, much less *fine*.

"Her recovery was miraculous. For the first few weeks the doctors weren't even sure she would survive." Winter wondered how much of Allison's survival was medical science and how much was her friend's incredible will, alive and fighting inside her motionless body. "But she *did* survive, and then there were months and months of recovery. Allison was out of school for a year. She had to learn how to read again, and how to write, and how to walk and talk."

"But she can do those things now?"

"Oh, yes. She has a slight limp, because of the pelvic fracture. I sometimes wonder if she still has pain," Winter said quietly. Allison never mentioned it, but Allison wouldn't. Even during those long, frustrating months of recovery, when there must have been so much pain, Allison rarely spoke of it. Winter's thoughts drifted to that year, to the beginning, to the most frightening part of all. She whispered distantly, "For a while, when you told Allison something, she wouldn't remember it five minutes later."

"She couldn't make new memories," Mark said.

"Couldn't make new memories," Winter repeated thoughtfully. "Is that the medical description?"

"Yes."

What is she thinking? Mark wondered as he watched the lovely violet eyes grow even more serious. Is she thinking how awful it would be to forget each second of life as soon as it was over, to never make a new memory? Or is she thinking just the opposite, that it might be better to forget than remember?

"But now she can?" Mark asked after several silent moments. He hoped to retrieve a sparkle as they talked about Allison's miraculous recovery. "Now Allison can make new memories?"

"Yes. Now she's fine." Winter started to ask another question, but instead she caught her lower lip with her teeth, tugging softly, debating.

"Ask," Mark commanded gently. He guessed that they had come full circle, back to the beginning, to whatever had prompted the search. Back to the beginning with the question still unanswered.

She obviously hadn't been checking on a prognosis: Will my friend ever be all right? And she wasn't an attorney seeking information about the appropriateness of the medical care: Can my client sue? She knew those answers. Allison was *fine*.

It was something else.

"This is going to sound silly."

"That's OK."

"Before her accident, Allison had no sense of color or style or design. None." Winter paused, then gave Mark a gentle command. "Imagine Ireland. Happy images."

"All right."

"What do you see?"

"Green . . ."

"Good. Green eyes, fair skin, freckles, a long mane of auburn hair. That's Allison. Born in the USA, but roots that are pure Ireland. So, before her accident she would wear magenta or fuchsia or crimson or purple, and she had no idea that the colors clashed horribly with her own coloring."

Winter used the word *horribly*, but there was no horror, no cattiness, only fondness and warmth.

"Before her accident," Winter continued, "Allison's handwriting was round, *plump*, like when you're making the switch from printing to writing. And her doodles—Allison has always been a doodler—were primitive and childlike. You knew the doodles were horses because what else would Allison draw, but that was the only clue. If you didn't know Allison, you really couldn't tell."

"And now?"

"Now? Now her handwriting is elegant and beautiful. Her doodles are sketches she could probably sell. And she has an astonishing sense of color and style and design. In fact, she graduated from here two weeks ago with a major in Design and is going to be a designer at Elegance, *the* interior design store in Beverly Hills." Winter tugged at a blade of grass and asked quietly, "So what do you think? Is that medically possible? Something to do with the head injury? Or—"

"Or?"

"—or is it magic? Is the new incredible talent a divine gift to replace what was taken from her?"

Mark gazed at the lovely violet eyes so soft with hope. She wanted to believe it was magic. She wanted to believe in a divine wand that could swiftly convert tragedy to joy, wave away sadness, make wonderful new memories.

Mark wondered what magic she was awaiting in her own life, what pain or sadness needed to be transformed into happiness.

"It seems like magic," he replied quietly. Some magical, wondrous healing power of the brain that modern science had yet to discover.

Winter started to speak again but stopped at the sound of nearby bell tower chimes. She listened, counting silently as the gongs marked the hour. Her eyes widened as the realization settled.

"Eight o'clock! I've got to go."

Winter stood up quickly and so did Mark. She probably — *doubtless* — was late for a date, but Mark conjured up more enchanted images: stage coaches turning into pumpkins and white steeds turning into mice.

"Would you like to go out sometime?" he asked impulsively before she vanished forever.

"Oh!" The question caught Winter by surprise. It was so out of context! This wasn't the usual way dates happened, the way she *made* them happen. She hadn't flirted or teased or played. Her eyes hadn't seduced, her lips hadn't beckoned, her voice hadn't whispered provocative promises. There had been no games, no pretense, no acting at all.

There had only been serious, quiet conversation about brains and blood clots and magic.

"OK," she breathed finally, uncertainly. *I guess.*

"Saturday? Dinner? A movie?" Mark pressed swiftly, sensing her reluctance, not wanting her to change her mind.

"That would be fine." Winter's mind spun as she struggled to shift to the familiar role of temptress. It was a role she had mastered, with every performance flawless, effortless . . . until now. Now she searched for a soft purr, but the words came before the tone did. She heard herself ask him as seriously as she had asked about neurosurgery, "I have to go to a wedding on Saturday. Would you like to come with me?"

"Yes. What time shall I get you?"

"The wedding's at four, so three-fifteen." Winter gave him the address on Holman Avenue and Mark wrote it in the margin of his neuroanatomy notes. "Oh, it's a garden wedding."

"All right. My name is Mark, by the way. Mark Stephens."

"I'm Winter. Winter Carlyle."

Then she was gone and Mark was left with images. A graceful gazelle disappearing across a savannah . . . a soft pastel mirage in a harsh desert . . . serious violet eyes and a wish of magic . . . Cinderella at the stroke of midnight . . .

For two days Mark's mind had danced with the images. Now he was at the address she had given him on Holman.

The address—the glass slipper left by Cinderella before she dashed away. The address might or might not belong to Winter Carlyle, whoever she was, if she even existed.

Mark parked his car behind a powder-blue Mercedes Sports Coupe and felt a mixture of apprehension and anticipation as he walked to the entrance of the security building. He hoped she wasn't a phantom; but if she was, he didn't want the dream to end.

Mark scanned the names beside the intercom buttons and found W. Carlyle next to 317. As he pressed the button, anticipation vanquished apprehension, gaining strength as it pulsed unopposed through his body.

"Mark?"

"Hi."

"I'll be right down."

Winter took a final critical look in the mirror and wondered why she was so nervous. Because . . .

Because for the past two days her mind had replayed that summer twilight interlude again and again. She almost hadn't spoken to him at all. He had been so absorbed in his studying, concentrating intently, a slight smile on his lips. He had no idea she was there, watching him, envying his obvious joy at what he was doing. He was happy, like Allison had been happy when she was riding; doing what he wanted to do, concentrating, *loving* it.

Winter almost hadn't interrupted him, but when she had he had been so kind, so patient, and . . .

Whatever it was that made her heart race. Winter hadn't felt the full effect of him until after. Then she remembered the dark black curly hair and handsome face and strong, slender hands. Then she remembered the deep, seductive voice and sensuous smile and interested, curious pale blue eyes that made her ask about magic. Were his eyes really cornflower-blue? Were they really identical in shade to the most valued of sapphires, precisely the color of the magnificent sapphire earrings she wore now?

Or was her mind playing tricks?

Winter sighed. He's a man, she told her pounding heart as she rode the elevator to the first floor. Just like any other man. Completely in your control.

"Hello, Mark." It wasn't a trick of her mind. His eyes *were* cornflower-blue. She had remembered perfectly. But she had forgotten the intensity.

"Hello, Winter." She was even more beautiful than he had remembered; more violet, more ivory, more velvet.

Mark and Winter walked in silence to the curb.

"Where's the garden?" Mark asked as he opened the car door for her.

"The Bel Air Hunt Club."

"OK," Mark replied calmly, but his mind swirled.

The Bel Air Hunt Club. *That* garden was the most expensive, exclusive, well-tended garden in Southern California. What was Winter's connection to the Bel Air Hunt Club? Maybe none. Maybe the bride or the groom was a college friend who belonged there.

But what if Winter belonged there? What if the powder-blue Mercedes Sports Coupe belonged to her? What if the stunning gems adorning her ears were real sapphires? What if the sleek lavender dress she wore was pure silk?

Mark would find out soon enough. The Bel Air Hunt Club was only two miles away, in the heart of prestigious Bel Air.

* * *

Allison arrived at the address on Montana Avenue at exactly three-twenty. She decided to wait in the car. Emily knew she would be there and was doubtless frantically dressing and gathering her camera equipment for this sudden all-important assignment.

Allison noticed the young woman appear from behind the palmettos that framed the stucco house, but until her hesitant steps brought her to the open window on the passenger side of the car, it did not occur to Allison that she had been watching Emily.

"Are you Allison?"

"Yes. Emily? Hop in."

"Hi." Emily slid into the passenger seat and set her camera on the floor at her feet. "I'm Emily Rousseau."

"I'm Allison Fitzgerald. Hi." Allison smiled warmly, successfully suppressing her shock beneath layers of well-bred politeness and instinctive kindness.

Emily wore baggy bell-bottom jeans and a baggier denim work shirt. The shirt and jeans were clean, neatly pressed, but to the social event of the season? To Bel Air's most lavish wedding?

Allison had noticed Emily the instant she appeared because her artistic eye had been drawn to the incongruity of what she saw. Emily's clothes were baggy and unstylish, as if designed to conceal, but her long golden hair glittered in the sunlight, a brilliant beacon that commanded attention.

Half-gold, half-denim; half-dazzle, half-drab.

And so anxious! Allison realized as Emily brushed a strand of gold off her face. Emily's hand trembled, her pale-gray eyes darting uncertainly toward Allison and back.

The same instinct that drove Allison to rescue and nurture wounded animals made her want to help Emily Rousseau. If it was just that Emily didn't have the proper outfit, the solution was easy. Allison had dresses, dozens of them, stylish, beautiful dresses, five blocks away. They would be big—long—on Emily, but . . .

It's not the clothes, Allison decided. Emily wasn't looking

self-consciously from her unfashionable denim to Allison's elegant Mardik chiffon. Something else made her chew mercilessly at her lower lip.

"It's lucky you were available today," Allison offered cheerily as she turned off Twentieth onto San Vicente Boulevard.

"I hope so."

"Have you photographed a lot of weddings?" Allison asked hopefully, guessing at the answer, worrying alternately for the obviously anxious Emily and the always anxious Meg.

"None."

"*Oh.*" *Meg, you and Cam will still be married. The pictures don't really matter, do they?* "But you work for Jerome Cole?"

"Yes," Emily answered swiftly, as if that made her qualified, as if Jerome's vast experience with celebrity weddings was contagious. "I've worked for him for three years, during my last two years at UCLA and for the past year since I graduated."

We're the same age, Allison thought. You, me, Winter. Allison and Winter would have graduated a year ago, like Emily, instead of two weeks ago, *if only* whatever it was hadn't caused Tuxedo to swerve with fright.

"So, you're a photographer."

Allison made it a simple statement of fact — firm, positive, indisputable. Two hours earlier, Jerome Cole had posed it as a frantic question: "You *are* a photographer, aren't you, Emily? You haven't bought my used cameras and darkroom equipment and chemicals for someone else, have you?"

The photography instructors at UCLA told Emily she was a photographer — a *talented* one — and Emily liked the pictures she developed in the makeshift darkroom in her windowless basement apartment, but . . .

"I'm a photographer, but I haven't really taken pictures of people." Emily's subjects were flowers and waves and the sun and the moon. She chose those subjects because they didn't mind if she took their pictures and they didn't get impatient if it took her an hour, or even two, to get exactly the image she wanted: the morning dew on a rosebud, the wind-caressed petals of a marigold, the fiery sun as it splashed into

21

the sea, the just-born summer moon. "Most of my photographs have been of flowers."

"What do you do for Jerome?" Jerome Cole was a celebrity photographer. Flowers played a small role in celebrity photographs: a bridal bouquet, a suite at the Beverly Hills Hotel overflowing with roses on Oscar night, a fragrant colorful float in the New Year's Day parade, a mantle of carnations for the first thoroughbred to cross the finish line at Santa Anita.

"I work in the darkroom. I've developed almost all of the wedding sets in the past two years. I just haven't taken them."

"So you do know."

"I know what they're supposed to look like, yes." Emily frowned. "To me, they always seem so posed. Posed shots and shots of groups."

Allison wondered if Emily's frown was an artistic one — the *artiste* who didn't like the posed shots — or simply a worried one — the frown of a timid young woman anxious about assembling a group, asking them to follow her commands, urging them to look at the camera in unison and smile on cue. Especially *this* group, Hollywood's most dazzling, Bel Air's most rich and powerful, the Wall Street financiers and Greenwich aristocrats who had made the trip after all.

"I think the purpose is just to have a record of who celebrated the marriage. It's probably not essential to take group pictures." Allison found group photos uninteresting, too; but they were tradition in Bel Air and certainly in Greenwich. Allison could imagine Meg's horror and her own confession: *Well, yes, Meg, I did tell Emily that I didn't think group shots were essential. I didn't realize she wouldn't get a picture of your mother-in-law. Not one picture. I know, Meg, an unfortunate oversight.*

"I really appreciate the ride," Emily said suddenly, as if remembering something she had rehearsed, a politeness, and then forgotten.

"It's no problem. I'll give you a ride home, too. The reception will go on for hours, but I don't care how long I stay. We can leave whenever you're ready."

"The reception would be a good time to get pictures of everyone, wouldn't it?"

"Oh. Yes, I guess it would."

It was obvious that, despite her anxiety, Emily wanted to do a good job. Most photographers, *including* Jerome Cole, took the obligatory pictures — the jubilant wedding party, the satin gown raised demurely to reveal the garter, the bride and groom cutting the cake, the frosting-laced kiss, the "old, new, borrowed, blue," the bride's last dance with her father and first dance with her new husband — and left.

Emily was willing to stay for as long as was necessary. She wanted to give Meg the best wedding pictures she could.

Allison wondered if Emily's photographs would be good. She hoped for Emily's sake as well as for Meg's that they would be great.

Chapter Two

"Dearly beloved. We are gathered here . . ."

Here. Vanessa Gold smiled appreciatively at the fabulous setting, listened to the familiar words of the wedding ceremony, and thought about the descriptions she would use in Monday's column.

All the usual clichés and superlatives, she decided without worry. Clichés and superlatives were old friends—reliable, comfortable, time-tested. Vanessa's gaze drifted skyward, above the towering pines, and she made a mental note: *flawless azure sky.* To this she added: *caressing ocean breeze, the fragrance of a thousand perfect roses, solemn vows whispered above the cooing of distant doves and the soft splash of honey-gold champagne cascading from a silver fountain.*

On the spot—the lovely rose-scented spot in the fourth row on the bride's side—Vanessa decided to devote Monday's entire *All That Glitters* column to this wedding. It was Vanessa's decision to make. *All That Glitters* was hers, and had been for forty years.

"Do you Meg . . ."

Meg. Vanessa smiled lovingly at the bride, a mother's

proud, gentle smile. Not a mother, Vanessa reminded herself. More like a *grandmother!*

By the time Meg Montgomery was born, Vanessa had already been well established as Hollywood's premier celebrity columnist. Vanessa was a celebrity herself, a feared and revered chronicler of the tumultuous and fabulous lives and loves of the rich and those who would be famous. Widowed by the War and childless, Vanessa had long since abandoned the idea of a family of her own. In the spring of 1960 she moved to Bel Air, to a "bungalow" on St. Cloud. Vanessa's new home was located an acre of lush gardens away from the Montgomery mansion and across the winding road from the Fitzgerald estate.

Vanessa was graciously welcomed by her new neighbors, Jane Montgomery and Patricia Fitzgerald. Fifteen years younger than Vanessa, Jane and Patricia had been best friends "forever" and very rich even longer. Both knew well the responsibilities of wealth and were relatively immune to the dangers that befell the newly rich and suddenly famous. Jane and Patricia were intrigued by Vanessa's provocative insider column and unafraid of exposés of their own lives.

A year after Vanessa moved to Bel Air, both younger women gave birth to baby girls. Meg Montgomery entered the world without drama, the third of five children; but Allison Fitzgerald's birth was a struggle. Sean and Patricia would be unable to have more children, the doctors said. Allison was their very precious only child.

Because of her friendship with Jane and Patricia, Vanessa Gold had the immense pleasure, the wonderful joy, of watching the lively little girls—Meg and Allison—become beautiful, lovely young women.

The bride, Marguerite "Meg" Montgomery, was stunning in an ivory gown of . . . Vanessa narrowed her eyes slightly, remembering Jane Montgomery's tease of yesterday afternoon. "Take a good look at the gown, Vanessa. I'm sure you'll recognize the designers!" Vanessa smiled. *Of course* she did. Meg's gown was undoubtedly designed by David and Elizabeth Emmanuel, the British couple who created the fairy-tale gown worn by Lady Diana Spencer the day she became the Princess of Wales. Wedding gowns for princesses . . . for Diana, for Meg.

Meg attended the exclusive Westlake School for Girls and graduated a year ago from Barnard College. While in New York, she met the groom, Cameron Elliott, of Greenwich, Connecticut. Cameron is vice-president of the Wall Street investment firm of Elliott and Lowe.

"For better, for worse . . ."

Worse. Meg and Cam would flourish in "better" and survive "worse," Vanessa decided. Meg and Cam were a splendid match. Meg had done well; she had found happiness and love.

Vanessa's gaze drifted from the bride to the other little girl whose life she had watched with such interest and care. Why had Allison broken her engagement to Daniel Forester? Theirs had all the makings of an ideal match, too; Bel Air and Hillsborough, real estate heiress and newspaper heir, old money and old money, very nice young woman and very nice young man . . .

Vanessa was confident that Allison had her reasons. The willowy coltish girl had grown into a striking beauty, but she had probably not outgrown, never would, the strong will and determination that had made her a champion. Perhaps Allison was searching for something to replace her shattered dreams. Maybe she had discovered in time that it wasn't Daniel Forester.

"For richer, for poorer . . ."

Poorer. That wasn't an issue in this marriage or, for that matter, in the lavish lives of the assembled guests. Vanessa thought about the guests and played with the question of who among them was the wealthiest. It was unanswerable, of course, but an intriguing exercise nonetheless; and Vanessa kept coming up with the same surprising name . . . Winter Carlyle.

When Jacqueline Winter died five years ago, her eighteen-year-old daughter Winter inherited everything. *Everything* included thousands of carats of diamond, emerald, ruby, and sapphire jewelry designed by Tiffany and Winston and Cartier, gifts from enraptured lovers; and priceless works of art, more gifts; and the magnificent mansion on Bellagio; and the millions of dollars earned by Jacqueline but never spent because there were always rich and powerful men to provide for her; and whatever Lawrence Carlyle had left. No one really knew how great a fortune Jacqueline had accrued in her dazzling and tragic life, but it was immense and now it all belonged to Winter.

Vanessa sighed softly, wondering about the legacy of pain that accompanied Winter's vast fortune. Vanessa could predict with great confidence that life would be happy for the Meg Montgomerys and Allison Fitzgeralds of the world; tragedy might befall them, as it had befallen Allison, but the foundation of love created by their parents would right them again. Vanessa foresaw with equal confidence only unhappiness for Winter Carlyle. How could it be otherwise? As far as Vanessa could tell, the foundation of Winter's life had been as solid and enduring as quicksand.

"Forsaking all others . . ."

Others, and the inability or unwillingness to forsake them. That was the inevitable problem in this town. Meg and Cam wouldn't fall prey to that cycle of anger and betrayal and sadness, Vanessa decided. They had made their vows and would keep them. Vanessa hoped Meg and Cam would also keep their *avant-garde* plan to forsake the reception line. Tradition was one thing, but a warm June day, four hundred guests, and her seventy-year-old legs were another.

"You may kiss the bride."

Vanessa returned a wink to a beaming Meg as she and her new husband walked happily down the satin-ribboned aisle.

"Meg, the ceremony was lovely." Allison gave Meg a brief hug. "You look absolutely beautiful. That gown!"

"Thank you! It did go well, didn't it? I was so afraid something would go wrong."

"Nothing did."

"No." Meg smiled happily at the shiny gold wedding band that snuggled against the three carat diamond on her ring finger. Her smile faded slightly, a tiny, *tiny* cloud on a vast horizon of euphoria, as her eye caught a glimpse of gold and denim.

"I don't know about this photographer, Allison."

Allison gave a reassuring smile, even though she didn't know either. Emily certainly was *trying.* She moved bravely through the rich and famous, taking many minutes with each photograph, waiting patiently until her eye saw the image she wanted. Emily didn't speak to the guests or smile. She just took her careful pictures, her gray eyes serious and intent. Emily's appearance drew an occasional arched eyebrow or disapproving frown—who was she? how *dare* she?—but was then promptly forgotten in the glittering glamour of the party.

"I think she's doing a good job," Allison offered hopefully, following Meg's gaze to Emily. "Who is that she's photographing now?"

"Rob Adamson. I'm amazed you don't know him, Allison. He owns *Portrait* magazine and moved here about a year ago from New York. He's with Elaina Kingsley, attorney for the

28

stars."

Allison recognized Elaina. Elaina was a familiar face, a familiar *force* in the lives of celebrity Los Angeles. *A shark cleverly disguised as an ingenue,* Winter had quipped once, accurately. Elaina blended her innocent Southern belle looks and her soft River Oaks drawl to create an image that distracted and amazed as she successfully negotiated the toughest movie and television contracts in Hollywood.

Allison recognized Elaina. And there was something hauntingly familiar about Rob.

"I wonder if I could have met Rob once, a long time ago. He's from New York?"

"From Greenwich. He and Cam have known each other forever. They roomed together at Exeter and at Harvard."

If Rob and Cam were boyhood friends, that made Rob thirty, seven years older than Allison. In the fleeting spans of childhood and teenage and college, seven years was another generation. It seemed almost impossible that their paths had crossed.

Allison *had* lived in Greenwich, of course, but it was only for the school year when she was fifteen. That year she had attended Greenwich Academy for Girls, an exclusive private girls' school renowned for its academic and equestrian excellence. The show jumping coach at the Academy was very good, but the year away was miserable. Allison was homesick and her parents were daughter-sick. Even Tuxedo was stable-sick, Allison decided. Her sleek black and white champion horse missed the comforts of his posh stall at the Bel Air Hunt Club.

Technically, Allison had lived in Greenwich, but in reality she never saw anything beyond the oak and pine forested campus of the Academy. When she wasn't in class and didn't have to be in the dormitory because of curfew or study hours, Allison was at the stable. There were no boys at Greenwich Academy, no *men,* not even guests.

Wherever it was that Allison had seen Rob Adamson before, it was not in his hometown.

But it *was* somewhere. She was sure of it. Allison looked

away for a moment, not wanting Rob to sense her stare and trying to prepare her mind for a fresh look. Then she turned back to the ocean-blue eyes and dark brown hair and high aristocratic cheekbones, and with the surprising clarity of the sun appearing from behind a dense dark cloud, her face brightened. She *knew*.

Rob was tall and strong and handsome, and *she* had been small and frail and pretty, but the resemblance was unmistakable.

"I knew his sister Sara. She was in grade twelve when I was in grade ten at Greenwich Academy. I wonder how she—"

"She's dead, Allison," Meg interjected.

"Dead? Oh, no." The memory, once rediscovered, had begun sending images of Sara, and with the images came emotion, warmth . . .

Meg's words pierced the warmth with an ice-cold shiver.

"She was murdered." The characteristic drama vanished from Meg's voice, leaving its tone eerily flat, sinister, *dead*.

"Murdered?" Allison echoed softly.

"She married a fortune hunter. The Adamsons are convinced he killed her. I don't know the details, I don't even know if Cam does, but it was a murder that didn't look like a murder—a clever, perfect crime. There was no proof, no evidence."

"So he's not in prison?"

"No. There wasn't even a trial. There was no public scandal whatsoever. He's rich and free and he probably won't do it again because he's becoming even richer on Broadway."

"He's an actor?"

"No. Well, maybe he is. Maybe that's how he got her to marry him, playing a role, being charming and seducing her. Anyway, now apparently he writes and directs."

"What's his name?"

"I don't know. If Cam knows, he didn't tell me."

"But the Adamsons really believe he murdered Sara?"

"Yes," Meg replied somberly. "But apparently it wasn't something they could prove."

"It must be awful for them." Allison didn't look back at Rob, but she remembered his face and thought about the torment that must certainly swirl beneath the calm facade.

"Cam is pretty sure it's why Rob moved *Portrait* from New York to Los Angeles. He just couldn't stand being anywhere near the man."

"A grim topic for a happy day," Allison whispered apologetically.

"It's probably just as well you asked me, not Rob, about Sara."

"I guess so."

Allison and Meg stopped speaking, listened to the sounds of the day—the laughter of friends, the soft chimes of crystal touching crystal, the splash of champagne, the melody of love songs—and willed the happiness to wash away the sadness. It happened for Meg more quickly than for Allison.

"I should probably go find my husband. We're trying to mingle together, but we keep getting separated!" Meg stood on tiptoes and scanned the sea of rich and famous. "I don't even see him. But, speaking of gorgeous men whom I would *not* want to be separated from unless I was the proud wearer of a wedding ring, who is Winter with? Or, actually, at the moment, *without?*"

This time Winter had been swept away from him by two "old friends from Westlake" who had to "tell her something important." Winter had cast a beautiful apologetic smile and Mark had replied with an easy laugh.

Of course he wanted to be alone with her, but that would happen later, after the reception. And he was learning new things about her, watching her in her natural habitat among the rich, famous, and glamorous.

Winter belongs here, Mark decided within moments of their arrival at the Club. As the afternoon wore on, he wondered if she owned the place. Winter more than belonged, she *controlled.*

The serious young woman who had frowned thoughtfully

31

at his neurosurgery text, posed intelligent, insightful questions, and asked shyly about magic had vanished. In her place was an alluring, confident vixen. Winter charmed them all, even the most celebrated and famous among them. Men flocked to her like moths to a brilliant flame, and women flocked, too, wanting to bask in Winter's golden rays but content even with her shadow. The men who noticed Mark assumed he was, like them, simply one in an endless series, captivated by the sensuous woman who beckoned like silk sheets to a canopied bed but made no promises.

Mark watched the seductive, provocative, bewitching Winter Carlyle and tried to reconcile this Cinderella with the serious, thoughtful one he had met at twilight in the Sculpture Garden.

It was really quite easy to reconcile the two *because she was so much like him.*

Mark, too, drew admiring stares. Even this afternoon he heard familiar stage whispers of "awesome" and "no wedding ring" and "those eyes." Mark could perform and charm and dazzle, too. He played the game magnificently, as she did; and, like Winter, Mark called the shots, playing, winning, beginning relationships and ending them, choosing when to begin and when to end.

They were both experts at a game that insured intimacy without emotion, sex without love, companionship without commitment; it was a game that was played a very safe distance from the heart, for whatever reasons.

Mark knew *his* reasons; he wondered about hers. Mark wondered who she was and why she belonged here and if *they* would play or if they were already way beyond that.

Whoever she was, she was looking at him now, sending a sparkling violet message of "Help." Mark lifted two full crystal champagne flutes from a silver tray and wove through the crowd toward her.

"Thanks," Winter whispered when Mark reached her. She turned to her "old friends from Westlake" and said, "I promised Mark a tour of the Club."

Winter cast *them* a beautiful apologetic smile and led

Mark down a short flight of brick stairs away from the crowd.

"I brought champagne in case we run into any thirsty roses on our tour," Mark said when they were alone.

"Oh, you noticed."

Of course he had noticed. He had noticed and he had wondered. Winter sipped, or pretended to, from each of the four glasses of champagne she had held during the afternoon. But most of the expensive bubbly had been gracefully poured onto the base of a rosebush as she bent to admire the magnificent blossoms.

"I noticed." And I notice that it embarrasses you. Mark rescued her quickly, "So, where are we now?"

"We're on a sort-of-secluded terrace in the champagne-drenched rose garden."

"Ah. And where are the beagles?"

"No beagles, no foxes, no bugles, no red-coated riders galloping across a fog-misted moor."

"So what kind of Hunt Club is this?"

"The best kind—all the wonderful traditions without the hunt. The Club was founded by several British producers and directors who made their fame and fortunes in the Golden Age of Hollywood but still longed for Merry England—horses, country riding, royalty, champagne brunches, formal balls, Yorkshire pudding . . ." Winter paused for a breath.

"It's very nice." Mark smiled slightly at his understatement.

"I like the British flavor. Of course there have been concessions to California *chic*. The guest rooms in the mansion are still pure Balmoral Castle—heavy forest-green drapes, carved armoires, four-poster beds—but the new bungalows beyond the pool and tennis courts are Malibu contemporary." Winter smiled wryly and added, with mock horror, "And now, on the same menu as beef Wellington, they offer platters of sprouts and yoghurt and fruit!"

"Oh, no." Mark laughed.

"Oh, yes!" Winter's eyes sparkled, met his, and held until

33

the intensity became too great, until all she could think about was that she wanted him to touch her, hold her, kiss her, make love to her. She continued, breathless, flushed, barely able to concentrate, "I've always thought it would be nice to change the name to something even more traditional, like The Royal and Ancient Club of Bel Air . . . ."

"Would you like to dance?" Mark spoke with a soft, seductive tone that told her he wanted what she wanted, all of it. They could start here, dancing in the rose-fragrant garden, their bodies swaying gently in a chaste hello.

A chaste hello, Mark mused as he set their champagne flutes on a white wrought iron table and extended his arms to welcome her. *Hello, Winter.*

They were already way beyond "hello." They had skipped a few chapters, beginning in the middle, in the enchanted part where there was magic and where they forgot all about playing and how important it was to keep a safe distance from the heart.

They danced in lovely sensual silence, saying that kind of hello, as the distant band played "Here, There and Everywhere."

Here, in this rose-scented heaven; there, in a four-poster bed in the mansion; everywhere . . .

Mark wanted to take her away *now,* but his logical scientific mind sought order. He forced himself to turn the pages back to Chapter One and fill in a few of the blanks.

Name? Winter Carlyle. Was that a real name or a stage name? *Blank.*

Age? *Blank.* But Mark had learned from Allison that she and Winter had both graduated from UCLA two weeks ago, so early twenties.

Family? *Blank.* Winter had made a point of introducing him to Allison and Allison's parents, and the introductions had been proud and fond, as if the Fitzgeralds were her parents and Allison was her sister. There were emotional links there but nothing genetic. The Fitzgeralds were red-haired and freckled and smiling and Irish. Winter's natural parents—whoever had given her the black velvet hair, violet

34

eyes, ivory skin, and elegant sensuality—were absent.

Occupation? *Blank*. Winter was rich. Everyone here was rich. Mark knew a little about wealth, and he knew that for some it was a goal in itself, but for most it was a by-product; what they *had* not who they *were*. Who was Winter? What was Winter? Today, among some of Hollywood's greatest actors and actresses, Winter acted, and her performance was dazzling. Mark hadn't been to a movie in years. For all he knew . . .

"You're a famous actress, aren't you?" His lips brushed her silky hair as he spoke, a gentle caress.

Mark held her close, already learning about her lovely softness and the instinctive way their bodies moved together. At his words, Winter stiffened, just for an instant; but Mark felt it as if it had been he, not she, recoiling at the question.

Mark pulled away to look at her face and saw a brief but unmistakable flicker of pain before she conquered it.

"No."

"A not-so-famous actress?" he suggested carefully. Maybe Winter had tried and failed. Maybe, if he had seen a movie in the past few years, he would have known not to ask.

"Not an actress at all," Winter whispered softly. *Only an actress . . . always an actress . . . never an actress.*

Mark regretted causing even a second of sadness and searched for a topic with a happy ending, one that would bring a sparkle. "I like your friend Allison."

"Do you want to be with Allison?"

"No." *You know I don't.* "I want to be with you."

"Why don't we do that? Go be someplace together."

"Would you like to go to dinner first?"

Winter shook her head, ever so slightly, her eyes never leaving his.

"OK. Shouldn't we stay until the bride and groom leave?"

"No. We should go now."

Chapter Three

Too much sadness for a wedding day, Allison thought. She sat on a wrought iron loveseat in a secluded alcove of lacy white lilacs; sitting because her injured hip sent angry messages, and in the lovely fragrant sanctuary because tears threatened.

Allison had expected to feel a little sad and nostalgic today because of Dan. But now that sadness was just a frivolous, trivial indulgence compared to the real sadnesses of the afternoon—the demons that plagued Emily Rousseau and the unspeakable tragedy of Sara Adamson. Daniel Forester and Allison Fitzgerald weren't tormented by demons and their broken engagement was not a tragedy. It was too bad—perhaps something Allison would always regret—but it was a choice, a decision. It wasn't a lurking pain, nor was it a senseless twist of fate.

Allison watched Emily and tried in vain to convince herself that the photographer was fine—just a girl with a preference for jeans and a little understandable anxiety about the important assignment that had been thrust upon her. Until the accident, Allison herself had had a strong preference for jeans; she had lived in jeans or jodhpurs, and whatever colorful sweatshirt or turtleneck or blouse she happened to grab from her dresser as she dashed to the stable. And Allison, too, was anxious about the important assignments that would be hers at Elegance.

Maybe Emily's just like me, Allison told herself hopefully.

But all the optimism in the world, all of Allison's unfailing ability to find the silver lining, could not force a troy ounce of similarity between them.

Emily's outfit was not a preference for jeans; it was a disguise, an obvious attempt to conceal. And Emily's anxiety was not just a simple case of "beginner's nerves"; it had depth and pain and fear woven through it.

Something troubled Emily, and it was surely much worse than the wedding-that-wasn't-to-be for rich and privileged Allison Fitzgerald; but even Emily's demons paled by comparison to the great tragedy of Sara Adamson.

Sara. Murdered. No.

Allison's mind filled with memories of Sara, clear, warm, vivid memories . . .

Allison could have spent the nine months at Greenwich Academy and never even met Sara Adamson. Sara was three years older, a senior when Allison was a sophomore. Sara didn't board at the Academy because her home was in Greenwich, and she didn't ride.

But Allison did meet Sara, and there had been a warm, quiet, special bond.

Sara was sitting on a wooden bench in the grandstand of the riding arena when Allison entered the ring at noon on her second day in Greenwich. Allison had studied the class schedule and study schedule and the required appearances at "gracious hours"—when they learned to be ladies—and decided that she would spend every noon hour at the stable, riding instead of eating. The pale, quiet girl who sat on the wooden bench had apparently made the same decision; except she *didn't* ride and she *did* eat lunch, slowly, gracefully eating food she removed from a pale pink cardboard box.

Sara and Allison exchanged awkward smiles the first day, and the second, and the third. On the fourth day, Sara introduced herself and asked shyly if Allison minded an audience. Allison introduced herself and replied gaily, "Of course not."

After that, there were days when Sara and Allison only smiled warmly, waved friendly waves, and uttered brief hellos. But there were other days when Allison spent more of the noon hour talking to Sara than riding. Allison explained to Sara about show jumping—the perfect arc, the oxers and verticals and walls, the carefully timed strides, the control of the horse's immense power—and Sara listened, fascinated.

Sara and Allison talked about riding and jumping and Allison's gold medal dreams; but when Allison asked Sara questions about her life, her dreams, the fragile older girl shrugged, smiled softly, and said little. Sara did tell Allison, apologetically but without elaboration, that she had to eat a special lunch and couldn't share it. Sara offered to have the cook at her estate prepare something for Allison, too. Allison always declined Sara's gracious offer for herself, but agreed, when Sara suggested it, that carrots and apples for Tuxedo would be nice.

"It looks like you're flying, Allison," Sara said one day as she watched Allison soar over jump after jump.

"It feels like that. Flying, floating . . ."

"Free."

"Yes, I guess. Free. Sara, I could teach you to ride, to jump if you want to."

"Oh." Sara's ocean-blue eyes sparkled for an uncertain moment and her pale cheeks flushed pink. She added quietly, "No. Thank you, Allison, but I can't."

Sara and Allison only saw each other at the riding stable. Their classes were held on different floors of the red brick building. A limousine dropped Sara at school each morning, minutes before the school day began, and was waiting when classes ended in the afternoon.

Allison was at the stable every day at noon. From September until late March, Sara only missed a few days. Sara was out of school for a week in November, and two other times she was gone for several days. Sara looked more pale and fragile when she returned after being away, Allison thought, as if she had been quite ill.

"I won't be here as much anymore," Sara told Allison on

the first day of spring term. "Most days, I'll be spending the noon hour off campus."

Allison smiled at Sara's politeness. It was nice of Sara to let her know, but certainly not necessary. Allison *almost* asked Sara where she would be, not wanting to pry but because she saw such happiness in Sara's dark blue eyes. Allison didn't ask, but on a splendid warm day in May, she learned the reason for Sara's happiness.

Sara Adamson was in love! Allison didn't see the man's face, only his silhouette in the distance. But she saw Sara's face, her pale cheeks flushed pink and her eyes glowing as she walked toward him, carrying her special lunch, to join him inside a battered forest-green Volkswagen bug.

Allison saw Sara for the last time in early June, the day before the school year ended. Sara was at the stable at noon, waiting for Allison.

"Hi, Sara."

"Hi. I just wanted to say good-bye. I enjoyed watching you. Thank you for letting me."

She is so gracious, Allison thought for a stunned, silent moment.

"I enjoyed having you watch," Allison replied finally, truthfully. "I heard that you're going to Vassar."

"Yes." Sara smiled. "And you're going back to Los Angeles."

"It's home," Allison murmured, not wanting to offend. After all Greenwich, with its icy winters and rigid rules, was Sara's home.

"Good luck in the Olympics, Allison."

"Thanks! Good luck at Vassar, Sara."

"Good-bye."

"Good-bye." Be happy, Allison thought as she watched Sara leave. Be happy. . . .

But Sara found something other than happiness, Allison thought sadly as she sat in the secluded alcove of lacy white lilacs. Sara fell into the arms of a murderous lover. Allison

39

narrowed her eyes and tried to see the face of the man in the Volkswagen bug, the man to whom Sara had gone with such joy. Was that the man, or had that love faltered only to be replaced by the lethal one?

"Oh, sorry!"

Startled, Allison looked up into dark blue eyes that were so hauntingly like his sister's.

"Hi."

"Hello. I didn't mean to invade your privacy." Rob had escaped, seeking privacy, too. Of the four hundred rich and famous wedding guests, he had decided, fully half wanted more fame, more wealth, more celebrity; and those two hundred seemed to believe that a profile in *Portrait* magazine would help.

An article in Rob's magazine would help—it always did. But Rob and Rob alone made the decisions about whom to profile. He remained calmly yet firmly uninfluenced by praise or pleas from agents, by "anonymous" callers who claimed to be "friends" of the magazine-hopeful, and most certainly by attempts to impress and woo at a wedding reception. Even Elaina, with her infinite charms and the luscious intimacy of their relationship, couldn't influence his choices.

Rob had been a little flattered by the obvious hints of so many celebrities—it was high praise for *Portrait*—but eventually he felt annoyance creeping in. He left Elaina to cope with the not-so-subtle onslaught, many of whom were her clients, while he sought a brief respite in the lilacs.

Rob wasn't alone in the lilacs, but he looked at the serious jade-green eyes—did they glisten with recent tears?—and her warm smile, and he instantly decided that this young woman would never try to convince him to put her in *Portrait*. Rob was quite safe here, but he gazed thoughtfully at the glistening eyes and realized that he had disturbed her.

"I'm just passing through, on my way to the next grove of lilacs," Rob said.

"No. Please. Stay. You're not invading my privacy." *I was thinking about your sister.* Allison wanted to tell Rob that she had known Sara and how much she had liked her and how sorry she was. But if she told him now, she would cry. Maybe she would always cry. She *would* tell Rob sometime — some safe time in the future in another grove of lilacs on another summer day, or at the Club's legendary Autumn Ball, or at Meg and Cam's fifth wedding anniversary — some *other* time. "I'm Allison Fitzgerald."

"I'm Rob Adamson. Allison Fitzgerald. Let's see. Aren't you the interior designer *extraordinaire?*"

"You've been talking to my mother!"

"No, although I did meet your mother and father. It was actually Claire Roland who told me."

Claire Roland owned Elegance, *the* design store of Southern California. Claire was fifty-seven and could have retired years ago to her "best address" home on Mountain Drive in Beverly Hills, but she grew restless at the thought of even slowing down. Claire's mission was incomplete; there still existed houses in the Platinum Triangle — Beverly Hills, Holmby Hills, and Bel Air — that needed an infusion of taste and elegance and style. That would be her legacy to Los Angeles, Claire hoped, and to a generation of designers trained by her.

Claire was the first designer in Los Angeles to offer apprenticeships to students majoring in Design at UCLA. On paper the apprenticeship was for one quarter only, complete with grades and credit hours, but Claire made rare exceptions for students with great promise.

When Claire had first seen Allison Fitzgerald's name on the class list eighteen months before, she had worried. It was more than a little awkward. Claire had to give a grade and she was known for her toughness; but Sean and Patricia Fitzgerald were friends and everyone knew about Allison's tragic accident.

Claire worried, but within three weeks of her arrival at Elegance, she was speaking to Allison as a colleague, with the no-nonsense approach never seen by clients but which delighted the other designers. "Customers *can* be wrong, Allison, remember that," Claire would confide with a sly smile.

41

"They can want mirrors over beds and trapezes and God knows what else, and that's *wrong,* so we politely suggest that they find another designer." Claire Roland was in the enviable but hard-earned position of being able to choose clients, as well as designers. Her designers were the best, and she wanted Allison to be one of them. "Taste and elegance, Allison. You have it. I have no idea why—you're so young, you were born and raised in California; it must be an instinct."

Allison knew that Claire's praise was genuine, but she knew from her riding that talent and instinct and natural ability had to be nurtured. Claire predicted a meteoric rise for Allison. In a year, maybe less, Claire announced confidently, Allison Fitzgerald would be *the* interior designer for the great homes of Southern California.

Three years ago everyone had predicted that Allison would be *the* equestrian Gold Medalist—she might even win three golds—of the 1984 Olympics. Allison feared predictions now. She had learned that crystal balls were very, very fragile.

"Claire gets a little carried away," Allison murmured uneasily to Rob. Her uneasiness increased as Allison wondered what else Rob had been told about her. Did he know that she had almost died, too? Except her death would have been an accident, not murder. "I don't even begin at Elegance until mid-August, after the Olympics."

Allison watched Rob's reaction when she mentioned the Olympics. Did he know about her shattered Olympic dreams? Would his dark blue eyes soften with sympathy? Would they flicker with the concern of an older brother: Do you really want to watch the Olympic Equestrian Team, Allison? Wouldn't that be too painful for you?

Rob's expression didn't change. His handsome, untroubled aristocratic smile didn't waver. If Rob knew about her, he politely hid the knowledge, just as Allison hid her knowledge about Sara.

"Claire didn't seem carried away," Rob observed mildly. A thought teased from a corner of his mind. These jade green eyes would never *try* to get in *Portrait,* but if Claire's prediction about Allison's future was even close to accurate, Rob would be calling *her*. Profiles about people like Allison were what distinguished *Portrait* from the other celebrity magazines. Rob chose strong, interesting, intriguing people; people who succeeded against all odds; people, like Allison, who were champions at whatever they did.

"Well." Allison was eager to change the subject away from speculation about her future. Or her past. Or *his* past. That left the present. She was only here searching for her emotions among the lilacs, instead of in the sanctuary of her own apartment, because of Emily. Surely, Emily would be finished soon. "Do you know if Meg and Cam are about to leave?"

"Soon, I think. Are you planning to catch the bouquet?"

"No." Allison softened her gasp with a slight smile. "I am planning to steer very clear of the bouquet. I'd like to wave good-bye, toss a little rice . . ." Go home.

"So," Winter whispered as she and Mark entered the living room of her apartment on Holman Avenue. Neither had spoken since leaving the rose terrace at the Club.

"So?" Mark's eyes and interest were on Winter, but he was aware of the modest furnishing in her nice-but-not-luxurious one-bedroom apartment; collegiate, not Hunt Club; Bruin chic, not Balmoral elegant.

"So, should I put on an album?"

"No. You should come here."

Winter obeyed. She had to. Her heart raced at the promise of Mark's touch; her body swirled with wonderful demanding sensations; and her mind had floated away, taking with it the vow she had made to herself to be in control . . . *always.*

Something else was in control now—her own desires.

And someone else was in control—Mark.

Winter stood in front of him, waiting in breath-held anticipation. But Mark reached for the gardenia in her hair, not for her. He removed the flower so gently, then unpinned the smooth, thick knot of hair until the black silk spilled loose and free down her back. Then, so delicately, he took the flawless sapphires from her ears.

"What are you doing?"

"I'm undressing you." Mark held the magnificent gems in his palm. "Where shall I put these?"

Anywhere. Just don't stop touching me. The gentle caresses as Mark's fingers brushed her hair and neck and shoulders sent warm — hot — tremors through her; dangerous tremors of desire, urgent, desperate . . .

"In the bedroom."

"Show me."

Winter led him to her bedroom. Mark set the earrings on the dresser, then joined her where she stood beside the bed. He reached for the zipper of her lavender silk dress.

"Hurry," she urged softly as his strong fingers touched her bare back.

"No," he answered with a gentleness that promised her it would happen — everything she wanted would happen — and it would be wonderful.

It would happen soon, because he wanted her so much, too. The exquisite pleasure of undressing her sent powerful rushes of desire through him. Her skin was so cool, so silky, and her violet eyes beckoned, and the soft sensuous curl of her lips . . .

Mark meant their first kiss to be a gentle hello, a soft whispered greeting, a tender promise. But there was too much passion, too much hunger, too much desire.

"Oh, Winter," he breathed as his lips touched hers.

"Mark."

They undressed each other quickly, kissing, touching, whispering, wanting.

When they were both naked, Mark pulled away. It was a monumental effort, defiance of a wonderful invisible magnetic force that willed their bodies to be together. Mark resisted the powerful force for a moment, knowing that soon and eagerly he would succumb to it, allowing it to win, marvelling in its strength. But now, in the soft summer twilight of her bedroom, he just wanted to look at her.

You are so lovely, Winter.

Winter trembled as his sensuous blue eyes caressed her, appraising, appreciative, full of desire.

Hurry, Mark.

Mark didn't hurry, even when they lay together between the cool sheets of her bed. He kissed a leisurely gentle path down her neck to the softness of her breasts, and slowly said hello *there*. And there were other gentle hellos, as his warm soft lips and his strong tender hands wandered, exploring, discovering, freeing ever-hidden desires.

Each new pulse of desire added to the last, crescendoing, hotter, stronger, wanting even more.

But how much more could there be?

More. Now her body was floating away! No, Mark held her and finally he put her exactly where he wanted her, exactly where she wanted to be. Her body floated up, just a little, as she welcomed him, all of him, at last.

At last, moving together in a rhythm of passion and desire. Hello, hello, *hello*.

And there was still *more*. Because, after it was over, Mark held her still—strong and gentle, close and tight. So close and so tight that there was no room left for the empty feelings of loneliness that were Winter's usual companions after making love.

"What are you thinking?" Mark spoke finally as he gently stroked her hair.

Winter moved her head slightly, a soft shake, a little shrug.

"Nothing?"

Winter raised up and gazed at him through a tangle of black silk. "No, I . . ."

Mark parted the tangle with amazing delicacy until he found her lovely violet eyes..

"You are wonderful," he told her.

"No." *I didn't do anything. You did.* "You are."

Mark tenderly traced a path around her eyes, down her cheeks, across her lips. His eyes were thoughtful as he studied her. Finally, he asked quietly, "Was that safe?"

Safe? Winter's mind reeled. No, it was dangerous, very, very dangerous. The danger was surfacing again as her skin responded to his touch, wanting more, and her desires willed her to follow wherever he led.

"Safe?" she whispered weakly.

"Are you on the pill?"

Oh. That kind of safe. Yes, of course. But there was nothing safe in the way Mark asked it! His voice was gentle and caring, assuming the responsibility if it wasn't safe, sharing that as they had shared everything else. There was nothing safe about Mark because he was so different from all the others.

"I have an IUD," Winter answered softly, marvelling that this discussion could feel so intimate, so tender, until he frowned. "Mark?"

"IUDs can cause problems, Winter."

I don't care! I'm never going to have children. The thought came to Winter swiftly—it had been part of her for so long—but the venom that usually came with it melted under Mark's gentle, worried gaze.

"Oh, well . . . Do they teach you this in medical school?"

"This?"

"How to ask intimate questions at intimate moments?"

Mark laughed softly. "They teach us how to take histories and do physicals."

"And you get A's in both."

"You think so?" Mark found her lips, starting the physical all over again.

"I know so."

Mark stopped the kiss with effort and whispered, "Would you like to go out with me sometime?"

"No." *I would like to stay in with you all the time.*

"How about dinner Monday night?" Mark ignored her words and read the message in her eyes.

"OK."

"I'll call you when I get home from the hospital, if you'll give me your unlisted number."

"I will." Winter made a move to get up.

"Where are you going?"

"To write down the number."

"There's no emergency."

"You're not about to leave?"

"No. I just wanted to get that settled before—"

"Before?"

"—before we make love again." And again. And again.

Chapter Four

Emily parted the heavy black curtains that divided her apartment into bedroom and darkroom and stared at the bedside clock. It glowed at her from the darkness of the windowless apartment that was barely lighter than the total inkiness of the dark-room: six-fifteen.

Six-fifteen. Was it A.M. Sunday morning, ten hours after Allison had driven her home from the reception? Or was it P.M., already Sunday evening? Or A.M. Monday morning, time to go to work?

Emily had no idea. The hours in the darkroom were timeless; enchanted, creative moments connected by a peace and joy that didn't belong to the rest of her life. Usually Emily set an alarm before she entered the darkroom, afraid to miss work, leaving reluctantly when the alarm sounded.

Emily opened the outside door and squinted at the fading rays of the summer sun. Sunday evening. Good. That meant she had more hours in the darkroom, with some hours to sleep, before work tomorrow.

Jerome would be pleased with the wedding photographs, wouldn't he?

Emily didn't know—she didn't have the confidence—but she liked the pictures. The bride and groom, caught in gazes of astonishment at what they had done and joy that they had done it; Allison, who had been so nice, so thoughtful, even though the day seemed to hold a special sadness for her; the stunning black haired-couple, violet eyes and sapphire ones, dancing amid the roses, falling in love; the confident sable-haired woman with the soft Southern accent and eyes that narrowed shrewdly if she wasn't on guard against that every moment; that *man* . . . that handsome man who watched her with smiling, curious dark blue eyes; and all the other celebrities whom Jerome would recognize and tell her about in intimate detail.

At first, Jerome simply stared at the photographs in stunned reverent silence. Finally, he murmured, "Uh, Emily, these are pretty good. Very good, really."

Spectacular, really, Jerome thought, staring at Emily as if seeing her for the first time. Jerome knew Emily worked magic in the darkroom, giving intriguing texture and imaginative richness to the photographs he took, but he had no idea . . .

"I'm glad you like them, Jerome."

"The Montgomerys will be very pleased."

Jerome studied the photographs for several more silent moments, his mind spinning as he realized the full measure of Emily's remarkable talent. Finally, he shifted his thoughts from the gifted photographer to her subjects, the celebrities whose lives fascinated him as much as they fascinated Vanessa Gold. Vanessa was a columnist, Jerome explained, but *he* was an unabashed gossip!

"My God, Emily! You got these two in the same picture? I thought they weren't speaking anymore. Do you remember what they were talking about?"

"No, I . . ."

"Think!"

"I really have no idea. I wasn't listening."

"Oh, well." Jerome moved on. "This is wonderful of Louis. He owns La Choix, you know. And look at Joan! Very flattering. She won the Oscar three years ago — or was it four — the sentimental favorite, of course."

"Who is this?" Emily pointed to a picture of the man with the smiling blue eyes.

"Oh! That's Rob Adamson. He owns *Portrait* magazine. Really a very nice shot, Emily. A masterful portrait of the master of *Portrait*."

"And is this his wife?"

"Elaina Kingsley? Not his wife yet, but it will happen. Someday soon, I'm sure, we'll be doing the photography for their magnificent wedding at the Bel Air Hunt Club."

"Oh."

Emily locked the door to her apartment and began the twenty-block walk to Mick's place. The day had gone well. Jerome had been pleased. If only tonight would go well, if only Mick wouldn't still be furious that she had agreed to do the Montgomery-Elliott wedding instead of going with him and his band for the two night "gig" on Santa Catalina Island.

Mick *would* be furious still, Emily knew it, but she knew, too, that by the time she reached his oceanside apartment, she would be able to handle his rage. The pill she had taken would be working its magic, numbing her, making anything possible.

The drug, a synthetic blend of mescaline and amphetamine, was already making the sky dance and the wind hum and the pastel hues of the summer evening pulse and glow and swirl. Cotton candy clouds floated close to the earth and streetlights were fine-cut diamonds scattering light like a thousand prisms. Houses stretched and melted and shrubs came to life, dancing and spinning and swaying in the balmy air.

Emily hallucinated easily. Her mind willingly embraced the drug-created monsters. The pulsing shapes and spinning colors and fantastic distortions didn't terrify her. They were old friends, soft, misty visions in a numb world, a welcome escape from the world she knew.

The mescaline let her hallucinate and the "speed" made her brave. She could appease Mick's anger. She could seduce him and recapture his love. Emily knew all the ways to give pleasure.

She had another pill in her pocket and Mick would give her cocaine if she needed it.

She could do it.

"Allison, *no.*" Winter frowned sternly at the telephone as if her expression of disapproval could be transmitted through the telephone wires to her best friend.

"I'm only telling you because I promised I would, not because I want you to talk me out of it."

"I just don't understand why."

"Because when riders fall off horses, they get back on."

"You didn't exactly fall."

"Yes I did!"

"The doctors really said it was OK?" Winter already knew the answer. She knew the exact day, six weeks ago, when the doctors told Allison she *could* ride — ride, but never jump — if she wanted to, if she was *very careful.*

Winter remembered the day with vivid clarity, because it was the day Allison began to change. The change was subtle — a quiet determination. Allison was making plans, but her solemn jade-green eyes artfully disguised the magnitude of the decisions she was making.

Allison didn't ask for Winter's advice or discuss her thoughts until the decisions were made. Then she simply announced them, three monumental decisions, all in row.

I've told Dan I can't marry him.

I said yes to Claire. I'll start working at Elegance after the Olympics.

I'm going to ride again.

"You can't jump," Winter reminded Allison gently now, as she had reminded her six weeks ago. What if that were Allison's fourth monumental decision?

"I know that," Allison answered with a soft sigh.

"Then why?"

"Because I want to. I *need* to."

"And I want — *need* to be there when you do."

"I'm just going to sit on Ginger and ride around the ring. Very safe. Incredibly boring. *And* incredibly early."

"That's fine."

"We really should be there by seven." At that hour on a Tuesday morning, Allison was assured of having the outdoor ring at the Club all to herself.

"I'll pick you up at six-thirty."

"Are you sure?"

"Positive. It's no problem. I'll see you then."

It's no problem, Winter thought after she replaced the receiver. I'll be awake because Mark will have just left.

Mark had left Sunday morning at six, rushing to his apartment to shower and change in time for seven A.M. rounds at the hospital. Mark and Winter had been awake at six because they had never been asleep.

Tonight they would sleep. Mark *had* to sleep. Winter heard the fatigue in his voice when he telephoned, moments before Allison's call, to say he would be late, too late to go out for dinner, but, if she were still awake . . .

Winter would be awake, exhausted from her own sleeplessness but unable to sleep. Ever since Mark had left her bed yesterday — only yesterday? — Winter's heart had pounded restlessly, missing him, wanting him, needing him.

Rob jogged effortlessly up the incline of the palm-lined path at the crest of the Santa Monica palisades. The exercise felt good — an invigorating interlude between the demands and challenges of the day with *Portrait* and the pleasures and challenges of the night that lay ahead with Elaina. The Pacific Ocean sparkled below, deep blue in the summer twilight, lapping gently on the snowy white sand. Rob inhaled a plumeria-scented breeze and thought for the hundredth time, or maybe the thousandth, how right it had been for him to leave New York and move to Los Angeles.

There was a softness here, a warmth, a promise of new beginnings. Maybe it was the golden sun. Maybe it was the distance from the painful memories. Maybe, as the poets wrote, it was the healing passage of time.

Or maybe his heart had told him, finally, in agonal rebellion, that it couldn't survive on hatred alone; a heart needed other nourishment—a little love, a little laughter, a little hope.

Rob saw a glitter of gold ahead on the path, a brilliant torch lit by the setting sun, a confusing image of long golden hair and baggy denim, conflicting messages. . . .

She was the photographer from the wedding. Rob had noticed her then, of course, and wondered. At first he assumed the amorphous tent of denim was worn in hostile defiance; a clear condemnation of rich people who sipped expensive champagne and tasted rare caviar and glided through life in designer dresses, silk tuxedos, and dazzling jewels.

But as he had watched, Rob decided there was nothing defiant in her manner—just the opposite. She seemed meek, timid, uncertain, and so *serious* about her task.

The baggy denim clothes were not worn in defiance, Rob had concluded. They were worn to conceal. And the long golden hair that hid her face? Were there scars too horrible to expose to the world? he had wondered, sadly, sympathetically.

But as her head had tilted to take the wedding pictures, the golden curtain had parted, revealing delicate porcelain features carved on the palest of alabaster skin. Her eyes— such *serious* eyes—were the lightest of gray, the color of early morning mist.

Rob had been intrigued with the fragile, ethereal, beautiful young woman who sent such a clear message to stay away.

And now she stood on the bluff near his ocean-view penthouse, still half-gold, half-denim.

But now she was not alone. And she was not so fragile or so timid after all.

She was with a man, and they should have been young lovers lost in the raptures of their love, marvelling at the glorious summer sunset; soft, romantic, gentle. But *he* looked mean—angry energy in black leather—and *she* looked hard and wanton. He leaned, sultry, sexual, against a palm, and she leaned against him. His rough hands roamed all over her, claiming their territory for all to see.

She allowed the intimate exploration without resistance, her golden head tilted toward the pink clouds overhead.

Rob passed them swiftly, as far away as the narrow path would permit. As he passed, he saw her eyes. The pale morning mist was dense smoky fog and the serious clarity had vanished beneath a glassy glaze. Her gaze shifted slightly toward him, without recognition, as he passed. The glazed, foggy eyes looked at him, but what did they see? Was he a monster, his face contorted and grotesque? Was he a swirl of light and color? Or was he nothing, unseen to the sightless eyes, a faded image in a misty haze?

Rob passed them swiftly and wished he could just as swiftly banish her from his thoughts. The memory of the fragile ethereal young woman from the wedding had stayed with him until now. Now that bewitching memory was shattered, the delicacy harshly corrupted by what he saw.

The new sullied memory lingered, as the pleasant one had, but now there was an accompanying emotion: anger. Rob was angry at them both; at the man for his blatant disrespect of her, at the woman for allowing him to treat her that way, and at both of them for insinuating their decadence on this gentle summer evening.

"Sorry," Mark said when he finally got to Winter's apartment at eleven P.M.

"Is this what it's like to be a doctor?" Winter asked with a gentle tease and a radiant smile. She was so happy to see him!

"No," Mark answered flatly. "If I were a doctor, I wouldn't have made it at all." *When I am a doctor, there will be much longer nights than this.*

"Oh!" The surprising harshness of Mark's voice startled her, extinguishing her smile, putting doubt in her sparkling

54

violet eyes.

Mark's tone reflected his fatigue and the incessant warnings that had bombarded his mind since the moment he left her bed. The warnings were simply reminders of the careful plans he had made for his life. *Do not get involved. Wait at least until residency is behind you. There will be no time for a love. It wouldn't be fair. You know too well what can happen.*

Mark had already dedicated the next four years to his career, just as he had dedicated the last three. It was not a sacrifice; it was a choice. Mark loved medical school and eagerly awaited the increased challenges and responsibilities of residency. He worked very hard, earned top grades, and his dream — a residency in internal medicine at Massachusetts General Hospital in Boston — was almost certainly going to come true.

There had been women, of course; a series of ideal relationships — sex without emotion, passion without commitment, laughter without tears, cancelled dates without regret.

Mark had made his choice, his plans; so far, it had been easy. Hard work, yes. Sleepless nights and exhaustion, of course. Dedication and resolve, always.

But Mark had expected that, planned on it.

Mark just hadn't planned on Winter Carlyle. He didn't even know he could feel this way. The warnings had bombarded his mind, but each missile had been intercepted — and exploded in midair — by the memory of Winter. She had already become a part of him; swiftly, confidently, she had found a home in his heart and in his mind.

And in his plans?

Mark gazed at the violet eyes that had been startled and hurt and confused by the harshness of his voice. He touched her cheek and whispered gently, "I missed you."

"I missed you, too," Winter murmured softly, but confusion and uncertainty lingered. She backed away slightly. "Are you hungry?"

"For you." Mark smiled, trying to reassure her.

"I went shopping after you called." It had been such fun, shopping in the gourmet stores of Brentwood and Santa

Monica for Mark; and setting the small kitchen table with mauve stoneware plates and crystal champagne flutes and a vase blooming with daisies; and preparing platters of smoked salmon and sliced pears and apples and cheese and caviar. Such fun, but now . . . "You said you hadn't eaten."

"Winter." Mark's lips found hers, showing her his hunger for her, apologizing. It wasn't her fault that she had turned his world upside down. He repeated hoarsely, "I missed you."

Winter gently touched the dark circles under his blue eyes. She whispered softly, her confidence a little restored by his kiss, "You're hungry for food, too, aren't you?"

"Maybe." Yes, he was famished, but if he could only satisfy one hunger, he would choose her.

Winter caught one of his hands and led him into the kitchen.

"We have rose food," she teased, holding up a bottle of chilled champagne. "And cheese, crackers, salmon, pears, smoked oysters—"

"Do you think we need oysters?" Mark extended his arms to her. She had let go, to get the champagne, and he missed her already.

"No, we don't need oysters." Winter curled against him and kissed the angle of his jaw. She could stay here forever wrapped in his strength, but . . .

The memory of his words and their hidden warning still haunted her. Winter wanted Mark to know that she already understood about his dedication to medicine. She had seen it the moment she saw him on campus, absorbed in his studying, a slight smile on his handsome face. She respected his dedication, admired it, and she envied his obvious joy.

"Have you always known you were going to be a doctor?" she asked, pulling away, sitting down at the table and motioning to Mark to do the same.

"No." Mark paused and added seriously, "In fact, I spent most of my life knowing I wasn't going to be a doctor."

"Really? I wondered if you were older than most third year medical students."

"I am. I'm twenty-nine. How about you? A little older than the usual recent college graduate?"

"A year older. I'll be twenty-four in January."

Mark waited for Winter to tell him about the missing year, but she didn't. He saw the soft seriousness in her eyes and realized she already had told him.

"You stayed out the year of Allison's accident, didn't you?" Mark asked.

"Her accident happened in September, just before Autumn Quarter of our junior year. Allison came out of the coma in the middle of October. I guess I had been in a coma, too, because I suddenly realized I'd been in the hospital, not in class, for the last six weeks."

Mark wondered why Winter couldn't simply say, I stayed out because Allison is my best friend, and she needed my help to learn to read again, and to write and walk and talk and make new memories.

"You took the year off to help Allison," Mark repeated gently.

"I guess so." Winter tilted her head thoughtfully. "We were talking about why you are so old."

Mark debated how much detail to give. His usual version of his unorthodox path to medical school was brief and unemotional; a sketchy outline of the chronology laced with humor at his apparent indecision and free of turmoil. Mark decided to tell Winter the truth. Someday—the day he said good-bye?—she might need to understand.

"My father is a successful—in fact, famous—heart surgeon. I was born while he was doing his residency in San Francisco. By the time I was six I had two younger sisters, a very unhappy mother, and an absentee father."

"Oh," Winter whispered softly. *A very unhappy mother. An absentee father. Just like me, Mark.*

What have I said that makes you so sad? Mark wondered, and waited. But Winter was silent and Mark continued his story.

"My father made his fame and fortune mending hearts, except at home, where he broke them. By the time he was established and could have spent time with us, the marriage was over and his children were angry and confused little strangers." Mark let the ancient emotions catch up with the words. "Home felt like war, a battle between my mother, who was good, and my father and medicine, who were the enemies."

Mark sighed as he remembered how everything had seemed so clear through his hurt young eyes.

"I graduated from Berkeley with a degree in business and joined the stampeding bull market as a broker with Merrill Lynch in San Francisco. It was lucrative, easy, pleasant, and—"

"Not who you are."

Mark nodded, marvelling that she understood. Usually when he recounted his journey from stocks and bonds to Hippocrates, the reaction was one of uncomprehending horror. *But . . . but . . . I thought that with HMOs and DRGs and malpractice insurance, medicine wasn't so . . . uh . . . attractive anymore. Couldn't you . . . don't really successful brokers make millions of dollars?*

"Not who I am," Mark agreed softly. "I returned to Berkeley, took the premed courses, and now I get the *New England Journal* instead of the one from Wall Street."

"And it feels right to be a doctor." Winter knew the answer.

"Yes. It feels very right." Mark reached for her hand, entwining his fingers with hers, and continued gently, "I just have to be so very careful not to—" He faltered, searching for the best words.

"Make the same mistakes your father did?"

"Put myself in a position where I can harm someone I care about. My father *did* make mistakes with his young family and the fragile feelings of his children, but so much of the time he was away from us was beyond his control. As a doctor, especially during residency, your life is controlled by the whims of illness. Like this evening, just as I was leaving to take you to a candlelight dinner in Westwood, three people who had been involved in a bad car accident on the

San Diego Freeway arrived in the E.R. The other trauma team was in the O.R., operating on a man who had been shot, so—"

"You had to stay. They needed you."

"Yes." *I wanted to stay. I wanted to help.* And something else, something that had made Mark's voice harsh when he saw her. For the first time ever, Mark had felt torn. He had wanted to stay *and* he had wanted to leave to be with her.

Mark had spent the next four hours with a twelve-year-old boy, the youngest victim. The boy had a severe open fracture of the femur. Mark stayed with him in the Emergency Room, during the emergency arteriogram in radiology, and until the orthopedic surgeons assumed his care. It was much more than babysitting; the blood loss had already been significant and the shattered thigh bone raised the ominous specter of fatty emboli to the lungs. Mark monitored the boy carefully, compulsively checking the measurable vital signs—the pulse, the blood pressure, the respiratory rate, the level of consciousness—and the immeasurable ones—the fright of an injured child. Will I live? Is my mother all right? Why can't I see her? Why does it hurt so much?

"There are the demands of long, unpredictable hours," Mark added quietly, "but the emotional demands can be even greater."

Winter nodded solemnly.

"I spent so many years blaming my father, as if he ignored us on purpose."

"And now?"

"I don't see him much. He's back in Houston, married to someone about your age." Mark smiled wryly. "We'll never be close, but the anger—my anger—is gone."

"And your mother?" Winter asked hesitantly, thinking about her own very unhappy mother.

"It's a happy ending. After the divorce and once my sisters and I were in our teens, my mother went back to school. For the past ten years, she has taught high school English and loves it. So—"

"So?"

"—now you know everything there is to know about me. What about you? Tell me about what you want to be and about your family."

Winter gazed for a thoughtful moment at their hands, Mark's strong fingers curled over hers. She felt safe now—almost safe enough to tell him her secrets and her dreams—but he had just finished telling her, so gently, that she couldn't count on him; he couldn't, wouldn't, always be there. Maybe he wouldn't even be there tomorrow.

Winter pulled her hand away, stood up, and began clearing the table. "It's late."

Mark joined her.

"OK. Your turn next time."

"Next time?"

"This weekend, if you're free. Starting Friday night, I'm on a break until after the Fourth."

"They give you vacation?"

"They give us a symbolic break between our junior and senior years. It's more than symbolism, though. They want us to have time to fill out our residency applications. Mine are almost done, because I'm spending next week in San Francisco. My sisters and mother and I haven't been under the same roof in years." Mark stood behind her, wrapped his arms around her waist, and kissed her neck as he spoke. "I don't have to leave until Monday morning. So I thought, if you're free, we could spend from Friday night until Monday together."

"I'm free."

"We could go somewhere."

"Yes." Winter turned to face him. "Or we could stay here."

"Or we could stay here."

Allison was strangely silent, Winter realized as she made the right turn off Bellagio between the brick pillars marking the entrance of the Club.

Allison had been cheerful and excited when Winter arrived promptly at six-thirty—eager to ride, confident of her decision—but as they drove from Santa Monica to Bel Air, her cheerful chatter stopped.

Allison's silence allowed Winter to drift—float—to her own thoughts, to the wonderful memories of last night and this morning. She and Mark had cleaned up the kitchen and gone to bed, to *sleep*. They hadn't made love. They had just kissed gentle kisses and curled close and fallen into necessary sleep and warm, lovely dreams. And then this morning, a half hour before the alarm would have sounded, they awoke together and made love, a tender good morning, a wish for a lovely day, a promise of next time. . . .

Winter parked her Mercedes in the nearly empty "members only" parking lot of the Bel Air Hunt Club. She heard the distant sound of tennis balls pinging off rackets and decided that the two other Mercedes, the Jag, and the Silver Cloud belonged to four of the Club's many tennis fanatics. Winter was about to make a comment about physical fitness addicts when she saw Allison's face.

The excited pink flush was gone. Allison's skin was tight and ashen around her bewildered jade-green eyes. She sat, stiff and frozen, her white-knuckled fists clenched in her lap.

"Allison?"

"I can't believe this," Allison whispered weakly. Her heart fluttered—a sparrow trying to flee her chest—her head swirled and her lungs gasped for precious air. *I'm afraid.*

No, Allison realized. It was more than fear, it was panic! She remembered learning about panic—and panic attacks—in the Introductory Psychology class she had taken to fulfill the social science requirement at UCLA. What if this was a panic attack? The symptoms fit: The panic came out of the blue, swift, powerful, without warning; her heart pounded; her world spun in dizzying fear; her breath was stolen; and she was consumed by a sense of doom.

No, Allison told herself. It's fear—panic *maybe*—but not a panic attack. *And whatever it is, I can control it.*

"You don't have to do this, you know," Winter said. "In fact, it's really a silly idea."

"No, Winter. I have to," Allison countered slowly. Speaking was such a struggle! Her brain was already completely consumed with the suddenly astonishingly difficult tasks of trying to breathe and trying to calm her heart. The additional task of searching for words and speaking them was almost impossible. "I have to."

I have to. I can't live my life with this fear. I can't never ride again because of *this!* Get in control, Allison told herself sternly. But how?

"You don't have to ride today, Allison."

"Yes I do," she breathed. Talking was a battle with her breathless lungs, a fight for the precious air. "Winter, I need you on my side."

"I am on your side, Allison, always. You know that."

"Yes." *Yes.* Winter's words reminded Allison of the other battles she had fought and won. Winter had been there, helping her, as she learned to speak again, and to read and write and walk.

This—this silly panic—was trivial compared to that, wasn't it? Trivial. Allison forced the word into her whirling mind, repeating it over and over, like a mantra. *Trivial. Trivial.* Miraculously, she felt a little more calm.

"I'm OK."

"Are you sure?"

"Yes." *Better, anyway.* "Let's go."

The miracle held. Her legs moved, unsteady, trembling, and she reined her heart in from a gallop to a canter.

Winter and Allison walked along the white marble chip path, lined with pale pink roses, toward the stable compound. As they neared the stable, the fragrance of roses faded in the smells of moist hay and polished leather and horses. The familiar once-beloved scents filled Allison with the memory of her dreams.

The dreams had died the day of her accident, but Allison hadn't known it, hadn't felt the emptiness, until much later. The long months of recovery were filled with their own goals, their own six-foot hurdles and conquests that felt like gold: reading, writing, talking, walking, remembering. Allison's heart and mind and strength and will were focused on being whole and healthy again.

Only after the bones mended as well as they were going to, and the crushed nerves only sent occasional angry messages of pain, and her auburn hair covered the scar on her skull and was a thick mane again, did the realization come. It was a feeling before it was a thought, an aching emptiness filling the place in her heart where her dreams had always lived.

The dreams were gone.

And then Dan was there. Dan, the kind, loving, gentle, young man who fell in love with her. Dan told her she was beautiful — yes, *beautiful* — and Allison laughed at his words with merry astonished eyes; but she had laughed again, at last. The empty aching retreated. *Yes, I will marry you Dan. Oh, well, they have design stores in Hillsborough, don't they? I'm not sure I'll even pursue a career as a designer. . . .*

It felt wonderful. Dan filled the emptiness. Dan became her new dream. Allison lost herself in Dan's love. *Lost herself.* That was the problem. Allison knew, from the aching that stayed in her heart after the horrible wounds had healed, who she *wasn't* anymore; but she had not yet discovered who she was, the new Allison.

She had to find out who she was, what she could do, what she wanted. Dan would help her, giving his proud, loving support, but it was his wonderful, generous love that gave Allison the confidence to be alone, to begin the journey to discover who she was all by herself.

I can't marry you Dan. I will always love you. You have given me so much.

Allison had said good-bye to Dan. In a month she would begin her career at Elegance, nurturing and challenging the incredible new talent that had risen like a phoenix out of the ashes of her shattered dreams.

And today she was going to ride. Allison had no illusions. She would never jump again, never compete, never win an Olympic gold medal, never spend her life riding and training and teaching others to ride.

Allison didn't want to resurrect the dream.

She only wanted to make peace with it.

Then she could go on.

When they reached the stable compound, Allison led the way to the tack room. Yesterday she had called to be sure that her key would still fit the tack room lock and that it was all right for her to ride one of the Club's horses. Of course, she had been told by a surprised voice. Why would the tack room locks have been changed? Why would the rules and privileges of the Club have been changed?

No reason, except that for Allison everything had changed.

"Hello, Ginger," Allison whispered ten minutes later, after she had taken a saddle and bridle from the tack room, signed the members' log, and walked along the rows of stalls to a once-familiar one. "Remember me?"

The horse whinnied and Allison smiled. Ginger's registered name was Bel Air's Ginger Lady. For years, Ginger and Allison—the flame-colored horse and the girl with the flame-colored hair—had been Bel Air's Ginger Ladies. Even after she got Tuxedo, and spent hours training, jumping, competing with him, it was Ginger who Allison still rode on the trails. Tuxedo dragged his champion thoroughbred heels at the prospect of a trail ride; Ginger always pricked up her ears, tossed her red-gold mane, and tensed with excitement.

Maybe today, Allison thought, she and Ginger could ride the trails after she rode in the ring.

After.

The panic came back in small, dizzying waves; each little wave carried the threatening promise that, if unchecked, it would swell into a monstrous one, crashing, consuming, destroying. Allison was on guard, fighting each wave.

Allison fought the panic and the memory of the sudden unexpected lurch of fright that could hurl her again into an immeasurable nightmare.

Ginger didn't lurch. She walked and trotted and cantered in amiable response to Allison's silent expert commands.

Winter watched from a distant corner of the outdoor ring, fingers crossed, breath held. After fifteen minutes, she relaxed a little, still vigilant but captivated by the grace and rhythm and elegance of horse and rider. Winter's eyes misted briefly, from sadness for Allison's shattered dreams, then from happiness as she saw her best friend's smile and sparkling eyes, despite the intense concentration. Allison's physical wounds had healed long ago. But, Winter realized, until this moment, Allison hadn't really fully recovered.

After thirty minutes, Allison brought Ginger to a halt in front of Winter.

"Wonderful." Winter smiled at her friend's flushed, happy face.

"Thanks. It felt good. In fact, I think Ginger and I are going for a ride on the Kensington trail."

The fabulous trails at the Club bore lovely British names: Kensington, Windsor, Knightsbridge, Covent Garden. Kensington was the sunrise trail, winding east through a forest of palmettos and ferns to a bluff overlooking the Los Angeles basin, the San Bernardino Mountains, the new dawn sun. Windsor was the sunset trail, meandering west to a breathtaking vista of the Pacific. The other trails criss-crossed like embroidery threads through a luxuriant tapestry of roses and lilacs and azaleas and rhododendrons.

Winter started to protest Allison's solitary journey, but stopped. Allison was fine, *better*.

"Shall I go have a cup of coffee at the Club and come back in an hour or two?"

"No. I'll call Mother when I'm done riding." Allison had spared her parents advance warning of this momentous decision, but now she was eager to let them know. Sean Fitzgerald was a passionate horseman; her loving father would hug her tightly, his understanding outweighing his fear. Her mother's embrace would be tight, too; Patricia didn't share the passion for riding, but she shared with her husband the wish for Allison's happiness above all else.

"OK. How about a celebration dinner at the Chart House in Malibu tonight?"

"I'd like that. Winter? Thank you for being here."

* * *

Winter clutched the leather steering wheel of her Mercedes. She had been sitting like this, in the parking lot of the Club, for the past twenty minutes. Members were arriving—elegant breakfast meetings, tennis lessons, teenagers planning a day at the pool, riders—and she was beginning to draw concerned stares.

Allison had found peace. Allison had conquered her demons. Allison was going to find a new dream.

What about you, Winter?

I'm not strong like Allison.

But remember what Mark said? "Your turn next time?" What are you going tell him? You can't lie to him. His eyes won't let you.

I know!

The mansion on Bellagio—Winter's mansion—was only a half mile away. How many times had she driven by in the past five years, forcing her eyes not to drift, even slightly, toward the opening in the ten-foot wall of bougainvillea and the winding drive that led to her home?

Winter's demons lived there. Winter's dreams had died there.

It's been five years. Why go back now?

Because you have to. You have to find peace with the lonely, unloved, frightened little girl who lives inside you.

Winter sighed softly and turned the key in the ignition. Only a half mile away . . .

Chapter Five

Los Angeles, California
January, 1961

The birth of Winter Carlyle was news, and Vanessa Gold printed it in *All That Glitters* before anyone else in the world, scooping the celebrity columnists in Los Angeles and, to Vanessa's great delight, scooping even the columnists of Fleet Street. This baby, the love-child of American actress and Hollywood darling Jacqueline Winter and the distinguished and extraordinarily successful British director Lawrence Carlyle, would make headlines from Hollywood to London. The love-child was due, appropriately, on Valentine's Day.

But Vanessa received the call from one of her most reliable sources shortly after midnight on New Year's Eve, moments after the baby's birth, as "Auld Lang Syne" played in the background and confetti still floated to the floor and champagne-flavored kisses among the celebrity revellers grew deeper and longer.

Vanessa left the New Year's Eve gala at Cyrano's moments after receiving the call. She rushed first to the hospital — a worthwhile trip because she was able to speak with a beaming Lawrence Carlyle — then to her office, and finally to the printing presses of the paper where she stood her ground and watched as the obviously annoyed typesetter exchanged the new words for ones that had been typeset hours before.

Then Vanessa drove to her bungalow on St. Cloud and poured herself a glass of champagne. Before taking a sip, she raised the crystal champagne flute first to the south, toward the hospital where the infant girl lay, and then to the east, toward England and her soon-to-be envious competitors, the columnists of Fleet Street.

CELEBRATED LOVE-CHILD
ARRIVES WITH NEW YEAR!!

Moments after the stroke of midnight, as the old year took its final curtain call, Jacqueline Winter gave birth to a baby girl. Winter Elizabeth Carlyle's birth comes just five months after the much-publicized marriage of stunning American actress Jacqueline Winter and celebrated British producer/director Lawrence Carlyle. Although the already famous love-child was not expected until Valentine's Day, the new papa reports proudly, "She's small and delicate and doing just fine."

The actress and director met two years ago during the filming of *Marakesh*. A passionate but stormy on-location affair—in Casablanca, no less!—ended "badly." Jacqueline and Lawrence were reunited by the Academy Awards, which garnered statues of Oscar for each for *Marakesh*. By August, passion vanquished storm clouds, and the never-married-ever-loved pregnant actress and the never-married-ever-secretive father-to-be director were married.

Carlyle will keep Laurelhurst, his fifteen-hundred-acre estate in his native England, but the couple will reside in the Bel Air mansion previously owned by legendary studio tycoon Ben Samuels and purchased by Carlyle three months ago. Two-time Oscar-winner Carlyle has just wrapped his latest sure-to-be-a-blockbuster epic *Destiny*. The actress mother plans to resume her acting career in April with the lead role in *Fame and Fortune*.

Fourteen months later, Vanessa reported the divorce. The "forsaking all others" vow had cast another celebrity marriage asunder. At least, the rumor that was leaked—a huge, gushing leak—to all concerned was that Lawrence Carlyle had been unfaithful and Jacqueline Winter had thrown him out. Vanessa suspected a "dysinformation" campaign, but she was unable *ever* to uncover anything else and had to conclude, with the rest of Hollywood, that the reason for the divorce was "as advertised." Lawrence Carlyle returned to England where, nine months later, he married British author Margaret Reilly, the unassuming, talented, very successful writer of murder mysteries.

The marriage of Lawrence Carlyle and Jacqueline Winter became just another Hollywood statistic, another failed marriage that, on the face of it, seemed less messy in its dissolution than most. But Vanessa wondered. According to everyone, Lawrence never saw his child after the divorce, and that was surprising indeed. It seemed so unlike what Vanessa knew of Lawrence Carlyle. And it worried her, because it meant that the little girl's only parent was Jacqueline Winter . . . and *that* meant the child had no parent at all.

It wasn't until she was four that Winter realized there was no one in her world whom she called Daddy. There was Mommy, of course. Mommy had flowing platinum hair and sapphire eyes, and she floated like a fairy princess, just beyond Winter's reach. Winter heard her mother's soft voice, but the softness was never for her, nor was Jacqueline's bewitching smile or her delicate touch. Jacqueline's smiles and softness were for her friends, the never-ending, ever-changing parade of handsome and powerful men who were there during the rare hours when Mommy was even at home.

There was Mommy—beautiful, fragrant, graceful, lovely . . . beyond Winter's desperate grasp.

But there was no Daddy. There were daddies on television

and in books, and although Winter had no friends, she was mysteriously invited to birthday parties in Bel Air and Beverly Hills—her nannies would take her—and sometimes there were daddies there, too.

At age four, Winter made the discovery that her Daddy was missing, but she didn't have the courage to ask her mother, or anyone, about it until she was six.

Winter was much too shy to ask—much too shy and terribly lonely. Jacqueline paid people—nannies and governesses and housekeepers—a great deal of money to pay attention to the daughter she herself rarely saw or wanted to see. The hired help cared for Winter dutifully and without affection. It was so difficult—impossible!—to feel warmth for the quiet, serious little girl with the sorrowful, judgmental violet eyes. Winter resisted warmth, they decided, *spurned it*, preferring her own private world of make-believe.

Winter lived in a fantasy world rich with wonderful adventures and loving friends, with whom she shared the feelings she was too shy to speak aloud. *Why doesn't anyone like me? Why doesn't anyone touch me? Why doesn't Mommy ever play with me?* The pain screamed silently from her small, shy heart; but her fantasy friends had no answers. And there were fears, too—horrible fears—nestled in her heart beside the pain. *What if I die? What happens when I die? What if Mommy dies? Is death cold and dark?*

Winter knew no one liked her—*please* like me!—but she didn't know why. And she knew that she had no Daddy, and she didn't understand that, either.

Finally, Winter summoned six months of courage and asked her beautiful mother a question she had rehearsed a hundred times in her mind.

"Mommy, where is my Daddy? Everyone else . . ."

Jacqueline looked up from her first screwdriver of the day and gazed with surprise at her daughter. Despite her enormously successful career and an unending stream of famous and powerful men who wanted her, Jacqueline Winter was unhappy with her life. Of the many things that displeased her, one of the most annoying was her daughter. Winter's

70

painful shyness was bad enough, an embarrassment, but add to that her looks . . .

Any daughter of Jacqueline Winter should have been at least pretty and adorable, and more likely enchanting and beguiling. But Winter was pale and gawky and her too-huge eyes stared critically at the world. Winter was, Jacqueline decided, really and truly an ugly little girl.

Ugly and sullen and serious, and now Winter was asking about her Daddy!

"Your Daddy," Jacqueline sighed as the memory of her marriage crashed over her like an enormous unwelcome wave on a sandcastle. How she hated Lawrence Carlyle for leaving her! She should have let him have Winter, even though . . . But Lawrence had wanted Winter, and Jacqueline had been determined to punish him every way she could.

"Where is he?"

"In England."

"What's his name? What does he do?" Winter pressed with uncharacteristic bravery. She had a Daddy!

"His name is Lawrence Carlyle," Jacqueline answered, amazed at her own patience. She was a little lonely. She had just finished filming *Roses are Red* and, as far as she was concerned, had also just ended the affair with her on-screen lover. Jacqueline was feeling the familiar, unwelcome let-down of reentering the real world. Maybe it would be diverting to talk to her daughter for a while. Another screwdriver would help, too. "He makes movies."

"Like you?"

"No, he's a director and a producer."

Winter frowned at the unfamiliar and so important-sounding words. Jacqueline wasn't in the mood to explain, but she didn't want to be alone, either.

"I'll show you."

Jacqueline and Winter were in the breakfast nook of the mulberry, cream, and heather-gray country kitchen. Jacqueline stood up, hesitated a moment, then moved decisively to a remote drawer and removed a key. She refilled her glass with more gin than orange juice and gestured for Winter to follow. They crossed the living room to a back hallway that led to a room Winter knew but that had never held much interest for her. It was a cavernous room, with peach-colored walls and cushiony chairs and sofas arranged facing a mural on one wall. Winter had spent an afternoon gazing at the mural, a faded Italian fresco, but couldn't understand its appeal.

Jacqueline flicked a switch on the nearby wall and the mural parted, revealing a huge screen. Next, she opened a gray panel built into the wall, inserted the key, and turned it, inactivating the special security system Lawrence had installed to protect the irreplaceable library of films stored in the peach-colored cupboards that lined the walls.

A state-of-the-art security system wired the entire mansion, but extra protection was warranted in the screening room. Some of the reels of films were original prints, rare studio copies, some purchased, some bartered, some stolen. Lawrence had bought Ben Samuels's film library at the same time he had bought the mansion, in a transaction that was separate and very expensive.

Jacqueline had fallen in love with the mansion because of its magnificent views of Los Angeles and the ocean, its palatial rooms, its crystal chandeliers and marble floors. Lawrence had fallen in love with the secret hidden gardens, the tranquil pond filled with koi, and the rare treasures buried in the film library.

Ben Samuels's film collection was already the best in the world, but Lawrence made it even better. He added prints of all his own movies and all of Jacqueline's, and he purchased contemporary "classics" to complement the ones of the Golden Era. Lawrence offered Jacqueline an enormous price for the library at the time of the divorce, but she refused all his offers because she knew how much his precious prints meant to him. Jacqueline held all the cards; Lawrence was desperate to get away from her. Jacqueline's fury and Lawrence's desperation meant he gave her everything she wanted . . . everything but himself.

Jacqueline hadn't set foot in the screening room since Lawrence left. Now she walked along the once-familiar walls, opened a cabinet, and removed the reels of *Marakesh*, the Oscar-award-winning Jacqueline Winter-Lawrence Carlyle collaboration. Winter followed her mother to the projection booth and watched as, after a few false starts, Jacqueline wound the reel and started the projector. Then she settled beside her mother in a cushiony chair in front of the huge screen.

When the first reel ended, Jacqueline briefly explained to Winter how to thread the next and disappeared to make another screwdriver. Winter's small hands threaded the projector quickly, then she scampered back to her chair and waited eagerly for Jacqueline to return so the magic could continue.

"You were wonderful, Mommy," Winter breathed when the last reel of *Marakesh* came to its end. "And my Daddy made that movie?"

Jacqueline nodded.

"Why is he in England?" *Where is England? Can we go there?* "When is he coming home?"

"He's never coming home."

"Why not? Doesn't he like us?" *Doesn't he like me? No one likes me, so why should Daddy?*

"No, Winter, he doesn't like us," Jacqueline said heavily, glowering at her empty glass as if it held the empty memories. Finally, she stood up. "Let's go."

"No! Can't we watch it again?"

"No."

"Please!"

"I said no."

"Are there other movies, Mommy?" She was being so brave, but she was so desperate. For the first time in her life Winter felt safe; in this enchanted place watching fantasy worlds come to life, she felt safe. And *happy*.

"Oh." Jacqueline shrugged. "I guess we could watch something else."

They spent the morning and afternoon watching Jacqueline's own girlhood favorites—*National Velvet*, *The Wizard of Oz*, *Gone With The Wind*. By the end of the day, Winter knew she was going to be an actress.

Until then, Winter had lived in the fantasies of her mind. Her imagination was vivid and creative, but this was even better.

Now Winter knew about Oz, and she could be Dorothy; and she knew about England—where Daddy was!—and she could be Velvet; and she knew about Tara, and she could be Scarlett.

Winter *was* Dorothy. She sang to the Japanese koi that swam lazily in the pond in a hidden garden beside the unused wing of the mansion. Winter joyfully serenaded the koi about places over the rainbow and the yellow brick road. The colorful, tranquil koi were her audience; Winter performed for them and talked to them, and they ate from her small hands. And she named them. The black one was Toto; the silver one, Tin Woodman; the white one, Belinda; the yellow one, Cowardly Lion; and the calico one, Scarecrow.

Winter was Dorothy and Velvet and Scarlett and a hundred other wonderful characters she discovered in the long, happy hours she spent in the screening room after she convinced Jacqueline to show her about the security system and promised to be *so* careful with the treasures.

Winter played all the roles to perfection. No one knew. No one watched her. If anyone had, if her audience had been other than the koi, they would have known what Winter knew: She was a gifted actress. Winter knew. She told no one because she was still shy and silent. Her shyness drove her deeper into the dreams that had become an obsession.

She was going to be an actress—she *was* an actress—but there was more! She was going to star in Daddy's movies and he was going to be so proud of her!

My Daddy will like me even though no one else does.

No one liked Winter. In the expensive private schools in Switzerland—in Geneva and Zurich—where she spent most of her life from the time she was eight, Winter finally learned why. The other girls stared at her and giggled and pointed. Their young eyes flashed with dislike and contempt and they hissed cruelly, "shy" and "weird" and "skinny" and "ugly" and "scaredy-cat" and "witch."

The vicious taunts stabbed Winter with excruciating pain. She stared at the other girls through tear-blurred eyes and wished she had the courage to say, But I'm Dorothy, I'm Scarlett, I'm Velvet! You like them, don't you? I can be them! I can be anyone you want me to be!!

Winter could, but no one gave her a chance because of the way she looked—so pale, so awkward, so serious. No one would listen, but it didn't matter because she didn't have the courage to speak.

Then everything changed.

Sometime between the time she flew from Los Angeles to Zurich shortly after her fourteenth birthday in January and the time she returned from the exclusive Swiss boarding school in May, Winter Elizabeth Carlyle became beautiful. Winter didn't know it. She never looked at herself in the mirror. And if the other girls at the school noticed, they were shocked into green-eyed silence.

Winter found out from a stranger on her way home. The stranger was a young man, although to Winter he seemed *so* mature. He stood beside her as she browsed through books in London's Heathrow Airport. Finally, he simply said, "You are the most beautiful creature I have ever seen."

He was handsome, and his eyes were brown and sincere, and he had a soft British accent, and he wanted nothing from her except for her to know that he thought she was beautiful. Winter smiled vaguely at his words. He returned the smile, then left. After a few moments, Winter went into the ladies' room and discovered that he was right.

The ugly duckling had become a swan; awkwardness had become grace; skinniness had become soft sensuality; pale, translucent skin had become rich cream; fine, stringy hair was black velvet; chapped, chewed lips were full and red; and the too-huge eyes were hypnotic, seductive, beckoning.

She was as beautiful as Scarlett O'Hara.

On the flight home, Winter thought a little about her

beauty and a lot about the man in the London airport. What if he had been Daddy? Winter knew he wasn't, of course. She had made a study of Lawrence Carlyle, carefully filling scrapbooks with articles about him and photographs of him. Winter had seen all his movies, over and over and over. She read the murder mysteries written by his wife — her stepmother! — and spent hours analyzing a rare, precious photograph she had found in a magazine, a picture of Lawrence and his two young sons, her half brothers. Winter tried to see the family resemblance, but her father was so handsome, and her rosy-cheeked half brothers looked confident and happy.

The young man at Heathrow hadn't been Lawrence Carlyle, but he had been British, like Daddy. And he had told her she was beautiful. Maybe it was a wonderful omen.

Suddenly everyone liked her. Strangers smiled at her, and so did the ever-before-hostile housekeeper at the mansion, and so did her mother. Jacqueline was delighted in a bittersweet way. She was envious of Winter's youthful beauty but happy that at last her daughter looked the way she should. Jacqueline embraced the new Winter — spiritually, not physically — taking her on shopping sprees to Rodeo Drive and to lunch at the Bel Air Hunt Club, the Polo Lounge, Benito, and L'Ermitage.

No one seemed to care any longer that Winter was quiet and shy; she was beautiful, ravishing, and that was enough. But Winter cared. She wanted to speak! She had been unheard for so long. Her shyness hadn't vanished, but her beauty gave her confidence.

At first her words were serious. She wanted to, tried to, share the pain and fears that had been imprisoned inside her for so long. She was like someone awakening from years of coma. What happened? Where am I? I've had the most horrible nightmares. . . .

Winter wanted to ask why, why, *why?* But when she did, Jacqueline and the housekeepers and the teenagers at the pool at the Club withdrew, suddenly uneasy, not liking her again.

Please like me!

Winter lapsed into thoughtful silence. When she spoke again, her voice was soft and purring, her words were charming and witty, and she was provocative and vivacious. Everyone loved Winter and it made her feel wonderful. The bright, clever words were hers, as much a part of her as the secret, hidden ones she couldn't utter, but for the dazzling delivery Winter borrowed liberally from the heroines she knew so well—the coquettishness of Scarlett, the dreaminess of Dorothy, the courage of Velvet, the passion of Lara, the boldness of Fanny, the will of Eliza, the soft loveliness of them all.

Winter was an actress. She created a magnificent, seductive, bewitching personality to match her stunning, provocative beauty. She wove a vivid tapestry of emotions and moods, but she was always confident, always golden, always in control.

It was better to be liked—much, much better—but Winter lived in fear that the lonely, frightened little girl who still dwelled in her heart would be discovered and she would be ostracized again. Winter didn't hate the little girl . . . it was who she was; but sometimes she ached desperately to tell someone about *her*, about how lonely and afraid she was, what wonderful dreams she had, how much she wanted to see her father.

By the time Winter was fifteen, her self-sufficiency and maturity had greatly surpassed that of her mother. She had long since abandoned hope that Jacqueline would love her, but as she realized the magnitude of her mother's despair, Winter's own anger began to melt into loving concern. It was a miracle that Jacqueline's career never wavered. She starred in major films every year, received four Best Actress nominations in addition to the one for *Marakesh,* and won one of them. Jacqueline Winter was a remarkable success. Her work earned her great wealth, but it paled by comparison to the fortune in jewels and other gifts lavished on her by the rich and powerful men who wanted her.

Jacqueline drank too much and too often, and she took

pills. Her life between roles was barren and desperate. She never remarried, despite constant offers. Winter couldn't recall a genuine laugh, not a happy one, just the on-cue laughter of a gifted actress. Jacqueline added her brilliant dazzle to Hollywood's parties, but when she arrived home at dawn, she was often restless, unsettled, reluctant to be alone.

It was then, as the new day sun peered over the San Bernardino Mountains and cast a golden beam across the Los Angeles basin, that Jacqueline and Winter became "friends." They weren't mother and daughter; they were more like the only two girls still awake at the slumber party, determined not to succumb to sleep, talking honestly because they were too tired not to.

Jacqueline's motherly advice to Winter sprung from her own mistakes. She never told Winter she had made a mistake by ignoring her little girl, but Winter let herself believe she saw that regret, too, in her mother's alcohol-blurred eyes. Jacqueline focused on her mistakes with men and on her foolish belief that her own stunning beauty was immortal and required no care.

"Stay out of the sun, Winter. Oh, I see that you already know that," Jacqueline added with a smile, as if she had just made an important discovery. It was mid-August and Winter's skin was still the color of fresh cream.

For the first fourteen years of her life, Winter lived in the darkened worlds of the screening room at the mansion and movie theaters in Zurich and Geneva. She left those enchanted caves to re-create the fantasies in the tree-shaded garden by the pond or in her Spartan dormitory room in Switzerland. Until her life-changing fourteenth summer, Winter had never walked on the white sand beach a few miles from her home or spent frolicking, splashing, carefree afternoons by the pool at the Club.

During that memorable summer, when she was beautiful and had fashioned a personality to match, Winter spent most days at the pool at the Club. But by then she was Scarlett. She wore elegant broad-rimmed straw hats, sipped lemonade in the shade of a pink umbrella, batted her long, dark lashes, and purred in a soft Southern drawl that she needed to protect her delicate skin from the harshness of the summer sun. Winter held court in the shade by the pool, Scarlett entertaining the Confederate Army on the verandah at Tara. The young men were enthralled and the girls frantically tried to imitate. The imitations failed. Winter's rich white skin was seductive and elegant; without tans, the other girls simply looked pale, anemic, unhealthy.

"I do stay out of the sun, Mother."

"And don't smoke."

"I don't."

"And," Jacqueline smiled wryly as she toasted herself with a half-empty glass of gin, "you probably shouldn't drink."

I don't. I won't. And I won't take drugs. Winter had made those promises years ago as she watched her mother's drug and alcohol-ravaged life. She added quietly, "Neither should you."

"But I do." Jacqueline gave a wobbly smile and a shrug that said, It's too late. She continued softly, speaking from her heart, "Be careful with men, Winter. They will want you. Oh, how they will want you! Have them, enjoy them on your terms, but be in control always. And never let them get too close."

Winter nodded solemnly. She had already learned that, but it applied to everyone, not just men. *Everyone* wanted something from her. The men wanted *her* and the girls wanted to be close, basking in her golden brilliance, hoping she had something to spare, an ounce of fairy dust to sprinkle on them, a small touch of her magic. Everyone wanted. No one gave. And they only wanted her if she was dazzling and beautiful. No one wanted to hear about her fears or her secrets.

Winter wished she could tell Jacqueline she was going to be an actress — *like you Mother!* — and that it would reunite her with her father. Winter didn't know why Lawrence had left or why in all these years he had never tried to see her, but she heard the bitterness in Jacqueline's voice when she spoke of him and assumed — prayed — it was something between her mother and father, nothing to do with her. *He doesn't like us,* Jacqueline had told her. But Winter had been so young! Surely Lawrence didn't leave because of *her*. No, she told herself. Lawrence left because of Jacqueline. Winter could go to him now, but that would mean abandoning Jacqueline. Winter didn't even consider it.

She would find him someday — they would find each other — and her Daddy would love her . . . even when she told him about the shy, frightened little girl who lived inside her still.

It was her mother's idea that she stop going to school in Switzerland and Winter gratefully agreed. She spent her last two years of high school in Bel Air, living in the mansion, attending the Westlake School for Girls on North Faring.

Winter's appearance on the first day of fall semester at Westlake drew amazed and delighted breaths from her classmates. They knew her from the pool at the Club and the starlit summer dances and sailing trips to Catalina. Winter was their idol, their *ideal;* envy didn't even enter in because what Winter had was so far beyond their reach.

The other girls wanted something, a ray of her sunshine; *all* the other girls except Allison Fitzgerald. Winter and Allison had both lived in Bel Air since birth, but before the day Winter enrolled at Westlake they had never met. Until then, the lives of Allison Fitzgerald and Winter Carlyle had no common threads.

Winter had lived in a dark cocoon until she became a butterfly. Then, during the summer days while Winter lazed demurely in the shade by the pool at the Club, Allison rode. And at night, when Winter teased seductively in the summer moonlight, Allison slept, because she would ride again at dawn. And at the time when Winter decided to lose her virginity — *to give it away* when she was sixteen and he was twenty-two — Allison still blushed uneasily when boys approached her and was most happy cantering across rolling green hills, her long red-gold hair tossed by the wind.

Allison was warm and friendly to the new girl in the junior class. She had no desire to bask in Winter's dazzle, no need for reflected glory. Allison had her own golden aura, a halo of love and happiness spun from loving parents and golden dreams and a heart that beat confidently with hope and joy. Allison wanted nothing from Winter, but she welcomed Winter into her life, sharing her warm, loving parents and her own dreams without expecting anything in return.

Allison became Winter's friend, her best friend, her only friend. Winter didn't tell Allison her secrets, but she believed she could and that Allison would still be her friend.

On the eve of her eighteenth birthday — New Year's Eve — Jacqueline gave Winter the powder-blue Mercedes Sports Coupe and the flawless sapphire earrings.

"You need the car, and I want you to have these earrings. Lawrence gave them to me when I went into labor, just about eighteen years ago this minute. He said they were the exact color of my eyes." Jacqueline's voice was soft and distant, lost in a lovely memory.

"They are."

"I thought you would like to have them." Jacqueline shrugged uncertainly, as the moment came too close to love. "I never wear them. There's a necklace, too, in the safe."

"Thank you." *Mother, thank you!*

"Happy New Year and early Happy Birthday."

Jacqueline touched Winter briefly — a rare, gentle, almost loving touch — before she left for a New Year's Eve Party. Winter was too stunned to touch back, and by the time she rushed to the door, to hug her, to thank her, to cry, Jacqueline was gone.

And Winter never saw her again. Just before dawn, Jacqueline's car plummeted over a cliff on Mulholland Drive and into eternity. Jacqueline's blood alcohol level was sky high. Her death was ruled an accident, but Winter wondered if her mother had known, if that was why she had given her the earrings, tacitly reestablishing the link with Lawrence after all these years of bitter silence. Winter wondered if Jacqueline had known she was saying good-bye.

"This is Jacqueline. I'm either not home or can't be bothered to answer. If you're calling about a role that has an Oscar attached — the statue, not just another nomination — leave a message. Otherwise . . ."

Winter listened to the tape in her mother's answering machine over and over. She had reels of Jacqueline's movies, but those were roles. The go-to-hell message on the answering machine was pure Jacqueline. Winter couldn't bear to erase it; but, finally, she stopped listening to it and put it, carefully wrapped, in the safe beside the boxes filled with jewels.

Allison and Patricia and Sean Fitzgerald wanted Winter to move in with them, to join their loving family, but Winter said no. She told all the live-in help to leave and resided alone at the mansion, grieving, waiting for her Daddy.

Winter expected Lawrence Carlyle to come to Jacqueline's funeral. All of Hollywood was there, all of Jacqueline lovers, all except Lawrence. It made Winter very sad, but in a perverse way it gave her hope. It was more proof that the reason Lawrence had stayed away all these years was because of whatever had happened with Jacqueline.

Three months after Jacqueline's death Winter sat in the living room of the mansion with Leo Stiles, the senior partner in the law firm handling the estate, and learned the staggering details of her enormous inheritance. The mansion, empty, was conservatively appraised at eight million. And then there were the five original Impressionist paintings, including two by Monet; the large bedroom safe filled with velvet boxes containing thousands of carats of precious jewels fashioned by Tiffany and Winston and Cartier; the priceless film library; Jacqueline's two Oscars; the millions of earned income shrewdly invested and never spent because there were always lovers who wanted to provide for her; the expensive furnishings; and Winter's trust fund provided by Lawrence Carlyle.

"Trust fund?" *From Daddy?*

"Yes. He has made substantial annual contributions since the divorce," Leo Stiles explained. "Since your mother was always able to provide for you, we just put the money in a special trust fund. The current value is about ten million."

"Is he still? . . ."

"Until you are twenty-one."

Winter bit her lower lip thoughtfully. It had been three months and each day she expected Lawrence to rescue her, his long-lost, long-loved daughter. What if he didn't even know about Jacqueline's death? Now there was a way to be sure.

"Do you know how to reach him?" Winter asked. She knew how. She knew the address of Laurelhurst and the address of Lawrence's film studio in London, and she even knew his phone number.

"Of course."

"Would you call him, speak to him directly, tell him that Mother died, and—" Winter paused. This was so important, sending a message to Daddy. "Thank him very much for all the money he has sent me, tell him how much it has meant to me, but tell him I don't need anymore." *I just need him.*

Two weeks later Winter called Leo Stiles to be certain the message had been conveyed.

"Yes. I spoke with him directly."

"What did he say?"

"He said fine and he thanked me for calling."

"Anything else?" *Anything about me?*

"No, that was all."

Winter waited for Lawrence Carlyle, aching with loneliness and fear, grieving her mother's death. But Lawrence Carlyle didn't come, and all the love and hope that had lived in Winter's heart turned into hatred.

The hatred tainted her dreams. She didn't want to be an actress anymore. How could she be? How could she find joy

83

in something that had caused a life of despair for her mother and might lead a path to the door of the man she now hated with all her heart?

Winter abandoned her dreams, as she had been abandoned by the father she dreamed about. Lawrence Carlyle was no longer a part of her life. She would simply have to forget about him. Winter threw away the scrapbooks, and she made a solemn vow never to read about him again or to see another of his brilliant movies.

During the nine months between Jacqueline's death and the first day of her Freshman year at UCLA, Winter took a hard look at the lessons life had taught her.

It is better to be liked than disliked. Even though it meant hiding her deepest feelings, it was better.

It is dangerous to care. She had cared about Jacqueline, and just as they were finally finding something—fragile and gentle and maybe close to love—her mother was gone. She had cared about Daddy, and when she discovered he *didn't* care, something inside her died.

People leave you. Daddy, Jacqueline, *everyone*, unless she was sunny and charming and beautiful. The ones who knew her the best left her, as if there were something wrong with her, something impossible to love and easy to leave.

Three weeks before Freshman registration, Winter made an appointment to see Leo Stiles. It was about the mansion, she told his executive secretary.

Winter thought about living at the mansion during college. Allison—her best friend Allison, who was still her friend because she hadn't made the fatal discovery—was going to live at home. Allison was happy with her parents, close enough in Bel Air to the UCLA campus, and very close to the important place, the stable at the Bel Air Hunt Club. Again, Allison urged her friend to move into her parents' home, but Winter declined. She couldn't live with the Fitzgeralds—it wasn't her home—but she couldn't stay at the mansion, the magnificent house that had never really been a home, either.

Winter was afraid to stay at the mansion. It would be so

easy to lapse into the fantasy days of her childhood, entombing herself in the dark screening room, isolating herself from the world, pretending the dreams hadn't died.

But the dreams *were* dead. Winter fought the self-destructive urge to stay in the mansion and die with them. She had to leave and find new dreams, something she wanted to do other than act. Surely there was something in the hundreds of courses offered at UCLA!

"Have you decided to sell the mansion?" Leo Stiles asked.

"No. Not yet. I assume it will just increase in value." Winter would sell it someday, when she found a new home for the priceless reels of film — celluloid dreams — and the Oscars, jewels, and paintings that were the only remaining symbols of Jacqueline's dazzling and tragic life. Until then . . . "I don't want to live there, but I want to have it maintained and safe. I have gardeners and a weekly cleaning service, but—"

"I don't remember offhand which services you have, but they probably are ones we recommended. If so, you don't have to worry about security. Anyway, I'll check if you like, and we can have the bills come through our office — we handle this for a number of the rarely inhabited homes in Bel Air — and send you quarterly statements."

"Yes. All right. Thank you." Winter paused. "There are fish — Japanese koi — in a pond in the garden. I had a man come out last week from a pet store in Brentwood. He says that there is enough natural food in the pond for them, but it's possible to set up reservoirs of food, just in case. I'd like to have him hired to come by once a month to check on them and set up the reservoirs. Here's his name and number."

"You'll be at UCLA?"

"Yes. I'm moving into an apartment on Holman Avenue in two weeks. I'll be sure you have the address and phone number."

Winter's hands trembled as she locked the front door of

85

the mansion. Her childhood was inside, along with her dreams, and she was leaving them behind. Winter took very little with her from the mansion on Bellagio to her apartment on Holman Avenue two miles away, just the gifts from Jacqueline—the car and the earrings—and the lessons life had taught her.

Winter spent four of the next five years carefully following the lessons of her life, revealing little, dazzling, enchanting, controlling, and playing games that kept a very safe distance from the heart. Winter was *the* belle on a campus known for its belles and starlets; Winter outshined them all.

Winter played and performed with everyone but Allison. And one year Winter didn't play at all. Winter spent that year helping Allison fight her courageous battle, silently crying for her friend, tormenting herself.

It is dangerous to care. People leave you. The words haunted Winter as she watched Allison struggle to be whole again. She had brought her own bad luck to her best friend! But, no, Allison was protected by that halo of love. Allison survived, and then Allison flourished, falling in love with Dan, discovering wonderful new talents to replace the shattered dreams.

Winter returned to UCLA after the year away, hopeful that her own frustrating search for new dreams would be more fruitful than it had been during the first two years. She studied the undergraduate catalogue carefully, resolutely avoiding courses in Drama, Theater, and Fine Arts, but sampling classes in virtually every other major.

Nothing intrigued her, nothing challenged her, nothing quieted the incessant whispers of her heart that told her she was an actress, she had to act, no matter what. To hell with Lawrence Carlyle!

How can I be an actress?

How can you be anything else?

Winter was still searching for something else—or maybe she was searching for the strength to become an actress *anyway*—the evening she took the final sentimental journey around campus. She was searching for guidance from the hallowed halls, guidance that had eluded her for five years.

Winter's journey took her to the Sculpture Garden, to intense sapphire-blue eyes that made her forget to play and tease; eyes that made her talk about magic.

Sensuous sapphire eyes that told her, *Your turn next time.*

Winter sat in her car at the top of the circular driveway gazing at the mansion. She couldn't go in. The front door keys were in a desk in her apartment . . . but she would bring them with her next time.

Your turn next time.

She had to tell Mark everything — about the unloved little girl who still existed, about her sad mother, about the father she hated, about her dreams. She had to tell Mark everything, because he wouldn't settle for less. She had no choice.

And if everything was too much, if Mark didn't want to hear her secrets, if they made him dislike her, too . . .

Winter shuddered. *People leave you.*

Chapter Six

Mark arrived at eight P.M. Friday night. He kissed her hello, and from that moment until noon Sunday, he and Winter lived in a world of love and passion, an intimate world without boundaries, a sensual world without time.

At noon Sunday, Winter whispered seductively, kissing him as she spoke, "Residency applications."

"Ah, yes," Mark whispered in return. "Are you going to help me?"

"Of course. I *can* type."

While Mark arranged the still-to-be-completed applications on the kitchen table, Winter studied the brochures. Each program in internal medicine boasted excellent educational experiences, fine faculty, extensive research funding, state-of-the art clinical facilities; and each provided in fine print the details of the "on call" schedule, the number of months spent on each clinical service, meals provided "on call," and vacation time.

"This is a different kind of Club Med, isn't it?" Winter asked after several minutes of serious study.

"Yes." Mark smiled. The colorful brochures were filled with pictures of white-coated doctors and elaborate intensive care unit facilities, not pictures of sailboards skimming across white-capped waves, glittering seaside discos, and smiling vacationers sipping piña coladas.

"How do you decide which trip-of-a-lifetime package to

take?" Winter asked, staying with the vacation theme, so far from the reality but amusing to Mark. "They all claim to be the best."

"These are the best," Mark admitted quietly. He was only applying to the most competitive residencies in the country.

"Oh." Winter smiled an appreciative smile. "Is there a best of the best?"

"That depends on who you talk to and what features you measure. Year after year, Massachusetts General Hospital seems to appear at the top of most unbiased lists."

"So that's where you're going? To Boston?"

"I'd like to. If they want me."

"They'll want you."

"Speaking of unbiased . . ."

"I admit it." Winter glanced through the ten brochures again, confirmed what she had already learned, and said, "You're only applying to East Coast programs."

"Yes." Mark had made that decision months ago, because he had never lived on the East Coast, because Mass General was the best, and because plans were so easy before Winter.

In the past few days, Mark had wondered about applying to UCLA, UCSF, Stanford, the University of Washington; but any top residency would be the same. The hours and emotions and responsibilities made it all-consuming; a journey to be travelled alone; a solitary voyage that was impossible to share and fraught with danger if one tried.

"I imagine Boston is wonderful. Charming, historic, misty salt air, the fragrance of clams and lobsters," Winter said.

"You've never been there?"

"No."

"I'm spending December and January in Boston," Mark said quietly, frowning slightly.

89

"Oh." It was bad enough that tomorrow Mark would be leaving for ten days. The thought of not seeing him for two months! *Too presumptuous, Winter,* she warned herself. It's not even July. By December . . .

"In December I'll be in the Intensive Care Unit at Mass General, and in January the Coronary Care Unit at Beth Israel."

"Busy."

"Very. The on-call schedule is every other night." Mark added quietly. "If you came to visit me, you might have to explore Boston on your own."

"That would be all right," Winter whispered as she gazed at the blue eyes that told her so eloquently, *I want you to come, Winter.* "I could visit at Christmas."

"That would be wonderful. But shouldn't you be with your family?"

Winter shook her head and gave a soft sigh. Mark hadn't asked her anything, not one question about *her* all weekend, but Winter knew he was waiting. And she was stalling, savoring every lovely moment they had together, fearing that when she told him, apologetically, that she hadn't always been beautiful or confident, and deep inside was still so shy and afraid, his eyes wouldn't fill with desire, and he wouldn't want to touch her and hold her and love her . . . because part of him would be touching a gawky, ugly little girl.

"Winter?"

As she looked at him, Winter felt tears in her eyes. *No!* She didn't cry, not with anyone watching, not since her huge eyes had filled with tears at the taunts of her childhood classmates and that weakness had made them tease her even more. Since then, the tears she shed for Jacqueline and for Daddy and for her dreams and for Allison had been private, hidden tears.

"Honey," Mark knelt beside her and cupped her face in his strong, gentle hands. Mark had sensed the pain and the secrets, hoping it would help if she told him, but not wanting to cause sadness. He started to wrap his arms around her, but Winter pulled away.

"After we're done with the residency applications, I have to take you somewhere," she said.

"Take me now, Winter."

Mark thought they might be driving to a cemetery, to a marble crypt that housed her beloved parents, but even before they left the apartment, as Winter retrieved a key ring from a far corner of a desk drawer, he revised his prediction. They were going somewhere else. And they were going in Winter's powder-blue Mercedes "because the Bel Air Patrol recognizes it."

Winter drove, following the same route they had taken last weekend, winding along Bellagio toward the Hunt Club. A half mile before the Club entrance, Winter turned through an opening in a wall of fuchsia and plum bougainvillea and onto a white pebble drive that led to a majestic mansion of stone.

Winter parked, got out, and led the way to the front door. Her hands trembled as she inserted the key. She knew what lurked on the other side . . . ghosts. Ghosts of her unhappy childhood and of her shattered dreams.

Winter opened the door and by reflex more than by thought moved swiftly to a gray steel panel in the foyer. She inserted a small key, turned it, and watched as a red light became a green one, a signal that the alarm had been disengaged. Winter paused for a moment, her eyes fixed on the green light, before turning to face the dark and sinister shadows of the house.

It had been so dark, an oppressive suffocating cave, in the months after Jacqueline's death, in those endless days and nights when she had waited for Lawrence. A huge dark monster waiting to devour.

Winter turned, and she realized that the dark monsters had been in her heart.

The foyer glistened with shining marble, and the pastel silks of the living room were light and cheery, and the summer sun streamed through the French doors, and a hundred roses bloomed brightly in the gardens beyond.

"Where are we?" Mark asked quietly, breaking the silence that had lasted since Winter had taken the keys from the desk drawer in her apartment. Mark had asked her such a question before; then they had been in the magnificent champagne-drenched rose garden at the Club. And now they were here, and this was even more splendid. But Winter's face was tense and troubled, and her ivory skin was rough with gooseflesh despite the summer heat.

"Home."

As she and Mark wandered from room to room, Winter told him her story. Her voice was soft and she spoke as if from a trance. Sometimes Mark wondered if she knew he was there. He tried to take her hand, but she wouldn't let him.

"I was ugly. See?" Winter showed him a rare photograph taken by a dutiful nanny—proof that she was doing her job—who had posed her in front of a birthday cake on her seventh birthday. It was one of the few pictures taken of Winter before her fourteenth summer. After that, there were hundreds of pictures, taken by admirers, given to Winter as gifts and carelessly tossed by her into dresser drawers.

"No, I don't see." Mark smiled at the little girl in the picture and her serious violet eyes peered back. He wanted to hold that little girl, to reassure her; and Mark wanted to hold the woman she had become and reassure her, too . . . but Winter wouldn't let him.

"No one liked me. I was very lonely, very afraid," Winter murmured as they walked along the plush carpet from her girlhood bedroom to Jacqueline's.

"Afraid of what?"

"What? Oh, everything. Of being alone, of being disliked, of dying, of my mother dying," Winter answered as they entered Jacqueline's bedroom. The bedroom ceiling was a skylight, now azure blue, but at night an ever-changing scene of moon and stars. The four-poster bed was dressed in lace and a thousand hand-painted wildflowers bloomed on the walls. "This was her room."

Winter paused at a gray steel panel near the door, identical to the one in the foyer. She inserted another small key and inactivated the alarm. Then she walked to the Monet, a pastel portrait of springtime, and pulled gently on the right edge. The priceless painting moved, revealing the safe in the wall. Winter spun the dial on the safe, testing a distant memory, and, on the second try, opened it.

Winter removed a box from the middle of one of the many stacks of burgundy, midnight-blue, and purple velvet that filled the safe. She checked to the see that the contents of the box—a magnificent diamond necklace—had been undisturbed. She read the note inside, written in Jacqueline's lavish script, a notation of who had given her the necklace and when, then gently closed the velvet and returned the box to the safe. Winter checked two more boxes at random—a ruby and diamond bracelet and emerald earrings—then shut the safe and spun the dial.

"I have the only keys to this alarm system and one downstairs in the screening room," Winter explained. "I just wanted to check."

Mark nodded. Winter was checking her staggering fortune. Her wealth was staggering but valueless, a collection of gems and property and money without emotion. No, that wasn't true. There *was* emotion attached to the fortune. Winter had a staggering fortune of pain and unhappiness.

Winter stood in front of the marble fireplace, gently touched the two glittering Oscar statues, their mirrorlike shine proof that the cleaning service was doing its job, and frowned.

"She was a wonderful actress, but . . ."

Winter began Jacqueline's story, speaking in a soft monotone, as they left the bedroom and walked down the spiral staircase. In the sunny kitchen, Winter told Mark about Lawrence, how she had found out about her Daddy, how excited she had been. She led him slowly, reluctantly, to the screening room, idly checking the security system and opening the panels that concealed the priceless reels.

A soft, dreamy smile crossed Winter's face as she told Mark about the enchanted hours she had spent watching movies.

"Then," she said as their journey continued, "I would go outside and re-create what I had seen. We can go this way. It's a shortcut. This part of the mansion was never used, never even re-decorated."

The interior landscape changed dramatically as they entered the unused north wing. The rooms were open and airy, but the wallpaper fell in sheets from the plaster walls and the carpets were threadbare. Instead of vistas of Los Angeles stretching to the ocean, these rooms opened to secluded gardens shaded by weeping willows.

"I always liked this wing of the mansion the best," Winter told him softly. She liked it because it was near her private theater and the pond of koi; but she liked it, too, because her lively imagination had populated these rooms with brothers and sisters—her brothers and sisters, the ones she would have when Lawrence and Jacqueline were reunited, before she learned that her father had another family, a wife and rosy-cheeked sons whom he loved much more than her. "Especially this room."

This would have been her room, sandwiched between her siblings, surrounded by their laughter. On the outside wall, double French doors opened to the garden and the pond. Winter opened the doors and drew a soft breath as memories swept through her, memories of a little girl performing for her koi.

Even when she was beautiful and performed at the

pool of the Club all day every day, even when her audience became enchanted men and admiring girls, Winter still spent hours here. She didn't perform for the fish any longer. She told them, as she put pellets of food in their eager mouths, the secrets and fears she didn't dare share with any living soul—until she found Daddy.

Winter had thought about coming back here—just to this spot, never stepping inside the mansion—a thousand times in the past five years. But she hadn't. She had to stay away.

But she thought about the fish! And now her eyes filled with fresh tears as she approached the edge of the pond and she held her breath.

"Toto," she whispered as his black nose broke the surface, curious, ever-eager for food. "Toto."

Winter got a handful of pellets from the food reservoir that had been installed and maintained just as she had wanted, then sat on the edge of the pond. She fed the sudden swirl of orange and gold and white and black, identifying each one with relief as they took pellets from her ivory fingers. "And Belinda! And Lion, a pig as always. Hello, Scarecrow, here, it's your turn. Hi, Woodman."

"You know these guys," Mark whispered, fighting emotion that swept through him for the lonely, frightened, unloved little girl whose best friends had been these fish. *Oh, Winter.*

Winter turned to him with a happy smile. "I've known them all my life. Koi live for fifty years, sometimes a hundred." Her smile faded slightly. *Longer than my mother lived.*

"Only in this century has man outlived the goldfish. They taught us that the first day of med school."

Winter nodded solemnly, then returned to feeding the fish, speaking to them as she finished her story. Winter had told the fish this story before, how the ugly duckling became a swan, how if she behaved in a certain way everyone liked and wanted her, how she and her mother were just beginning to become close when Jacqueline died, how she waited for her father, how she gave up her dreams.

Then her story was over, and Mark knew everything—her fears, her secrets, who she really was. Winter stopped speaking and stared at the fish. They eyed her expectantly, waiting for food, and she waited for Mark to speak. Maybe he wouldn't. Maybe when she finally forced herself to look toward him, he would be gone.

He hadn't left yet. Winter felt his magnetic presence and the heat of his sensuous blue eyes staring at her. Mark moved behind her. Winter trembled as he gently touched her bare shoulders.

"I'm not who you thought I was, am I?"

"You're exactly who I thought you were." *Lovely and sensitive and vulnerable and warm and loving.* Mark leaned over and kissed a soft place on her neck beneath the fragrant silky strands of her hair. He whispered, "Exactly . . ."

Winter nuzzled against his lips, hoping, praying, but she stiffened as reality crashed and she heard the unspoken "except."

"Except," Mark continued swiftly, between kisses meant to reassure, "I want you to be happy."

"I am happy." *Now. With you. Never before.*

"And I want to be right."

"Right?"

"About your being a famous actress. I was so sure when I watched you at the wedding."

"Mark . . ."

"Darling." *We are so much alike.* "We have both been very strongly and very negatively influenced by our absentee fathers. I spent too much of my life not doing what I wanted because of him, and you're doing the same thing. You were an actress long before you even knew about Lawrence Carlyle. You created a wonderful fantasy and somehow *he* became the goal, not your acting. When the fantasy disintegrated, you threw everything away."

"Maybe," she breathed. *Maybe.*

"You wouldn't have to do movies, would you? You could do theater. Chances are you would never meet him."

"I want to do movies," Winter said swiftly, her heart racing. *I am an actress. I want to do movies.*

"Then do movies." Mark laughed softly. "But I thought the most legitimate was theater, and television and movies fell in somewhere behind."

"It's like your residencies, Mark. It depends on whom you talk to."

"So why are movies best?"

"Because a movie—a *motion picture*—is just that, a painting created by an artist, exactly the way he wants it. You don't drop by the Louvre to see if *Mona Lisa's* smile is a little more crooked or more demure or more sly than it was the last time you looked. You *know* her smile. I'm not explaining this well . . ."

"Yes, you are. Rhett *always* doesn't give a damn the same way, and Scarlett muses about tomorrow with that famous determined look every time."

"Yes."

"So."

"So?"

"So, it's movies."

"You really think? . . ."

"I do think. Movies it is." Mark wrapped his arms around her. "I have some other thoughts if you'd like to hear them."

"OK."

Mark sat beside her and gazed at her with serious, gentle eyes.

"I think the greatest loss was his. Lawrence Carlyle never had the joy of knowing you."

"Mark." Winter's eyes filled with tears again, but she didn't try to hide them. "Thank you."

"You're welcome." Mark smiled. "And I think, I *know*, I can't imagine spending the next ten days without you."

"But your mother and sisters . . . You have to go."

"Do I have to go by myself?"

"No."

A strand of long black hair clung to her tear-dampened cheek as she shook her head. Winter started to reach for it, but Mark stopped her, moving it gently himself.

"Didn't you ever take an infectious disease course in medical school?" he teased, glancing meaningfully at the delicate fingers that had been dabbling in pond water and mouths of hungry fish.

"Oh, Mark. Toto doesn't have germs!"

"I'm sure Toto doesn't, but still, we need to wash our hands, don't we, before we finish filling out residency applications and eat smoked oysters and . . ."

"Mark," Winter teased, giddy with the joy that had been building — *You're exactly who I thought you were. . . . Then do movies. . . . Do I have to go by myself?* — and now overflowed in a cascade of laughter and love. "Look at Toto's eyes. He doesn't believe you. Feed him, Mark. Show him!"

Mark never finished his list of thoughts. Maybe it was just as well. Mark's most important thought was one for which he couldn't predict a future, at least not a future brimming with the joy and love that pulsed through him now.

Winter Carlyle, I love you. For as long as we have together . . .

Until my dreams take me to Boston and your dreams keep you here.

Chapter Seven

"I'm really going to do this, aren't I?" Winter asked quietly the next morning as she and Mark drove to San Francisco. Mark had started talking about her acting, encouraging her to make specific plans, as soon as they were north of the rush hour traffic of Los Angeles.

"Yes. If you want to."

"I want to."

"So?"

"So. I guess I should go back to UCLA and take all the drama classes I never took. I wonder if I can."

Mark pulled over at the next gas station.

"Why don't you find out? Call UCLA."

"Right now?"

"Why not?"

Ten minutes later Winter returned to the car with a sparkling smile.

"I told them I was a recent graduate in good standing! They said I could register for Autumn Quarter as a 'special' student."

"That sounds appropriate." Mark smiled. "What about auditioning for roles now?"

"I'm not in a rush anymore, Mark." Winter's desperate search for a new dream was over, and she felt so calm, so happy with the old familiar one. After a moment, she teased, "Why, do you think by the time I finally get in front of a camera they'll have to put a ski sock over the lens?"

"A ski sock?"

"They put gauze, or something a little more glamorous like silk stockings, over the camera lens to block out wrinkles. It works, and if it doesn't they can always do the close-ups a little out of focus so it's a romantic blur!" Winter smiled, then added thoughtfully, "I guess I *could* look at announcements of open casting calls."

"Unknown actresses do get cast, don't they?"

"Yes, it happens, but I think it's rare." *It happened to Vivien Leigh, didn't it? The other Scarlett.*

"It couldn't hurt to look at announcements."

"No, it couldn't."

So it was decided. Winter would take drama classes at UCLA in the fall. Over the summer she would look at casting calls in the paper and *maybe* even answer one. And she would spend time at the mansion. During the warm summer days when Mark was doing Orthopedic Surgery at Harbor General and Gastroenterology at Wadsworth, Winter would read Jacqueline's gilt-edged leather-bound scripts, watch movies, and practice by the pond.

After Winter's plans were decided, the couple lapsed into peaceful silence, holding hands, exchanging gentle smiles and loving glances as they drove through the hot San Joaquin Valley.

"Have you ever tried birth control pills?" Mark asked, breaking the peaceful silence with a worried thought.

"Yes. They made me sick." Winter didn't know how much was hormonal and how much was simply her aversion to pills of any kind. Jacqueline had taken so many drugs—pills and alcohol—and they had never helped. They had only slowly, relentlessly killed her.

Winter couldn't, or wouldn't, take birth control pills.

She wanted a tubal ligation, but the doctor she saw refused to do the surgery. And, he told her, he expected any good doctor would refuse, too; she was young, healthy, and even though her eyes were so serious when she said she wasn't going to have children *ever*, she might change her mind.

Winter knew she would never change her mind. Her own childhood had been too sad. Winter was unwilling to risk such unhappiness for another life. Even if she was there to protect her baby from sadness, one day she might die, as Jacqueline had died, and her child would be alone, frightened, bewildered . . . as Winter had been.

"There really are problems with the IUD, Winter," Mark said seriously.

"Problems with fertility. I know, Mark." Winter had listened impatiently as the doctor had explained the risks. It didn't matter; she didn't want to be fertile! "I've only had the IUD for a year. Aren't problems related to having it for a long time?"

"The risks increase the longer you have it, yes, but—"

"Let's not talk about it now!"

"There are other things we can do, Winter."

"*Things,* doctor?"

Mark started to elaborate, but Winter stopped him. "I know. Let me think about it, OK? Please?"

"OK."

Silence—not as peaceful as before—prevailed for five miles. This time Winter broke it with a worry of her own.

"Tell me about your family, Mark. What should I know before we get there?"

"You should know that they'll be *very* interested in you."

"Why? Don't you usually bring girls home with you?"

"No." Mark smiled at her. *Never.*

101

"Don't . . . if you wouldn't tell them who I am."

"I won't tell them about your parents if you don't want me to. But they'll know who you are, Winter, how wonderful you are, and they'll like you very much."

Mark's family *did* like Winter and she liked them, too. Mark's mother Roberta, and his sister Gayle, who was studying with the San Francisco Ballet, and his other sister Jean, who was a first year law student at Dartmouth, welcomed Winter with open arms and easy smiles. Roberta and Gayle and Jean *were* interested in the lovely young woman who obviously made Mark so happy, but their curiosity was gentle, not probing, and their laughter was frequent and merry.

They welcomed Winter, carefully explaining the "in" jokes and allusions that were part of their private family history — the history of four people who had weathered life's storms together and had survived, strong and close and loving.

"Joanne had twins, little girls, not identical," Roberta announced casually one evening over blueberry pie. Turning to Winter, Roberta added, "Joanne is my sister's daughter."

"Mother has grandbaby lust, Winter," Jean explained lightly.

"Grandbaby lust," Gayle agreed amiably. "That *may* have sounded like a perfectly innocent comment, simply updating us on the life of our cousin, but it is dripping with hidden meaning."

"Not at all!" Roberta laughed, but her twinkling blue eyes fell for a thoughtful moment on Mark, her oldest, the one for whom childhood had been the most difficult. What a wonderful father Mark would make!

* * *

102

Mark and Winter spent five days in San Francisco. They stayed in a motel because Mark insisted on their privacy, but they spent most waking hours with his family. Winter's eyes filled with tears as she said good-bye to Roberta and Gayle and Jean. She was eager to be alone with Mark, but the visit with them had been so nice.

The drive north from Los Angeles had taken five hours. The trip home took five days. Mark and Winter meandered along the Pacific Coast Highway, spending the nights in quaint hotels in Carmel, San Luis Obispo, and Santa Barbara, strolling at sunrise and sunset on white sand beaches, talking, laughing, touching, loving. . . .

"You brought this blouse on purpose, didn't you?"

"My silk blouse with a thousand buttons?" Winter answered innocently. She loved the way Mark undressed her, *so slowly*, gently kissing each patch of bareness as he uncovered it, his talented lips making her tremble with desire that she knew would be fulfilled. "Yes."

On the third evening, Mark and Winter watched the summer sunset from the porch at Nepenthe as they drank champagne. Winter drank champagne now, enough to flavor their kisses, because she felt safe with Mark. Safe and warm and giddy.

But the wonderful, giddy, euphoric feeling wasn't the champagne, Winter realized. The euphoria was there *all the time* when she was with Mark . . . because of Mark.

"A penny for your thoughts," Winter whispered as she shifted her gaze from the red-orange sunset to his serious sapphire eyes.

"No. It's an irrational thought."

"OK. I'll give you ten million dollars."

"It's a worthless thought, Winter."

"Then it's a very highly leveraged one. Worthless, but

I'm willing to pay ten million for it. I think you should take me up on it."

"How do you know about highly leveraged?" *Highly leveraged* was a term from Mark's previous career.

"I took courses in everything—except drama—in college," Winter answered. "I even did well in them."

"I'm sure you did."

"So, you're stalling. Ten million. I think it's a fair price, maybe even a steal for such a rarity. I didn't think you had irrational thoughts."

"I didn't used to." *Before you.* Mark smiled. Then he told her quietly, "I was thinking about your doing love scenes."

It was more than a thought, it was a vivid image. Mark imagined her lovely breasts artfully silhouetted but *revealed,* her graceful elegant body, her soft loving sighs, the desire in her violet eyes; and he imagined all the men who would watch her, and perhaps talk about her, and certainly *want* her.

"It's just acting."

"I wasn't thinking about you and the actor. I was thinking about all the people who would see you. I told you, completely irrational." *The irrational thought of a man very much in love.*

Winter smiled. She was so happy that Mark wanted their love, their intimacy, to be theirs alone.

"Why are you smiling?"

"Because that was definitely worth ten million." Winter's smile faded slightly. "Mark, what do you think about all my money?"

"What I think about money in general. It doesn't buy happiness, but it *can* buy freedom."

"Freedom?"

"Freedom to do what you want, be what you want, be *where* you want to be." Mark kissed her gently. "If I had

104

all the money in the world, there is nowhere I'd rather be than right here, right now, with you."

"And in three days, there is nowhere else you'd rather be than doing Orthopedic Surgery at Harbor General, setting—what did you call the ones from the roller-skating accidents?—Colles' fractures?"

I want that, too, Mark thought. I want you and I want medicine. Mark wondered if it were really possible to have them both.

As soon as the first boarding call for PSA's July Fourth flight to Phoenix was called, Mick was on alert, eager to be on his way, restless, showing no regret that he would be away from her for the next two months. Mick's band was going on tour, playing at the many summertime rock concerts that dotted the country.

Mick curled his strong hand around Emily's fragile neck and pulled her to him for a final kiss—rough, possessive, without tenderness. He released her, smiled a mean smile, and removed a brown pill bottle from his tight jeans pocket.

"A little going-away present." Mick shoved the bottle containing an assortment of illegal hallucinogens and amphetamines into her hand.

"Thank you." Emily slid the bottle into her loose jeans and hoped she wouldn't need to take pills this summer. Maybe she wouldn't, with Mick gone.

"See you in September."

Emily nodded, but she thought, *I hope not.* She needed to find the courage to say a final no to Mick. *Good-bye, Mick. I want to be by myself. I feel better, more peaceful, when I'm alone.*

Emily would rehearse the words all summer, but if she was very lucky, she would never need to say them. If she was very lucky, Mick would find someone else and not want her anymore.

Lucky, Emily mused as she wove her way through the Fourth of July crowds at LAX. Had she ever been lucky? If there had ever been luck in her life, or joy or happiness or hope, Emily didn't remember it.

"Are you awake?" Winter asked when Allison answered her phone at seven-thirty A.M. on the fifth of July.

"Of course! Welcome back. Did you have a nice time?"

"Wonderful." Winter's voice softened with the memory. "Really wonderful."

"You liked Mark's family?"

"Yes. Very much."

"That's nice."

"Yes. Oh, and Allison?"

"Yes?"

"I made a career decision."

"Really?" Allison had watched Winter's frantic search for a career with sympathy and concern. Each quarter Winter enthusiastically declared a new major, but neither her boundless energy nor her fervent desire could urge the small flickers into flames. Nothing ignited her, nothing held her interest. Allison had heard the pronouncement—"I've made a career decision"—a hundred times. But now there was a new softness in Winter's voice. "What have you decided?"

"I'm going to be an actress."

"Good," Allison replied swiftly. *At last.*

"Good?"

"Well, I . . ." Allison faltered slightly. It had been so obvious in high school! Winter loved performing in the school plays, chattered constantly about movies, and by the beginning of senior year was already planning the

Drama courses she would take at UCLA the next fall. But after Jacqueline's death . . . "You were so terrific in the plays at Westlake."

"Oh. I'd forgotten about those. Anyway, I'm going back to UCLA in the fall and begin with Drama 101." Winter smiled wryly. "Of course, Mark thinks I should start auditioning for parts now."

"Why not?"

"That's what he says."

"I could talk to Vanessa," Allison offered. "She always seems to know about casting calls."

"Thanks, but no. They're in the paper, anyway. I do plan to look, and if there is something, who knows?" *Who knows?* "Anyway, enough about me! How are you? Are you still being crazy?"

"Is that your incredibly subtle way of asking if I'm riding?"

"Perhaps."

"I am riding. I'm also reading mounds of novels and stacks of *Architectural Digest, Design, Arts and Antiques, Interior,* you get the idea." With each day Allison felt better, more confident of the decisions she had made, more eager for the challenges that lay ahead. "Oh, Meg called yesterday. She and Cam are back from their honeymoon. They leave for New York on Saturday, and Meg wants us to come over tonight to see the wedding pictures."

"You're kidding!" Winter's gasp crescendoed into a laugh. "To see the wedding pictures? Why in the world would we want to do that?"

"Meg thought we might want copies," Allison replied solemnly, suppressing a giggle with effort.

"No! Something in a poster, perhaps? Meg and Cameron saying their vows? I'm sure I'll want three or four for my apartment alone, not to mention the wonderful gifts they would make!"

"Stop!" Allison laughed. She continued thoughtfully, remembering Emily, happy for her, "Apparently, the pictures are wonderful. Not just of Cam and Meg, but of all of us. Besides, it's a chance to see the newlyweds before they move back East. Mark's invited, of course."

"He's on call," Winter sighed softly. The wonderful leisurely days were already a memory. Mark left for the hospital an hour ago. He would call her today if he had a chance and *hopefully* would see her tomorrow night.

"Do you want to go? Meg said about seven."

"Of course I want to go! Who knows, maybe they'll have a slide show of the honeymoon!"

Even before they reached the Montgomery estate on St. Cloud, Allison and Winter decided that the silver Jaguar they had been following since they turned off Sunset through the East Gate of Bel Air was also en route to view the wedding pictures.

"Rob Adamson and Elaina Kingsley," Winter murmured as Allison parked behind them.

"Oh." *Oh.* Allison had hoped to have a chance to talk to Meg, or even Cam, about Sara Adamson. Thoughts of Sara had been with Allison since the wedding, troublesome thoughts, sometimes weaving themselves into her dreams. The dreams usually vanished with dawn, vague disturbing memories without substance, but there was one recurrent dream that survived the light of day.

In the dream Sara was riding Tuxedo, her dark blue eyes glowing and happy. Then, as she jumped a green and white railed fence, Sara was hurled to her death. But it wasn't a tragic accident. It was *murder!* A man—a theatre-type, dressed as a Harlequin but *evil*—had sliced the leather girth of the saddle with a sharp bloody knife. The menacing Harlequin smiled wickedly as Sara fell, and he erupted into raucous laughter as she died.

As Allison felt more peaceful, and more eager about her own life, her own second chance, her thoughts drifted often to Sara . . . Sara who never had a second chance.

"It looks like Rob and Elaina are waiting for us," Allison said as she returned a friendly wave to Rob.

"Great. I never tire of talking to Elaina," Winter whispered through a sweet smile. Winter's dislike of Elaina was based on instinct and emotion, not experience. It was unfair, but she couldn't shake the image of a young Elaina Kingsley throwing taunts at a frightened Winter, leading the assault, laughing when Winter cried. It wasn't fair to Elaina; and it especially wasn't fair to Rob, who Winter liked and respected, but . . .

"Winter," Allison warned as they got out of the car.

"I'll be nice," Winter promised. Why not? She was in love, and somehow the mean little girls who had hissed at her, together with all the horrible sadness and fears of her childhood, had brought her to where she was now: in love . . . happy . . . with Mark.

"Hi, Allison." Rob smiled as Allison and Winter approached. "Hello, Winter. Do you both know Elaina?"

"Sure. It's nice to see you, Elaina."

Allison met Rob's warm, smiling eyes and thought, *I won't find out about Sara tonight.*

And why should she? Why should she ever find out about Sara? Why did Allison Fitzgerald need to know? What would she do with the knowledge? *Nothing,* but if she knew the facts, however horrible, she could deal with that reality and put an end to her own terrifying imaginings.

A selfish reason.

Allison looked at Rob and realized there was another reason, not selfish, just fantastic. Somewhere in her imagination—perhaps it was a dawn-vanquished dream—Allison had trapped the sinister Harlequin into a confession.

A silly reason.

"It looks like quite a crowd," Winter offered as they strolled toward the house. "Allison, at least your parents and Vanessa can just walk over."

"My parents are in Argentina."

"Oh, that's right! It's polo time."

"Polo?" Rob asked.

"It's really quite a group. Kings, crown princes, dukes . . . the whole monarch set," Winter explained merrily. During the summer between the junior and senior years of high school, Winter and Allison had gone with Sean and Patricia on the yearly pony-buying and polo-playing trip to Argentina. "And their *consorts,* too, of course."

"Fabulous," Elaina breathed.

"Yes, it is."

"Speaking of fabulous, Meg says the wedding pictures are fabulous," Allison said. Then, recalling Meg's exact word, a word Allison had never heard uttered by her famous-for-hyperbole friend, she added, "Actually, Meg called them *extraordinary.*"

"That's what she told me, too," Rob said with an uncomfortable twinge. As he had watched a fragile, timid, serious Emily Rousseau taking pictures at the wedding, Rob had hoped the photographs would be good; he sensed how important it was to her. But now, Rob's image of Emily was tainted and he hoped *what? Nothing.* Rob had no wish to cause her harm. Still, it made him strangely uneasy to hear that her photographs were extraordinary.

Extraordinary, Meg's word; dramatic Meg. Surely . . .

But the photographs *were* extraordinary. Meg and her mother had carefully displayed the photographs on tables

110

and chairs and window sills and mantels throughout the first floor of the Montgomery estate. The displays were uncluttered, a few photographs in each location, because each shot deserved attention. The guests wandered from room to room with the hushed, reverent silence of museum-goers at the opening of a spectacular art exhibit.

"Meg," Winter whispered. "These are magnificent."

"Yes," Meg answered solemnly. She had been very moved by the photographs—a careful, loving, artistic celebration of her wedding. "As far as we can tell, Emily took at least one picture of each guest."

"One incredible picture of each guest."

"There are several breathtaking pictures of you, Winter, and Mark. That's his name, isn't it?"

"Yes, Mark," Winter answered. Breathtaking pictures of *Mark,* she thought, and a photograph of the two of them dancing on the "sort-of-secluded" terrace. Emily had invaded their privacy, but Winter didn't mind. To all other eyes, it would be a picture of Mark and Winter dancing; a lovely, graceful, melodic moment among the roses, but Winter knew better. Emily had captured the precise intimate moment when Winter had whispered, *We have to go now.* "There are breathtaking pictures of everyone, Meg. I'd like to have a copy of this one of you and Cam, and the one of Sean and Patricia by the ice sculpture, and the one of Allison . . ."

Allison admired the photograph for several moments before she realized she was admiring a picture of herself. The summer sun glittered off her long red-gold hair and her eyes were dark jade and her expression was thoughtful and she looked almost beautiful. Emily had captured a look of serene beauty, yet Allison knew the thoughts behind her pensive expression had not been serene. At the moment Emily took the picture, Allison had been thinking about Sara.

"I know your parents would like a copy of this," Vanessa Gold said quietly as she moved beside Allison. "It's very lovely."

"Oh, thank you, Vanessa." Allison shrugged slightly. "Emily has really mastered the art of trick photography."

"Not at all." Rob overheard Allison's remark and joined them. He had already lingered many minutes admiring the photograph of Allison. He repeated firmly, "Not at all."

She's just mastered the art of portrait photography, Rob thought for the hundredth time that evening. Emily Rousseau *had* mastered it; her wonderful, talented, creative photography was the best Rob had ever seen — and he'd been looking.

Portrait was staffed by a talented group of writers who reliably created magnificent portraits in words; in-depth, honest, intriguing profiles of the people they interviewed. Each beautifully written article was accompanied by a photograph, a portrait that should have been as articulate as the words, but often wasn't. Rob used free-lance photographers because he had been unable to find a photographer he wanted to hire full-time, one whose talent matched the exceptional quality of the journalism.

Rob had been looking for a photographer for *Portrait,* and now he had found her. Emily Rousseau took the kind of portraits — unposed, insightful, honest, multi-layered — Rob had always envisioned for the magazine.

Even the way Emily developed her photographs was creative, the texture and clarity a reflection of how she saw the mood, personality, and essence of each subject. Some portraits were sharp, clear, and glossy, as if reflecting unashamed ambition and power; Rob smiled as he noticed Emily had chosen to develop the photographs of Elaina that way. Other portraits — Meg and Cam, Winter dancing with Mark, and even the one of *him* taken while he was watching *her*—were soft, muted, romantic, like delicate pastel watercolors. Still others, including the beautiful, serious one of Allison, had great richness and texture, as if painted in oil.

Rob had been looking for a photographer for *Portrait,* and here she was.

Emily Rousseau. Drug addict, and whatever *else* made her look and behave the way she did. Rob couldn't imagine sending Emily all over the world to homes, offices, studios of the rich and famous and powerful, except . . .

Except Rob had to imagine it, because he had to have Emily's incredible talent, her remarkable gift, for *Portrait.*

"These are the best photographs I've ever seen of these frequently photographed people," Vanessa said. "I assume Emily Rousseau will open her own studio. The minute word gets out, she'll be in constant demand."

Allison listened and decided she had better call Emily soon to arrange to have another portrait done. She didn't want to give her parents this one. Even if no one else saw the sadness in it, Allison did. If Emily could take another one, a happy one, it would make a wonderful present for Sean and Patricia's wedding anniversary in October.

Winter had already decided to schedule an appointment with Emily, too. She would need portraits for her portfolio. Even though Winter doubted she would answer a casting call this summer, or even next summer, there was no harm in being prepared.

Chapter Eight

Vanessa spent a few minutes each day reading her *All That Glitters* column in the newspaper. She wasn't checking for accuracy — she did that on the galleys — and of course she knew what the column said; but Vanessa liked seeing and reading the words the way her readers did. The smudged newsprint, the bold-faced type, the plump exclamation points, and the italics gave her words life and character; so much more interesting than the same words in neat double-spaced lines on the pure white typing paper on which the column had been created.

Vanessa devoted her entire July sixteenth *All That Glitters* to *Love*, the "hottest property" in Hollywood. As she read the printed column at her desk overlooking Sunset Boulevard, Vanessa thought about the remarkable script and how smart Steve Gannon had been to have let her read it for herself in June, a full month before hundreds of copies floated around Hollywood, topping the teetering stacks on every agent's desk and lying beside the swimming pools and in the boudoirs of Hollywood's best young actresses.

Usually a producer presented Vanessa with an encapsulated version of his latest project. He would take her to a martini lunch at the Cafe Four Oaks or Ma Maison or Rebecca's and rave about the "incredible script" and the "dynamite director" and the "unbelievable cast" he was going to assemble; then he would expect Vanessa to begin the preproduction *hype* of his movie-to-be.

But Steve Gannon was an old friend and he knew the script was pure gold. The script had won Vanessa's enthusiasm, but she liked Steve's approach; she liked being included; she very much liked being allowed to arrive at her own conclusions. As soon as Steve gave her the firm dates for the open casting call, Vanessa ran the column she had written a month before, the moment she had finished reading the script.

PETER DALTON'S
ASTONISHING *LOVE*

Love, a screenplay by Pulitzer-Prize-winning playwright and three-time Tony-Award-winning director Peter Dalton, is a stunning exploration of the enormous treasures of the heart and the magnificent gifts of love. For a writer of lesser stature or lesser genius to give a script such a title would be an insufferable presumption. But the title is apt. Dalton has written a definitive work.

With *Love,* Dalton displays his six-octave talent. His previous work has proven his remarkable ability to plumb the depths of human despair, to venture into the caves of darkness in the soul, to rip apart the tender threads that seam the gossamers of sanity and madness. Now, with *Love,* Dalton's genius soars from murky darkness to the brilliant clarity and untainted splendors of love. The voyage is breathtaking and not without peril, but Dalton uncrosses the stars and delivers a happy ending.

At 32, Dalton is surely the brightest light in an impressive galaxy of talented young playwrights and screenwriters. His remarkable theater career began nine years ago, when his critically acclaimed one-act plays were first produced at La Mama's and the American Place Theater in New York. Since then, Dalton has garnered recognition for excellence in both writing and directing.

Merry Go Round, his first full-length work, was produced off Broadway in 1979 and won the New York Drama Critics Circle Award for best new play. The following year he won two Tony Awards—Best Director and Best Original Play—for *Storm Watch.* In 1981, he won a third Tony—Best Original Play—for *Echoes.* In 1982, Peter Dalton entered the rarified world of literature with *Say Good-bye,* a chilling study of hopelessness and despair, for which he was awarded the Pulitzer Prize. An anthology of all Dalton's produced work, including *Say Good-bye,* was published earlier this year by Random House.

Now there is *Love.* One might logically assume the writer gave the world this gift in penance for *Say Good-bye,* but apparently *Love* was written before *Say Good-bye.* When Steve Gannon, President of Brentwood Productions and Executive Producer of the film, approached Dalton last January about making a movie of *Merry Go Round,* Dalton responded with a counter offer: first, *Love*—the manuscript for which lay in a remote corner of a desk drawer—then *Merry Go Round.* One can only wonder what other treasures Dalton has hidden away!!

Dalton will take time—a *little* time—away from his remarkable Broadway career to direct *Love.* He will move to Los Angeles in December to begin preproduction activities for the picture—over which he has "total artistic control." *Love* will be filmed entirely on location in LA between January and April. Dalton returns to New York in April to assume directorial responsibilities for his recently created company, Shakespeare on Broadway, which begins its inaugural season this summer, opening with *Hamlet* and showcasing the greatest stars of the New York and London stage.

Although the screenplay has already been circulated to Hollywood's best young actresses, Gannon says, "We are fully prepared to cast an unknown actress in the lead. Julia is a rare blend of innocence, courage, love, and magic; we will know her when we see her." The male lead will go to one of five top actors, already selected and waiting only to see which has the best chemistry with the lucky actress chosen to play Julia. So, aspiring actresses, if you believe in love and magic and the gifts of the heart, Gannon and Dalton want to see you during the first two weeks of August. Interested? Contact Brentwood Productions at . . .

Winter's heart raced, beating faster as she read *All That Glitters* the second time.

I believe in love and magic and gifts of the heart. I know about love. I'm living it.

Winter wondered what a camera—zooming in for a close-up of enraptured violet eyes—would have seen if she had tried to act "love" before she met Mark. How convincing could she have been? Not very, Winter thought, because even in her most romantic fantasies of love she had not imagined the feelings she felt now.

I wonder if I'm Julia? Winter decided to find out. She would type up a résumé—that would take no time—and attach one of the wonderful portraits Emily had done last week, then she would appear at the casting call to see if she was who Steve Gannon and Peter Dalton were looking for.

Winter had a very strong feeling that she was.

Emily saw the *All That Glitters* column from a too-far-away-to-read distance as she rode the bus along Wilshire Boulevard to the Beverly Hills office of *Portrait* magazine. She had an appointment with Rob Adamson . . . about a portrait, Emily assumed. His secretary, Fran Cummings, had been quite vague, except to say it had something to do with a job and he wanted to meet her in person. Fran had given her several options—lunch anywhere, a meeting at Jerome Cole's studio, dinner anywhere—but Emily selected a noon meeting in Rob's office.

Emily knew who Rob Adamson was now—Jerome had raved about the portrait she had taken of him at the wedding—and she couldn't very well ask *him* to come to the studio, nor could she dine with him. Emily was uneasy about seeing Rob again, remembering the curious dark blue eyes that had followed her at the wedding; but it was a *job*, a portrait of him, an engagement picture of him and Elaina Kingsley . . .

Emily noticed a clock inside a car dealership as the bus lumbered by. She was going to be on time. Good. She was lucky to have caught this bus. She had been late, but the bus was, too, delayed just long enough by a malfunctioning stop light.

Good . . . lucky, Emily mused. Those unfamiliar words again, but now they *almost* applied to her life. The past two weeks had been a busy, creative swirl—taking pictures, developing them the way she wanted, taking more pictures. If she could spend her life like this—taking beautiful pictures, too busy to think, lost in a timeless enchanted world of color and texture and images—then she might even be . . . another unfamiliar word . . . *happy*.

Emily reached the Beverly Hills offices of *Portrait* three minutes before her twelve-fifteen appointment.

"My name is Emily Rousseau," she told the receptionist. "I have an appointment with Mr. Adamson."

"Oh, yes," the receptionist barely concealed her skepticism. Why would Mr. Adamson have an appointment with *her?* The men and women who usually had appointments with Rob Adamson were of a type; they exuded confidence and power and success. This woman exuded *nothing*. No, that was wrong. She exuded the certain knowledge that she *was* nothing. "Mr. Adamson's secretary, Fran, is at lunch, but he is expecting you. His office is at the end of this hall. I'll let him know you're here."

Rob appeared in the doorway and smiled as Emily approached.

"Hello. I'm Rob Adamson." *I watched you at the wedding—you remember because you finally turned camera on me. And I saw you another time—but you then were in a foggy, faraway world. I saw you—how well I remember—but I wonder if you saw me.*

"Hello. I'm Emily Rousseau."

"Please come in." Rob gestured to a conversation corner, a blue leather couch and matching chairs arranged around a glass top coffee table. Rob never met with anyone across the impersonal expanse of his carved oak desk.

"Thank you."

Rob thought about her voice. It was surprisingly soft and refined. Rob had expected—had prepared himself for—harsh, abrasive, street-tough, and life-wise. There was nothing harsh about Emily today. Her shiny golden hair swayed in silky waves as she walked, her gray eyes were clear, and her baggy denim jeans were topped with

119

a billowy long-sleeved white cotton blouse.

Long-sleeved, despite the summer heat. Perhaps the long sleeves were necessary to cover knotted purple veins, scarred and damaged from years of intravenous drugs. Heroin? Cocaine?

Rob looked at the gray eyes beneath the strands of gold silk and forced the image away. Today Emily bore no resemblance to the glassy-eyed woman he had seen on the bluffs of Santa Monica; today she was the young woman at the wedding — fragile, timid, serious, ethereal.

Emily obviously didn't remember seeing him that balmy evening, and Rob wondered if it had all been a mirage.

Do you have an evil twin sister, Emily? Dr. Jekyll, do you happen to know a Ms. Hyde?

"Your secretary said you were interested in having me do some photographs?"

"More than some. I would like you to be the staff photographer for *Portrait* magazine."

"Oh!" Emily's surprise quickly became confusion. She didn't really know about the photographs that appeared in *Portrait*. She had seen the magazine in stores, of course, and she knew Rob owned it, but she had never opened a copy.

Rob correctly interpreted Emily's confusion. Why would she be familiar with *Portrait?* Rob guessed she had very little money. *What money she has probably goes for drugs,* he thought with an ache, *not for clothes or food and* certainly *not for an expensive magazine like* Portrait. Even as an aspiring portrait photographer, Emily wouldn't be lured to the pages of *Portrait* for inspiration; her work was already better than the best he had to offer.

Rob reached for the July issue of *Portrait* that lay on the coffee table.

"Each month we profile between ten and fifteen people, accomplished men and women in all fields — celebrities, leaders, innovators—talented people with vision and imagination. We explore who they are and why they are, what drives them, what motivates them." Rob explained the purpose of *Portrait* without trying to sell it to her. He didn't use any of the words the critics had been using since the first issue hit the newsstands two years before: "unique," "stunning," "exceptional," "intensely committed to quality journalism," "one of the best."

Rob handed the July issue to her. As Emily's fingers uncurled from the tight ball of white knuckles in her lap, Rob saw her bitten-short nails and her thin, pale fingers. He winced slightly—a wince of the heart, nothing Emily could detect.

Emily looked through the magazine, carefully examining the full-page color photographs that accompanied each article.

"The portraits don't match the quality of the journalism. That's why I need you," Rob said finally. Because you have the unique ability to peel away the veneer and find the essence, he thought, remembering how she had captured the graceful sensitivity of Allison Fitzgerald, the soft vulnerability of Winter Carlyle, the surprising toughness of Elaina Kingsley, and even his own unmenacing curiosity.

"You think I can take better pictures than these?" Emily asked weakly. She thought the portraits were excellent. He thought she could do better?

"These aren't terrible, I know that. I've got some of the best free-lance photographers in the world available to me. But, yes, I'm sure you can." Rob expected, hoped for, a slight smile—if smiling was something Emily Rousseau ever did—but saw only confusion and doubt. *Doubt?* "I realize you're probably about to open your own studio. . . ."

"My own studio?"

"I assume there has been a large demand for your

work since the wedding."

"Well, yes, but . . ."

It obviously hadn't occurred to Emily to leave Jerome Cole. Why not? Rob wondered. Surely she knew that her place as photographer to the stars was secure. Was it lack of ambition? No, Rob decided, remembering the patient, careful pictures she had taken at the reception, staying longer, doing so much more than was expected. Lack of confidence? Yes, probably. *Why?*

"You may prefer to open your own studio," Rob said, firmly planting that idea in her mind, deciding if Emily said no to working for him, he would get Elaina to help her set up her own business. Elaina had plenty of confidence to spare. "But let me tell you what I can offer, OK?"

"OK."

"An excellent salary. We can discuss the specifics of that now if you'd like." Rob was prepared to pay her a great deal, probably more than she would ever imagine.

Emily shook her head.

"All right. Let's see. You'd have quite a bit of creative freedom. Naturally, I have final approval on everything that goes into the magazine, but I saw the photographs you took for the Montgomery-Elliott wedding, and I obviously like your work or I wouldn't be offering you the job." His words only worsened her uncertainty. Smiling, Rob changed tack, "I guess I should define the job. Ideally, I would have you do all the portraits for every issue, but I know that is impossible. We profile people all around the world, important people with difficult schedules. I honestly don't know how many portraits any one photographer can do each month. We'll just have to see. Having told you it's an impossible job and you'll be frantically busy, I can also tell you there will be slow times. I'm sure five or six portraits a month, or even fifteen, won't be enough photography for you. So I have no objection to your doing outside work, as long as your top priority is the magazine."

"I wouldn't do outside work."

"There can be very slow times," Rob repeated, sensing interest in her eyes, not sure what it was he had said that was beginning to intrigue.

"There would be travel?" Emily asked softly.

"Of course. All first class, all around the world, five-star hotels." The promise of luxury worried more than appealed, but traveling interested her. "As you can see, for the July issue we went to Rome, London, New York, Buenos Aires, Tokyo, and Paris."

"Paris." It was almost a whisper.

"Are you French?" Rob asked. *Rousseau* certainly was French, but her soft voice was unaccented.

"My father was French. I was born in Quebec."

"Is Paris a favorite city?"

"I've never been to Paris," Emily answered quietly. "But I've always thought I might live there someday."

It was then, when Emily spoke of living in Paris, that Rob learned she could smile. Her lips curved softly, just the beginning of a smile, and it came with a deep light in her gray eyes. *So beautiful.*

"I can promise you trips to Paris. And if you fall in love with the place, we can base you there."

Emily never officially said yes, but the soft glow in her gray eyes when Rob spoke of trips to Paris gave him his answer.

"When would you like to start, Emily?"

"We have so much work at the studio, at least until the middle of September . . . ."

So much work because of *you*, Rob thought. He knew Jerome Cole would make a great deal of money from Emily's work, but Rob guessed *she* would simply get whatever small salary she had always gotten.

"How about the beginning of October? That would

give you a break between jobs." Rob wished Emily could start today. He doubted that Jerome Cole felt a sense of loyalty to her, but it was bad business to appear to be stealing her away.

"The middle of September is fine."

Rob walked to his desk and consulted his calendar. "September seventeenth? That's a Monday."

Emily nodded.

"About your salary . . ."

"Whatever you think."

"OK." *I think I want to pay you a lot, but please don't spend it on drugs. Please spend it on something that makes you smile.*

Emily stood up and extended a small, thin hand. "I'll see you in September. Thank you, Mr. — "

"Rob," he interjected swiftly. "Thank *you*, Emily."

As Emily rode in the bus back to the photography studio, she thought about what she had just agreed to. Mostly it scared her. What if she couldn't take the kind of pictures Rob wanted? She had to try, that was all, because it was her escape to Paris.

Emily didn't know why Paris meant so much. It was something vague and distant in the past or in the future. Emily didn't remember a time in the past when she had been happy, when her heart had been full of laughter and trust and hope. She didn't *remember* that time, but it had existed, in the first ten years of her life, when she had lived in Quebec. She had been happy then . . . a happy, golden-haired French girl.

After Emily left his office, Rob glanced through the newspaper while he waited for Elaina to arrive for their one-thirty lunch date. The headlines of Vanessa Gold's *All That Glitters* column — Peter Dalton's Astonishing *Love* — caught his eye. After a few moments, Rob forced himself to read it.

As Rob read the column, his fists clenched into angry bloodless knots and his strong body braced for the full force of his fury. It was a horrible sinister joke, an evil sham. Peter Dalton knew *nothing* of love.

Except to betray it.

Peter Dalton. How Rob hated the man responsible for the death of his beloved little sister. . . .

Chapter Nine

Greenwich, Connecticut
November, 1954

Jeffrey and Sheila Adamson greeted the birth of their son, Robert Jeffrey, with relief, joy, and pride. A beautiful firstborn son! An heir!

Even before his birth, Rob's life as heir to the Adamson empire was destined to follow an inevitable path. It was a path paved with gold and lined with privilege, luxury, and success. The golden path led from boyhood in Greenwich, to prep school in New Hampshire, to college and business school at Harvard, and back to Greenwich and Wall Street. The path meandered, apparently shapeless and with no purpose beyond pleasure and privilege, but the shapelessness was an illusion. The path had a definite shape: it was a circle, beginning and ending in the same place. And it had a purpose: to prepare Rob to become the successor to the Adamson empire. And it had expectations: Rob had to be perfect.

For the first twenty-two years of his life, Rob followed the path without the slightest deviation, unaware that there was a path, effortlessly excelling in everything he did. Sheila and Jeffrey watched their brilliant, charming, handsome son with smug approval. They didn't have to worry about

Rob, not ever. They could devote their worrying, their coddling, their protectiveness to Sara.

Sara Jane Adamson was born four years after Rob. At age six, as her family watched in horror, she went from consciousness to grogginess to coma in a matter of minutes and was rushed Code Three to Greenwich Hospital. The diagnosis was diabetic ketoacidosis.

Sara recovered quickly from her first episode of diabetic ketoacidosis and coma; but there would be other episodes, the doctors told Sheila and Jeffrey. Sara had "juvenile-onset diabetes." Her diabetes was "insulin-dependent" and "very brittle" and "very severe."

From the moment Sara returned home from Greenwich Hospital, she relinquished what little control she previously had over her own life. Sara had always been delicate and fragile and passive. She offered no resistance to the careful regimentation and supervision that greeted her when she arrived home, smiling bewildered reassurance at the sudden army of hand-wringing, ever-watchful nannies that surrounded her, napping when she was told, eating all of the prescribed food, no more, no less.

The doctors warned the Adamsons that Sara might rebel against the precision of her life. She was a child, after all, and it was quite normal—in fact *typical*—for young diabetics to test the rules by skipping meals or drinking sugary soft drinks. It was a logical defiance against the constraints placed on them by their disease. They wanted to play and eat and frolic like their friends.

But Sara didn't rebel. Sara was an angel. She lived like a precious, fragile bird in a gilded cage and never offered a peep of complaint. She wasn't allowed to have pets, because pets carried diseases and infections were dangerous for diabetics. She wasn't allowed to ride horses or ice skate or climb trees, because injuries, even minor ones, were dangerous, too.

Sara didn't have playmates, not children her own age, so

she didn't really know what she was missing. When Sara played, she played with the army of kind, hovering nannies with the sympathetic worried smiles, or with her parents, or with Rob.

Even before Sara's diabetes was diagnosed, Rob protected his little sister. He instinctively sensed her fragility and amiably channeled his lively, healthy energy into quiet games he could play with her. Rob and Sara assembled jigsaw puzzles, played word and board games, made enchanted kingdoms out of blocks, and invented stories to go with the kingdoms. Rob roughhoused with his friends, Cam Elliott and the other young golden heirs, but he enjoyed, even more, the quiet times with bright, imaginative Sara.

When he was thirteen and Sara was nine, Rob was sent to Phillips Exeter Academy in New Hampshire. Rob *had* to go to Exeter; the golden path led there. Before Exeter, Rob attended Greenwich Country Day School and Sara was educated at home. Every evening, Rob and Sara would eagerly share what they had learned during the day.

But now, Rob was far away and Sara missed him terribly. Rob missed Sara, too, but he was caught up in the scholastic challenges of Exeter and the intriguing new feelings of a boy becoming a young man. When Rob saw his frail, lonely little sister at Thanksgiving, tears of love and guilt filled his eyes. His life was so exciting, so exhilarating, so full of wonderful adventures. Sara's life was empty and lonely, and she looked to Rob for hope.

"Why doesn't Sara go to school?" Rob asked his parents one afternoon while his sister was resting. "She could go to Greenwich Country Day through Grade Six and then on to the Academy. I think she'd really enjoy it."

"It's too dangerous, Rob."

"I don't understand."

"Her diabetes." *We don't know how long Sara will live.* Jeffrey Adamson thought about saying those words to his bright thirteen-year-old son, but decided against it. Perhaps it was too much of a truth for a thirteen-year-old. Besides, it was a truth laced with unknowns.

All the doctors — all the specialists — agreed. Sara's life expectancy was unpredictable. It depended on when the "complications" developed and how rapidly they progressed. The doctors talked about when, not if. Although the many specialists disagreed on several important aspects of Sara's diabetes — including, even, how "tightly controlled" she should be — they all recognized the severity of her disease. They gave the Adamsons gentle warnings, preparing them for the inevitable.

"Has something happened?"

"No." Jeffrey smiled thoughtfully. "Sara is doing very well."

No she's not! Can't you see how lonely she is? She's withering here, alone in her cage. Or maybe she's dying. Rob shivered at the thought. It was a private, secret worry. What if Sara weren't alive when he came home at Christmas? On impulse, Rob decided he wouldn't return to Exeter. But, he realized, that was precisely what everyone was doing to Sara — watching her, breath-held, waiting for her to die.

"Sara doesn't even have one of those bracelets," Rob murmured sadly.

"She doesn't need to. She's always with someone who knows about her diabetes," Sheila replied to Rob's seemingly out-of-the-blue observation.

"But that's wrong, don't you see?"

"I beg your pardon?" Sheila bristled.

Rob sighed. It was pointless to launch into a philosophical discussion. Pointless and dangerous. They were talking about Sara's freedom — he was — but Rob might start talking about his own freedom, about the dangerous feelings inside him that made him wonder if he really wanted to spend his life on Wall Street after all.

"The administrators and teachers at Country Day, and

I'm sure at the Academy, are extremely responsible. They would watch Sara carefully. Her meals could be prepared here. Why don't you just ask her? Maybe I'm wrong. Maybe she wouldn't want to."

Sara cried, tears of joy, when Sheila and Jeffrey asked her if she wanted to go to Greenwich Country Day School. Sara's tears shocked them all. Sara *never* cried, not ever, not even when needles poked her delicate skin.

"I expect letters from you," Rob told Sara the day before he returned to Exeter.

"About what?" she asked eagerly.

"The people you meet. I want to know all about the people, what they look like, who they are inside."

"You want portraits," she said quietly. "You want me to paint their portraits with words."

"Yes," Rob breathed, ever amazed by his brilliant little sister. "Portraits."

"Will you write to me, too, Rob?"

"Of course, Sara. I promise."

Rob kept his promise, and Sara kept hers. Rob loved the "portraits" from his sister. He learned about her teachers and classmates and the postman and her doctors. Sara gave wonderful descriptions, full of insight and humor and care. She defined the *essence* of the people she met. Rob felt as if he knew them, even though Sara never gave their names. *I agree with Juliet,* she wrote. *What's in a name?*

Sara never mentioned Allison Fitzgerald by name, but Rob learned a great deal about the magnificent fifteen-year-old rider with the flame-colored hair, the determined champion with the heart of gold. As Rob read the descriptions in his dormitory at Harvard he thought, *Thank you, whoever you are, for being so nice to my beloved little sister.*

Beginning in late March of Sara's final year at Greenwich Academy for Girls—Rob's senior year at Harvard — the frequent descriptions of the girl who flew over the jumps were replaced by descriptions of the new rose garden at the Adamson estate.

Mother is finally getting the rose garden she has wanted for the library courtyard, Sara wrote. *And I am helping the gardener select the flowers! Do you know about roses, Rob? Each has its own color and fragrance and the names are so lovely. Yes, yes, "What's in a name?" and "A rose by any other name . . ."—but Juliet can be wrong! My favorite rose is Pristine. She (!) is creamy white with delicate pale pink edges and so fragrant. We're planting one named Portrait (deep rich pink) and others—Smoky, Sterling Silver, Christian Dior, Summerwine, Blue Moon. . . . They'll bloom into a magnificent kaleidoscope of color and fragrance, every day a little different, every day a new miracle! You'll see, Rob, when come home in June.*

Sara wrote about the garden and the roses — the happiest letters she had ever sent — but she never sent a portrait of the gardener who was letting her help with the garden's colorful, fragrant design.

Rob assumed the gardener was Joseph Dalton. He was surprised that a portrait of the Eastern European immigrant who had designed gardens for the estates in Greenwich for years wouldn't intrigue Sara. Rob expected a sensitive, thoughtful, insightful portrait of the rugged white-haired gardener; the man whose blue-gray eyes had seen the ugliness and horrors of War, but who created lovely, exquisite kaleidoscopes of flowers. But Sara told Rob about the garden, not about the artist who created it.

In April, Sara wrote, *I've decided to go to Vassar instead of Radcliffe. I know we had planned to both be in Boston next year, Rob, but can we do one more year of portraits? Poughkeepsie is very close to New York City, so, the year after, when you're on Wall Street, I'll come visit you all the time!*

Sara punctuated her letter with frowning faces and smiling ones and never, Rob realized, offered an explanation for her last minute change in the plans they had talked about for years.

But plans changed. Rob knew it, and Sara's decision helped him make a decision of his own, one that had been teasing him, preventing sleep, for months. Rob wouldn't go to Harvard Business School . . . not this fall, anyway, and maybe *never.*

He didn't *have* to become President of Adamson and Witt, did he? Or President of the New York Stock Exchange? He didn't *have* to spend his life commuting between Greenwich and Wall Street, did he? Did he?

Rob told himself no. He could be whatever he wanted to be. He could pursue his interests in writing and literature and journalism. He could travel, meet new people, learn about the world that existed beyond the golden walls.

Long before Rob received the letter from Sara announcing her plans to attend Vassar, he had applied for the Hathaway Fellowship. The prestigious, highly competitive fellowship awarded three years of "advanced study of liberal arts" at Oxford University in England. What am I doing? Rob asked himself as he stayed up night after night carefully preparing the detailed application. What if I get accepted? Will I really go?

Yes.

Rob made the decision not to attend Harvard Business School before the Hathaway Fellowship recipients were announced in June. He told no one of his decision, not even Sara, but his heart quickened, restless and eager, as he thought about the infinite possibilities that lay ahead.

A week before Rob graduated summa cum laude from Harvard University, he received the letter from London. The trustees of the Hathaway Fellowship were pleased to announce . . . They particularly liked the clever, insightful collection of essays Rob had written about his trip to London the summer before, and they were intrigued by his proposal that he publish a collection of essays—his views of England—during his fellowship. In fact, members of the

132

board had already spoken with the editor-in chief of *The London Times*. If the quality of Rob's future essays matched the quality of the essays they had already read, *The Times* would publish them as a series under the title Rob had proposed, "The Connecticut Yankee."

Rob wired a prompt acceptance to the Hathaway Foundation in London, informed Harvard Business School that he would not be attending in the fall after all, cancelled plans to spend July and August sailing the Caribbean with Cam Elliott, and couldn't wait to tell his parents and Sara the thrilling news.

As Rob drove between the imposing stone pillars of the Adamson estate in Greenwich, he faced the taunting worry that Sheila and Jeffrey Adamson might not greet his news with great pleasure. Rob decided to tell Sara first.

"I'm so proud of you, Rob! I expect frequent portraits!"

"You'll get them. Will I? From Vassar?"

"Of course. Rob, are they really going to publish what you write in *The London Times?*"

"That's what they say . . . assuming it's any good."

"It will be. It always is. And I love 'The Connecticut Yankee' as a title."

"That was a middle-of-the-night whimsy, and I inked it onto the application before I had time to reconsider."

"It's wonderful."

"Speaking of wonderful, Sara, I love your garden."

Rob and Sara were sitting on the warm grass in the courtyard, amid the fragrant, colorful collage of roses.

"Thank you. It's really Peter's garden."

"Peter?"

"Peter Dalton. Joseph Dalton's son."

"Oh."

"How often will you be home, Rob?" Sara kept the discussion on Rob's plans, not daring to mention hers.

"I'm not sure."

"I think I'll come visit you."

No, Rob thought, instinctively protecting her.

"I've always wanted to see Rome," Sara continued eagerly. "We could meet there."

Rob gradually became aware of another presence in the walled, private courtyard. A presence . . . a shadow . . . a long, dark, twilight shadow cast by a tall, dark stranger. Rob stood up and silently greeted the intruder's dark brown eyes with surprise, and then concern. The other man responded with matching surprise; then, sensing Rob's disapproval, the dark eyes sent an ice-cold message of defiance. The proud, defiant scowl for Rob became a gentle smile as the man turned to Sara.

"Sara, I'm sorry. I didn't mean to interrupt."

"It's fine, Peter. I want you to meet my brother. Rob, this is Peter Dalton. Peter, this is Rob."

Peter shifted a dark blue wire-bound notebook from his right hand to his left and extended a taut-muscled arm to Rob. The two men shook hands firmly, silently, appraising each other without smiles.

"I can come back later," Peter told Sara.

"No." Rob spoke to Sara, not to Peter. "It's time for me to tell Mother and Father about my plans."

"Let me know, Rob."

"I will. It will be fine." Rob smiled confidently at Sara and left the magnificent rose garden without looking at Peter Dalton again.

It wasn't fine. Sheila and Jeffrey sat in the elegant great room of the estate and stared at Rob with unconcealed horror.

Didn't their golden son know that the path-paved-in-gold had no detours, no intersections, no stop signs? Apparently not! They would have to make it clear.

"You have to go to Harvard Business School, Rob."

"I may, Mother, I probably *will*, but not this fall."

"This fall." *Not even a yield sign.*

"This fall I will be at Oxford." *This fall and two falls after that.*

"No."

"Yes. You don't understand," Rob whispered. He needed to give them more details. He needed to explain about his restlessness and his unhappiness when he thought about the life they planned for him. Surely . . .

"We do understand, son," Jeffrey countered solemnly.

Rob looked at his father hopefully, but the hope faded as his father continued.

"Perhaps you're worried that you won't make the grade at Harvard Business School."

"I'm not worried about that at all!"

"You don't have to be the top in your class in business school, too," Sheila murmured with obvious disappointment. Maybe Rob, perfect, confident Rob, was just feeling a little insecure. Sheila didn't like that sign of weakness— *any* sign of weakness in her strong handsome son—but it was better than the alternative, that Rob was rebelling. She added unconvincingly, "We don't expect you to be."

"But you do expect me to go Harvard Business School, join the firm, run the firm someday. . . ."

"Yes," Sheila and Jeffrey answered in unison.

Rob stared at their resolute faces and a series of realizations, each more shocking and more painful, pulsed through his body. They didn't understand and they weren't even going to try! They didn't care about his unhappiness or his restlessness. They only cared that he met their expectations. *Their* expectations, not his, as if they believed *they* had been the driving force behind his excellence all these years! Didn't they know that no one expected more of Rob than he himself did? Didn't they know that whatever he chose to become he would be the best he possibly could be?

The Hathaway Fellowship was very prestigious. There were far fewer Hathaway Fellows *ever* than there were stu-

135

dents in one class at Harvard Business School. Couldn't they be proud of that accomplishment?

No. The realization pulsed through Rob and wrapped around him like a thick, golden rope, imprisoning him in his parents' expectations of what—*who*—he was to be.

"I've accepted the Fellowship and I'm going," Rob breathed finally, with great effort, as if the rope bound his chest, constricting his breathing, smothering him. "I'm leaving tomorrow."

"Don't you dare," Sheila whispered.

"Or what?" Rob demanded as he backed toward the door. He had to get away, fast, before he was doomed to a prison of wealth and luxury and despair.

"We cut you off," Jeffrey answered simply.

"Disown me? You would do that?" As Rob gazed at his parents, another realization swept through him, and it was the most painful of all. They were his parents, but he didn't know them and they didn't know him. All the years of proud smiles and loving praise were smiles and praise for themselves, for what they had created, not for him.

"We might."

"Then do it! You do what you have to do, and I'll do what I have to do."

Rob left the great room quickly. He had to get away! He dashed to his bedroom to get his passport. It was all he really needed. He could buy clothes in New York tomorrow, before he left, or in London after he arrived. What he needed was to leave.

But he had to say good-bye to Sara.

Sara was still in the rose garden and so was Peter, sitting beside her, reading to her from the dark blue notebook.

"Rob! What happened?"

"I think they're going to disown me," Rob whispered with disbelief.

"They won't. It's just an idle threat. They're afraid."

"And I'm not?" Rob hadn't been afraid—he had been

only excited—until now. Now the rope had been cast off and he was adrift, following wherever the currents led, to a distant horizon and beyond.

Sara stood up, wrapped her pale, thin arms around her big, strong brother, and hugged him.

"They'll be fine and so will you, Rob. You are going still, aren't you?" Sara's tone was urgent, as if it were very important that Rob do what he wanted to do.

"Yes."

"Good." Sara smiled. "Being disowned really *is* an idle threat, you know. Unless you've somehow squandered the twelve million already!"

Rob and Sara had each inherited twelve million dollars on their eighteenth birthdays. Usually such trust funds established by grandparents for their destined-to-be-wealthy grandchildren came under the grandchild's sole control at age twenty-one, or even twenty-five. But, because of Sara's illness, the inheritance age for both Rob and Sara was eighteen; it seemed a young age to inherit such a fortune, yet no one knew if fragile Sara would even live to her eighteenth birthday. But she had. Rob had inherited his twelve million dollars just over four years ago, and Sara had inherited hers in February.

"No. I haven't touched it."

"Well, if you ever need more, let me know."

"Thanks." Rob gave her a brief kiss on the cheek and a final hug. "I'll send you my address as soon as I have one."

"OK. Rob?"

"What, honey?"

"I expect portraits!"

"So do I."

The following morning Rob flew to London. As the jet carried him swiftly to his destination, he forced the ugly scene with his parents from his mind, courageously replacing it with exciting visions of the life that lay ahead. Rob succeeded in suppressing the scene with Sheila and Jeffrey, but as it faded, another scene from the previous day came into clear, vivid, troubling focus.

The scene was of Sara and Peter in the secluded rose garden.

What the *hell* was Peter Dalton doing there?

Chapter Ten

Oxford University, England
December, 1976

Rob wrote long, enthusiastic letters to Sara at Vassar. He loved Oxford; he loved studying poetry and literature; he loved exploring England; he loved writing "The Connecticut Yankee" for *The London Times;* he had made the right decision. Sara sent enthusiastic letters in return, writing more about plays and poetry than about people. By Thanksgiving, the letters that flew frequently across the Atlantic were filled with intricate interpretations of *Finnegan's Wake,* reverence for the gifts of William Shakespeare, joy in the simplicity of Robert Frost, and critiques of plays they had seen in London and New York.

New York. Sara obviously spent a great deal of time in New York. It worried Rob to think about his sister in Manhattan, but her letters were so happy and full of joy that he suppressed his fear.

By Christmas, the anger that had driven Rob from the estate in Greenwich was a distant cloud on the vivid brilliance of his new life. He was safe, wandering an enchanted path that would lead to a career in journalism, *loving* it. Sarah knew how happy he was. Something made Rob want his parents to know, too.

Perhaps it was the Yuletide cheeriness of London, the Christmas Eve carollers at Harrod's, the enraptured rosy-cheeked children mesmerized by fairytale displays, and the scents of pine and bayberry. Or perhaps it was nostalgic memories of Christmas shopping in Boston and New York for just the right presents for Sara. Rob didn't know, but *something* compelled him to make the call.

Christmas had always been a time of joy and happiness at the Adamson estate, hadn't it? That was Rob's memory; but, of course, Christmas was also when he always returned home from school, the conquering hero, another perfect all-star semester at Exeter or Harvard behind him.

Even if his parents wouldn't talk to him, Rob was eager to talk to Sara, to *tease* her about the letters that had fallen victim, he assumed, to Reading Week and final examinations at Vassar. Sara's last letter had been postmarked from New York on the tenth of December.

"Mother?"

"Rob! Jeffrey, it's Rob. Are you coming home?"

She sounded so desperate, so uncertain, so unlike Sheila Adamson.

"No, Mother. Not yet."

Jeffrey picked up the extension in the library and asked the same question.

Silence prevailed for a few moments after Rob gave Jeffrey the same answer he had given Sheila. Finally Rob said, "I wanted to wish you all Merrry Christmas. Is Sara there?"

"Sara is gone," Sheila whispered.

Gone? Rob's heart stopped and his mind screamed, *No!* Sara had the address of his flat at Oxford, but Sheila and Jeffrey didn't. If anything had happened to Sara . . .

"Gone?" *No, please.* Sara had looked so well that summer day in the garden, so beautiful and radiant, and she hadn't been hospitalized for two years.

"Sara doesn't live here anymore." The *either* was unspoken, but it was there, a heavy, sad sigh eloquently transmitted across the Atlantic.

Relief pulsed through Rob. Relief, elation, and finally curiosity.

"Where does she live?"

"Don't you know?" Jeffrey asked sarcastically. Jeffrey and Sheila assumed their two rebellious children would have been in touch, perhaps encouraging each other, ever strengthening the resolve that kept them away.

"No."

"She lives in New York City—in Greenwich Village—with her husband."

"Husband?"

"Peter Dalton, the gardener's son. They eloped two weeks ago."

"You couldn't stop it?" Rob asked, suddenly bonded to his parents in their protectiveness of Sara, forgetting that he was calling from London, the defiant son, the son *they* couldn't stop from *his* folly.

In a horrible, uneasy moment Rob wondered if he could have prevented Sara's marriage. If only he had spent the summer in Greenwich! If only he hadn't been blinded by his own selfishness!

He should have seen it that day in the rose garden— "Peter's garden"! Sara was so radiant, her voice so soft when she spoke Peter's name and her ocean-blue eyes so bright when they greeted the sensuous dark ones.

That summer day Rob had been consumed with his own desperate escape; but his subconscious mind had formed images of Peter and they came to him now, angry and menacing. There was a wildness about Peter Dalton, his strong, cougar-sleek body, his dark, defiant eyes, his sultry sexuality.

If only Rob had been home this summer *where he should have been!* He could have explained to his precious little sister, so carefully, so gently, so lovingly, that Peter didn't love *her;* he only loved her money, her fortune, the twelve million dollars Sara and Rob had discussed so casually in front of him!

Rob had let Sara down. He should have known . . . he should have stayed home despite the storm that tossed inside him . . . he should have protected her!

"We couldn't stop her," Jeffrey replied heavily.

"Do you have her phone number?" Maybe it wasn't too late.

"Yes."

Sheila read the obviously unfamiliar number to Rob, then began awkwardly, "Rob . . . "

"Yes?"

Sheila sighed softly. It was something you didn't tell a brother about his sister—it was so private—but now it could be the difference between life and death.

"Mother?" Rob sensed that Sheila had an important message for her estranged daughter and that he was the messenger.

"Sara should never have children, Rob. Pregnancy would be too dangerous for her."

"Does she know?"

"Oh yes." The doctors had hinted about this to Jeffrey and Sheila from the very beginning, and they had told Sara when she was fourteen. Most women with diabetes could have children quite safely as long as they were carefully followed throughout the pregnancy, but Sara's diabetes was so "brittle" and there were already signs of "complications." The physiologic stress of pregnancy for Sara might be lethal. Sheila had watched as the doctors had very gently told her fourteen-year-old daughter about the dangers of pregnancy. Sara had nodded politely but her dark blue eyes were wide with amazement. She didn't have boyfriends! She couldn't imagine a time when she would. But now Sara was married to a man about whom the Adamsons knew virtually nothing, except that the relationship had been kept secret until it was much too late stop, until Peter had stolen their precious daughter from them. "Sara knows, but I don't know if he does."

"I'll discuss it with her, Mother," Rob promised uneasily.

"Thank you."

"I'm sorry," Rob told his parents before he said goodbye. For a moment, Rob wished he could rush to Heathrow, catch the first plane to JFK, and joyfully enroll in Harvard Business School. He couldn't do it, unless . . . *If I knew that if I returned home so would Sara, then maybe . . .* "I'm sorry."

Rob paced in his flat for five minutes before dialing the number in New York. He was searching for a gentle way to convince Sara to leave Peter *now*.

It's not too late, Sara! You're so young!

But I may never get old, Rob.

Finally, without really knowing what he was going to say, Rob took a deep breath and dialed.

Peter the gardener, Peter the fortune hunter, Peter the man with the dark, defiant eyes, Peter who Rob hated with an intensity that frightened him, answered. Rob identified himself and asked for Sara.

"Rob! Merry Christmas!"

Rob had steeled his heart for grief, regret, despair in her voice, but all he heard was joy—joy and happiness and love bubbling from the soul of his fragile sister.

"Merry Christmas, Sara. What the hell have you done?"

"I've out-rebelled you!" Sara laughed.

"I think you have." Rob laughed a little because Sara's merry laugh demanded it. "Although I was the first to be disowned."

"I'm sure they didn't disown you! I think they really *did* disown me."

"Sara . . ." Rob began gently, seriously.

"Rob . . ." Sara matched his serious tone briefly, then warned lightly, "No lectures, Rob. I'm sorry I didn't tell

143

you. I almost did, the day you left."

"You knew then?"

"Yes. I wanted to tell you then. I wanted you to understand and approve, but—"

"But what?" *You knew I would try to stop you?*

"—you glowered at Peter that day."

"I did not."

"You did! Anyway, we're married now." Sara's voice softened. "We love each other, Rob. We're very happy."

"I'm glad," Rob replied without conviction. "What are you doing in New York?"

"Peter's a playwright and a director, and he's wonderful at both."

"Last spring Peter was a gardener," Rob murmured as evenly as he could, trying to banish images of *Lady Chatterley's Lover* from his mind.

"Is there something wrong with being a gardener?"

"No, of course not." Unless it was a ploy to meet an eighteen-year-old heiress who had just inherited twelve million dollars. Wouldn't twelve million dollars be helpful in launching a Broadway career?

"Why is it so hard for you and Mother and Father to believe that Peter loves *me?*" The anger was gone and Sara's voice was so sad, so bewildered. *Can't I be loved for me?*

"Oh, Sara, no," Rob answered swiftly, his heart aching with guilt. He did assume Peter had married Sara for her fortune and, by telling her that, by even suggesting it, implied that she couldn't possibly be loved for who she was. Of course that wasn't true! "It's not hard to believe at all. We're just so used to protecting you, I guess."

"You don't need to protect me, not anymore, especially not from Peter. He's a wonderful man, Rob. I know you'll like him very much. He didn't marry me for my money. We're not even touching it, but we will if I have medical bills. We live in a cozy brownstone. I'm not going back to Vassar. Most of the books and poems and plays I wrote to you about were ones Peter and I read together or saw together, not ones from my courses anyway. Those are the answers to the usual questions. Do you have others?"

Lots, Rob mused, but he decided to focus on the most critical one.

"Does he know about your diabetes?"

"Of course he does! Before we were married, we met with Dr. Williams, the specialist I've been seeing in New York. Peter knows everything."

Rob hesitated, still aching from inadvertently hurting her in the name of caring, reluctant because it was so private, so intimate . . . but so important.

"Sara, does Peter know you shouldn't have children?"

"Yes," she answered softly, sadly, but without anger. "Peter knows I shouldn't have children. I take it Mother told you that?"

"Yes. She told me because she's worried about you. They miss you very much, Sara."

"Remember your delusion about them being excited about the Hathaway Fellowship? Peter and I had a similar fantasy that they might be happy for us, perhaps would even want to witness our marriage. Pure folly! They responded to the news by first trying to pay Peter off and then by trying to demand a pre-nuptual agreement."

"As a wise sister once said to me, 'They were afraid.' "

"You certainly are being magnanimous, Rob."

"It's Christmas, Sara. And I can afford to be, because I'm free."

"So am I, but it's much too soon."

"I thought I might send Mother and Father the odd postcard."

"Go ahead! Perhaps the Tower of London?"

"Very funny. Speaking of the odd postcard, you owe me a letter, Sara."

"I know. May I send you a portrait of Peter? I've been wanting to since last spring."

145

"Please do."

Peter Dalton was born on a bitter cold November night. Peter's humble birth in a small cottage in Danbury, Connecticut occurred exactly two years before Robert Jeffrey Adamson's golden birth in a magnificent estate in nearby Greenwich.

Peter's home was cold in the harsh, icy Connecticut winters, but he didn't even notice. His childhood was filled with the warmth of his loving parents. Peter's mother, Anne, taught him about the majesty of words. In her soft voice with its wonderful British accent, Anne read Peter her favorite poems and plays. Shakespeare, Brecht, Tennyson, O'Neill, Williams, Longfellow, Shaw. Anne joyously shared her great love of language and literature with her very bright young son.

From his well-educated mother, Peter learned to love the treasures of language. From his father, Joseph, Peter learned the mysterious secrets of flowers. As a little boy, Peter accompanied his father to the magnificent gardens of the Greenwich estates where Joseph worked. Peter helped Joseph plant bulbs in the warm, rich soil, and he listened in wide-eyed amazement as his father made promises about the fate of the small, bland bulbs. Joseph was a man of few words, but to Peter, that made each word his father uttered so important. Joseph spoke in broken English and his voice was very deep. The heavy accent and rich tone gave a mystical quality to the promises Joseph made.

"This one," Joseph would say, holding a taupe bulb that looked to Peter like all the rest, "will be bright blue, like a summer sky."

The flowers always blossomed *just as Joseph promised*. How did his father know the secrets of the flowers? Peter wondered. Was Joseph a wizard like Merlin? Or a gypsy with magical powers?

146

For six years, Peter lived in a world of beautiful words and beautiful flowers, a world of warmth and laughter and love. It didn't matter that the Daltons were poor and sometimes cold. Joseph designed the gardens of the great estates of Greenwich, creating colorful, fragrant works of art, but he made little money. Joseph designed only a few gardens each year; he was an artist, and his art took time and patience and loving care. Anne planned to teach as soon as Peter was in school. Until then, it was too important to be at home with her bright little boy, teaching him. The Daltons were poor and their cottage was sometimes cold in winter, but they were rich in love and happiness.

When Peter was six, everything changed.

Anne became ill and then, suddenly, in the dark of night, she died. Joseph fell into troubled, tormented silence, and the tiny cottage that had been filled with such laughter and joy became a dark, suffocating coffin.

Peter watched his father's anguish in bewildered silence and grieved the loss of his beloved mother in the privacy of his small bedroom. It was then, at the age of six, that Peter Dalton began to write. The eloquent, emotional words flowed like tears from his confused, lonely heart.

Two months after Anne's death, Peter was awakened by a noise — a cry in the darkness — and he found Joseph huddled, sobbing. Joseph's sobs pierced the agonizing silence that had lived in the cottage since Anne's death; for Joseph, the sobs were a final, desperate attempt to escape a silent madness that threatened to destroy him.

Peter wrapped his small arms around his father and listened in the icy darkness as Joseph told Peter the grim stories of his life.

Joseph had been forced to flee his home — his homeland, everything he loved — by the soldiers of the most horrible war of all time. Joseph had escaped with his young bride, his first wife, and they were *almost* free! But, as Joseph watched, helpless, screaming, the woman he loved was

147

murdered before his eyes.

Joseph fled again, this time to England. He found work there, in the country gardens of Kent, and a new name, and a new love. Joseph met Anne in England, and after the war they sailed together to America. Joseph and Anne made a wonderful life, rich in happiness and joy and love, until Anne, too, was taken away.

Six-year-old Peter listened to the torments and horrors and loves of his father's life. After that, the bond of love between father and son became even stronger. Each was an artist, driven by silent passions and visions. Joseph poured his soul and emotion into the fragrant pastel gardens he so lovingly created. Peter eloquently translated the confusing, inexplicable tragedies of life into words. Peter helped Joseph create the wonderful gardens—never very many each year . . . just enough to keep them warm in winter—and in the long winters, Joseph proudly read the plays, stories, and poems written by his talented son.

Peter went to Yale University, on scholarship. After graduation, he moved to New York City. Peter lived in Greenwich Village, but he travelled frequently to the small cottage in Danbury to visit Joseph.

Eighteen months after Peter moved to New York, six months after *The Village Voice* raved about his first one-act play, his father was hospitalized with pneumonia. Joseph never fully recovered from the pneumonia, because there was cancer, too. Peter returned to Danbury to be with Joseph and to help him create the gardens he had promised for that spring. Sheila Adamson wanted a rose garden for her library courtyard. Peter and Sara gave her one, a beautiful one, one that Joseph would have loved.

Joseph never saw the rose garden Peter and Sara created. He was too ill to leave the cottage. Peter and Sara told him about it in the long hours they spent with him until his death. Peter and Sara were with Joseph when he died, and he died with a soft smile on his rugged face, a

148

smile for Peter, a smile for Sara.

Sara knew the stories of Peter's life, and the stories of Joseph's life, too. In the portrait she wrote to Rob, Sara didn't give the details, just the essence of the father and son who were so alike, the proud, talented artists whose visions of the world had been shaped, sometimes brutally, by the inexplicable whims of fate.

Sara began her portrait of Peter the way William Shakespeare began *Romeo and Juliet:* "The two houses, both alike in dignity . . ."

As Rob read Sara's portrait in his flat near Oxford, he searched between the lines and found more that worried than reassured.

The houses—the Adamsons and the Daltons—were both alike in dignity, proud and strong, but weren't they also at war? Weren't the stars inevitably crossed? Didn't the dark, talented, sensitive son of the proud, tormented father harbor resentment toward the wealthy and privileged Adamsons of the world?

Rob worried, even though Sara's letter brimmed with love and joy and happiness. Sara ended the ten page letter with: *And in case you don't know, Rob Adamson, in case you didn't notice while you were glowering at him, Peter Dalton is the most handsome man alive (relatives excluded from this analysis for obvious reasons!!!).*

The day after Rob received Sara's portrait of her husband, he received a short letter from Peter.

Rob,
If Sara were my sister, I would doubtless feel the way you must. Please believe I know how special she is, how precious, how much I love her. I promise I will take care of Sara. I will love her with everything I have and give her everything I have to give.

Peter

Rob met Peter the following summer. Rob returned "to the Colonies" for a long Fourth of July weekend. Rob's visit had purpose: He hoped to begin mending fences with his parents, and he wanted to *really* meet Peter. Rob needed to see if the boundless joy Sara sent across the Atlantic in letters and over the telephone was real.

Sara's happiness *was* real. Sara was obviously very much in love with Peter. Although Sara's great joy was quiet and private as Sara always was, Rob could tell because he knew her so well. It was more difficult to tell about Peter, who Rob didn't know, and who was distant and wary with his brother-in-law. Peter's dark eyes always softened when they gazed at Sara, though, as they had that day in the rose garden. Rob decided, because his sister believed it and because he *wanted* to believe it, that Peter was very much in love with Sara, too.

Rob and Sara attended performances of two of Peter's one-act plays at La Mama's, and he saw for himself his brother-in-law's remarkable talent. Rob served as liaison between Sara and their parents, calmly reassuring Sheila and Jeffrey that their daughter was fine, happy, safe.

But was she safe? The question taunted Rob as he flew back to London on the eighth of July. *Was fragile Sara really safe with the dark, silent stranger who took her horseback riding in Central Park and ice-skating in Rockefeller Center and on wind-tossed rides on the Staten Island Ferry?*

Rob hoped so. Rob *prayed* so.

"Sara, what's that noise?" Rob asked when he called to wish her a happy twenty-first birthday. The noise sounded like a bark.

"That's Muffin. I think the phone startled her."

"Muffin?"

"Maybe the name is too preppie, but she really is a Muffin." Sara laughed. "Come here, honey, say hello to your Uncle Rob."

"Sara?"

"She's a blond cocker spaniel puppy, suddenly shy. She's curled in a wriggling ball of fur in Peter's lap."

"Sara . . ."

"Rob, there is no reason whatsoever that I can't have a puppy. Mother and Father were unbelievably paranoid about the lurking dangers."

"They just wanted you to be safe."

"I know," Sara replied with surprising softness.

"Have you spoken to them?" Rob asked hopefully.

"Yes. I used your ploy of sending them the odd post-card. I think it was the Statue of Liberty that did the trick. Not terribly hidden symbolism, but it worked. Mother and Father and I had lunch together last week. I think we've reached a cease-fire, if not a truce."

"That will happen. I've made it to the truce stage with them." After a moment, Rob added quietly, "I think we may be headed for peace."

"That would be nice," Sara said wistfully, knowing it was a long way off for her. Sheila and Jeffrey still harbored the unconcealed hope that Peter Dalton would disappear from their lives and Sara would return to Greenwich. When she spoke again, Sara's voice was filled with pride, "I just sent you the reviews for *Merry Go Round*. The critics loved it!"

For her twenty-first birthday, Sara got Muffin. For her twenty-second birthday, Sara travelled to Rome.

Sara sent the telegram to Rob in his office at *The London Times,* where he had worked full-time in the eight months since the Hathaway Fellowship ended.

Rome. On My Birthday. Be There. Sara.

Rob smiled as he read Sara's telegram. Then a slight

151

frown crossed his face as he realized with amazement that he hadn't seen his sister for two and a half years. Rob felt so close to her—through frequent letters and phone calls--but he couldn't wait to see her. Rob had something to tell her, plans to discuss with Sara and Peter when he met them in Rome in two weeks.

But Peter wasn't in the lobby of the Lord Byron when Rob arrived. Only Sara was there.

Peter let Sara come alone! How could he? Rob's instant reaction was anger. If Peter loved Sara, how could he let her travel all that distance by herself? What if she became ill? What if the plane were delayed and she got behind on her meals? What if the plane were *hijacked?*

Rob's anger was swiftly subdued by Sara's words and the way she looked. His sister had never looked healthier, happier, more radiant, more beautiful.

"I don't know which of my strong, handsome men is the bigger worrywart—you or Peter!" Sara teased the horror from Rob's deep blue eyes. "As you can see, I'm fine!"

"I admit you look fine—no, you look wonderful."

"Peter wanted to come, of course, but he's in the middle of rehearsals for *As You Like It.* And, I waited to tell you this in person: *Storm Watch* is going to be produced on Broadway next fall! It's an incredible play, Rob, and Peter's going to direct as well."

"I can't wait to see it."

"You'll come?"

"For opening night." Rob smiled. "By then, I should be living in New York. I have a plan that I need to talk to you about."

"I need to talk to you, too," Sara said quietly. That was why she was here, alone, to see her brother.

Rob and Sara spent the week exploring Rome, visiting the happy sites—the sparkling fountains where wishes made are destined to come true, the Spanish steps, the Sistine Ceiling, the Borghese Gardens — and strolling along the Via Condetti and through the Vatican. Sara looked wonderful but she fatigued easily. "Too much fresh air," she exclaimed lightly. Sara napped between their morning and afternoon excursions, and they ate early dinners so she could be in bed before nine.

They explored, and they talked, and Rob told her about the idea that had been dancing in his mind for over two years.

"It's a magazine. I'm going to call it *Portrait*. We'll paint portraits with words, like you and I have always done, although there will be photographs as well."

"Rob, this is so exciting!"

"I'm glad you think so." Rob was excited about his magazine-to-be. It would take hard work and it would be risky, but if he insisted on quality — quality writers, quality photographers — and if he selected the right people to feature . . .

"Do you need my twelve million?"

"No! That's for you and Peter."

"We don't need it, Rob. We're happy."

"Well, I don't need your money, but thank you. I do, however, need you."

"Me?"

"I hoped you would be one of the writers."

"Really?" Sara's eyes widened and sparkled.

"Of course. I imagine there will be many interviews to be done in New York City. I don't plan to send you gallivanting all over the globe. I'm sure Peter wouldn't want that, either."

"No, he wouldn't."

"I thought a portrait of Peter, written by you, would be nice for the first issue."

Sara smiled lovingly at her older brother. "I know you will like Peter when you really get to know him, Rob. I

153

know you're still a little skeptical about him."

"No."

"Yes!" She continued very softly, her eyes dreamy, "I want to know that you and Peter will be friends always, no matter what."

"Sara . . ." Rob wanted to stop the ominous tone of her voice. It was so incongruous with how she looked—healthy, robust, with flushed cheeks and sparkling eyes, as if she had never been ill in her life and would live forever.

"Promise me, Rob."

"I promise, Sara." Rob made the promise because he wanted an end to the sudden mood of gloom. He would like Peter, for Sara's sake. The three of them would become good friends. Together they would take New York City by storm.

Rob made the promise swiftly, easily, in good faith.

But it was a promise he could not keep.

Two months later Sara was dead. It happened too quickly for any of them—except Peter—to be with her. From the moment the bleeding began to the moment Sara died at Columbia Presbyterian Medical Center was less than one hour.

Dr. Williams, Sara's specialist in New York, made the call to the Adamson estate in Greenwich and to Rob's flat in London. "Bleeding, shock, overwhelming sepsis, uremia, renal failure," he explained to Jeffrey and Sheila, and again to Rob.

Why? Why? *Why?* they asked in disbelief.

Didn't they *know?* Weren't they prepared? Hadn't Sara told them?

Apparently not. Apparently, they didn't know that Sara was five months pregnant.

"How dare you come here!" Rob hissed when he opened the door of his parents' home and saw the gaunt, anguished face of Peter Dalton.

"I wanted to explain," Peter whispered.

"Explain? I know how women get pregnant, and I know that any man who loved Sara would never have allowed this to happen."

"Rob, I love Sara!"

"Love? Sara is dead, remember? You never loved her. You only loved her money."

"No! How can you say that? Please, Rob, let me explain!"

"Get the hell out of here." As Rob stared angrily into Peter's eyes, powerful, unfamiliar feelings swirled inside him. The strong, terrifying feelings were urging him to harm Peter.

Finally, because he was afraid of what he might do, what he *wanted* to do, Rob slammed the door.

Two weeks after Sara's death, Rob and Sheila and Jeffrey met with Dr. Williams. It was a desperate attempt to make sense of the senseless.

"Sara told me that she and Peter met with you before they were married and that Peter knew everything, including the dangers of pregnancy."

"That's right. I was quite blunt about the risks."

"So Peter couldn't have misunderstood."

"No. He understood. In fact, he decided to have a vasectomy. I told him—them—that they should think about it, but Peter was quite firm. Before they left my office that day I arranged an appointment for him with a colleague."

"The operation failed?" Was that what Peter Dalton had wanted to explain? Was it all a horrible, tragic accident?

"No. I checked last week. I assumed that Peter followed through with it—he seemed so definite—but he didn't. My colleague keeps his records for five years, so I had him check. The appointment was cancelled three days after it was made."

"And you never asked Peter about it again?"

"I didn't see Peter again until the night Sara died. She always came to see me by herself."

"Peter didn't come with her?" Sheila whispered. She had been with Sara, her precious daughter, for every appointment until the horrible announcement that Sara was getting married. If Peter cared about Sara at all, he would have been with her!

"No. I urged Sara to bring him with her." Dr. Williams frowned slightly. "In the past year her condition deteriorated quite rapidly. There were decisions to be made about hemodialysis and—"

"But she looked wonderful!" Sheila interjected. "She spent the weekend with us two months ago, just after she returned from Rome, and she looked so healthy." *So happy, so loving as she said good-bye.*

That was why Sara arranged to meet me in Rome, Rob realized. She knew that she was pregnant and how great a risk it was.

"Sara did look wonderful," Dr. Williams agreed. "But she wasn't." He added, because it was the truth, because it might help, "Sara was dying. Even with heroic interventions she wouldn't have lived much longer."

"But that made pregnancy even more dangerous!"

"Yes," Dr. Williams answered grimly.

"Sara knew?"

"Of course she knew. We tried very hard to convince her to terminate the pregnancy."

"We?"

"Sara's obstetrician and I."

"What about Peter? Where was Peter?"

"I don't know."

"Why didn't you call him? Or us?"

"I couldn't, not without Sara's permission. You know that."

156

But who was taking care of Sara? Who was protecting her?

Not Peter Dalton. Not the man who claimed he loved her.

After Dr. Williams left, Rob and Sheila and Jeffrey sat in the great room as twilight fell, darkening the room, forcing them deeper into their dark, unspeakable thoughts.

Finally, Sheila's voice broke the eerie stillness.

"He killed her. Peter killed her."

"Mother . . . " But it was what Rob had been thinking, too.

"Sheila," Jeffrey whispered weakly.

"He pretended to have the operation, and when she got pregnant, he probably pretended the surgery had failed. Peter knew Sara would never have an abortion." Sheila's voice broke. After a moment, she whispered, "And he knew what would happen if she didn't."

"Sheila, Dr. Williams told us that Sara was dying. She was going to die, dear, even if she hadn't been pregnant."

"But maybe Peter didn't know! Sara looked wonderful. She looked as if she would live forever." Sheila's words ended in a soft sob.

Or maybe Peter did know, Rob thought grimly. Maybe he didn't want to waste any of his inheritance on costly heroic measures. *Either way . . .*

"Peter murdered Sara," Sheila whispered, finishing Rob's thought. *Peter murdered her as surely as if he had fired a bullet into her heart.*

Sheila Adamson believed Sara's death was cold-blooded, premeditated murder. The Adamsons' high-powered attorneys listened to Sheila's words, perhaps even shared the horrible belief, but knew that legally there was nothing to be done. It was pure supposition; not a shred of evidence;

157

nothing that could be proved.

The attorneys strongly advised the family to mention "the theory" to no one. The accusations were libelous, and if Peter Dalton was the kind of man the Adamsons believed him to be, if he heard their accusations, it might be *very dangerous*.

Rob and Jeffrey heeded the attorneys' warnings, and Sheila did eventually, after she told Victoria Elliott, her closest friend.

The Adamsons mourned in dignified silence. The hatred lodged in their hearts, burrowing ever deeper, killing them slowly.

Rob moved to New York and created the astonishingly successful *Portrait* magazine. But it was a joyless triumph. *Portrait* glowed with stories of remarkable, talented, creative men and women; people like Peter Dalton, whose career was as dazzling and distinguished as Sara proudly predicted it would be. Peter was the toast of Manhattan, although he rarely heard the toasts himself, preferring private shadows to the brilliant glitter of Sardi's, Lutece, Le Cirque, or The Brook Club.

Rob watched Peter's success, heard the toasts, and pulsed with helpless rage. Rob answered the frequent query, "When is Peter Dalton going to appear in *Portrait?*" with stony silence and a private vow: *Never.* Not that that would hurt Peter. Nothing Rob could do would harm Peter. And what harm, what hurt, could begin to match what Peter had done to Sara?

Finally, because New York held neither joy nor peace, only powerless torment, Rob moved to Los Angeles.

Rob blamed Peter for Sara's death. As time passed, as emotion was tempered by rationality, Rob saw Peter's crime as the carelessness of a self-absorbed man, not cold-blooded murder. Rob couldn't believe such evil lived in a human heart. And, if such evil existed, Rob didn't *want* to believe that lovely, gentle Sara had been its victim.

Peter Dalton's crime was a careless betrayal of trust, not cold, calculated murder . . . but the result was the same. Peter should have protected Sara. He *promised* he would. Peter had broken that promise and Sara was dead. And for that, Rob hated Peter Dalton with all his heart.

Chapter Eleven

Los Angeles, California
August, 1984

I don't belong here, Allison realized, finally diagnosing what was wrong.

Here was the paddock on the first day of equestrian events at the 1984 Summer Olympics.

The paddock area was an excited, energized bustle of horses and riders. Allison had been sent a special pass by the United States Equestrian Show Jumping Team. They were her friends, the men and women who would have been her teammates.

The special paddock pass was a thoughtful gesture, and her riding friends had welcomed her so warmly — "Allison, you look wonderful!" But they wore jodhpurs; and she wore a light cotton dress. Their bodies were sleek and fit and strong; and she was slender, but not strong enough anymore, and damaged. Their hearts pounded with restless, eager energy as they neared their dreams; and her heart ached with the realization that she was now merely a visitor in a world that for so long had been her home.

And was that pity Allison saw in their eyes? Pity for her and surprise that she had actually come?

These ten days in August were going to be the final chapter in the story of Allison Fitzgerald, Champion

Equestrian. Allison had spent the summer making peace with the dream. And she *did* feel at peace — at peace with what she had lost and hope for what lay ahead.

Allison believed that spending these days watching her friends — and Tuxedo — compete for gold and silver and bronze, being a small part of the energy and excitement one last time, would be the perfect ending to the story.

But she was wrong. The story — *her* story — had ended three years ago.

They belonged here. *She* didn't.

As Allison hurriedly left the paddock area, she expected to feel the heat of tears in her eyes. But there were no tears! Instead of emptiness, Allison felt relief.

And then the once-familiar, almost-forgotten rushes of determination and joy. Determination and joy were old friends. They had always accompanied Allison to the stable, and now they were with her as she left.

Determination and joy stayed with Allison, gaining strength and energy as she navigated the sluggish freeways across the Los Angeles Basin to Beverly Hills. By the time Allison eased her car into a parking space in the patrons' lot behind Elegance, her eyes sparkled and she was smiling.

"Allison!"

"Hello, Claire. I'm reporting for duty."

"Today? The Olympics just started."

"Today."

"Terrific. Except I haven't gotten your work area set up yet. The partitions have been ordered but haven't arrived. I'm planning to create a space over here." Claire wove among the colorful samples of carpeting, wallpaper, and fabric that perpetually cluttered the floors of Elegance. Elegance was a workshop, without pretense or glamour. Allison's "office" was going to be a cubicle created by partitions.

"See?" Claire extracted an ivory business card from a small box on the floor. In gold script, above the name, address, and telephone number of Elegance, were the words *Allison Fitzgerald, A.S.I.D.* "Proof positive that this will be your spot."

"It looks perfect!" Allison added seriously, "The work area isn't terribly important, Claire, but I would like some work."

"You've got it." Claire glanced at her watch. "Arriving in fifteen minutes."

"Really?"

"Yes. This has been your project from the very beginning. I've been filling in until you arrived."

"What is it?"

Claire gave a sly, knowing smile. "Bellemeade."

"Oh!"

Bellemeade was a landmark in Bel Air, an exquisite French Country cottage built in the late 1930's by movie producer Francois Revel for his paramour, the famous Celeste. Bellemeade was small by Bel Air mansion standards, a romantic, charming love nest with private views of dazzling golden sunsets over the sapphire-blue Pacific.

"Bellemeade was recently purchased by Steve Gannon. He's President of Brentwood Productions and also happens to be a very good friend. Steve bought Bellemeade as an investment—it's bound to appreciate—and he can write it off his taxes by using it to house the studio's imported talent in the meantime."

"Imported talent?"

"Actors, actresses, directors who need a place to stay while they're here filming or writing or accepting their Oscars. *Important* imported talent, of course. An elegant house in Bel Air is a giant step beyond even the best suite at the Beverly Hills Hotel."

"Mr. Gannon wants us to decorate Bellemeade?"

"He'll want you to call him Steve, and yes, he does. It's a beauty make-over, really. The house is structurally solid, but the interior is a fixer-upper. It was last decorated in the mid-fifties, so you can imagine, but an elegant face-lift and a tasteful amount of make-up will make it the show-case of Bel Air." Claire smiled. "And it's all yours, my dear."

"Mine?"

"Steve has given you a very nice close-to-seven-figure budget — we'll go over that later — and total freedom, unless this Peter Dalton fellow has strong ideas."

"Peter Dalton?"

"He's the first imported talent who'll be living there. He's the one who wrote *Love* and is moving here for the winter to direct it. I'm sure, if you've spoken to Vanessa Gold recently, she has mentioned him."

Allison nodded. She had seen Vanessa at a welcome-home-from-Argentina dinner for her parents, and Vanessa *had* raved about the "astonishing" screenplay and its "incredibly gifted" author.

"Dalton is due to arrive December first, which means you will be very busy."

"That's fine." *That's good.* "What's happening today?"

"Dalton is in town because they're casting *Love* this week. Steve is going to bring him by, after he sees Belle-meade, to meet us — you — in case he has any preferences for the decorating style." Claire twinkled. "Steve knows there are things we *will not do,* but he thinks Peter Dalton will have very traditional tastes. Oh. Here they are now."

Claire led the way back through the maze of samples to the office foyer.

Steve Gannon looked like a movie producer — rich, powerful, energetic. Allison was instinctively comfortable with such men because they reminded her of her rich, powerful, energetic, and loving father. She smiled warmly at Steve as Claire made the introductions.

Then it was time to meet Peter Dalton.

"I'm Allison," she told the long-lashed, dark brown eyes.

"I'm Peter."

"Hi." Allison smiled, and Peter smiled, too, but she thought she saw flickers of sadness in the dark eyes. No,

163

that *had* to be wrong. This very handsome man was the writer who was giving the world the definitive work on love *complete with a happy ending*. He wouldn't be sad.

"Hi."

"Allison will be the designer for Bellemeade," Claire explained. "Did you have a chance to see it?"

"We were just there," Steve answered. "I gave Peter a whirlwind tour of Bel Air and the Club and UCLA."

"Do you have ideas about how you would like it decorated, Peter?" Allison asked.

"No," Peter answered. After a moment, he added quietly, "I . . . I'm sure whatever you do will be very nice."

"I hope so."

The conversation faltered quickly. Claire murmured something about how talented Allison was, and Steve said something similar about Peter, and the "prized students" exchanged awkward smiles. After a few moments, Steve announced that he and Peter had to rush off to a meeting with the casting director for *Love*.

"Peter could have been a *little* more enthusiastic about Bellemeade, couldn't he?" Claire asked with obvious disapproval after Steve and Peter had left. "Admittedly, the interior is somewhat drab and oppressive at the moment, but he knows that will be fixed—for him!—and the setting itself is absolutely breathtaking."

"I'm sure Peter is quite preoccupied with the movie," Allison said.

"So is Steve, but that doesn't prevent *him* from being polite, does it? No, I imagine Peter Dalton is wondering why he's leaving his penthouse on Fifth Avenue and his estate in the Hamptons to spend four months in *déclassé* Bel Air in *déclassé* California. If Peter were our client, not Steve, I might suggest to the arrogant writer that he find another designer!"

"I didn't think Peter seemed arrogant," Allison countered

softly. *He just seemed sad and lonely.*

"No? Well, aloof, at least. Anyway, Bellemeade is the project of a lifetime for you, Allison. It's just a shame that it has to be such a rush, especially since I'm not sure Peter Dalton will appreciate it no matter how fabulous it is. I wonder if I should just tell Steve that December first is impossible and let him put Dalton at the Beverly Hills Hotel like everyone else!"

"December first is fine, Claire."

"Well, there *is* the dog."

"The dog?"

"Dalton is bringing his dog with him. That's why he wants a house, not a hotel. The dog is probably a designer-eating Doberman!"

"Claire . . ." Allison began, then stopped. She was about to say, I think it's nice that Peter wants his dog with him. I'm sure he's a very nice man. *Sure?* You're the one who thinks his dark eyes are sad and lonely, not aloof and arrogant. Aloof and arrogant makes sense — "incredibly gifted" Peter Dalton has ample reason to be aloof and arrogant — but sad and lonely doesn't. "Do you have the keys to Bellemeade? I'd like to go take a look right now."

"I have the keys and the code for the alarm system, but I don't think you have enough time before your next appointment."

"My next appointment? Claire, I'm at the Olympics today!"

"I know, isn't this working out well?"

"Claire, it will be a miracle if I can finish Bellemeade by December first — and that's assuming I spend every single minute on it!"

"I know. Don't worry. Your next client doesn't want you to begin until December second."

"Who is my next client?"

"His name is Roger Towne. He owns the Chateau Hotels. You've heard of them — small luxury hotels, very elegant, very upscale, all around the world. The Chateau St.

Moritz is the most famous, but perhaps it will be surpassed by the Chateau Bel Air, for which, hopefully, we are doing the interior design."

"Hopefully?"

"It depends on what Roger Towne thinks of your work. He lives in San Francisco, but he flew down for the Opening Ceremonies. We arranged that I would show him photographs of what you've done—the Doheny mansion, the March library, Fairchild House—and he could meet you on his next trip if he's interested."

"Why me?"

"He was specifically referred to you."

"Who referred him?" It had to be Dan. Dan lived in Hillsborough, just south of San Francisco.

"Rob Adamson." Claire talked as she walked, leading Allison toward her office. "The appointment is in ten minutes. Why don't you use my office? The notebook with the photographs is on my desk."

As Allison waited for Roger Towne she thought about Rob. Before Meg's wedding, Allison had never even seen Rob; now she saw him all the time!

Allison recalled how, as a little girl, she would learn a strange new word—"asylum," "indigo," "Serbia," "requiem"—and suddenly everyone would be using it. Allison always wondered if the new word had been there all along and she had just been inattentive, or if it was a remarkable coincidence. Now the same thing was happening with Rob Adamson; once discovered, he was everywhere. But Allison knew she had never seen Rob Adamson before Meg's wedding; she knew he hadn't been there all along and she had simply been inattentive.

Rob hadn't been there before, and now he was, all the time, by remarkable coincidence.

Allison and Winter would be having Sunday brunch at the Club, and Rob and Elaina would appear on the path that led from the garden terrace to the tennis courts. "Elaina in Ellesse," Winter would whisper as she cast a cheery smile. Or Allison would be browsing at Giorgio or Chanel or Gucci on Rodeo, and she would look up and Rob would be there, browsing, too. One Monday night they had both been in the express lane, buying a six-pack of sugar-free soft drinks, at Ralph's in Santa Monica. And last Saturday Allison had seen him jogging on San Vicente.

On those frequent chance meetings, Allison and Rob would acknowledge each other, as well as the coincidence, more with twinkling eyes, warm smiles, and friendly waves than with words. . . .

Just as it had been with Sara. Not many words, just a lovely warmth, a special bond.

And now Rob was sending her important clients, looking out for her, just like an older brother would. How thoughtful of him!

"Hello?" A deep, pleasant voice interrupted her reverie.

Allison looked up into pale blue eyes, sun-blond hair, an easy smile, and the unmistakable look of confidence worn by someone who has created his own empire through hard work and vision. Rob had the same confident look, and so did Steve Gannon, and Allison's father; and Dan would look this way, too. As Allison smiled at the pale blue eyes, her thoughts drifted briefly to a man who *should* have been on that list, but wasn't. Peter Dalton didn't wear the easy confidence of tremendous success. Peter searched the emotions of the heart and soul, and he wrote eloquently about that voyage, but his dark eyes didn't sparkle with confidence. Instead, they flickered with uneasy sadness at the visions they saw. *Didn't they?*

"Hello."

"I'm Roger Towne."

"I'm Allison Fitzgerald."

"You come highly recommended." Roger settled into a chair across from her.

"Rob doesn't have the foggiest idea about my work!" Allison exclaimed with a soft laugh.

"He actually doesn't claim to. It's *you* who comes highly recommended."

"Oh!"

"Rob says if even a tenth of who you are flows over into what you design, I will be delighted with the result." Roger delivered the compliment effortlessly.

"Oh." Allison felt the warmth rush to her cheeks, but she remained steady under the pale blue gaze, strangely comfortable, strangely bold. She tilted her head and asked, "Roger, have you known Rob long?"

"For about two years. We met at my hotel in New Orleans. Why?"

Allison's eyes widened and sparkled. "Rob's crazy, you know."

"We have the Chateau Bel Air," Allison told Claire an hour and a half later.

"You dazzled him. I could hear the coquettish laughter."

"We just hit it off. He's very nice, very funny." *Very nice.* Allison had decided that about Peter Dalton, too. Roger Towne and Peter Dalton, such different men. Both very nice? "Besides, I don't think I could really dazzle anyone with this mane, do you?"

Claire's silence told Allison what she already knew. It struck her as she caught her image in the Kentshire mirror that leaned against the wall in Claire's office. The long red-gold hair belonged in a paddock or galloping across field or floating over a jump—places she no longer belonged—but not here, not on the exciting young designer of Beverly Hills!

"I was in Rinaldi's today. Normally, they are booked every day from dawn until dusk, but the fear of Olympics gridlock has driven the regulars out of the city, so the place is empty. I'm sure you could call right now and get an immediate appointment."

"You'd let me off early?"

168

"I think you've done a fair day's work!"

Allison had planned to think about it for a day or two, but . . .why not?

"I guess I will then."

"Let me just give you the keys to Bellemeade and the instructions for the alarm, so you can stop by on your way in tomorrow morning. Take a long, leisurely look at Bellemeade and *maybe* you'll have an office by the time you return."

Allison had forgotten about the curls! They had been there as her hair grew out after the neurosurgery, but she had been so eager to feel the weight of her mane again that she had hardly noticed.

Allison smiled as she watched soft curls appear where before there had been a long, sleek wall. Curls, suddenly freed, bouncy, somehow hopeful.

You're not a filly any more, Allison thought. Good-bye Bel Air's Ginger Lady.

"You like it," the stylist murmured as he noticed Allison's smile.

"Oh!" Allison had been intrigued, mesmerized, by what was happening to the suddenly freed short curls. She hadn't thought at all about how the new cut made her look.

"I know women who would kill for these curls, this look!" the stylist continued. "Very soft, very feminine, but still so *chic*. And, of course, with your eyes . . ."

Allison gazed at her suddenly huge jade green eyes and the soft red-gold frame around her face, and she had a sense of déjà vu—a recent memory of looking at an image of herself, a beautiful image, and appreciating the image before she realized it was *her*. When was that?

Allison remembered—the beautiful but sad picture Emily had taken of her at Meg's wedding—and that memory recalled something else that she had entirely forgotten.

169

Emily was coming to her apartment at seven-thirty tonight to do the portrait for her parents' anniversary—a happy, exhilarated portrait of Allison after her first day at the Olympics.

Allison had forgotten, and that scared her because of those horrible months after her accident when she couldn't remember *anything*. But Allison swiftly calmed her fear. *It's been an eventful day and you* did *remember.*

Allison smiled away the brief frown and replaced worries about the past with plans for the future. Bellemeade was her top priority. The Chateau Bel Air would come later, and working with Roger Towne would be easy and fun.

And Bellemeade? Easy and fun? Perhaps not . . . but, somehow, Bellemeade was terribly important.

The interior design Allison would do for Bellemeade would be French, of course, something light and cheery and floral, with wonderful wallcoverings and drapes by Charles Barone and pastel silk chaises and delicately carved blond woods and Lalique crystal. Perhaps Emily had some lovely photographs of roses or lilacs or wild-flowers.

I want to make Bellemeade very beautiful and very happy, Allison thought. The thought continued before she could stop it.

I want to make Bellemeade very beautiful and very happy for Peter . . . for sad, lonely, nice Peter Dalton.

Chapter Twelve

"The Dynasty Room has excellent food," Steve told Peter when he stopped the car on Hilgard Avenue in front of the Westwood Marquis. "I assume you can have it served in your suite. Are you sure you don't want company?"

"No, thank you, Steve."

"All right. I'll pick you up at seven tomorrow morning."

"Fine. Good night."

As Steve drove from the Westwood Marquis to his home on Mountain Drive in Beverly Hills, he wondered again if he had made a big mistake when he decided to produce *Love*.

Everything about this project was different, beginning with the remarkable concessions he had already made to the very serious, very quiet Peter Dalton.

The very serious, very quiet, very *decisive* Peter Dalton. Peter knew precisely what he wanted—demanded it—and Steve agreed. Peter wanted to choose the principal cast, especially Julia, himself; Peter wanted an agreement in writing that he wouldn't give interviews or make promotional appearances; and Peter wanted absolute approval of the final product with power to block release if he wasn't happy with it.

Steve had made those phenomenal concessions to Peter Dalton because *Love* was the best script he had ever read. Before making the concessions, Steve had done some checking on Peter—beyond the impressive credentials of three Tony awards, a Pulitzer Prize, and nonstop successes on Broadway. Steve spoke with actors and actresses Peter had directed—famous ones and not-so-famous ones—and with producers. And Steve was more than reassured.

Peter Dalton was the best. The actors and producers made the pronouncement swiftly and with great respect. Peter was tireless and energetic, they told Steve. A perfectionist, of course; but Peter had a remarkable ability to gently lure the best out of everyone. He was always calm, they said, always serious, never temperamental.

The men and women with whom Peter worked on Broadway smiled when they spoke of him—warm, thoughtful smiles, but not smiles of close friendship. No one seemed to know about Peter's private life—except that when he wasn't *in* the theater he *had* to be somewhere writing, because the remarkable plays kept appearing despite his full-time directing commitments.

A private man, a private genius, *and* a man who knew precisely what he wanted. Even for this trip, to choose the cast, Peter requested a hotel near the UCLA campus rather than the usual suite at the Beverly Hills Hotel.

Everything will be different with *Love,* Steve thought as he turned into the drive of his home in Beverly Hills. I hope it's worth it.

Peter poured himself a glass of bourbon from the full decanter in his suite at the Westwood Marquis and took a large swallow. In moments, he felt the effect of the bourbon on his exhausted mind, loosening thoughts, freeing memories.

Peter *was* exhausted. He hadn't slept last night, driven as always into wakefulness by his nightmares. Usually Peter spent those dark, wakeful hours writing, but last night he read the words he had written four years before, for Sara, and hadn't read since. And after, as dawn had light-

172

ened the summer sky, Peter wandered around the UCLA campus, restless, wondering what the hell he was doing.

Keeping your promise to Sara, he reminded himself.

Peter sighed, drank more bourbon, and thought uneasily about the exhausting day that had followed the sleepless night.

Steve had been so polite, so gracious, but Peter didn't need to be treated like royalty! He didn't need — or want — guest privileges at the Bel Air Hunt Club. And he certainly didn't need a house as splendid as Bellemeade.

Peter chided himself for not acting more impressed, more appreciative, more gracious. His tired mind had been so consumed with his own memories.

If Steve found Peter's lack of enthusiasm rude, he probably dismissed it as artistic temperament, or maybe simply jet lag. Steve had only one concern . . . that Peter deliver the movie of the decade. That was the bottom line. Everything else — the creature comforts, the gracious pleasantries — were fluff.

Steve didn't care if Peter was effusive about the Club or Los Angeles or Bellemeade, not really, but someone else *had* cared. Peter narrowed his dark eyes, frowning at the uneasy memory, thinking it was the one scene of the day he would do over if he could.

It was the scene at Elegance. The designer, Allison, had seemed so nice, so enthusiastic, so eager to make Bellemeade something he would like. Allison, whose coloring reminded Peter of the richness of autumn — luxuriant jade, sunlit red, radiant gold — and whose merry eyes and full lips sent a wonderful, healthy promise of a bountiful harvest. Peter had dampened that marvelous spirit, made uncertainty flicker in the remarkable jade eyes.

He *should* have been more positive about Bellemeade, more appreciative, more polite, but the words hadn't come.

Peter was sorry, but it didn't matter. Nothing mattered, not where he lived, or if he caused a moment of disappointment in lovely jade eyes, or if they all thought he was arrogant and rude.

Peter was in Los Angeles for one reason . . . to keep his promise to Sara.

Peter had made three promises to Sara. One—this one—he would keep. The second he would try *again* to keep. And the third he would never keep.

Promises to keep. It was a line from Sara's favorite poem by Robert Frost. *The woods are lovely dark and deep/ But I have promises to keep/ And miles to go before I sleep.*

Sara's favorite poem, and what Peter's life had been since Sara's death; a desperate wish to sleep—to find lovely dark woods and fall asleep forever—but there were miles and promises, because of Sara.

Sara, Sara . . .

There had always been girls in Peter's life. From the moment his young, healthy body wanted girls, they were there. In junior high and high school, in Danbury, there were girls like him, girls with little money whose parents worked for the wealthy, privileged inhabitants of Greenwich. Sex was a free pleasure, a wonderful pleasure, a desperate, frantic pleasure in lives that had little joy. At Yale there were girls, smart girls who were going to be doctors and lawyers and Supreme Court Justices and President. Sex with the smart girls wasn't so frantic or so desperate, or so uninhibited.

Then Peter moved to New York, and there were the uptown girls with the go-to-hell looks and the incredible confidence. They had never met anyone like Peter. They loved his wildness, the dark, restless part that could never be tamed. And they loved the passion—the passion of a tormented poet—in his sensuous dark eyes. The uptown girls tried to tame the modern-day Heathcliff, knowing it was impossible but loving the exciting, provocative game.

There had always been girls in Peter's life, but there had

never been love.

Then Joseph became ill, and Peter returned to Connecticut because his father had promised Sheila Adamson a rose garden. Peter met Sara and fell deeply, astonishingly in love. Neither Peter nor Sara had expected love in their lives, certainly not then, maybe not ever. But they fell in love quietly, confidently, joyously.

"I have diabetes," Sara told Peter a month after they met, two weeks after they first whispered *I love you*.

"What does that mean?" Peter asked gently. His eyes told Sara the question was, really, *What does that matter?*

Sara told Peter what it meant, what it had meant for her: living in a glass cage, being watched so carefully, a precious specimen on display until it became extinct. And what it would mean for them: She might not live very long, she couldn't have children.

Peter listened, fighting tears, making silent vows that he would never make Sara feel trapped, feeling contempt and anger toward the family who had imprisoned her, a family he disliked *already* because of their wealth and privilege.

But even before Peter and Sara were married, Peter realized how difficult it would be for him to keep those vows. He wanted to protect Sara—Peter even felt a begrudging closeness to the family who had only wanted the same thing—but he had promised to let her be free.

"I don't want you to have the vasectomy, Peter."

"Sara, I want to."

"But, Peter, what happens when they find the cure?" Sara's dark blue eyes glistened with hope and love.

"All right," he whispered gently, holding her close. Peter blinked back tears and wondered if it had anything to do with a cure, or if Sara simply wanted *him* to be able to have children, someday, after . . . "Sara."

Sara pulled away and looked at him with serious eyes.

"Peter, I've never had any control over my life. Let me be responsible for this, please."

"For our birth control?"

"Yes."

"All right. But, Sara, I want to go with you for your regular appointments with Dr. Williams."

"No, Peter. Diabetes is my disease. It's part of me—a friendly rival—but I don't want it to be part of *us*. I'll take good care of myself, Peter, I promise. But . . ."

"But?"

"Someday, there may be decisions to make. You have to trust me to make them, Peter."

"You have to trust me to help you."

"I will. If I need help."

Peter touched Sara lovingly on her pale cheek, and Sara took his strong hand in her small one and whispered, "Make love to me, Peter. I'm not that fragile."

Peter and Sara lived in a private world of love. Peter became a brilliant star in the glittering galaxy of stars who lived in Manhattan. Some of the stars sought the limelight, the dazzling galas, the ever-flowing champagne, the attention of adoring, interested media and fans; other stars, like Peter, preferred quiet, anonymous solitude. In Manhattan, both life-styles were allowed, both were respected.

"Are you a happy man?" Sara asked Peter as they celebrated their second wedding anniversary in their made-cheery-by-Sara apartment in Greenwich Village.

"My God, Sara, don't you know how happy I am?"

"I know." Sara did know, and she knew that Peter's life before their love hadn't been happy, and that was why he wrote what he did. "It's just that your plays are so—"

"Grim? Tragic? *Real?*"

"—tormented, dark, heart-stabbing," Sara added with a loving smile.

"Van Gogh painted flowers and he was *not* a happy man."

"Van Gogh painted tormented flowers."

"Ah."

"Look at William Shakespeare. Tragedies, comedies."

"You're comparing me to Shakespeare? You are so good for me!" Peter laughed softly and gazed lovingly into her eyes. "OK, Sara Dalton, someday I'll write a happy play, just for you, hearts that aren't broken and flowers that aren't tormented. But I can't do it yet. It would destroy my image as the author of darkness. OK?"

"OK. I love you, Peter."

"Oh, Sara, I love you, too."

Peter loved Sara too much and he fought that silent battle within himself. He wanted desperately to protect her, but he had promised to let her be free. Sara wanted to ice-skate, so Peter took her to Rockefeller Center and hand-in-hand they skated around the rink. Then Sara told him about a girl she had known at Greenwich Academy, a champion rider, and how she floated over jumps, so happy, so free. Peter held his breath and prayed that Sara would be safe as, together, they learned to horseback ride in Central Park. Sara *was* safe, and her pale cheeks were rosy and her eyes glowed with such happiness.

Peter kept his promise, loving Sara, letting her be free; and Sara kept hers, taking good care of herself, living a delicate balance.

They were going to live and love forever. Peter began to believe there would be a cure—or that maybe their love was the cure. . . .

Then Sara got sick. Peter noticed the change—weakness, fatigue, strain in her lovely eyes—immediately.

"Darling, how are you?"

"Fine." Sara forced a loving smile, but her ocean-blue eyes misted briefly.

Peter knew Sara was dying, and battling with the horrible choices that might prolong her life but cause great pain.

"I love you, Sara."

"I love you, Peter. I need—"

"You need what?" he asked gently. *Anything, darling. My life, if I could give it to you.*

"—I need to know that you trust me to make the right decision."

"I trust you, but can't I help you, please?"

"You do help me, Peter."

Two weeks later Peter wondered if it had all been a mirage. Sara looked better again, *fine*, in fact; but that only lasted a few weeks. A new pattern emerged—good times and bad times—subtle changes Peter pretended not to see because he knew how hard Sara was fighting. But they both knew, and they held each other even tighter and touched each other more often—*almost always.*

Then, four months before Sara died, everything changed again. Sara looked wonderful, glowing, healthy, happy. Her energy soared and her eyes sparkled with joy and hope. She insisted on going, alone, to Rome, and Peter held his breath. But she would be with her brother, and even though Peter sensed that Rob was uneasy about him, he felt a kinship with the brother-in-law who loved Sara, and who shared the conflicting instincts to protect her and allow her to be free.

Sara returned from Rome, safe and happy; and then she spent a weekend in Greenwich making peace with her parents; and then Sara came home to spend the rest of her life with him.

"We're going to have a baby, Peter."

"Sara?"

"I'm three months pregnant."

"Honey." *No.* He should have had the vasectomy! But Sara had wanted to be in charge of that intimate part of their lives, and Peter had let her, and something had gone wrong. Peter looked at Sara's glowing blue eyes and her proud smile, and he realized it wasn't a mistake. "You got pregnant on purpose."

"Yes."

"But, Sara." The doctor had told them it was a great risk

178

three years ago, and now . . . *No.*

"I want to have our baby, Peter." *I want you to have our baby.*

"I only want you, Sara. This is too much of a risk."

"Peter." Sara fought tears. *You can't have me much longer anyway, my darling.*

"Sara." Peter held her close to him and kissed her hair as tears spilled from his eyes.

After a few moments, Sara pulled away and gently kissed his tears.

"Peter! I'm going to be fine and the baby's going to be fine. Our only problem will be that this place is too small for the four of us!" Sara cast a loving glance at Muffin, who observed the entire somber episode with sad, knowing eyes and now wagged her tail at the familiar lilt in Sara's voice.

Pretend with me, Peter, please.

"Would you like to move to a penthouse on Park Avenue?" *I'll pretend, darling. We'll make these the happiest days of our life, our love.*

"Perhaps." Sara smiled, then curled up quietly against him.

The next day, Peter arrived home from the theater with an announcement.

"I've decided to take the next few months off."

"*As You Like It* opens in two weeks," Sara countered quietly, but it was a weak protest and it told Peter what he feared.

"That's not as important as what I'm going to be doing." *I'm going to be spending every second I can with my beloved Sara.* "I've decided, by popular demand, to write a love story."

"Peter! A happy ending and everything?"

"Everything."

Peter and Sara spent their last two months together in their brownstone in Greenwich Village, loving each other so gently, so tenderly, each knowing that they were saying good-bye, each pretending that Sara and the baby would be fine, both *believing* it because their love was so strong, so magical, so joyous.

Peter finished *Love* in six weeks. He gave it to Sara to read, but she gave it back and asked him to read it aloud to her. *Love* was Peter's lovesong to his beloved Sara, a loving, joyous celebration of what she meant to him and of their forever love.

"I'm not Julia," Sara said softly when Peter told her that *she* was the magnificent heroine. Did Peter really believe she was that lovely, that loving, that generous?

"Yes, you are, darling."

"I'm not, but thank you."

"You are, and you're welcome." Peter kissed her tenderly.

"What are you going to do with the play, Peter?" Sara asked after a few gentle, loving moments.

"Read it to you, over and over, and to our baby—our *babies*—and to our grandchildren. By then, you and I should be able to do the parts by heart."

"I think the whole world needs to hear the words."

"You do?" Peter had known Sara would want him to produce *Love*. That was why, even though it was Peter's lovesong to Sara, the story bore no resemblance to their own. Julia was Sara—Sara's loveliness and innocence and courage—but only the people who loved Sara—Peter and the Adamsons—would see her in Julia.

"Yes. Peter, you have people standing in subzero weather hoping to get last minute seats for your plays about tormented souls. Don't you think it would be lovely to share this?"

"Maybe."

Two nights later, Sara awakened Peter at midnight.

"Peter, we have to go to the hospital."

"Sara?" Her voice was so calm it terrified him. Sara had made peace with what was going to happen. Peter hadn't. *Please, no.* "What is it?"

"I guess it's labor. And I'm bleeding. I already called an

ambulance."

Peter took Sara's hand and didn't let go until after she died. The doctors and nurses swirled around, working frantically and in vain to save Sara and her baby. Peter and Sara were in the eye of the storm, gazing lovingly, whispering, oblivious to the chaos, lost in their own private world for a final time.

"Peter, promise me that you and Rob will be friends. Go to him, become his friend, please."

"All right, darling. The *three* of us will become best friends. Rob will be living in New York, too, remember?"

"You and Rob, *please.*"

"I promise."

"And Peter?"

"Darling?"

"Promise to make a movie of *Love.*"

"A movie? You want to go to Hollywood?"

"A movie, just the way you wrote it. A happy ending, OK?"

"OK." Peter smiled through tears at the slight twinkle in her blue eyes.

"And Peter?"

"Yes?"

"Find someone else to love. Find someone lovely with whom you can share your life."

I'm sharing my life—my love—with you!

"Sara . . . "

"Thank you for letting me be free." *Thank you for allowing me to make this choice. It's what I wanted.*

"Sara . . . "

"And Peter, thank you for loving me."

"Oh, Sara, I love you so much." *Don't leave me, please. I can't live without you.*

Peter almost didn't live without Sara. He felt himself slipping into the silent madness that had possessed his father in the months after his mother's death.

Silent madness.

The oppressive stillness was pierced by the telephone two weeks after Sara's death. Sara's attorneys wanted to talk to Peter about his enormous inheritance. Peter didn't even want to hear about it. He told the attorneys to give everything to the Juvenile Diabetes Foundation. Peter didn't want Sara's money; he wanted Sara. Even though Peter hated the disease that had stolen his wife from him, he knew Sara didn't hate it. Sara had been calm about her fate — her lifelong battle with her friendly rival — not bitter. The bitterness and rage belonged to Peter.

It was probably Muffin who saved Peter. In mechanical silence, Peter cared for Muffin, feeding her, walking her, nothing else. Peter took care of Muffin in the same distracted, silent way that Joseph Dalton had cared for his six-year-old son in the months following Anne's death.

Then, one day, Peter *looked* at Muffin. Muffin, who Sara had loved. Muffin, who had been the baby Peter and Sara would never have. Muffin, whose tail hadn't wagged and who lived in the somber silence, curled up in a corner, quietly bewildered by how her world had changed.

Peter's sad dark eyes met Muffin's bewildered ones. The sudden attention — a *look* from Peter — caused a hopeful, uncertain tilt to Muffin's blond head.

"Muffin," Peter whispered. He had fed her and walked her, but he hadn't spoken to her for almost six weeks.

Muffin's small blond tail moved a little, a tentative wag.

"Come here, Muffin."

She bounded joyfully, gratefully, across the room and into Peter's lap.

"Oh, Muffin, you miss her, too, don't you?" Peter's words ended with a sob and he cried into Muffin's soft fur. "You miss her, too."

That evening, with Muffin curled up in his lap, Peter began to write again, carving anguished words from his soul. The first play he wrote after Sara's death was *Say*

182

Good-bye, for which he won the Pulitzer. Peter's entire life became his work, writing, directing, writing more. Peter directed during the day, and in the long, lonely nights, when he was driven into wakefulness by the nightmares that were his constant companions, he wrote.

Two years after Sara's death, Peter and Muffin moved from the bright, cheerful apartment in Greenwich Village, where there had been such love, to a small flat in Chelsea. The flat was dark and barren, and Peter did nothing to decorate it, but it had a garden and was a short walk to the theater district.

Peter wrote, Peter directed, Peter succeeded.

Peter survived.

Even though part of his heart—most of it!—wanted to join his beloved Sara in the dark, lovely woods and a forever sleep.

Peter survived.

He had promises to keep.

Promises to keep. In his suite at the Westwood Marquis, Peter filled his glass with bourbon for the third time.

I will make the movie, Sara.

I will find Rob and try to become his friend—again. Peter had tried, two years before, when his brother-in-law was still in New York, but Rob had refused to take his calls.

But the third promise—*find someone else to love*—could never happen. Peter didn't even want it to.

That promise, darling Sara, I can never keep.

Chapter Thirteen

"I really love your hair!" It was the third time Winter had made that pronouncement during the short drive from Holman Avenue to Bel Air. Winter had worried that she wouldn't like Allison's short hair. She remembered the red-gold curls that had appeared, finally, after Allison's operation, and the huge, bewildered jade-green eyes that had stared from beneath the curls. Allison had been so haunted then. Winter was afraid the short hair would recall that awful time.

But Allison's eyes weren't bewildered, and the whole look was beautiful and confident and full of hope. Allison's were the eyes of a champion again, envisioning new golden trophies and blue satin ribbons, something that made Allison look wonderful.

"Thank you," Allison laughed. "I like it, too."

"So, we're heading for Bel Air. Why?"

"We have to take a look at my first official project."

"You're doing a house in Bel Air? I'm impressed!"

"Not just a house, Winter, *Bellemeade.*"

"You're kidding. How exciting!"

"How scary."

Allison turned off Perugia onto the cobblestone drive that swept to the French Country cottage.

"I've always loved this place." Winter smiled. "So romantic, so charming."

"Have you ever been inside?"

"No. I can't wait."

As Allison and Winter wandered from room to room in Bellemeade, Winter's enthusiasm waned and Allison's crescendoed.

"It's dark and dank and grim," Winter whispered.

"But the spaces are wonderful! And the cathedral ceilings and circular staircase and marble fireplaces and hardwood floors. And look at the windows, Winter! Done right, Bellemeade can be very lovely." Allison frowned. "Done right *and* in record time. Everything has to be ready by November thirtieth."

When Allison finished explaining the reason for the rush, because Peter Dalton was arriving, Winter made a quiet confession.

"I wasn't going to tell you this until it was all over, Allison. I thought I'd just tell you *after* where I had placed—one hundredth runner-up, or one thousandth, whatever—but . . . I answered the casting call for *Love*."

"You did? And?"

"And I still don't know. I've been called back three times, and last Friday they did a screen test."

"That's terrific, isn't it?"

"I guess. I think I was the only unknown actress to get a screen test. The well-known actresses were screen-tested, too. Apparently, Peter Dalton doesn't spend a lot of time at the movies. He doesn't even know the big stars."

"So that gives you an equal chance."

"Maybe." Winter smiled. "Actually, I feel that I have an unfair advantage. When I read the scenes, I just pretend I'm talking to Mark."

"Is it really the love story of the decade?" Allison asked.

"Me and Mark?"

"I know you and Mark are. I meant *Love*."

"Probably. I've only read the parts of scenes they've given me, not the entire script. But the parts I've read are stunning, breathtakingly beautiful."

185

"When do you read the entire script?"

"I *could* read it now. There are plenty of copies floating around, but it seems presumptuous. If they're interested in me, they'll give me a copy of the script. Peter Dalton is supposed to be in town this week looking at the screen tests, so we'll see."

Allison didn't tell Winter she had met Peter. Winter would want to hear what Peter was like, and Allison really didn't know what to say.

Peter and Steve moved forward in their chairs at the same moment, as if pulled by a powerful magnet. The magnet was on the screen, a lovely, bewitching woman with violet eyes and ivory skin and such softness when she spoke of love.

"My God," Steve whispered.

Peter simply nodded. At last they had found Julia.

It was Friday afternoon. Peter and Steve had spent the past four days viewing the screen tests. Now the search was over.

"Who is she?" Peter asked. He assumed she was a well-known star, unknown, as they all were, only to him.

"I have no idea."

Steve turned on the screening room lights from the control panel in the center of the room, looked through the stack of folders on the table, and removed the one with the number that corresponded to the number on the test. As Steve started to open it, reminded himself that *Peter* had absolute control over casting, suppressed his curiosity and handed the folder to Peter.

"It looks like no acting experience," Peter said as he scanned the standard bio sheet prepared by the casting staff. Under previous performances was written *None*.

Christ, Steve swore silently. It was really amateur night at the movies. The best goddamned script *ever,* perhaps Broadway's best director, but theater was theater and film

186

was film. A novice film director was worrisome enough, but an unknown inexperienced actress, too? "You mean no film experience."

"No. No acting experience. No, wait," Peter said as he turned to Winter's brief résumé attached to the bio sheet. Peter smiled. "Here she has written 'a few plays in high school,' followed by two exclamation points and a smiling face."

"A smiling face? Great. What's her name?"

"Winter Carlyle."

Steve's frown turned upside down. Winter Carlyle. Maybe she didn't have the acting experience, but she sure as hell had the genes.

Winter Carlyle. Steve's mind searched for a memory of her. He had a recent memory; a somber memory of black hair, a black dress, a black veil. Steve hadn't gotten close enough at Jacqueline's funeral to see the face beneath the veil. He had that recent memory, along with a distant one. How long ago had it been? Ten years . . . no, twelve, before he met his wife. He and Jacqueline were doing *The Last Time* together, she as actress, he as director; and they had made more than the movie. For three wonderful months they had been in . . . in *passion,* at least. Steve had seen Jacqueline's daughter only once, from a distance, but he remembered huge, shy violet eyes.

What a beautiful woman that little girl had become! Beautiful like her mother, with Jacqueline's incredible talent. Steve wondered what else Winter had inherited from her mother.

"She's the daughter of Jacqueline Winter and Lawrence Carlyle," Steve told Peter. Then Steve turned to the casting director, who sat in smug silence two rows back. Four days ago she had told Steve that there was a promising unknown, but he had insisted—logically—that they begin with the screen tests of Michelle and Madolyn and Paula and Rachel and all the other talented, established actresses who wanted to be Julia. "Did you know that? Did you know who she was?"

"No," the casting director replied. "She never said a word. She was quiet, serious, not the least bit pushy. I don't even think she has a copy of the script."

"Well, let's get one to her," Steve said. "And a contract to her agent. We should probably give them the weekend."

Steve looked at Peter. He knew Peter was eager to get back to New York. Peter had interrupted rehearsals of his new play, *Shadows of the Mind,* to cast *Love.*

"If you like, Peter, assuming we can get it set with Winter and her agent, we can meet for coffee at the Garden Terrace at the Marquis Monday morning, instead of for martinis at the Polo Lounge Monday afternoon." *Why not?* Steve thought. Everything was different about this project. Why not seal the deal over black coffee instead of dry martinis? "Then, if Winter's on board and you trust me to decide which of the five actors we've already lined up reads best with her, you'll be back in New York Monday night."

"That would be fine." Peter looked again at Winter's résumé. "I don't see an agent's name listed."

"Really? Then we'll just send everything directly to Winter Carlyle."

Mark let himself into Winter's apartment at five-thirty Sunday afternoon. He had been on call Saturday night at the VA. Winter was expecting him, but she didn't hear him come in. Mark found her, sitting on her bed huddled over the script, crying.

"Darling." Mark kissed her lovely damp eyes. In the past two months there had been tears—sad tears and happy ones—flowing without shame from emotions that had been hidden for a lifetime. "This is what I call a sodden heap."

"Hi." Winter smiled through her tears. "This is at least the fifteenth time I've read this and it still makes me cry."

"Is it sad? I thought it was supposed to be happy."

"It is happy." *It reminds me of us.* "I don't know if I can even say these beautiful words without crying, much less say them the way they deserve to be said."

"That good?"

"Yes. This motion picture has to be painted with the most delicate brush in the world and every tiny stroke has to be perfect."

"But you want to try?"

"Yes, I want to try. I want to paint a perfect Julia if I can." Winter added quietly. "And if I don't have to do love scenes."

"Oh, Winter, I should never have mentioned that."

"Yes, you should have." Winter curled up close to Mark and whispered softly, "I'm going to tell them, over coffee at the Marquis, no nudity."

Winter arrived at the Garden Terrace early, ordered black coffee, and waited. She spent the anxious moments before Steve and Peter were due to arrive rehearsing what she would say, wondering for the hundredth time if she should have asked attorney-agent-shark Elaina Kingsley to represent her, and hoping she would not be disappointed with Peter Dalton.

Winter hoped Peter Dalton wouldn't be wearing an open-collared, vivid print shirt, heavy gold chains, a smug sleazy-sexual smile, and dark glasses. Winter didn't want Peter Dalton to be a commercial love guru, a smooth savvy writer who wrote the beautiful words only to pluck heartstrings and put mega-dollars in his bank account.

Winter wanted Peter Dalton to look like . .. .

. . . the dark, handsome, serious man who was approaching her table with a soft smile and sensitive dark brown eyes. Someone, like her, who knew about love.

"Winter? I'm Peter Dalton."

"Hi."

Steve Gannon was with Peter. Steve introduced himself,

and he and Peter sat down. After they ordered coffee, Steve got right to business.

"Winter, have you read the script?"

"Yes." Winter smiled at Peter and said softly, "It's really wonderful. I would very much like the part."

"Then this is easy," Steve said. "We plan to start filming in early January, wrap by late March, and release by August. That's a tight schedule, lots of hard work, maybe seven days a week, long hours every day."

"*Love* will be filmed entirely in Los Angeles?" Winter asked. That was what she had read in Vanessa's column, but Winter wanted to be sure. She didn't want the part if it meant being away from Mark. They would be apart, because of his clerkships in Boston, but she would visit him at Christmas, as soon as her Autumn classes at UCLA were over. Then, in January, she would be so busy with *Love* that Mark's second month in Boston would go quickly.

"Yes, entirely in LA." Steve paused. "Are we waiting for your agent?"

"No."

"Did you take a look at the contract? It's all quite stand-ard, of course, but I want to make sure that you under-stand."

"I did look at it." Winter had spent three hours Saturday afternoon at the mansion, carefully comparing the contract that had arrived by courier Friday afternoon with Jacqueline's, which were filed, alphabetically by movie title, in an oak cabinet in the library.

"And?"

"There are two problems." *Three,* Winter thought, if you count the fact that my heart is about to jump out of my chest. *Come on, Winter, let's see some acting here.*

"Oh?"

Winter smiled sweetly, as if the problems were very mi-nor, before she spoke.

"No nudity."

190

"*What?*"

"And no love scenes that are . . . suggestive. Kissing is all right, but nothing else."

"Winter, we don't want anything pornographic, but there have to be love scenes. There have to be bare breasts and—"

"Then I can't do it."

"Virtually every actress in Hollywood . . ." Steve started naming names.

"Then you should ask one of them to be Julia."

Winter stared bravely at Steve, but she turned when she heard a soft laugh from Peter.

"It's all right, Steve," Peter said.

"What's all right?"

"There doesn't have to be nudity."

"Christ," Steve breathed, relenting because he had to, because Peter had artistic control. "I can just see this movie coming out with a G-rating."

"I don't have a problem with love being for general audiences," Peter said quietly.

"OK." Steve sighed heavily, for the record. "What's the other problem, Winter?"

"I would like a piece of the movie."

Steve gazed at Winter for a stunned moment, then laughed. "Just when I was wondering if you were really Jacqueline's daughter."

Jacqueline Winter had never had a problem with suggestive love scenes—on or off screen—or nudity, and she had always demanded a piece of the movie. Of course, that was a demand Jacqueline could make. As an established actress, it was standard for her to receive a percent of the profits. But for an unknown actress!

"Did you know my mother?"

"Of course." Steve saw the sudden sadness in Winter's eyes and said gently, honestly, "I was very sorry about her death."

"Do you know my father?"

191

"Yes. Not very well. I see him at Cannes every year or two. I *would* see him at the Academy Awards, except he never bothers to come to pick up his Oscars."

The issue of Lawrence Carlyle—if it was an issue—had worried Steve ever since he learned he was about to cast Winter in *Love*. Steve didn't know the real details of the swift divorce of Jacqueline Winter and Lawrence Carlyle—no one seemed to know; but, even years later when Steve and Jacqueline had had their affair, Jacqueline had still spoken of Lawrence with great bitterness. If Winter shared Jacqueline's bitterness, the press would go crazy, searching for skeletons, exploring the estrangement of the famous director father and his destined-to-be-famous actress daughter.

"Do *you* know him?" Steve asked Winter after a moment.

"No. He left when I was one. I don't remember him."

"And you haven't seen him since?"

"No."

"Do you want to?"

"No."

This was bad; very, *very* bad. The press would have a field day. If *Love* and Winter Carlyle were the sensations Steve expected them to be, the issue of Lawrence and Winter Carlyle would have to be dealt with, head-on, long before the Academy Award nominations were announced.

Of course, Steve thought wryly, without breasts or erotic love scenes, and with a novice actress and director, he probably had nothing to worry about . . . except having paid a huge amount of money for the flop of the year!

"We'll give you a piece of the movie," Steve sighed finally. *Why not?* "How much did you have in mind?"

Allison looked at the photographs on the desk of her recently completed cubicle at Elegance and thought, smiling, *Emily Rousseau, you are so talented!*

Emily had managed more trick photography with her—

the portrait she took the night Allison had gotten her hair cut was wonderful, radiant, happy—and a week later, at Allison's request, Emily had provided her with a selection of magnificent photographs of flowers, sunsets, moons, and the sea.

Allison finally chose six of Emily's breathtaking nature shots to have enlarged, signed by Emily, and framed for the walls of Bellemeade. No matter what else, Peter Dalton would have six lovely, peaceful photographs to look at. No matter what else . . .

Allison rested her hand on the telephone on her desk before dialing. In the past three weeks she had gotten so good—so *bold*—at using the phone. Allison had called Rob Adamson to thank him for referring Roger, and that had felt easy and comfortable; and she had laughingly told Roger, when he called long distance with ideas for the Chateau Bel Air, that she couldn't think about his hotel *yet* because of Bellemeade; and she had firmly and decisively placed rush orders—insisting on guarantees of delivery much sooner than was their *usual* policy—with Lalique and Charles Barone and McGuire and Stiffel.

Allison was becoming an expert at using the phone.

So dial, she told herself.

"Brentwood Productions," a voice answered on the third ring.

"This is Allison Fitzgerald calling for Steve Gannon."

"Just one moment please."

Steve answered promptly and with a slight tease.

"Allison? You want more money after only three weeks on the job?"

"Hello, Steve. No, I just have a silly question."

"Shoot."

"Do you know what kind of dog Peter has? What size?"

"Are you building a dog Bellemeade to match?"

"Not exactly." Just pillows, cozy places to curl up, custom-made to match the bedspread in the master bedroom, the cheery curtains in the kitchen, the expensive sofa near the marble fireplace in the living room. Frivolous, elegant, silly.

"It's a cocker spaniel. I know that because my daughter wants one."

"Thank you." Not a Doberman, Claire, Allison thought with a smile. Just a nice, lovable cocker spaniel.

"Anything else, Allison? More money?"

"No, thank you, Steve. Not yet."

Chapter Fourteen

Donald Alexander Fullerton died of leukemia on the seventh of September. Mark watched him die. Donald's death marked the end of a courageous battle; a war fought with everything medical science had to offer and the gallant spiritual weapons of a dying young man.

Donald was twenty-nine, Mark's age. Donald's wife, Mary Anne, was twenty-seven and pregnant. Mark had been on the Hematology-Oncology inpatient service at UCLA for seven days. Donald had been Mark's patient. Mark had gotten to know Donald and Mary Anne very well.

And now it was over. A life ended after twenty-nine years. *Why?*

Mark held Mary Anne Fullerton for a long time after Donald died. Then Mary Anne's family led her away, to begin the rest of her life. Mark took care of the paperwork, the red tape of death, made rounds on his other patients, signed out to the on-call team, and walked out of the hospital into the glaring autumn sun. It was late afternoon, almost evening, but the sun was still too bright, too hot, too brilliant on a day that was filled with so much sadness.

Mark walked to his apartment on Manning and quickly changed into his jogging clothes.

He had to go to the beach and run, until the physical ache matched the emotional one, until the salty tears were dry, until the powerful urge to scream with helpless rage was exhausted.

Then Mark could go to Winter.

This was the solitary voyage of medicine; impossible to articulate, unfair to share.

Since July, Mark and Winter had virtually lived together in her apartment, but he kept his apartment for necessary sleep and necessary privacy.

Necessary sleep. Mark would call Winter just before he left the hospital, after he had been up all night and it was eleven the next night and he *had* to sleep because it would start again the next day.

"I'm going to my apartment to take a long hot shower and collapse into bed," he would say.

"OK."

"I'll call you tomorrow."

"OK."

Winter never pushed or pouted or sulked. Mark could have said good night then but he didn't want to, because he had been thinking about her, missing the soft promise of her voice, feeling warm and alive as memories of her came to him.

"How was your day, Winter?" he would ask, not wanting to say good night.

And they would talk. And thirty minutes later, still at the hospital, Mark would whisper reluctantly that he should go. And Winter would say, so softly, "You could take a shower here, Mark, and collapse."

Mark didn't use his apartment for necessary sleep. He slept, always, with Winter.

Necessary privacy. The past two and a half months had been amazingly free of the kind of tragedy that had befallen Donald and Mary Anne. Until today, Mark hadn't felt the need to stay away from Winter until his emotions were spent.

And now . . . It wasn't fair to take the sadness, or his troubled silence, home to her. *Was it?*

Mark drove down Westwood Boulevard to Wilshire. He

should have turned right on Wilshire, toward the ocean. But Mark continued on Westwood and in a few blocks turned left onto Holman.

Mark let himself in the main security door but knocked when he reached Winter's third-floor apartment. He had a key, of course, but she wasn't expecting him.

"Hi. You didn't have to knock." Winter smiled and searched the troubled blue eyes.

"Come jogging with me, Winter."

"Jogging? *Moi?*"

Winter never exercised, but her body was sleek and slim and her energy seemed limitless. She bounded up stairs without breathlessness, and her gait was gazelle-graceful and buoyant. Mark imagined the muscles beneath the beautiful skin, like coiled springs of a black panther, naturally strong and fit and healthy.

"Someday, Winter . . ."

"Someday, I will fall victim to the design flaws, just like every other woman on earth."

"Design flaws?"

"Breasts that can't forever defy the laws of gravity. Cellulite — the ultimate symbol of planned obsolescence! — appearing out of nowhere. Why are you smiling?" Winter was glad the blue eyes smiled a little, but they were still *so* troubled.

"You."

"I'm not impressed that jogging changes anything, and that's based on years of observing the results on the jogging path on San Vicente. However, I *will* go jogging to be with you."

Mark sat on the bed while Winter disappeared into her closet. When she reappeared, she was wearing a clinging gold tank top and peacock-blue nylon shorts — both emblazoned UCLA — and tennis shoes.

Winter twirled a model's twirl and asked, "How do I look?"

"I see no design flaws."

"I think I'd better braid my hair." Winter stood in front of the dresser mirror, her back to Mark. As she braided her long black hair, she caught glimpses of his thoughtful expression in the mirror.

Mark looked at Winter's perfect body and let his thoughts drift to a distant time . . . Winter with strands of white in her coal-black hair; Winter with wrinkles around her eyes from years of laughter; Winter with pink-white marbled lines on her abdomen from the children she had borne; Winter with breasts that fell from life and nursing.

It was a lovely image because Mark was there, sitting on their bed, watching her braid her black and silver hair, waiting for her sparkling violet eyes to look at him again. Mark was there, in that distant scene, and it meant that *they* had survived. They were together, and their magnificent love had history and age and wonderful, comfortable wrinkles.

Mark smiled, but it was a wobbly smile. His own happy vision was clouded by the memory of Donald and Mary Anne, whose forever love was over.

"Is there a price tag on that thought?" Winter asked gently as she turned.

"No. It's not for sale. The investment is much too speculative." Mark saw a flicker of hurt in Winter's eyes and added gently, "OK, for *free,* I will tell you I was thinking how lovely you will look with cellulite."

"Good, then that settles it. I will set a leisurely pace along the sand, possibly in the water, and you can jog in circles around me, or to the horizon and back if you want." Winter took a broad-rimmed straw hat from her dresser. "Shall we go?"

She led the way to the apartment door. Winter turned to face Mark before she opened it.

"Something terribly sad happened at the hospital today, didn't it, Mark?"

"Yes."

"Will you tell me?"

Mark wrapped his arms around her, held her close, and whispered softly, "Yes, darling, I will."

Allison was on the phone when Winter appeared in Elegance just before noon on the twelfth of September. She smiled and gestured for Winter to come into her cluttered cubicle.

"You are guaranteeing delivery by November fifteenth. Will you please confirm that in writing? Yes, I'm serious. Good. Fine. Thank you."

"You're beginning to sound like an attorney," Winter observed when the conversation ended.

"I have to. Who knows if it will make any difference? The furniture and chandeliers and drapes and rugs will arrive when they arrive."

"How is Bellemeade going?"

"*I'm* on schedule. I just hope everyone else is. How are you? Shopping, I see."

"I just wanted to see what the Rodeo Collection had for its fall line of campus casuals."

"They had some things." Allison smiled at the bulging sacks with designer labels that Winter had set on top of the stacks of sample books in her office.

"Some. I'm not sure what the well-dressed special student is wearing this fall. I guess I'll find out on Monday. So, can you *do lunch* today?"

"I'd better not."

"OK. I really stopped to say that Mark and I would like to take you to dinner Friday night."

"That's not necessary, Winter!"

"We were thinking Spago Friday night, and then you and I could have dinner — Mark's on call — at the Club Saturday."

"Winter." Allison smiled. "You and my parents. They suggested dinner both nights, too, although not at the actual sites of the rehearsal dinner and wedding that aren't to be."

"I thought that was a nice touch," Winter replied. "You're the one who believes in getting back on the horse no matter how hard the fall."

"Winter, I *chose* not to marry Dan and it was the right decision. I'm not going to spend this weekend moping around, wishing I was getting married."

"That's good, but Mark and I still would like to have

dinner with you Friday."

"Why don't you and Mark have dinner with me and my parents?"

"We'd love it."

"I *am* selecting china, silver, crystal, and linens this week," Allison said after a moment.

"For what?"

"For Bellemeade. The china's easy — Minton's *Bellemeade* — but I haven't decided yet about the rest. I'm going to spend Saturday morning at Pratesi, Geary's, Neiman-Marcus. Would you like to help?"

"Sure. And shall we plan to have a memorial dinner at the Club Saturday night?"

"I'm having dinner with Emily."

Winter waited, trying to interpret Allison's hesitance. Finally, with a laugh, Winter asked, "So? May I join you?"

"Of course, Winter." Allison frowned slightly.

"But?"

"But Emily and I were planning to eat in Westwood — Alice's, The Old World, maybe the Acapulco. I'm not sure Emily has clothes that would be right for dinner at the Club. It might be awkward for her."

"Westwood's fine, jeans are fine," Winter replied swiftly, but her reassurance didn't erase the worry in Allison's eyes. "Now what?"

"Emily begins working at *Portrait* on Monday. On Tuesday, she leaves for her first assignment — in Hong Kong."

"So you and Emily were planning to see *Hong Kong,* Lawrence Carlyle's latest blockbuster."

"I'm sure Emily really doesn't care."

"No, Allison, I would like to see *Hong Kong.* I'll probably be required to see a number of the great Lawrence Carlyle's movies for my Contemporary Film seminar. It's fine, really."

"Are you sure?" Allison didn't know why Winter hated the father she had never known, but the bitterness had appeared in her friend's voice — where before there had been such pride — in the months after Jacqueline's death.

"I'm sure." Winter stood up to leave. "Jeans Saturday

night, Allison, but I plan to be *very* dazzling for dinner Friday."

After Winter left, Allison thought about her best friend. She chided herself for hesitating, even for a moment, before telling Winter her concern that Emily might feel uncomfortable about dinner at the Bel Air Hunt Club. As if Allison didn't know that Winter's reaction would be one of sympathy and compassion!

Winter didn't cut a millimeter of slack for the Elaina Kingsleys of the world, but for someone like timid Emily Rousseau — someone who might be ridiculed for how she looked — Winter was as protective as a mother bear.

Allison smiled softly as she thought about Winter.

What a friend Winter had been when Allison needed her the most . . .

Winter talked to Allison — all day, every day — as her friend lay in a coma. Allison couldn't speak to answer, but she heard Winter's words and her mind and spirit answered, fighting even harder.

Sometimes Winter scolded her, and Allison heard Winter's heart-stopping fear, "Allison Fitzgerald, don't you *dare* die! Don't you dare. I will never forgive you if you die."

And sometimes Winter whispered softly, lovingly, and Allison heard the tears, "I love you, Allison. You're my best friend, my *sister.* Don't leave me, please."

When Allison finally awakened from her coma, it was still just the beginning of the nightmare. Now Allison could *see* the fear in the eyes of her beloved parents. Sean and Patricia's eyes would fill with fresh tears as they patiently gave their precious daughter words to remember and she couldn't. At first, Allison didn't understand the game, or her parents' incredible sadness when she couldn't play. But, as she improved, Allison *knew* that she couldn't remember, and she, too, was filled with bewildered terror.

When Sean and Patricia had to leave the room because they couldn't stop their tears, it was Winter who stayed, loving and scolding.

"Allison, it's almost Christmas. Do you know the most wonderful gift you could give your parents? Your memory. Now pay attention." Winter shook a slender ivory finger at her friend, just as she had waved a tiny finger at the greedy koi years before. "Pay attention and remember these three things, OK? Candy canes . . . tinsel . . . a partridge in a pear tree."

On Christmas Eve, three days later, Allison whispered, "Winter?"

"Yes?"

"Is this right? Candy canes . . . tinsel . . . a partridge . . ."

Winter was there, helping Allison fight to awaken from the coma, then helping her fight to remember. And Winter was there, too, during the long, painful months of recovery. Winter helped Allison learn to read again, and write, and talk and walk.

"Don't walk if it hurts, Allison."

It always hurts, Winter. It always will. If I let the pain become an obstacle, I will never walk. I have to get beyond the pain.

It was then that Allison explained to Winter how champion riders urged their horses, and themselves, over walls and fences that seemed too high and too wide and too dangerous to ever clear.

"If you focus on the jump that's right in front of you, Winter, you'll never get over it. So you think about what's *beyond* the jump, on the other side, and you make *that* a place you want to be. That way, when you jump, you're flying from where you are to where you want to be."

With the words she and her riding friends used when *they* talked about it, Allison explained to Winter how champions soared over the impossibly high jumps. Allison didn't tell Winter her own private wording: *You send your dreams over the jump first, then simply follow after them.*

Allison didn't know—and never would know—why on that fateful September day when she joyfully sent her dreams ahead of her over the green and white railed fence *she* had been unable to follow.

* * *

Now Allison had unwittingly put an imposing obstacle — *Hong Kong* — in front of her dear friend. Could Winter find a way to soar over this hazardous jump? Was there a place *beyond*, a place of dreams, where Winter wanted to be? Allison didn't know, and it worried her.

"Are you sure this is OK, Winter?" Allison asked as she, Winter, and Emily approached the brightly lighted marquee of the Odeon Theater on Lindbrook Avenue in Westwood on Saturday afternoon. Allison had asked the same question the evening before, at the wonderful dinner with her parents, Winter, and Mark, and earlier today as she and Winter looked at silver, crystal, and linens in the elegant shops of Beverly Hills.

"It's *fine*," Winter murmured. She smiled bravely, first at Allison, then at Emily. But Emily looked confused. Apparently, Allison hadn't told her about Winter's connection to *Hong Kong*.

By way of explanation, Winter silently led them to one of the huge glassed-in posters that advertised *Hong Kong*. The poster was a vivid collage of scenes from the movie: the Hong Kong skyline, quaint junks in the harbor, glittering statues of jade, the famous actor and actress entwined in a passionate embrace. The names of the stars were in large teal-blue letters, but one name was even larger, because he was even bigger box office: Lawrence Carlyle.

Winter tapped her finger on the glass over his name and whispered quietly, "Daddy." After a moment, she turned to Emily and embellished unnecessarily, "We're not very close."

"We don't have to see *Hong Kong*, Winter," Emily replied swiftly. "Why don't we see what's playing at the Bruin or the National or the Westwood Village?"

"No, Emily, really. I want to see *Hong Kong*. You just need to be aware of the situation in case I do something crazy."

"Such as?" Allison asked.

"I don't know." Winter laughed uneasily. "I might hurl Milk Duds at the screen, something embarrassing like that.

Allison, don't worry! It's not as though the great Lawrence Carlyle himself is going to be in the theater."

Allison, Emily, and Winter had the Odeon Theater almost to themselves. They had chosen a matinee to be certain they could get seats, but this was Westwood on the Saturday before UCLA began its Autumn Quarter. The students had arrived and were busy patrolling the dormitories, meeting roommates, sharing the highlights of their life stories, *flirting*. Not even the best movie of 1984 could entice the undergraduates away from those provocative endeavors.

After they selected their seats, Emily disappeared without a word. When she returned, five minutes later, she was carrying three very large, very *expensive* boxes of Milk Duds.

Emily cast a questioning smile at Winter as she handed her one of the boxes.

"I just want you to know, Winter, that if you want to throw Milk Duds, I'm with you all the way."

"Me, too," Allison agreed. "Hand me my ammunition, please."

"Thank you, Emily," Winter whispered softly, quite moved by Emily's shy, thoughtful support. "Thank you."

Ten minutes into *Hong Kong*, Winter announced quietly, "It's safe to eat your Milk Duds, ladies. I'm OK."

Winter wasn't OK, not really. She clutched her unopened box of Milk Duds tightly, squishing the candy inside.

Winter had been wrong when she'd said it wasn't as if the great Lawrence Carlyle himself would be in the theater! Lawrence Carlyle *was* here, in the only way Winter had ever known him, in the way she had grown to love him, through the sensitive genius of his movies. Lawrence Carlyle, the wonderful, talented artist who painted magnificent motion pictures.

Winter *felt* the movie more than she saw it, tossed by emotions and memories, finally calming the storm with a fantasy.

Someday — a million moments from now — she would meet Lawrence Carlyle. It might be on the white-sand-dotted-with-pink-umbrellas beach at Cannes, or in the Dorothy

Chandler Pavilion on Academy Award night, or afterwards at Swifty Lazar's gala winner's party at Spago.

Mark would be there, and Allison, and even Emily. Winter smiled as she envisioned Emily's role in the fantasy. Emily would have her camera, of course, to capture Lawrence's bittersweet expression of great love for the daughter he had abandoned and deep regret for all the lost years. Emily would have her camera, but stuffed into the back pocket of her baggy jeans would be a huge box of Milk Duds just in case.

As Allison watched *Hong Kong*, she cast careful glances at Winter. Despite the brave announcement that she was fine, Allison sensed Winter's tension and saw the strain on her friend's beautiful face. Allison was just about to suggest—insist—that they leave, but when she glanced at Winter again, the tension had vanished. Winter's lips curled into a soft smile and her violet eyes gazed dreamily at a lovely distant vision.

Somehow, Allison realized with relief, Winter has found a way to get beyond this enormous hurdle.

After the movie, Allison, Winter, and Emily walked around the corner to the Acapulco Restaurant.

"Would you like margaritas?" the waitress asked.

"A Diet Pepsi for me, please," Winter said. Winter drank champagne now, a little, but only with Mark.

"That sounds good," Allison agreed. The sophisticated tests done at UCLA showed that Allison still had altered depth perception from the accident. That was why the doctors had told her it would be too dangerous for her to jump again, and that was why Allison never had anything to drink when she was driving.

"Diet Pepsi for me, too," Emily said. Emily hadn't had a drop of alcohol or any other drug since Mick had left on July Fourth; and it felt good, *better*. Mick had returned and that was good, too, because he had found someone new and didn't want Emily anymore.

When the Diet Pepsis arrived, Winter raised her glass and smiled.

"Here we are, each on the brink of our new careers, and it's exciting and scary, is it not?" Winter's violet eyes sparkled. More exciting than scary!

"Yes."

"Absolutely."

"So, we should make toasts to us and our tremendous success, shouldn't we?" Winter smiled and turned to Emily. "To Emily, and her great success with *Portrait*."

"Thank you," Emily whispered as the three glasses clinked.

"To Allison," Winter continued, "and her great success with Bellemeade."

After the glasses clinked again, Winter gave a soft smile and looked at Allison. Allison had to make the toast to her best friend, but Winter didn't need to tell her what to say. There was that *one perfect word*, the word that described what Winter's life had become since Mark and the word that was the title of the magnificent movie in which she would star.

Allison knew what to say.

"And to Winter, and her great success with *Love*."

Part Two

Chapter Fifteen

Bel Air, California
November, 1984

"Allison, this is unbelievable," Steve raved as he, Allison, and Claire walked from magnificent room to magnificent room. It was noon on the thirtieth of November. The new interior design for Bellemeade had been finished exactly on time. "Claire, you knew."

"Of course!" Claire beamed. She had steadfastly forbidden Steve see Bellemeade until everything was done. Claire knew Steve would be thrilled, and she knew, too, that the triumph was all Allison's. Claire had been there, the safety net beneath the high-wire, but Allison's pure gold instincts hadn't even wobbled. "A masterpiece."

"It really is," Steve agreed.

"I'm glad you like it, Steve," Allison murmured without much energy.

Allison was exhausted. How many visits had she made to Bellemeade, just to see if the morning sun — and afternoon and evening — caressed the pastel fabrics as she had imagined? How many times had she travelled up and down the elegant circular staircase that swept to the spectacular master suite? How many phone calls had she made, reminders, *threats?*

As Allison looked at the finished product now, her exhausted mind remembered the battles. The wallpaper in the kitchen hadn't been hung perfectly and Allison had insisted that it be done again. She had driven to the warehouse herself to help locate the mysteriously misplaced fabric for the dining room chairs. The first hand-painted trousseau trunk from France had been cracked and the replacement had arrived only yesterday.

Allison wasn't like a homeowner who had done the work herself and knew, uneasily, where the flaws were hidden. It was just the opposite: *Allison knew there were no flaws in Bellemeade.* Allison hadn't permitted flaws, even though the cost to her was high. Now her exhausted mind cried for sleep and her hip sent hot, angry, relentless messages of pain.

It was nice, at least, that Steve was pleased.

"I'm going to call Paige the second I get back to my office," Steve said.

"It does have *Architectural Digest* written all over it, doesn't it?" Claire smiled knowingly.

"I am also going to call my wife. She'll either want us to move in here after Peter leaves or—what Claire has been pushing for for years—she'll want our house completely redone. Allison, are you available?"

Allison replied silently with a smile that wavered a little because of a sharp pain in her hip.

"Allison has to turn her attention to the Chateau Bel Air," Claire told Steve. "First, however, she is taking a well-deserved week off, starting *now.*" Claire turned to Allison with a warm smile. "I'm serious, Allison. Then you will return, revitalized, to face the Chateau and the ever-expanding list of people who want you to do their homes."

"A list to which my name will be added?" Steve asked.

"Of course."

When Steve, Allison, and Claire reached the front door, about to leave, Steve said, "Shall I take the keys now?"

"I need to come back this afternoon," Allison answered. "A few finishing touches."

"What more can there be?"

Allison gave a slight shrug. She just wanted to fill the

magnificent Lalique vases with fresh roses. Perhaps the beautiful French crystal vases filled with fresh pastel roses would become the signature on every home, every hotel, every penthouse she designed; Allison was thinking about it. But, no matter what, she wanted roses in the vases at Bellemeade, so it would be lovely and bright and fragrant tomorrow when Peter arrived.

"I'm going to put roses in the vases. I'll drop the keys by your Brentwood office after I'm done, Steve. Is that all right?"

"Of course, but there's no hurry, Allison. I have an extra set I can give Peter in the morning."

"I'll drop them off today. I don't need them."

Allison picked up the gold-foil boxes of roses at the florist in Beverly Hills, met Winter at the Westholme Avenue entrance to UCLA, and together they drove to Bellemeade.

"Allison, I can't believe this is the same dark, dungeony place. It feels like a springtime meadow. So romantic."

Romantic? Allison's weary mind spun. She wanted Bellemeade to be light and lovely and peaceful and happy, but romantic? Had she overdone?

"Allison, your hip is really bothering you, isn't it?" Winter asked bluntly when she returned from her tour of the house. Allison was in the kitchen arranging the roses. Winter saw the strain in her friend's eyes and was reminded of those long months of recovery when Allison had never complained as she fought a private, silent, determined battle against her pain.

Allison looked surprised at the bluntness of Winter's question. Then she answered honestly.

"It hurts."

"Can you rest?"

"Yes. Claire has given me next week off. I'm planning to soak in hot bubble baths and sleep and read." Last week, at a bookstore in Century City, Allison had bought the recently published collection of plays by Peter Dalton. The collection included all of Peter's produced works—his one-act plays and his full-length ones: *Merry Go Round, Storm Watch, Echoes, Depth Charge, Say Good-bye,* and three others. The book did not contain his just-produced-on-Broadway *Shadows of the Mind* or the soon-to-be-produced *Love.*

Allison planned to curl up in her bed, relaxed after a hot bath and with a cup of tea, and read the gifted words of the man she had met last August . . . the man for whom she had worked so hard to make Bellemeade lovely, happy, flawless.

"Good," Winter said firmly. She tilted her head and asked, with a twinkle, "Do you think you'll feel like making Christmas cookies on the fifteenth?"

"Sure. Why?"

"I told Mark I'd bring Christmas cookies with me to Boston." *And I've never made Christmas cookies.* No one had taken the time to show painfully shy Winter Carlyle how to make Christmas cookies. No one had cared if Winter had that childhood joy. In fact, the cook at the mansion had never wanted to muss her kitchen for the quiet, gawky child. There were always Christmas cookies at the mansion, of course, exquisite delicacies that arrived in ornate boxes and hand-painted tins from the best bakeries around the world. "Do you realize that Mark has only been gone for six hours and I'm already counting the minutes until the sixteenth?"

"I realize that."

Winter walked across the plush teal-blue living room carpet to the framed photograph of a new moon signed E. Rousseau. She gazed admiringly at the photograph for a moment, then asked, "Do you think Emily would like to help make Christmas cookies, assuming she's not in Hong Kong or wherever?"

"I . . . we should ask her."

"I'll give her a call," Winter said. "She is really talented, isn't she?"

Emily gathered the just-developed portraits from the dark-room in her Santa Monica apartment and carefully put them

212

in folders. In a few moments, she would leave to catch the bus to Beverly Hills for her four o'clock meeting with Rob.

As she put the photographs in a manila folder, Emily's gaze fell on her fingernails. They were long now, and gently tapered. For Emily, to have fingernails that were long and tapered, instead of bitten-short, was such an incredible accomplishment! Her fingernails looked presentable now and she didn't wear jeans anymore. Emily wore *outfits,* identical to the stylish ones displayed on the mannequins at Bullock's-Westwood. Emily bought her new outfits — slacks, blouses, sweaters, and sweater vests — in subdued colors, and in sizes that were loose and unrevealing. But still she was more stylish, wasn't she?

Emily wondered if Rob noticed.

Of course not!

Rob Adamson *expected* women to have long, tapered fingernails, stylish, elegant clothes, and dazzling jewels. Rob expected women to be beautiful and confident. Rob would never notice *her;* but he liked her photographs and that meant so much to Emily.

As Emily stepped out of her night-dark apartment into the bright November sun, she thought about the women Rob did notice . . . beautiful, dazzling, confident women like Elaina Kingsley. . . .

Emily had done a portrait of Elaina in early November — a "surprise" birthday present from Elaina to Rob. She had taken the photographs in Elaina's luxury condominium on Roxbury in Beverly Hills — Elaina's condominium, or Rob and Elaina's?

Elaina had positioned herself on the couch in the elegantly decorated peach and cream living room, staring critically at Emily as she tested lenses and filters. Elaina's critical gaze was unconcealed, as if Emily's eyes became unseeing and her heart could feel no pain when she viewed the world through the lens of her camera. Maybe Elaina didn't care if her critical stare caused Emily pain. Why *should* she care?

At first, Elaina had been impatient, restless, irritable with Emily's slowness. Elaina's phone rang incessantly, but the calls were answered by her machine. Emily and Elaina heard each message as it was recorded; high-powered messages from high-powered people for high-powered Elaina, the all-important, ever-shrewd negotiator. In the midst of the high-powered messages came a warm one, in a voice familiar to both women, Rob's voice. "Hi, kiddo. I've made dinner reservations for eight o'clock at the Bordeaux Room. I'll be by to get you at seven-thirty."

Eventually, Elaina's nervousness about the camera, along with her impatience with Emily's slowness, dissipated. Elaina relaxed, and like most people Emily had photographed, she began to talk—openly, honestly, without inhibition—to the camera . . . as if Emily wasn't even there. It was then, in those unposed, unguarded moments, that Emily took the magnificent, natural, revealing portraits.

Most people eventually relaxed and chattered to the camera, enjoying the release of nervous energy, unconcerned that Emily was a silent witness. But there were exceptions. Allison had talked to Emily, not to the camera. Allison had smiled warmly and asked Emily questions about *herself*. When Emily hadn't been forthcoming with answers, Allison had shifted cheerfully to a discussion of Emily's talent, and how much she would like to put her photographs in the beautiful homes she designed. Allison hadn't chattered about herself, and neither had Winter. Winter had sat patiently, without a trace of irritation or restlessness. Finally, when Emily asked if Winter knew what she wanted her portfolio portraits to look like, Winter had simply posed, quietly, perfectly.

Elaina chattered, a breathless outpouring on a number of subjects, including her relationship with Rob and how much they loved each other. "I hope you'll photograph our wedding, Emily. I know Rob would want you to." Elaina had frowned briefly, then admitted to the camera, "Of course, Rob hasn't proposed yet—not officially—but he will. We'll probably be married in June, at the Club."

Rob expected women to be beautiful, confident, dazzling, like Elaina, Emily reminded herself as the bus travelled along Wilshire from Santa Monica to Beverly Hills. Rob wouldn't even notice Emily's tapered fingernails or her sort-of-stylish clothes. The nails and clothes were Emily's own private badges of courage, small, brave signs that her life was better.

Better. So much better. Mick was with someone else and Emily spent her life taking beautiful pictures. And once a week, if she was lucky, she met with Rob. Emily felt better, happy, at peace. She didn't even think about moving to Paris anymore! It was too important to be here, taking beautiful pictures and meeting with Rob, seeing his smiling blue eyes, hearing his gentle voice tell her how much he liked her photographs.

A very nice way to end the afternoon, Rob thought with a smile as he waited for Emily to arrive for their four o'clock meeting. Meeting with Emily was completely unnecessary, but Rob enjoyed seeing her, looked forward to their meetings, regretted the weeks when his travel schedule or hers prevented them.

Rob didn't need to meet with Emily at all. She could— *did*—get all her assignments through Fran. And Rob certainly didn't need to tell Emily the kind of portrait he wanted her to take. He didn't even know what he wanted until he saw it—Emily's latest remarkable portrait.

Remarkable. . . Emily took photographs of the world's most glamorous women without make-up, and they looked more alluring, more beautiful than ever. She captured a sparkle of laughter in the eyes of men who never smiled and thoughtful reflection on the faces of men who always laughed. Her magnificent portraits were glimpses—careful, gentle, loving glimpses—into the spirit and the soul.

Rob didn't need to meet with Emily before her assignments to tell her what kind of picture to take, nor after to select together which photograph should appear in the magazine. *That* was Rob's decision, but he always asked Emily and she always pointed to the one he had already selected.

There was no need for Rob to meet with Emily — ever — except that he wanted to.

So Rob and Emily would meet each week, if it could be arranged. They would talk about *Portrait* and her photographs. Quiet, serious, business conversations. Sometimes, Emily Rousseau would smile. Emily's soft, lovely smiles were rare, but her pale gray eyes were always clear. Rob wondered about drugs and about the man on the bluffs at Santa Monica. Rob hadn't seen Emily and her lover again, but he hadn't even wanted to run the risk. The day Emily had agreed to work for *Portrait* Rob had changed his jogging route entirely, following the well-worn grassy path along San Vicente Boulevard, avoiding the Santa Monica Palisades altogether.

Rob glanced at his watch. Emily would be here in five minutes, exactly on time as always, for their unnecessary — but for him somehow so necessary — meeting.

"Rob?" Emily appeared in his open doorway, a little flushed, a little late. "I'm sorry. There was a traffic accident."

"It's fine. Hi. Come in."

"I brought the photographs of the Prince."

"Oh, good." Rob had been tempted to tell Emily to come empty-handed. They could just talk, couldn't they? Rob wasn't sure. They used Emily's photographs as a focus — a crutch! — but the conversation never strayed far. Maybe, without the photographs, there would be nothing to say.

Nothing to say, but so many questions to ask.

Who are you, Emily Rousseau? May I do a portrait of you? May I try to discover who you are and why you are the way you are?

Rob admired the photographs Emily had taken of the Prince, told her which one he liked the best, and when that business was done, he said, "I promised you a trip to Paris."

"It's not . . . it doesn't matter."

"I've decided to profile four top fashion designers in Paris — LaCroix, Chanel, St. Laurent, Dior. How good is your French?"

"It's good."

"So, you can be my interpreter."

"You're going?"

"*We're* going. I'd like to do the interviews myself, with you as interpreter if necessary. And, of course, you have to take the photographs."

"When?"

"The third week in January, if it can be arranged. I have commitments the weeks before and after, but at this point that week is entirely clear. I thought you might like to stay in France for a while, maybe take a vacation? I need you back by mid-February, of course, by the time the Academy Award nominations are announced."

Now that *Portrait's* home was Los Angeles, Rob had decided to establish an Academy Awards issue. This would be its inaugural year. Rob planned to profile fifteen people — the five nominees in the categories of Best Actress, Best Actor, and Best Director. The issue had to be on the stands before the Academy Award ceremony, which meant five frantic weeks from announcement of nominees to publication.

"Emily? Is there a problem about going to Paris?" Rob had thought Emily would be pleased. He had even hoped for a rare, beautiful smile. But her pale gray eyes were uncertain.

"No, Rob. It's fine."

Two weeks later, just before four o'clock on the fourteenth of December, Rob looked at Emily's name on his appointment calendar and frowned slightly. He and Emily *had* been scheduled to meet today at four, but Emily had been delayed in San Francisco.

"She's on your calendar for next Friday," Fran replied when Rob asked if they had set a new time when Emily had called to cancel. "It would be very tough to get her in before then."

"Oh. All right."

At four-thirty, Fran appeared at Rob's door, smiling coyly. "Yes?" Rob asked, returning her smile, curious.

"Peter Dalton is on the line." Fran's smile flattened as she watched Rob's reaction . . . Rob's lack of reaction. Rob looked completely blank, almost stunned. "Rob, Peter Dalton. You know, the Broadway sensation who is here doing *Love,* the movie of the century. Rob? I put him on hold because I thought you would want to take the call. I mean, I assume he'll be in the Academy Award issue in '86, but that's over a year away, so . . . Rob?"

Fran screened all calls very politely, but she was a brick wall. She rarely even put an unsolicited caller on hold, usually just taking a message no matter what Rob was doing.

But *Peter Dalton?* Fran assumed Peter Dalton would be the exception to the rule, someone Rob would be happy to talk to, undeniably the type of talent he loved to feature in *Portrait.*

"I'll just take a message," Fran murmured finally.

"No. Put him through."

Rob closed his office door while Fran returned to her desk to transfer Peter's call. Then Rob waited, fists clenched, unable to stop the ancient emotions that swept through him.

"What do you want?"

"Hello, Rob."

Silence.

"I will be in Los Angeles for the next four months," Peter continued finally. "I thought—hoped—that sometime we might talk."

"About what?"

"About Sara. I promised her . . ."

"You promised *me* that you would take care of Sara, that you would protect her and love her." Rob paused. When he spoke again, his voice was ice, "I will make you a promise, Peter, and I will keep it if I can. I don't know if it's possible for you to love—to ever care about anyone but yourself—but if you do and I learn of it, I promise you I will do everything I can to take that love away from you."

"Rob . . ."

"If I can hurt you, Peter, if I can make you ache until you want to die because the loss is so great, I will do it. That is my promise to you."

Rob hung up then, quietly, gently, his rage more frightening in its control than if it had been violent. Rob's fury was ice-cold, strong, powerful. His hatred toward Peter hadn't lessened with the passage of time or distance or the golden warmth of the California sun. The hatred was evergreen, its roots strong and healthy, burrowing ever deeper into his heart.

Rob made the threat and meant it, but he knew its emptiness. If Peter ever found someone to love, Rob wouldn't even know it. Rob's rage had not become an obsession. He wouldn't allow it to be. He wasn't going to spend his life tracking Peter Dalton, hoping for a chance at revenge, because revenge — Peter Dalton's pain at the loss of a great love, even Peter Dalton's death — would be so empty, so joyless, so trivial compared to the irreplaceable life of beloved Sara.

Rob's eyes fell on his open appointment calendar. How he wished this hour had been spent with the lovely gray eyes and soft voice! Rob's thought continued. It was a surprising thought, but it brought such peace. . . .

How Rob wished Emily would walk into his office, even now. Perhaps Rob would tell her why his face was ashen, his body trembling, his eyes dark and stormy. Or perhaps he wouldn't tell her, but, still, just having Emily here, with him . . .

"Thanks for the ride." Winter grasped the passenger door handle and started to lift it as they neared the United terminal at Los Angeles International Airport.

"Winter! Sit and stay!" Allison commanded with a laugh. She had last tried that command on a recalcitrant Labrador retriever when she was nine and the puppy was a puppy. Winter looked at her friend with startled eyes that reminded Allison of the surprised-but-trying-hard-to-understand puppy. "I haven't stopped the car."

"Then stop it!" Winter laughed.

The laughter—the giggles—had begun last night, while Allison, Emily, and Winter made Christmas cookies. Allison's and Emily's were true masterpieces—*designer cookies,* Winter announced happily—and Winter's were simply culinary reflections of her restless euphoria about seeing Mark.

"We are two hours early for your flight. Of course, it may take that much time to find a place in the baggage compartment for your bulging suitcase," Allison teased. She knew what was in Winter's suitcase. Winter had popped in and out of Elegance almost daily for the past week to show Allison her purchases. Winter called the new wardrobe of luxurious cashmere sweaters and stylish wool skirts and slacks and a camel's hair coat her foul weather gear for snowy Boston.

"Do you think Mark will remember me?"

"After sixteen days?"

"Seventeen. Seventeen desolate days and nights."

"Daily and nightly phone calls notwithstanding, I think Mark *will* remember you." Allison gave her friend a brief hug before Winter opened the car door and hailed a porter. "Have a wonderful time. Merry Christmas. Happy Birthday. Give Mark my love."

"You, too. Thank you."

Allison carefully negotiated the traffic, impressive for seven-thirty Sunday morning nine days before Christmas. The sky awakened as she drove north on the San Diego Freeway and made plans for the day that lay ahead. The sky was becoming robin's egg blue, promising sun and an invigorating crispness.

A beautiful day for a trail ride, Allison thought. She hadn't ridden in months, not since before the Olympics, before Bellemeade. Allison's hip was better after the week of rest and so was she, eager again and energetic. The Chateau Bel Air was so well in hand that Allison was even working on additional projects.

You can relax, Allison told herself. Everything is under control. You can take a nice, long, peaceful trail ride.

* * *

The woods are lovely, dark, and deep. The words floated in Peter's mind as he rode along the Windsor Trail. From the stable compound, the trail wound through a dense, lush forest. After a mile, as the trail steepened, pale blue sky replaced the evergreen ceiling. At its crest, the trail opened to a panoramic view of the ocean.

Peter dismounted, tethered his horse to a nearby branch, and walked to the cliff edge.

So peaceful, except Peter's mood didn't match the tranquility of the setting.

I am trying to keep my promises to you, darling Sara.

Peter gazed at the ocean and the sheer cliff below — one step into eternity — and his dark eyes hardened angrily as he remembered Friday afternoon's conversation with Rob.

It hadn't been a conversation. Rob wouldn't give him a chance! Perhaps Peter didn't *deserve* a chance to explain. Peter blamed himself for Sara's death; he had loved her too much, allowed her to be free . . . too free? Peter blamed himself and always would. Rob obviously blamed him, too. Fine. Peter was willing to accept the blame. But couldn't he and Rob even *try* to get beyond the blame . . . for Sara's sake, for her memory, for the promises?

Apparently not, and Rob's unwillingness to try filled Peter with anger, frustration . . . and hatred.

Ginger whinnied at the sight of Peter's horse — a stablemate — and Allison started to smile as she recognized Peter. But her smile faded when she saw Peter's eyes — dark, turbulent — glaring at her without recognition and with a clear message that she had intruded.

"I'm sorry."

"Don't be. I was just about to leave."

"I can just ride on."

"It's not necessary." Peter unwrapped the reins of his horse and, without mounting, disappeared into the green maze of palmettos and ferns.

Allison watched in stunned, disappointed, *angry* silence. After Peter vanished into the lush forest, she dismounted and walked to the edge of the cliff.

You have no right to be angry! Allison reminded herself as the surprising and so unfamiliar emotion swept through her. *Peter Dalton didn't ask you to make a lovely, happy place for him to live. He never even pretended to care.*

Had Allison really expected to hear from Peter? After all, Steve was her client, not Peter. And Steve had been effusive in his praise of Bellemeade; but it would have been nice to hear from Peter, too . . . if he even liked his new home, if he even *noticed*.

Claire's instincts about Peter—aloof, arrogant, impossible to please—were obviously entirely accurate. And Allison's kinder instincts—sad, lonely, nice Peter—were obviously entirely wrong.

But, until this moment, Allison had been unwilling to revise her initial impressions. She had read Peter's plays, read them and cried, and had spent long, quiet hours thinking about the unhappy man who had written the beautiful, unhappy words. And now . . .

"Allison?"

The storm had vanished from his eyes, leaving just dark uncertainty.

"Hi, Peter."

"I didn't recognize you. I'm sorry."

"My hair." Allison ran a hand through her soft curls. *My hair and whatever it was you were thinking about when I arrived.*

"Yes." Peter smiled. "I feel like I'm living in a French Impressionist painting."

"I guess I overdid."

"No, not at all. Bellemeade is lovely . . . magnificent." Peter added quietly, "I should have let you know before this."

"It doesn't matter."

"Well, it does." Peter had been overwhelmed by Bellemeade, but his thoughts had been, *I don't need to live in this lovely place!* And now, as Peter looked at the thoughtful jade-green eyes and pink-flushed cheeks, he realized he should have told her how wonderful it was. Perhaps he didn't deserve to live there, but Allison Fitzgerald deserved to know. "It *does* matter and I apologize. So, belated thank you."

"You're welcome."

"Muffin loves her pillows. She's not used to such elegance."

Muffin? Peter Dalton, writer of such dark, tormented dramas as *Say Good-bye,* has a cocker spaniel named Muffin? *How nice.*

"Oh, well." Allison blushed. "I'm glad Muffin likes them."

The silence was filled by soft whinnies and uncertain smiles.

"I really do have to go," Peter said finally. "Steve and I have a few more locations to chose."

"It was nice seeing you again, Peter."

"It was nice seeing you, too, Allison."

"It must not have made the connection at O'Hare," the man at the lost baggage counter at Logan Airport told Winter and Mark. He had already told fifty other passengers the same thing, only two hours into his shift. "If you can fill this out, we'll have the bag delivered to your address in Boston as soon as it arrives."

"When will that be?"

"Probably first thing tomorrow morning."

Winter shrugged amiably, took the form, and moved to a counter to fill in the information. It didn't matter. Nothing mattered. She was with Mark and the desire in his blue eyes told her how much he had missed her.

"Could I borrow a shirt or something? My new silk negligees—wait until you see them!—are in Chicago."

"I like the idea of you without clothes," Mark whispered as he pulled her close and kissed her.

"I like that idea, too . . . soon."

Winter didn't need anything, just Mark, *except* . . .

Winter and Mark had agreed to *no Christmas presents.* Winter knew Mark would be too busy to shop in Boston and she didn't want him to spend precious time before he left—time *they* could be together—looking for gifts for her! No presents, they agreed, just each other.

So it wasn't a present, just a surprise, something to erase the worry she sometimes saw even though he hadn't mentioned it since that sunny morning in the San Joaquin Valley. *I had the IUD removed, Mark. Now I—we—have a diaphragm.*

But the diaphragm was in the suitcase in Chicago. Winter had simply, happily, unthinkingly tossed it in amidst the romantic silk negligees.

Winter thought now, as she curled up in Mark's arms as the taxi neared his apartment, *This is Mark. I need him. It will only be for one night of love, a night I wouldn't miss, not for anything in the world.*

4 BESTSELLING HISTORICAL ROMANCES BY YOUR FAVORITE AUTHORS CAN BE YOURS, FREE!

Kensington Choice brings you historical romances by your favorite bestselling authors including Janelle Taylor, Shannon Drake, Rosanne Bittner, Jo Beverley, and Georgina Gentry, just to name a few! Each book is filled with passion, adventure and the excitement of bygone times!

To introduce you to this great club which is part of Zebra Home Subscription Service, we'd like to send you your first 4 bestselling historical romances, absolutely free! And once you get these 4 free books to savor at home, we'll rush you the next 4 brand-new books at the lowest prices available, as soon as they are published.

The way the club works is that after your initial FREE shipment, you will get our 4 newest bestselling historical romances delivered to your

doorstep each month at the preferred subscriber's rate of only $4.20 per book, a savings of up to $8.16 per month (since these titles sell in bookstores for $4.99-$6.99)! All books are sent on a 10-day free examination basis and there is no minimum number of books to buy. (A postage and handling charge of $1.50 is added to each

shipment.) Plus as a regular subscriber, you'll receive our FREE monthly newsletter, *Zebra/Pinnacle Romance News*, which features author profiles, subscriber benefits, book previews and more!

So start today by returning the FREE BOOK CERTIFICATE provided. We'll send you 4 FREE BOOKS with no further obligation: A FREE gift offering you hours of reading pleasure with no obligation...how can you lose?

Chapter Sixteen

Mark's on-call schedule in the Intensive Care Unit at Massachusetts General Hospital was every other night. The first two weeks of December had been "quiet," the ICU beds virtually empty, as if a divine wand had waved, banishing sickness for the holidays.

The day after Winter arrived the pace at the hospital became frantic. The ICU beds swiftly filled with desperately ill patients. On the alternate nights when he *could* leave the hospital, Mark didn't return to the studio apartment until after midnight, exhausted, apologetic.

"Isn't it better to be busy?" Winter asked. "This way they really get to see how terrific you are."

"Yes, but what about you?"

"I'm fine. Boston is a charming, wonderfully historic city. I love the snow and I'm perfectly happy wandering around, rehearsing my lines, gazing at the MGH from across the Charles River and thinking of you inside saving lives."

Winter tried to reassure him. *Mark, I have been on my own all my life! Until now.*

Being this close to Mark, touching him for six hours out of forty-eight, seeing his sensuous blue eyes, was so much better than being a continent apart.

It was better for Mark, too . . . better and worse. Better, *wonderful* to know that he would hold her soon. And worse, because he felt guilty that he had so few hours to share with her.

I'm sorry were the two words Winter heard the most. Mark greeted her with "I'm sorry" when he called to say it would still be an hour or two; and when he arrived home four hours later, or five; and as he drifted off to necessary sleep before they made love because he was exhausted and in six hours it would begin again.

I'm sorry. The words echoed in Winter's mind as she roamed the romantic city of Jennifer and Oliver. Winter wanted to remind Mark gently, lovingly, "Love means never having to say . . ."

But Mark had never said "I love you," and Winter had never told him, either; and Jennifer and Oliver's was a different love story, one with a sadder ending than theirs would ever have. Besides, those were someone else's words of love. Winter had to find her own way of letting Mark know that she was happy—so happy—just to be near him.

"I'll be able to leave the hospital at noon on Christmas Eve—if I don't get any admissions that morning. We could plan on dinner somewhere that evening."

"A candlelight dinner right here would be nice." Winter smiled coyly.

"Smoked oysters?"

"Even better. You'll see." Winter had already been to the best restaurants in Boston, examined their menus for Christmas Eve dinner, and made arrangements with the chef at the Colonial Inn to prepare a feast *to go,* something she could reheat in the small oven in the apartment whenever Mark was free.

By ten-thirty Christmas Eve morning, Winter had gotten the food, set a festive holiday table, and heard from Mark that *so far* it looked like he would be able to leave at noon. On impulse, she decided to walk to the hospital to meet him as he left.

Mark had promised Winter a tour of "The General," but it hadn't happened yet. One day she had stood in the circular drive in front of the immense red brick building topped like a

Christmas tree with the red neon letters MGH—Massachusetts General Hospital—but she hadn't ventured inside. It seemed too imposing.

But today, on Christmas Eve, as the light snow softened the morning chill and as she thought about the man she loved so much who was inside, "The General" seemed more like a home than a hospital.

A gigantic home with slick linoleum floors and pale yellow walls and fluorescent lights and colorful signs that attempted to decipher the intricate maze of corridors. Winter studied the signs for familiar words. She would avoid the Intensive Care Unit. Winter didn't want to disturb Mark. She would be waiting for him, at the Main Entrance, at noon.

Winter wandered to the Phillips House, the private hospital within the hospital. As she entered the Phillips House, the slick linoleum changed to plush carpeting and pale yellow plaster was covered by Laura Ashley wallpaper. It looked like something Allison might have decorated! Next, Winter went to the Bullfinch, the historic open ward with the lovely name. Winter expected cheeriness, the echoes of chirping birds, but the ward was desolate and disturbing, filled with men and women with vacant eyes and sallow skin.

At eleven forty-five, Winter followed signs—thinking, with a smile, that she should have left a trail of bread crumbs—back toward the Main Entrance and the Emergency Ward. Emergency *Ward* not Emergency *Room*, as it was called on the West Coast. As Winter walked along the corridor past the "E.W." and toward the Main Entrance, she saw Mark.

Mark was in the Emergency Ward with a patient, an admission that meant it would be hours before he could leave the hospital. Winter's immediate reaction was disappointment mixed with anger, frustration, and a strong feeling that it wasn't *fair;* but, as she watched, unnoticed by Mark who was wholly involved with his new patient, the ice in her emotions melted into love and pride.

The patient was an elderly woman with frightened eyes and gasping breath. *Someone's grandmother,* Winter thought as she remembered what Mark had told her the afternoon

227

Donald Fullerton had died. Mark hadn't jogged at all that autumn day. Instead, he and Winter had walked along the white sand beach for hours, talking, touching. *If you treat every patient the way you would want someone to treat your mother or father or children or sisters or brothers or best friend — someone you love — then you'll always do your best. You can't give more than that, Winter, but you have to give that much, always.*

Mark's new patient was someone's grandmother, afraid, perhaps in pain, perhaps dying. Mark smiled at the woman with gentle, reassuring eyes, wrapped his strong fingers around her frail wrist, and appeared so calm as he studied the cardiac monitor that beeped irregularly over the stretcher and quietly gave medication orders to the E.W. nurse.

As Winter watched, a miracle happened. The woman's terror subsided and her breathing slowed. The intravenous medications were working their magic and Mark was working his. Mark's attention was entirely focused on his patient. There was no restlessness, nothing that told the woman if she had only chosen to come thirty minutes later, he would be on his way home. Mark's eyes and smile and calm voice sent only one message: He was here to help her.

If Mark's patient had only chosen to come to the hospital thirty minutes later, Winter thought, then analyzed her own thought. The woman hadn't *chosen* to be sick! On this day of all days, the woman would choose to be home, baking cookies, wrapping presents, surrounded by the love and laughter of lively grandchildren. The woman didn't choose to be sick or be here, not today, not ever.

But she was here, and she was so lucky that the sapphire-blue eyes and gentle smile and strong hands and brilliant mind of Mark Stephens were caring for her. *Caring*, Winter mused. It was the right word. Mark cared. It was so obvious.

This — the chaos of the Emergency Ward, the drama of the hospital, the battle waged between doctors and disease — was Mark's natural habitat. Mark belonged here, was happy here, thrived, contributed.

Winter started to withdraw, afraid that Mark might sense her loving stare, but she stopped as she saw a young nurse move close to Mark—closer than was necessary!—and speak softly to him swaying slightly toward him, her admiring eyes searching his handsome, serious face. Mark answered the question, but his eyes kept their calm vigil of his patient, the cardiac monitor, and the carefully calibrated drops of lifesaving medication that dripped slowly into her veins.

Oh, Mark, Winter thought. This is where you belong, even though it takes you away from me for so many more hours than we can share and even though there are hazards—young, beautiful hazards—here, too.

Winter withdrew quickly. Outside the snow was falling heavily, a quiet, fleecy, enveloping fog. Winter didn't walk back to the small apartment. Instead, she walked toward Beacon Hill and its elegant, brightly lighted old houses. As she walked, her thoughts swirled like the snow.

She had actually begun to *resent* the unknown patients that kept Mark away from her! As if they were conspiring against her and her love. How selfish, how foolish. How natural, Mark would say quietly if she told him.

She had actually begun to resent the nameless, faceless patients. What was next? Resenting Mark? Believing that he stayed away later and longer than was really necessary? That was why doctors' marriages failed, wasn't it? That was why Mark's parents' marriage had failed.

But now she understood! As Winter trudged through the soft snow, she vowed that Mark's patients would never again be anonymous. They would be, as Mark had told her they had to be, someone's mother, someone's grandmother, someone's *love*.

Mark finally left the hospital at five o'clock that evening and arrived at the apartment six minutes later.

"Hi. Merry Christmas Eve," Winter said.

"Hi. I'm—"

Winter stopped the "sorry" with a long, hungry kiss. *Love means* . . .

"Don't be," she breathed finally.

"OK," Mark whispered as he pulled her back to him for more.

Mark showered and changed into jeans. Winter wore a provocative wine-red satin negligee that looked like an evening gown. Mark and Winter ate the gourmet Christmas Eve dinner by candlelight.

"What do you think, Mark? Is Mass General the best?" Winter asked when they finally finished the elegant meal. They had eaten very slowly, far more interested in loving gazes and long, deep champagne-flavored kisses than in gourmet food.

Mark considered Winter's question for a moment. Is MGH the best? Yes. Is it the best for me? Yes. Is it the best for us? *No.*

"I think you should do your residency here," Winter continued before Mark answered.

"You do? Why?"

"Because it's your dream."

So are you, darling Winter.

"Well. We'll see, Winter. Maybe they won't want me."

"They will," she whispered softly to the eyes that hadn't slept all last night and were so exhausted, but trying so hard to fight fatigue to be with her. So hard, too hard.

Winter fell silent, lost in thoughts that had been tormenting her since the scene in the Emergency Ward. It wasn't fair to Mark that she was here. It wasn't like Los Angeles, where the apartment was hers and Mark didn't feel responsible for her when he was away. Here, in Boston, Winter was a visitor, a *guest*, Mark's guest—at least in his gentle, tired mind. It wasn't fair to him. This all-important month in the ICU was Mark's audition for his dream, *his* casting call! And as much as Winter reassured him that she was quite happy wandering around Boston by herself, Mark still felt torn, compelled to be awake with her, even if it meant sacrificing necessary sleep.

Mark saw the worry in Winter's lovely eyes, as well as the sadness, and he wondered if this were the beginning of the end. Was she going to tell him she couldn't stand having so little of his life?

Winter's frown fell on their plates. Mechanically, she began clearing the table, still lost in thought.

"Winter?"

"I want to get the rest of the turkey in the refrigerator so we don't get salmonella," she answered distantly.

Mark smiled and moved behind her as she wrapped the leftover turkey in tinfoil. He wove his fingers through her long black hair and gave a soft tug. "Hey, Winter Elizabeth Carlyle, talk to me."

Winter turned and gazed into his eyes.

"I think I should go back to LA, Mark."

"OK." Mark couldn't object. He couldn't promise that tomorrow would be better.

"You think I'm leaving because I'm upset that I see so little of you, don't you?"

"That would make sense," Mark answered gently. *I don't blame you, Winter!*

"But that's not why!"

"No?"

"No. I was there today. I saw you in the E.W. and—"

"And?"

"—and this is so important for you, this month, and I think it's hard for you to have me here to worry about, even though you don't have to worry about me, but I know you do." Winter stopped, breathless, wishing she had rehearsed this, desperately wanting Mark to understand that it wasn't because she didn't care about him; it was the *opposite*.

Mark pulled her close until their lips almost touched, smiled into her glistening violet eyes, and asked quietly, "Did I ever tell you how much I love you?"

"No," Winter breathed.

"Well, I do. Very, very much."

"I love you, Mark."

"I have something for you."

Winter couldn't believe Mark left her then, but it was only for a moment, and he returned with a gold box tied with a violet velvet ribbon.

"No Christmas presents," she whispered, remembering her own Christmas surprise. Winter had told Mark about the diaphragm *after* they had made love her fourth night in Boston. He hadn't noticed—the doctors had promised her he wouldn't—and it hadn't occurred to him that it had been in her lost luggage, not her purse; and he had been so pleased that she'd given up the IUD.

"It isn't a Christmas present." Mark smiled. "It's for your birthday."

Winter's birthday present from Mark was a music box, a delicately carved quaint English cottage in a bright, lovely garden of roses. When Winter gently lifted the carved thatched roof, her wonderful music box played "Here, There and Everywhere."

"Mark."

"So?"

"So?"

"May I have this dance?"

Mark and Winter swayed gently to the music that recalled a rose-fragrant terrace and a June wedding and the enchanted beginning of their magical love. They kissed as they danced, kissed and whispered.

"How is the woman you admitted?" Winter's lips touched Mark's as she spoke.

"Better. I think she'll be fine."

"And the nurse?"

"The nurse?"

"The one with the fawn-eyes and too-small dress who kept brushing against you."

"I didn't even notice."

"Good. That's nice."

"This is nice."

"I still should leave, shouldn't I?"

Mark's blue eyes answered lovingly, *Yes, I guess, but I will miss you.*

"I'm leaving on one condition."

I don't want you to leave at all, Winter. Don't give me conditions!

"Yes?"

"When you call and wake me up in the middle of the night because you finally have a chance to call—and I want you to!—or when you haven't been able to call for two days, please don't begin with 'I'm sorry.' "

"OK."

"Please begin with 'I love you.' "

"That's very easy. I love you, Winter."

"I love you, Mark. I wonder if we could tell each other that when we make love."

"For me, it would just be a matter of whispering what I'm already thinking."

"For me, too."

"Shall we try? Right now?"

"Yes. Right now."

Allison loved the Club at Christmas! The twinkling lights and flickering candles and wreaths of holly and scents of pine and bayberry and nutmeg . . .

And the tree. As a little girl Allison had sat where she now stood, in front of the glittering tree, mesmerized by the lights and colors and exquisite enchanted ornaments from around the world. Allison wondered if her remarkable eye for color and design had always been there, simply jarred back to life by her fall, because the memories of the Christmas tree and the prisms of light were so vivid; sparkling memories of red and green and blue and gold; memories of color, of emotion, of little-girl wonder.

Allison gently spun a gold ball. As it twirled, it sent bursts of color, a tiny private display of fireworks. Allison was so glad she had stopped here on her way to Christmas Eve dinner with her parents and Vanessa. The red-orange fire crackled, soft carols filled the air, and in the distance, like delicate wind chimes, sterling silver gently touched fine bone china. How peaceful it was, how beautiful, and what a luxury to be alone in this lovely place. . . .

"Good evening."

Whoever he was, whoever owned the soft, low voice, he

shared the same impulse to be in this enchanted place.

"Peter. Hello." Allison felt warmth in her cheeks as she turned and met his dark eyes.

"Hello, Allison. It's very beautiful, isn't it?"

"Yes. Very." Allison searched for more words to describe the lovely room, but for her it was a room of feelings, not words, a place of private memories, a page from her girlhood diary. Allison couldn't find words for those private feelings, but she found other words, happy words, to speak to Peter. "How's Muffin?"

"Muffin is terribly spoiled lounging around on her designer pillows."

"Good."

"And I'm terribly spoiled lounging around in my designer house." Peter smiled.

Good. Allison smiled, too.

"Have you selected all the location sites for *Love?*" she asked. "Winter says you start rehearsing right after the New Year."

"We have them pretty well lined up. You know Winter?"

"She's my best friend. She's very excited about the movie." Allison added softly, "Winter says the script is wonderful."

"Oh, well . . ."

The compliments had been exchanged—Bellemeade, Allison's triumph, and *Love,* Peter's triumph-to-be—and neither searched for more words. They smiled soft smiles and gazed at the twinkling lights of the magnificent tree and listened to the distant sounds of carollers and silver and china. Neither Allison nor Peter searched for more words, because neither was restless with silence in this beautiful, peaceful place.

Finally, because she was already late for dinner, Allison said quietly, "I have to go. Merry Christmas, Peter."

"Merry Christmas, Allison."

Chapter Seventeen

Beverly Hills, California
January, 1985

Rob probably won't be in, Emily told herself. He'll be at lunch, but . . .

If he was here and not busy, she could show him the photographs she had just developed of Cecelia Fontaine. In the four months Emily had worked at *Portrait,* she had never "dropped in" on Rob. In fact, *she* never even made an appointment to see *him.*

Rob and Emily were leaving for Paris in the morning. If Rob wasn't in, she would just leave the photographs on his desk with a note, *I thought you might want to see the pictures of C. F. before Paris. Emily.* She might even add something bold like, *I'm looking forward to the trip.*

Rob's office door was open, and Emily heard a familiar, soft Southern drawl . . . Elaina.

"You'll be at the Ritz?"

"Yes, at the Ritz," Rob answered. There were more words, more deep tones, but they became indistinct, as if Rob had walked across the huge office, farther away from the door. Or maybe his words became muffled because his lips had found Elaina's. Emily put the envelope of photographs on Fran's desk and wrote a brief explanatory note: *Fran, Photos of Cecelia Fontaine, Emily.* She was turning to leave when she heard

Elaina's next question.

"Is *she* staying there?"

Emily froze. Elaina was talking about her! And her voice held such contempt — contempt to match the criticism Emily had seen in her eyes the day she had done Elaina's portrait. Emily should have left — an instinct for self-preservation — but she didn't. She heard Elaina's diatribe, all of it, a scathing, breathless critique.

"She is? In those clothes? I admit, her new Annie Hall look *is* an improvement over the wilted flower child image, but *still*. She must embarrass you, Rob. No matter how wonderful her photographs are, you can't really want her to be an ambassador for the magazine! I don't understand why she doesn't do something about it. She may have been poor last summer, at the wedding, but you certainly are paying her more than enough to get decent clothes, do something with her hair. I could talk to her if you want."

There was a pause — silence. If Rob spoke, his voice was too low, or too distant, for Emily to hear.

Finally, Elaina continued, softly, seductively, "I know you're not looking forward to this trip, Rob, being with her. But, if I can't be with you, there is no woman in the world I'd rather have you be with than Emily. I won't have to spend one second feeling jealous!"

Tears streamed down Emily's cheeks as she pushed her way out the heavy front door of the office building and into the bright January sun.

Did Rob dread going to Paris with her? Was he embarrassed to be seen with her? Did he pay her all that money because he hoped that she would make herself look better and stop humiliating him and the magazine he loved?

Probably, Emily realized miserably. *Of course*.

Rob was dreading the trip to Paris and *she* had been unable to sleep because she was so excited. Emily practiced her French, the language of her childhood, reviewed French history, and studied guide books of Paris so that she might be knowledgeable if there were times when she and Rob were together other than the interviews with the couturiers. Emily

236

had no expectations beyond the hope that Rob would smile at her and be pleased with how well she spoke French and how helpful she was. Emily didn't expect Rob to notice her, but she also never expected that he would notice and hate what he saw.

But, of course he would!

Emily stood in the winter sunshine on Wilshire Boulevard. She was only a few blocks from Rodeo Drive and only a half block from Elegance. She had money, lots of Rob's money, in the bank. She could find Allison—Allison who was so stylish, so fashionable. She and Allison could go to Rodeo Drive, buy beautiful clothes, make Emily look . . .

But she was probably an embarrassment to Allison, too! Allison and Rob were alike—impeccably bred, polite, kind— too polite and kind to let their real feelings show.

Emily didn't go to Elegance, and she didn't go to Rodeo Drive. Instead, she crossed the street to the bus stop to wait for the bus that would take her back to Santa Monica, to her lightless basement apartment and the bottle of drugs she hadn't opened—hadn't *needed*—since Mick left last summer.

There was no *point* in going shopping. All the money in the world, all the fabulous clothes on Rodeo Drive, couldn't make her worthy of Rob Adamson. Emily had no idea what was wrong with her, but there was *something* deep and painful; and it crashed like a lethal tidal wave over the fragile feelings—hope, joy, happiness—whenever they dared to find a home in her heart.

Emily hadn't even thought about packing the bottle of drugs in the small suitcase she would take to Paris. But as the bus rolled along Wilshire and dark, ugly feelings wiped away her excitement about the trip, Emily decided it was safer to bring the pills. In case the pain became too great.

"Rob, please don't be angry!"

Rob had listened to Elaina's tirade with a quiet fury that erupted—"Don't talk about Emily like that!"—just seconds after Emily left.

Elaina was stunned by Rob's reaction. Stunned and frightened.

"Rob, I wasn't being hurtful. I offered to talk to her, to help her, remember? I wasn't being critical of *her*, just of how she looks. Rob, please don't be angry!"

Rob looked at Elaina's confused, startled, *anxious* brown eyes and forced himself to examine his own anger. He was as angry with himself as he was with Elaina. Hadn't he, too, worried in the beginning about hiring Emily? Hadn't he conjured up images of drugs and denim and wantonness walking into the homes of celebrities around the world with the imprimatur of *Portrait?*

Yes. And now, Rob didn't *care* about Emily's clothes. He only noticed—and *cared*—that her gray eyes were clear and sometimes she smiled.

"I'm sorry, Elaina. I overreacted. But, for the record, Emily does not embarrass me. I'm proud to have her working for the magazine. I do *not* want you to talk to her."

And—something Rob didn't tell Elaina—*I am very much looking forward to Paris.*

A week later, Rob strolled along the Left Bank of the Seine and mentally measured the success of the trip to Paris.

From a *business* standpoint, it had been pure triumph. The interviews with the four top couturiers had gone beautifully, candid conversations laced with humor and insight and personality. The ease of the interviews had been because of Emily. She listened, attentive and smiling, quietly providing the correct translation when the designers' English faltered, speaking in soft, flawless French, unobtrusive and intriguing.

The designers *were* intrigued with Emily, with her perfect French, the physical delicacy so much like Parisian women, the dazzling sun-gold hair, the exquisite face. But the clothes . . .

Rob watched each designer react to the paradox of Emily, wondering if her meant-to-conceal clothes were an *avant-garde*

238

fashion statement from some renegade Californian designer whose creations had yet to make the pages of *Vogue* or the runways of New York and Paris. Rob watched as the Parisian designers discounted that possibility, frowning slightly, and how each, as the interview progressed, wanted nothing more than to dress Emily in his own magnificent silks, satins, and chiffons.

Rob's high school French was good enough to enable him to understand the designers' offers of gifts to her—"*Un petit cadeau, cherie, s'il vous plait. Une blouse, une robe elegante, les pantalons à la mode*"—and Emily's polite, quiet, *amazed* refusals.

Rob didn't know if Emily eventually relented, accepting a silk blouse or scarf or some token, because he left at the end of the interview and she stayed to take her famous portraits. Rob wouldn't see her again until the next morning, when they met in the lobby of the Ritz moments before they taxied together to the design studio.

From a business standpoint, the trip to Paris had been an immense triumph, but from a personal standpoint it had been a disaster.

Rob had hoped this trip would enable him and Emily to get to know each other, to feel comfortable outside the realm of work. But it hadn't happened. Even before they'd left Los Angeles—at four-thirty the day before they left—Emily had Fran rebook her airplane seats in Coach, not First Class with Rob, and cancel her reservations at the Ritz. Rob knew Emily never travelled First Class, never stayed at the Five-Star hotels he was happy to pay for, but he had thought that this trip, travelling with him, she would.

Perhaps her boyfriend, the menacing man from the bluffs of Santa Monica, was travelling with her, Rob decided when Fran told him. But at LAX the next morning, Emily was quite alone and quite uncomfortable with *him*.

Rob had hoped he and Emily would meet each morning for breakfast in the dining room at the Ritz. They would drink rich black coffee, and eat fresh-baked croissants frosted with sweet butter and orange marmalade, and talk at least about the day ahead. Perhaps they would even have a chance to stroll along the Champs-Elysées or through the Tuileries or the Jeu de Paume or the Louvre. And, in the evening after Emily returned from the afternoon photosessions, they could have dinner together in the Latin Quarter.

Rob had hoped that he and Emily would become friends.

But it had been a total failure. Emily appeared in the lobby at the Ritz each morning, just moments before their "work day" began; she sat through the interviews, making them a great success; then Rob left and she took the photographs; and that was all. Rob suggested dinner once. Emily looked surprised, confused, *troubled,* and finally she shook her head no. Rob spent the evenings in his suite at the Ritz, writing the profiles on the designers, sipping champagne, gazing at the City of Light, and wondering what she was doing, where she was hiding.

The operation was a success, Rob thought now as he strolled at twilight along the Seine, but the patient died.

Rob walked along the Boulevard Saint Michel into the heart of the Latin Quarter, its sidewalk cafés alive with students from the Sorbonne, laughing, talking. Discussing Sartre and romance, Rob mused hopefully. But, he thought, like youth everywhere, the students were probably actually discussing the stock market, money, fast cars, and good sex.

Years ago, Rob had spent a romantic evening here, in the shadow of the Sorbonne, discussing the existential dilemma. The girl had been beautiful, French, with wide, intelligent eyes and provocative lips. She and Rob had spent that spring night together, in a swirl of cheap wine and Gaulois cigarettes and profound, profound conversation about the meaning of life, or its meaninglessness. And it was probably all just flirtation, because afterward they made love, again and again, and that was Rob's most vivid memory.

As Rob turned off the Boulevard Saint Michel onto the Boulevard Saint Germain, he caught sight of Emily in a bookstore. She looked very French. Her loose pantaloons and shapeless smock were perfectly acceptable in the Latin Quarter. Rob hesitated a moment. Emily hadn't wanted to be with him. She had made that abundantly clear. They had said good-bye after the interview at Dior today. Rob was returning to Los Angeles tomorrow. Emily was remaining in France for another week.

Rob started to turn away, to leave the French girl alone in her city, but Emily looked up and saw him. Rob smiled uncertainly as he joined her.

"Hi."

"Hi."

"Did the photosession go well this afternoon?" Rob asked, knowing that business was safe ground.

"Oh, yes. Fine."

"I think all the interviews went very well, don't you?"

"Yes. I hope the photographs will be all right."

"They will be." Rob smiled, then commanded gently, not allowing her the option of saying no, "Come have a cup of cappuccino with me. I'd like to hear your thoughts about Paris."

Emily told him, as they drank cappuccino in the Café de Flore, how much she liked Paris, how strangely at home she felt here.

"Are you planning to move to Paris?" Rob asked. His emotions were mixed. He would miss seeing Emily—he would get her magnificent photographs by mail instead of in person—but that selfish reason was offset by the soft glow in her eyes. Emily did seem at home, relaxed here, relaxed at last even with him.

"I don't know." *Should I? Do I embarrass you, Rob?* Emily looked bravely into the smiling dark blue eyes—eyes that were too polite to reveal their disapproval—and repeated softly, "I don't know."

"How long are you planning to stay this trip?"

"I'll be back in Los Angeles on Saturday, a week from tomorrow."

"The whole time in Paris?"

"Paris, Versailles, the Loire Valley." Emily frowned slightly, debating. Finally, she added, "I'm doing some moonlighting."

"For the Chateau Bel Air. I know. It's perfectly fine with

me, Emily. I told you that."

"Did Allison tell you?" Emily asked quietly. Had Allison checked with Rob to make sure he really didn't mind as long as her work for *Portrait* didn't suffer? Emily hoped not. She hoped that Rob and Allison didn't talk about her like Elaina and Rob did.

"No. Roger Towne told me. A euphoric, thrilled, *acquisitive* Roger Towne."

"Acquisitive?"

"I'm quite sure Roger would like to acquire your talent full-time for Chateaus all over the world."

"Oh, well . . ."

"I will more than match any offer Roger makes." Rob knew Roger wouldn't try to lure Emily away from *Portrait,* not that he wouldn't want her. It simply wasn't done, not among gentlemen, not among friends. It wouldn't happen, but pretending it might gave Rob a chance to remind Emily—because he wondered if she really heard his praise—how valuable she was to him.

"I wouldn't ever leave *Portrait.*" *You.*

"I hope not." Rob smiled. "So, this coming week isn't a real vacation."

Emily tilted her head and smiled shyly.

"What?" *What are you thinking, Emily?*

"I shouldn't tell you this, Rob."

"Tell me."

"Taking photographs isn't work." *Living the rest of my life is work. Taking beautiful pictures is escape, happiness. . . .*

Rob and Emily walked beside the Seine along Le Quai de la Tournelle. When they reached the Pont de la Tournelle, Emily stopped.

"Well, my hotel is this way. Thank you for the cappuccino, Rob."

"You're on L'Ile de Saint Louis?" On the *dark* L'Ile de St. Louis, Rob thought as he looked beyond the bridge Emily was planning to cross. The bright lights of the Latin Quarter were far away.

"Yes."

"Let me walk with you, Emily. It looks a little dark and deserted." *And I'm in no hurry to leave you. Are you in a rush to get away from me, as always?*

"Oh, all right. Thank you."

Across the Pont de la Tournelle, on L'Ile de Saint Louis, the streets became darker, shadowed by magnificent ancient buildings, classical majestic reminders of the grandeur of Old Paris.

"Here it is."

Emily's "hotel" was a house whose small, inexpensive rooms were rented to those—almost exclusively French—who knew to look there. The front door was opaque glass and it opened directly to a poorly lit, very steep flight of stairs.

Rob walked up the stairs with Emily. The hotel was probably safe, but . . .

Emily's room was at the top of the stairs on the right. It was a garret, austere, windowless. Broken springs protruded from beneath the small, narrow bed and it sagged in the middle. An unshaded lightbulb hung from the ceiling and provided the room with its only light. A crooked chair was shoved under a dilapidated table. Guide books anchored the corners of a map of Paris that lay open on the narrow bed.

"Vintage Paris," Emily whispered, suddenly embarrassed that Rob had seen the room. *I feel more comfortable here, Rob, than in a suite at the Ritz.*

Emily bent her head, sending a golden curtain of fine silk across her face, hiding her eyes. Rob wanted to find the gray eyes, smile at them, reassure them.

Very gently, and without giving it much thought because it felt so right, so natural, Rob moved the silky gold away from Emily's face.

At his touch Emily stiffened, and the gray eyes beneath the golden curtain were no longer simply shy and embarrassed . . . they were terrified.

"Please don't." Emily backed away, two steps. In another step she would reach the bed.

"Emily?"

"*Please.*"

"Emily, what's wrong?"

Rob took a step toward her and watched the terror crescendo. *You're afraid of me, Emily? Why?*

"Please go away, please go away, don't hurt me, please. . . ." Emily's voice was soft and distant, like a little child saying an incantation that no one would heed, a prayer that would be unanswered, a final weak plea not to be hurt.

"Emily." He was the cause of her fear! The more he pushed, the greater her fear. Finally, Rob whispered helplessly, bewildered, "All right. I'm leaving, Emily. I'm sorry."

Rob closed the door behind him as he left and Emily stared at it through a blur of tears. Then she began to tremble, shaken by the emotions that swept through her. *Relief . . . disappointment . . . pain.*

Relief, because Rob had left.

Disappointment, because she'd believed Rob was different — so different — and he wasn't. *Yes,* he was, just a little, because he had listened to her pleas. *No,* mostly he was the same, and there was no hope.

Pain, the screaming, unbearable pain deep inside her.

Emily reached into a corner of her small suitcase and removed the bottle of drugs Mick had given her. Her hands shook as she twisted off the cap and the pills spilled onto the narrow bed and the colorful map of Paris. Emily picked a gray pill with green speckles off Monmartre and swallowed it quickly. She put two other pills in her coat pocket for later, in case the first pill lost its magic before she was ready to return from her dark walk into the night.

Emily felt more calm now. She was going to escape. The pain would be numbed for a few precious hours. The pill was in her stomach. *Good.* In a few minutes she would begin to feel its effect. Emily made herself forget about Rob and think about the lights and colors of Paris, the shapes that were out there, the intriguing hallucinations that awaited her, the friendly monsters.

Calm, calm . . .

Rob stood on the Pont St. Louis glaring at the flying buttresses of Notre Dame—eerie forms in the darkness—trying to make sense of what had happened.

What the hell did Emily think he was going to do?

Please go away, don't hurt me! How could Emily possibly think he would hurt anyone, much less *her?*

Rob had left the tiny garret because that was what Emily wanted—her pleas had been desperate—but it couldn't end like this.

He strode quickly back toward the small hotel, climbed the stairs two at a time, and knocked on the splintered wooden door to her room.

"Emily, let me in."

No! Fear seized her at the sound of his voice and the sudden violence of the pounding. Fear and more disappointment: Rob wasn't any different at all. At least she had taken the pill. That would make it better, but still . . . *no.*

"Emily?"

Emily opened the door slowly, a reluctant acceptance of her destiny of pain. She tilted her delicate face up to him and her gray eyes met his, proud and defiant, but so wise, so painfully wise. *I know what you're going to do, Rob, and I will do it, whatever you want, because I have no choice.*

Rob gazed at her lovely face and the gray eyes that sent a proud message of hopelessness. *Hopelessness? Why?*

"Emily, please, tell me what happened."

Emily felt little rushes, evidence that the pill was beginning to work. *Please hurry!*

"Emily?"

"You know what happened."

"I don't."

"You wanted to"—Emily searched for a polite way to say it—"have sex with me."

"What? Emily, no." *Yes, if that's what you wanted. If your eyes had told me I could kiss you, I would have, but . . . .* "You seemed embarrassed about the room. I pushed your hair off your

245

face so I could see you while I convinced you not to be embarrassed. That's all."

Rob's thoughts drifted to that balmy summer evening on the Palisades in Santa Monica. Emily's lover's hands had roamed all over her delicate body—intimate, explicit, ugly—and she had allowed it . . . or the drugs had allowed it.

"Tell me, Emily."

"Tell you what?"

"Tell me why you thought I wanted to make love with you."

Tell me why you assumed I would force myself on you.

"Make *love?*"

Such bitterness! Emily, talk to me.

The pill was beginning to work. *Good.* She was beginning to feel a little strong, a little brave.

"Make love," Rob repeated softly. Emily *might* have seen desire in his eyes, but to react to his gentle touch with such terror! "Why did you think that?"

"Because that's what all men want," Emily replied simply.

"Maybe your boyfriend, Emily . . ."

"My boyfriend?"

"I saw you with him last summer, a couple days after the wedding. You were on the Palisades in Santa Monica."

So you know all about me, Rob. Emily's heart ached. *You've always known.*

"Emily, maybe all *he* wants is sex, but—"

The drug was working now and her illusions—that Rob had been warm and kind because he saw something good in her that no one else had ever seen—were shattered. There was nothing more to lose. *Tell him everything, Emily. Why not?*

"Sex is all that any man has ever wanted from me." Then, because there was nothing more to lose, no more illusions to protect, she added defiantly, "There have been a lot of men, Rob. It goes way back."

"How far back?" Rob asked gently, fearing the answer.

Emily had never told anyone. Memories swirled, tossed by the drug, and she remembered the people who had asked her this before. There were the doctors when she had tried to kill herself. Is someone touching you, Emily? Is someone making you do things you don't want to do? Is someone making you feel bad? No, she had told them. He's touching me because he loves me, and I want to do these things, don't I, to earn his love? And I am bad, because if I weren't, he wouldn't want to do these things to me, would he?

Emily hadn't told the doctors or social workers or psychologists at the hospital or the teachers at school. They learned nothing from her about why she had taken the handful of pills that had almost killed her. But Emily learned something. She learned about pills. She learned that just before she was about to die there was a wonderful foggy floating feeling. If she could feel that way, again and again, without dying . . .

And if she took too many pills, if she died, it didn't really matter.

"Emily? How far back does it go?"

Emily had never told anyone and now she was going to tell Rob *of all people*. Rob, who she desperately wanted to believe was different. And maybe *he* was, but *she* wasn't, even with him.

"My stepfather."

Oh, Emily.

"Do you want to talk about it?" he asked quietly.

Rob looked for an answer in her eyes, but the clear gray had become cloudy. He looked beyond her to the pills scattered on the narrow bed. "Emily, what have you taken?"

"Something gray and green."

"You don't know?"

"Some specially designed hallucinogen." She smiled bravely, defiantly. It doesn't matter what it was, Rob! It's working.

Rob felt helpless, and very angry. He was angry at the men who made Emily fearful of *him*, and angry at Emily for counting him among them, and angry at himself for ever leaving her.

Emily was leaving him now, escaping into another world.

"Let's go for a walk," Rob suggested. He wasn't going to leave her again. He was going to stay with her, protect her, until she was in control.

Maybe then she would want to talk—or maybe not—but if she did, it wouldn't happen in the tiny, poorly lit room with the bed covered with drugs. Rob would return to the glitter of Paris with her, to protect her from the demons of the night and, if he could, to protect her from the demons of her heart.

Rob could tell Emily was hallucinating. She would stop and stare, tilting her head, smiling softly, mesmerized by a light or a shape or a color. Then it would be gone. She would look confused for a moment, then she would walk on until she found something else.

Emily led and Rob followed. She was Alice in Wonderland admiring all the creatures. Rob wasn't sure Emily knew he was there. She would look at him, as if making a surprise discovery, and carefully study his face. Rob guessed she saw a kaleidoscope of a thousand faces in his own. He hoped the faces Emily saw in his were friendly ones. Rob hoped, too, that deep down, beneath the layers of drugs and the layers of pain, some part of Emily knew that he cared.

Finally, the drug-world began to fade. Emily gazed at him uneasily and they were back to what had started this all—a shy, embarrassed look, Rob's attempt to reassure, a gentle touch that recalled a lifetime of pain and fear.

Perhaps Emily Rousseau had never felt the gentle touch of a man who cared.

Rob and Emily sat in a remote corner of a café, still crowded and alive at two in the morning, and he ordered espresso for both of them. No wine, he thought. No more drugs. Talk to me, Emily.

"Do you want to talk about your stepfather?"

"There's not much to say."

Hours ago they had sat in a café, drinking cappuccino, and Emily had seemed so relaxed, so at home. Now her gray eyes were clear of drugs, and in that clarity Rob saw sadness and resignation.

I've already told you everything, Rob. You know the horrible truth of my life.

Wouldn't it help for Emily to talk about it? Rob wondered. He knew nothing about this! It was in the news, of course, but it was so much easier, so much more pleasant, to deny it existed. At the very least, it belonged to other people, women he didn't know, never would know. But now it belonged to this beautiful woman, and Rob was ill-equipped to help her, except that he cared.

"Emily, you can trust me. I'm your friend. I really am. I think it would help to talk about it."

"What do you want to know?"

"How old were you?" Rob answered her question aloud. Silently, his mind gave another answer. *Nothing. I want to know nothing. I want it never to have happened to you.*

"I was ten and eleven and twelve."

"It happened more than once?"

"All the time." Emily added softly because she wanted Rob to know, "I tried to stop him, Rob. I pleaded with him."

"You couldn't stop him, Emily. How could you? He was a grown man and you were a little girl. It wasn't your fault."

"He made me believe it was," she whispered distantly.

"It *wasn't*. Hasn't anyone ever told you that before?"

"No one knows. No one knows but you. Please don't ever tell anyone." *Please don't tell Elaina . . . or Allison.*

"I won't. I promise." Rob smiled gently. He wanted to touch her, to hold her, but that would frighten her, a betrayal after all. "You never told the police . . . anyone?"

"No."

"But he stopped when you were twelve."

"He left." Her stepfather had vanished the day after Emily tried to kill herself. He simply disappeared, which had made her mother terribly unhappy, and Emily had felt even more guilt because that was her fault, too. "And I left four years later, right after I took the final exam of my senior year of high school."

"That was in Quebec?"

"No. We moved to a small town in northern California

249

when my mother married my stepfather. My stepfather was—is—American. He adopted me. I changed my name back to my real father's name when I was eighteen. My real father was French . . . a fisherman. His boat capsized and he drowned when I was three."

"I'm sorry." Rob wondered how different Emily's life might have been—joyous and full of laughter—if a storm-angry wave hadn't crashed on a fragile fishing boat.

Emily smiled softly, wistfully. There was so much she couldn't change.

"You ran away from home?" Rob asked after a few silent moments. *He* had run away—sort of—with twelve million dollars in the bank and dreams of gold that were more wonderful than the luxurious promises life had held since the day he was born.

"No one tried to stop me, Rob." Emily shrugged. "I had been accepted at UCLA, but I needed more money for tuition and living expenses than I was able to save from the jobs I had during high school."

Rob held his breath, hoping Emily hadn't run away from a loveless home to the streets of Los Angeles. But she hadn't. She found work—working two or three jobs at a time—and a tiny basement apartment in Santa Monica that no one else wanted; and one day she saw a "Help Wanted" sign in the window of Jerome Cole's photography studio.

"And then, one Saturday in June, Jerome got food poisoning, and I got to take wedding pictures, and—" Emily smiled. *And then I got to work for you.* The smile faded, remembering that Rob knew everything about her—he always had—even though his eyes were still kind. "I don't see Mick anymore."

"Mick?"

"The man you saw me with."

Good. It was a start, but it wasn't enough.

"Emily, if you've never talked to anyone . . . don't you think it would help? There are people who are trained—"

"You think there is something wrong with me." Emily stared at her espresso, looking for a shape or a color, some proof that the pill was still working. But there was none, no cushion for the pain.

"*No*," Rob answered swiftly, decisively. He gazed at her until she lifted her eyes and met his. "I know there is nothing wrong with you, Emily. You were an innocent victim." *And you still are.*

"I'm all right, Rob."

No you're not! Rob thought, remembering her reaction to his gentle touch: pick a drug, any drug, to escape.

It was three-thirty A.M. when Rob and Emily returned to her tiny room on L'Ile de Saint Louis. Rob stood a safe distance as Emily opened the door to the apartment and flipped the switch for the bare lightbulb that hung from the ceiling.

"Thank you, Rob."

Rob smiled as his mind searched for the right response. *You're welcome, Emily. I enjoyed the evening.* The polite response would have been a lie. His own helplessness, his inability to really help her, had tormented him all evening as he watched her cast about, adrift, alone, desperate. Rob hated that, but—*but being with her* . . . Rob didn't want *that* part to end.

"My flight back to LA leaves at four tomorrow afternoon. Would you like to have lunch with me?"

"Yes."

"Good. I'll be here at eleven."

"All right."

As he started to leave, Rob's eye caught sight of the map of Paris strewn with pills.

"Emily, promise me you'll throw the pills away."

Emily answered with a sad smile. *I can't promise you that, Rob.*

Chapter Eighteen

"Are we still going to Aspen, Rob?" Elaina heard the soft plea in her own voice and wondered if Rob knew it wasn't a seductive pout, but rather ice-cold fear.

Elaina wasn't so tough when it came to Rob Adamson. Elaina had spent her entire life wanting it all and *getting* it all. And she had never wanted anything more than she wanted Rob. The blowup before Rob left for Paris—his surprising anger when she merely spoke the truth about Emily Rousseau—had terrified her. Rob's anger had abated quickly, but the next day he left for Paris and the memory of his inexplicable fury had lingered. When Rob called Elaina from Paris, his voice sounded pleasant, normal, but they needed to be together, touching, loving, passionately erasing the nagging vestiges of the angry words.

Elaina and Rob had been planning the week-long vacation in Aspen for months. They would leave the Friday following Rob's return from Paris and stay in a suite at the just-opened Chateau Aspen. It would be a perfect vacation, a wonderful week of passion and luxury in Roger Towne's newest Chateau.

When Rob returned from Paris, he was preoccupied and distant. It had nothing to do with her or them, Rob assured Elaina. But even in bed she felt the distance.

"Of course we're going to Aspen, Elaina. There are just some things I need to take care of before we go."

Then take care of them, please!

There weren't "things." There was just the one thing: How Rob could help Emily. During the five evenings between Rob's return from Paris and the trip to Aspen, when he and Elaina could have been dining by candlelight at Adriano or the Cafe Four Oaks, Rob was in the Health Sciences Library at UCLA, reading. It was a painful, agonizing read—the story of Emily's life and thousands of others—but the search was worth it because there was hope and help.

And the help was nearby! Dr. Beverly Camden, a leading authority, herself a victim, had an office in Santa Monica two blocks from St. John's Hospital. Rob read both of Dr. Camden's books: *Little Girl Lost,* which revealed the tragedy, the betrayal, the loss of joy and trust and innocence; and *Little Girl Found,* which told of the hope.

Rob met with Dr. Camden on Wednesday, two days before he and Elaina were to leave for Aspen. Dr. Camden listened in silence as Rob told her about his "friend," carefully revealing nothing that would betray his promise to Emily that he would tell no one about her.

"I've read your books," Rob told Dr. Camden when he finished. "And I think she could be helped."

"I know she could. It sounds as though she has made great progress on her own."

"Does it?" Rob asked hopefully.

"Yes. For one thing, she told you about it."

"She told me because she had taken some kind of drug."

"No. Drug or no drug, Rob, she knew she was telling you. And there are other very positive signs: her clothes, her fingernails." Dr. Camden looked at the concerned dark blue eyes that had noticed what many others might have dismissed as trivial. The short-bitten fingernails that had been allowed to grow were an important symbol of his friend's desperate wish to rediscover the joy and happiness and confidence that had been so harshly, so inexplicably, stolen from her. "She's searching for a little pride, a little self-worth."

"She should have so much!"

"Of course she should. *Everyone* should. But she has none."

"As if she's to blame," Rob whispered. "She's just an innocent victim, like a little kitten playing in a storm who is suddenly struck by lightning."

"Not like a little kitten, Rob. A kitten would have known instinctively not to play in a storm, that there were dangers in doing so. There were no warnings for your friend, no instincts she could draw on. That makes it all the more devastating, because it was so *unexpected,* so contrary to everything her life had taught her. She probably was a trusting, happy child. She may have been thrilled that she was going to have a new daddy. And he was probably charming to her, told her how much he loved her, how much fun they would have."

"In therapy, does she have to go through all of that, what actually happened?" *So much pain, too much.*

"No, not necessarily. Only if it's helpful to her. Many women block out the abuse all together, remembering only years later, after multiple failed relationships or marriages. But your friend already remembers. What she needs to focus on is the little girl who played hopscotch on the playground and laughed with her friends and smiled at the golden sun and giggled at the thought of ice cream cones and soft puppies. I need to help her find that innocence again. I need to help her believe that the joy and hope and happiness she felt — and the *trust* — were real, and that what happened was a horrible fluke, a bolt of lightning that would never happen again."

"But I think it *has* happened to her again and again. She believes that all men will hurt her."

"You said she wears clothes that are unrevealing, *concealing,* and that she is very beautiful. She is obviously trying not to send a message of sexuality, but it's backfiring because it makes her look like a victim and that attracts cruel men."

"I never thought her clothes made her look like a victim,"

Rob murmured almost to himself. Vulnerable, *yes*. Precious and fragile, *yes*. But to want to *hurt* her?

"That's because you're not that kind of man." *You're the kind of man that your friend doesn't believe exists.*

"Why would she be with men like that?"

"She needs to be loved, Rob, just like everyone else in the world. I'm sure these men tell her they love her; I'm sure her stepfather told her that, too. For her, sex has always been an act of violence, not an act of tenderness and love. She's known nothing else. But now a deep instinct is telling her there *has* to be something better. She knows about real love—some fragile, resilient corner of her heart knows about it—but can she trust that knowledge?"

"Trust," Rob echoed softly. That was the central issue. How could Emily trust any man? Why *should* she? The first man she had trusted with her love and her innocence and her joy had brutally betrayed her.

"She trusts herself the very least," Dr. Camden said. "And she doesn't trust men. Does she have women friends?"

Rob considered the question for a moment. Allison Fitzgerald—warm, generous, kind Allison—was Emily's friend, wasn't she? Rob got the impression more from the way Allison spoke of Emily—pride in her talented friend and perhaps a sigh of concern—than when Emily spoke of Allison. Rob remembered the conversation in Paris about Emily moonlighting for the Chateau Bel Air. *Did Allison tell you?* Emily had asked. Rob remembered that there had been a flicker of disappointment in Emily's eyes, as if she were about to learn that she couldn't trust Allison, either.

"There are people who would like to be her friend," Rob said.

Dr. Camden nodded thoughtfully. It was quite obvious that Rob Adamson wanted to be the young woman's friend—*at least*—and Dr. Camden guessed there could be much more. She wondered if the woman knew it. Of course not, she thought. Even if Rob told his friend how much he cared, she wouldn't believe it because she had no confidence in herself. Dr. Camden looked at Rob and felt a sense of urgency about his friend. There was a wonderful life waiting out there for her.

"Will she come see me?"

"I don't know. I thought I could do a portrait of you." Rob paused, not wanting to reveal too much about Emily. Many people worked for him; it wasn't a betrayal. "She's with the magazine. I could arrange for you—"

"Don't trick her, Rob," Dr. Camden interrupted. "Don't ever give her a reason not to trust you."

"So I should—?"

"Tell her the truth. Tell her you read everything you could and met with me and that I would very much like to see her." Dr. Camden added a serious, quiet warning, "It may backfire, Rob. She may consider even this a betrayal. She may be very angry."

"I can't imagine her being angry."

"Oh, Rob, then you don't know about the rage of an innocent victim."

But Rob *did* know. The rage of innocence betrayed lived in his own heart because of Sara.

"I guess it's a risk I have to take," Rob said. "To help her."

"Yes."

"I'm serious about doing an article on you and your work for *Portrait*. It's something I should have done—should have known to do—a long time ago."

"Well, after she's fine, then I'd be delighted. I think that now it might muddy the waters, perhaps discourage her from coming to see me."

"All right." Rob stood to leave. "Thank you very much. I appreciate you taking the time to meet with me."

"You're welcome. And Rob? She's very lucky to have you as a friend."

"I haven't scheduled your next appointment with Emily," Fran told Rob when he returned to his office after seeing Dr. Camden. "She's due back from Europe the day after you leave for Aspen. You'll be in Aspen, then she'll be in

New York. Oh, but that reminds me. Lawrence Carlyle is certainly going to get the Best Director nomination for *Hong Kong*. I checked with his studio in London. He's leaving in two weeks for a three-month shoot in Africa. Wouldn't it make sense for Emily to take his picture in London now? I know she'll call before she leaves Europe, to see what I have scheduled for her. I could arrange to have her stop in London on her way back."

"Lawrence Carlyle hasn't been nominated yet."

"But he will be! And then Emily—or whoever, although Emily would be the best because Lawrence Carlyle photographs are always so *unrevealing*—is going to tramp into the bush?"

"I guess. If need be." Rob had already decided—as much as he, too, would love to see what Emily Rousseau could do with Lawrence Carlyle—that Emily would just do portraits of the nominees who happened to be in Los Angeles. That way she could keep daily appointments with Dr. Camden. "So, when can I meet with Emily?"

Fran flipped the calendar two weeks ahead. It was Rob's calendar, but Fran made notations in the margins about the travel schedules of Emily and the staff journalists.

"You want to meet with her before the nominations are announced?"

"I want to meet with her as soon as a meeting can be scheduled."

"OK. Let's see. She'll be in New York and you'll be in San Francisco. The afternoon of the fourteenth looks OK." Fran tapped a tapered finger on the calendar, on a date around which she had drawn a large red heart. "Like at three?"

"All right. Make it three and block out the rest of the afternoon. What's the red heart?"

"God, you're such an incurable romantic! February fourteenth, Rob Adamson, is Valentine's Day."

"And you're such a skeptic," Rob countered lightly, reaching a quick decision. He wanted to talk to Emily alone, in private, without the possibility of interruption. "I think, as a Valentine to all the staff, I'll just close the office at three that day."

"You're kidding."

"No. Why don't you generate some cute little heart-shaped memo and send it around?"

"With pleasure. You still want to meet with Emily at three that day?"

"Yes."

Allison sat at the huge picture window in the plush dining room of the just-opened Chateau Aspen and watched the dawn awaken to a blizzard of snow. She curled her hands around a mug of rich hot chocolate and smiled.

I probably look like a contented cat. Warm and cozy and completely happy to sit by a window and watch windy, snowy swirls.

Warm. That was the adjective Allison would apply to this moment, this weekend, every moment she spent with Roger Towne. It had been that way since they first met — warmth, not fire, nothing dangerous, just wonderful comfortable feelings.

Just as it had been with Dan.

Warmth without fire, but maybe the warmth would become fire. Maybe the warm smiles and easy laughter were kindling that someday would explode into flames. Allison thought it might happen, but she was in no hurry. It was so nice this way, touching with smiles, eyes, and words, not hands and lips; happy together but not desperate apart; working harmoniously on the Chateau Bel Air.

Allison wondered if Roger's expectations differed from hers. If they did, *he* was respecting *her* wishes. When Allison arrived yesterday for a long weekend in Aspen, Roger showed her promptly to her own elegant suite, instantly assuaging any worry she might have had that he expected them to share a room.

After Allison was settled in her suite, Roger gave her a tour of the hotel, followed by a sleigh ride through Aspen, followed by a candlelight dinner and a nightcap in front of a roaring fire, complete with roasting chestnuts. Then Roger escorted Allison to her suite, caressed her only with his handsome smile, and wished her good night.

Allison awakened early, arrived in the dining room before the skiers—if *anyone* was going to ski today—and found a window seat from which to drink hot chocolate and gaze happily at the swirling blizzard.

"Good morning, Allison."

"Rob! Hi. You made it. Roger was worried."

"We got in late last night. There were long delays in Denver because of the storm, which, I see, has now arrived in Aspen."

"I feel like I'm inside one of those glass balls—a chalet scene—that someone has just turned upside down." Allison smiled. "I love it, but I guess the skiers won't be happy."

"It will probably pass through quickly, leaving blue sky and powder snow. You aren't a skier?"

"No."

"May I join you? Is Roger on his way down?"

"Yes, of course. I don't know about Roger." Allison frowned briefly. *Roger and I aren't lovers.* Rob wouldn't know that, and he would *assume.* Since New Year's Eve, Roger and Allison had had dinner with Rob and Elaina twice, and three days before Rob and Emily left for Paris, Allison, Roger, and Rob had had a leisurely lunch together at The Bistro. "Will Elaina be joining us?"

"I doubt it. I imagine Elaina won't be up for hours." Rob sat down across from Allison and told the waitress he would like a mug of hot chocolate, too. He leaned over to study Allison's almost-full mug and asked, "Have you already eaten the marshmallows?"

"There weren't any!"

"No? And Roger calls this a luxury hotel?"

"It *is* a luxury hotel. Except for the marshmallow problem—and those may be available on request—there are virtually no flaws."

"Virtually?"

"Well, I was just thinking that an overstuffed chair, suitable for curling one's legs under while spending an entire day drinking hot chocolate, right here, would be nice."

"In the dining room."

"Yes! Do you think that's just too bold a design statement?"

"Not at all. Any other flaws?"

"I guess I would have a few photographs by our friend on the walls."

Our friend, Rob mused. How he wished Emily knew she had friends.

"Do you know her very well?" Rob asked, trying to sound casual but delighted to have an easy entrée into a discussion of Emily with Allison.

"Emily?"

"Yes."

Allison hesitated before answering.

"I think of Emily as a friend," Allison began after a few moments. "I like her very much, but I guess I really don't know her very well. She's quite private."

"And it's not your style to pry."

"No, I guess not." Allison wondered if she should say the next, but she saw the gentle concern in Rob's eyes and continued thoughtfully, "I've wondered if there was something—something very troubling—in Emily's past. That's just a feeling." Allison frowned slightly. "And, for as nice and as kind as Emily is, and as talented, she doesn't really have much confidence."

"No, she doesn't," Rob agreed quietly.

"I do know how much Emily enjoys working for *Portrait,*" Allison said after a moment.

"Really?"

"Yes." Allison added something she believed to be true, although Emily had never actually said it, "I think it's really how much she enjoys working with you."

"Oh." *I hope so.*

Rob and Allison watched the snow swirl in silence for several minutes.

"Speaking of *Portrait*," Rob began as he turned from the stark whiteness of the blizzard to the smiling jade eyes, red-gold curls, and pink-flushed cheeks, "I would like to do a portrait of you. Interior designer *extraordinaire*."

"Me?"

"Of course. I'd like the article to appear after the Chateau Bel Air is open, perhaps the August or September issue?"

Bellemeade was going to be featured in *Architectural Digest* in June. That had been Claire and Steve's decision to make. The focus of the *Architectural Digest* article would be Bellemeade—its architecture, its history, its recent interior design . . . Bellemeade, not Allison. An article in *Portrait* would be quite different—*her* story, not the story of Bellemeade or the Chateau Bel Air.

"I'm very flattered, Rob."

"Is that a yes?"

"It's a no," Allison said softly. "It's too soon."

"You think you're a flash in the pan?"

"No . . ." *But I've learned not to count gold medals before I've won them.*

"Is it because of your accident?" Rob asked gently.

So Rob knew. He probably had known from the very beginning, from the day last June in the fragrant alcove of lilacs.

"It would be hard to do a very thorough article about you without mentioning your riding and your accident," he added truthfully.

"I know. That wouldn't be a problem as long as I wasn't portrayed—*portraited!*—as a courageous heroine."

"But it did take courage, Allison."

"No, Rob. I just did what I had to do to survive."

"So?"

"I guess I just want to keep a low profile for now."

"Fair enough. You probably won't give me a call when it's time, will you?"

"Probably not."

"I'll check back every six months or so, OK?"

"Sure." *Tell him, Allison. Tell him now, gently, that you knew*

Sara. "Rob, there's something I've wanted to tell—"

At that moment, Roger appeared. For the next hour, Roger, Rob, and Allison talked, marvelled at the silent power of the snowstorm, and drank hot chocolate. Then Rob left.

Some other snowy morning, I'll tell Rob how much I liked Sara and how sorry I am, Allison thought after Rob was gone.

Or will I? Allison wondered as she analyzed her feelings, a mixture of relief and guilt. Relief, because it would be difficult, emotional, for both of them. And guilt. Why guilt? she asked herself. Was it really wrong not to want to recall Rob's pain? Was it really impolite not to want to see sadness in his dark blue eyes?

No, Allison decided. It wasn't wrong . . . it was right.

That snowy morning in Aspen, Allison decided that she would never tell Rob she had known Sara. Rob, who Allison would never want to hurt; Rob, who was her friend; Rob, with whom there had always been a special bond.

"Come to bed," Elaina whispered softly, hiding the plea as well as she could. Rob stood at the bedroom window gazing out at the snowstorm. He was just across the room, *but so far away.* And she wanted him, needed him so much! A day in bed—a day of breathless sex and daring intimacy— would bring Rob back to her, wouldn't it?

"It's nine A.M., Elaina. Time to get up."

"And do what, Rob? We're snowed in. Let's enjoy it. Bed and room service and long hot showers and more bed. . . ."

"I told Roger and Allison we would meet them for cocktails at seven and dinner at eight."

"*Tonight!* Ten lovely sensual hours from now. We should be famished by then. Rob? . . ."

Rob barely heard Elaina's words. He was thinking about Emily, worrying about what he would say to her on the fourteenth. *Happy Valentine's Day, Emily. Oh, by the way, here are some books you should read because you don't know about love or valentines, just violence and betrayal. And here's the name of a doctor you should see.*

Rob worried about how he would say what he needed to say and how she would react, but his thoughts about Emily went way beyond that. Rob ached for her. He wanted her to be happy. He wanted so much to help her.

Rob wished Emily were here right now, in this elegant suite, warm and safe beside the fire, protected from the icy winter storm. Rob wished he could spend however long Emily needed with her, in these luxurious rooms, talking to her, listening to her, helping her purge the pain from her heart.

He and Emily could hide in this perfect place, and when they emerged, the blizzard outside would be over, and so would the blizzard within. And Emily's life would be golden and sunny *always*.

Fantasy, Rob told himself. Emily would feel so *trapped* here! Emily didn't believe she deserved beautiful things. She would want to run away from this beautiful, luxurious place.

Would you lock her in? Rob's mind demanded of the part of him that had created the wonderful fantasy. Would you *force* Emily to stay against her will? Wouldn't that make you one of *them*, the evil men who had harmed and imprisoned her?

And even, if by some miracle, Emily would agree to be here with him, words were only words, promises only promises. Emily had years of emotion and experience and pain—all *real*—that would eloquently refute anything Rob promised her about love. Rob knew Emily's healing couldn't happen overnight. It would be a long, painful process with many setbacks; a dream constructed from a lifetime of nightmares; a delicate belief that would take faith and nurturing and patience and time. *Time* and the feathery weight of new, wonderful experiences to counterbalance the oppressive weight of the old, horrible ones.

Rob wanted to make everything right and gentle for Emily *now*.

He wanted, he realized, to *show* Emily about love.

But it was Elaina, not Emily, who was here with him. Elaina, who was in his bed. There had been many women in Rob's life and in his bed. Making love had always been such an easy pleasure; a welcome sharing of ecstasy . . . effortless, exciting, *good.*

It had never been that way for Emily. For Emily, there had been only terror.

"I'm going for a walk," Rob said, finally answering Elaina's plea for him to join her in bed.

"Rob, there's a blizzard! It's very dangerous."

"I'll be back."

Rob trudged through the deep, fresh snow, whipped by the icy wind, acutely aware that the beacons that guided the path to safety were lost in a white fog of snow.

This is what Emily's life is like, Rob thought sadly. Every day of her life is like walking in a blizzard without beacons, a foggy, turbulent world of harm and danger.

Rob had always known about Emily's lovely fragility, but now he realized her remarkable strength. What courage it must take to venture into the world—a world of danger—day after day! What an effort to be always wary—to know there are no safe ports in the storm—and yet to go on, in a brave, solitary search for peace and beauty.

Oh, Emily. Let me help you. Let me show you about love.

"Why don't you go ahead, Elaina? I need to make some calls. Please tell Roger and Allison I'll be along soon."

"All right." Elaina didn't tease him—"It's Saturday night, Rob, forget the magazine!"—she just kissed him softly on the lips before leaving for Roger's suite.

That afternoon, after Rob returned from his long walk, had been . . .

Elaine had no words to describe the tenderness of their lovemaking. Rob had been so gentle, so careful, so loving. He had never made love to her like that before. It was as if . . .

Don't think it, Elaina warned herself. But it was impossible to suppress the horrible thought. *It was as if Rob were making love to someone else.*

After Elaina left to join Roger and Allison, Rob dialed the number he had memorized before he left Los Angeles. Emily's number was in Fran's Rolodex, of course, and E. Rousseau was also listed in the telephone book.

Rob just wanted to say hello—maybe more—if Emily was home. She was due back from France sometime today.

The first time he dialed, Rob let Emily's phone ring fifteen times. He waited ten minutes, redialed, and this time listened through thirty rings before hanging up.

Perhaps it was just as well. It was an impulse and it might have confused or worried her.

Just concentrate on what you're going to say to her when you see her, Rob told himself as he walked to Roger's suite. *Just be sure you have rehearsed, over and over, those so very important words.*

Chapter Nineteen

By Valentine's Day, *Love* was ahead of even the optimistic filming schedule Steve and Peter had planned. Steve was on the set most days, watching without interfering, marvelling at the genius of Peter Dalton.

Peter was calm, serious, never temperamental or even the least impatient. And Peter's calm professionalism was contagious. The crew was calm and serious, the cast was calm and serious; they were all serious, dedicated professionals working harmoniously to create the movie of the decade.

Even Bruce Hunter. Bruce was a party boy. He was famous for off-screen romances with his costars and was the gold standard for egocentrism in Hollywood. Bruce had reason to be egocentric: He was *huge* box office. Bruce's enormous success was attributable to his Greek God looks, his stunning sexuality, and to the remarkable fact that, in addition to everything else, he could act! Bruce Hunter had been selected to play Sam, the male lead in *Love,* because his on-screen chemistry with Winter Carlyle was sensational.

Peter's style as a director was to allow the actor great freedom in defining and exploring the role. He provided guidance and direction as necessary. Peter's style presupposed that the actor had a serious interest in the character he was portraying. The actors and actresses with whom Peter usually worked—the *best* of the London and New York stage—had such a commitment.

Bruce Hunter did not. Bruce spent no time thinking about his character's motivation; he simply awaited direction. And like a gifted natural athlete—"What shall I do now, Coach? A long bomb into the end zone for a TD? OK, no problem."—Bruce could deliver.

"Give that last line with a little more sincerity, Bruce," Peter would say.

"More? All right. Like this?"

Bruce would deliver Peter's magnificently crafted lines exactly as the director told him to, every scene perfect, every scene bringing Bruce Hunter closer to an Academy Award.

"Look more loving, Bruce."

"More loving? What do you mean, Pete?"

"I mean," Peter answered softly, "you need to look at her as if you would give your life for her."

"Jesus!"

"Do it."

"OK, you got it."

Peter's working relationship with Bruce was easy but uninspired. His working relationship with Winter was what he preferred—a serious, analytical, artistic collaboration. Winter cared *so much* about Julia and about Peter's astonishing script. Winter wanted to speak every line as well as it could be spoken, to make every emotion exactly right. In the beginning Winter was obviously uncertain about her talent, but with Peter's calm support her confidence blossomed and her wonderful natural talent matured.

"Were you happy with that scene?" Peter would ask, joining Winter during a break, waiting patiently for her honest reply.

"Not completely," Winter would admit truthfully.

"What didn't you like?"

"I don't know, Peter. It just didn't feel right. What did you think?"

Peter and Winter would discuss it quietly, gifted actress to gifted director, and when they did the scene the next time, it would be better, and eventually, when Peter and Winter were both satisfied, the scene would be perfect.

"Cut," Peter said just before noon on Valentine's Day. "Let's break for lunch."

The crew dispersed. As usual, Bruce Hunter looked a little lost. On most sets, "breaks" were a time for flirtation, even sex in a costar's trailer, but not on this set. Bruce had imagined, assumed, that he would have an affair with the beautiful Winter Carlyle. But Winter was remote, interested only in her work. After a confused moment, Bruce shrugged and ambled off to have lunch with the crew.

Within two minutes of Peter's announcement of the break, the sound stage was empty, except for Winter, who hadn't moved from the sofa where she had sat during the scene, and Peter, who had joined her there.

"You're green."

"What?" Winter turned to look at Peter, moving her head slowly. Fast movement sent waves of dizziness and nausea.

"Green," Peter repeated with a gentle smile. "Even with filters, the camera is seeing green."

"Flu."

Peter nodded. "I'll drive you home."

"Peter, we're not done filming for the day."

"Yes we are."

Peter and Winter could have driven to the set together

every day—Bellemeade and Holman Avenue were very close—but that would have changed their relationship. In those predawn and after-dusk hours, Peter and Winter might have easily drifted from discussions of the movie to more personal topics.

During the early morning and late evening commute, Peter *might* have asked Winter questions about her best friend, Allison.

Tell me all about Allison, Winter, Peter might have said. Then he might have even asked, *Does Allison have someone? Is Allison in love?*

Winter could have easily answered those questions, but she would have been unable to answer the most perplexing question that danced in Peter's mind about Allison Fitzgerald: *Why do I keep thinking about her?*

Peter and Winter didn't speak at all on their Valentine's Day drive from Burbank to Westwood. Peter could tell that Winter's energy was focused on her battle with nausea. He sent sympathetic smiles but didn't disturb her concentration by talking to her.

When they reached Holman Avenue, Peter walked with Winter to the door of her third-floor apartment.

"I noticed a Westward Ho a few blocks away. I'm going to buy some chicken noodle soup and ginger ale, and then I'll be right back."

Winter smiled a wobbly appreciative smile.

"I have soup here, Peter. I'm fine, really. Thank you."

"You sure?"

"Yes."

"OK. Steve and I agree we'll make this a three-day weekend. Call me Sunday and let me know how you feel about working Monday."

"I'll feel like working Monday."

"Call me."

"OK."

Peter drove to Bellemeade, distractedly tossed a tennis ball for a lively Muffin, and thought about Allison Fitzgerald.

Answer your own question. Go see her.

"Allison?"

Allison looked up from the photographs she had just carefully spread out on her desk. Two hours ago she had moved the latest catalogues from Henredon, Clarence House, Baker, and Brunschwig and Fils onto the floor to make room for the twelve long-stemmed red roses that had arrived from Roger. An hour later, when Emily appeared with the photographs she had taken in France, Allison hastily removed everything else from the top of her usually cluttered desk.

Allison's desk had been transformed from the clutter of success to tranquil elegance, from catalogues, fabric samples, sketches, phone messages, and idea lists to fragrant long-stemmed roses arched over spectacular photographs of Paris, Versailles, and the Loire Valley.

"Peter," Allison breathed. What was *he* doing here? "Hi. No movie today?"

Try to speak in complete sentences, Allison told herself. Peter is a talented writer, remember? But it was hard enough to speak *at all* to the sensuous dark brown eyes.

"Winter is ill. The camera crew tried every filter they had, but she still looked pale green."

"Oh!" Allison stood up. That was why Peter was here. Winter had sent him. "Did Winter want me to—"

"No, Winter's fine. It's the flu, or something she ate, or the fact that she's pushing too hard. I just gave her a ride to her apartment and extracted a promise that she would have some soup and take a nap." Peter continued, with a voice that didn't exude the confidence one would expect from the extraordinary man that he was, "I decided to drop by and see what you're doing."

"Oh." Good. *Why?*

"So, what are you doing?"

"I was just looking at these photographs, trying to decide which ones are the best."

Peter moved beside Allison to look at the photographs.

"They're all the best," Peter said after a moment. "All masterpieces."

"That's what I thought, too."

"These must have been taken by E. Rousseau, the photographer who did the pictures for Bellemeade."

"Emily Rousseau. Yes. You probably also recognize her work from *Portrait* magazine. Beginning with the December issue, Emily has taken most of the portraits." Allison looked at Peter for a smiling confirmation, an "ah, yes, of course," but his handsome features were somber. "Don't you read *Portrait?*"

"No," Peter answered quietly. He looked from a magnificent photograph of Le Petit Trianon at Versailles to Allison's slightly puzzled but smiling jade-green eyes. Her smile encouraged him. Peter was here today, testing his instincts, not believing it was possible, and Allison was passing his test with flying colors. "I wondered if you would like to have dinner with me tonight."

"Oh!" *Yes.* "I . . . have plans."

"The red roses?"

"Yes, he's—" Just a client? Allison couldn't say that about Roger any longer. It wasn't true. "Yes."

Now Peter had the answers to his questions.

Why do I keep thinking about her? Because she is so lovely, so special.

Does she have someone in her life? Yes.

"I'd better go. It was nice seeing you, Allison. Good luck deciding about the photographs." *Good-bye.*

271

"Thank you," Allison whispered. "Good-bye."

Allison watched Peter weave through the maze of the office and out the door into the afternoon sunshine and the bustle of Wilshire Boulevard . . . gone.

But not forgotten. Now Allison would have this memory to play and replay in her mind, just as she replayed the three other times she had seen Peter Dalton. Allison replayed the scenes and she changed the endings. Before Peter, Allison had only wanted to change one scene in her life story, the dream-shattering scene of the jump with the green and white rails.

But now, because of Peter, there were other scenes she wanted to change. Why hadn't she ridden back to the stable with him that December morning? Why hadn't she asked him to join her family for Christmas Eve dinner? What if Peter had been alone, and lonely, on Christmas?

Allison tormented herself about the ways she could have — *should have* — changed the scenes with Peter. *And she imagined new scenes.* Just last night, at Von's in Santa Monica, Allison had seen a red-ribboned dog toy — for Valentine's Day — and had wondered if she should buy it for the famous Muffin.

Of course not! Reality had crashed swiftly. Pure silliness. You don't *know* Peter Dalton. Just because you keep thinking about him.

Allison looked at the vase of red roses from Roger. More reality, wonderful reality. On that snowbound weekend in Aspen, her relationship with Roger had become more than warm. There had been long, lovely kisses in front of fires and softer laughs and gentler gazes. And since Aspen, in nightly long-distance phone calls, Roger and Allison had talked about the two days they would have together, beginning tonight. The two days, and nights, would start with a Valentine's Day dinner at Adriano with Rob and Elaina. Tomorrow would be spent looking at Emily's photographs, making those decisions and others for the Chateau Bel Air, and afterwards, beginning tomorrow night and ending with Roger's Saturday evening flight to Chicago, they would be together.

And tonight, or tomorrow night, or both nights and Saturday until he left, Allison and Roger would make love. And it would be gentle and warm and lovely and right, *wouldn't it?*

In a month, *Love* would wrap. Peter Dalton would return to New York. And Allison would never see him again.

But would she replay this scene—Peter's mysterious appearance at Elegance on Valentine's Day—over and over. Would she want to change its ending, too?

Yes! So change it now! The urgent command came from deep inside, from a place other than her brain. The message from Allison's brain was loud and clear and logical: *Roger is real, wonderful, right.* The illogical command came from somewhere else. Her heart, perhaps?

Allison didn't know and didn't analyze. She simply obeyed the powerful command.

By the time Allison walked out of Elegance into the February sun, Peter had almost reached the corner. He was about to turn, about to vanish.

"Peter!"

Somehow Peter heard her soft call above the harsh noises of Wilshire Boulevard. He turned just as Allison caught her heel in a grill in the sidewalk. Allison gasped silently as the twist sent a sharp stab of pain into her hip. She recovered her balance quickly and walked toward him, smiling as he approached.

"Are you all right?" Peter asked as he rushed to meet her. "You're limping."

"I'm fine." Allison frowned briefly. Peter had never even seen her walk enough steps to realize she had a limp! *You*

273

don't know Peter Dalton and he doesn't know you, her brain reminded, *warned.* "I always limp."

"Oh." Peter smiled reassuringly. He was so happy to see her! In the moments since he had left her, Peter had felt such a loss. He had been just about to return to Elegance. "Did I forget something?"

"Yes." *Courage,* Allison told herself. When Rob had described her as courageous that snowy morning in Aspen, Allison had replied honestly, "I just did what I had to do to survive." Perhaps this was survival, too, something she *had* to do, something her heart knew more than her mind. So bravely, so softly, Allison told Peter, "You forgot to ask me if I wanted to go riding with you on Sunday."

"I did forget that, didn't I?" Peter replied gently. "Do you want to?"

"Yes." *Very much.*

Emily arrived thirty minutes early for her three o'clock appointment with Rob and waited in the lobby until it was time to take the elevator to the suite of offices. She sat quietly, almost immobile, but her heart pounded restlessly, anxiously, and terrifying thoughts paced back and forth across her mind.

What if Rob's memories of Paris were ugly? What if Rob's enduring images were of Emily's drug-glazed eyes and the horrible things she had told him about herself? What if Rob didn't want her to work for him anymore? What if he couldn't even look at her anymore?

Please, please, please, just let it be the same, Emily's heart cried. Emily didn't dare wish for more. She dreamed, though — lovely dreams — that the new concern and gentleness in Rob's voice would be there still, but, if not, just let it be the same as before.

At two-fifty-eight, Emily took the elevator to the sixth

floor. Rob was there, near the elevator, when the door opened. He had been pacing between his office and the elevator as he waited for her to arrive.

"Hi." He smiled. *Hello, lovely Emily.* Rob took the armful of folders from her. "Here, let me take these."

"Hi. Thank you. I have the portraits of the Paris designers and the work I did this week in New York."

"Great."

The first thirty minutes of their meeting was like any other. Rob admired the magnificent photographs, Emily smiled shyly, and together they selected which portraits would appear in the magazine.

"I wanted to talk to you about the plans for the Academy Award issue," Rob said after they were done with the portraits from Paris and New York. He was easing into the uncharted, dangerous, so important territory—Emily's *life*, Emily's *happiness*—through the familiar route of business.

"OK."

"I'd like you to just do the portraits of the people in town. For all I know, that will be all nominees except Lawrence Carlyle, who's already in Africa. If none of the nominees is in town, we'll have to adjust, but—"

"All right."

"All right?" Rob was about to deliver the next rehearsed lines, convincing her despite her reluctance, but Emily had said all right. She would be in LA. Good. That meant she could begin to see Dr. Camden right away.

"Yes. All right." *If I'm here and you're here, working on the Academy Award issue, we can meet every week. Everything can be the same as always.*

"Good." Rob smiled. That was easy. Now came the difficult part, the delicate part, the important part.

Rob walked to his desk, removed the two books from the locked side drawer, and returned to the chair beside

275

her.

"I got these books for you, Emily."

Emily looked at the books Rob held in his hands: *Little Girl Lost*, the story of the destruction of young, innocent lives, and *Little Girl Found*, the story of hope for those victims. She read the words on the books. As the meaning of the words sank in, her reaction was instant — defensive, angry, hurt — a reflex from someone who had known only hurt and betrayal for so long.

"Emily, I read the books and I met with Dr. Camden who wrote them."

"You told her about me?" *You promised! Did you tell Elaina? Allison?*

"I told Dr. Camden that I had a friend — "

"A friend?"

"A very good friend. I told her nothing that would identify you in any way. Emily, she wants to see you. She's a victim herself. She understands. She can help you."

"Help me? Or help you? You're the one who's embarrassed to have me work for your precious magazine! You're the one who thinks there's something wrong with me, something that needs to be fixed!"

"There's nothing wrong with you, Emily. My God, how can you think I'm embarrassed because of you?"

"I know you are." Emily stood up, shaking, her fists clenched in tight balls.

"*No.* I care about you, Emily. Very much. There's nothing wrong with you. You've been harmed and you can be helped. You can be happy."

"*Happy?* Happy is for people like you, Rob, not me." Emily paused, and when she spoke again her voice was a soft hiss, a whisper of ice, cold and empty and dead. "I wanted to trust you, Rob." *So much.*

"You *can* trust me, Emily."

"No. I can't. But don't worry. You and Elaina don't have to endure another day of mortification. I don't work for you anymore. Good-bye, Rob."

Emily was almost to the door when Rob's voice stopped her, startling them both because it was suddenly full of his own rage.

Emily turned to face him. Her gray eyes flickered with fear and acceptance. She knew he was going to hurt her, and she accepted it. The look in her eyes made Rob's rage even greater.

"Take these." Rob forced the books into Emily's hands. She took them but recoiled instinctively, as if even that were an act of violence and betrayal. Rob closed his eyes for a second, forcing control, preventing the instinct that made him want to hold her, to keep her with him until she understood, agreed, acquiesced. Rob's instinct was compassion, but to Emily it would only feel like more violence, more brutal intrusion on her will. Rob sighed heavily and breathed through gritted teeth, "Please, Emily. Take these and read them. Please think about seeing the doctor."

"I don't work here anymore. It doesn't matter."

"It matters, Emily," Rob whispered as he watched her *escape from him.* "It matters very much."

For two hours after Peter left, Winter sat in the living room of her apartment, fighting waves of nausea and fighting what she knew to be the cause. Both fights were losing battles, but Winter finally controlled the nausea enough to walk two blocks—a million twirling miles—to the pharmacy on Westwood Avenue.

Winter bought three different kits, for a second opinion and a third, not that any confirmation was necessary. Winter knew. She had known for at least a month.

Winter gazed at the deep purple color. "Definitely positive," the directions read. "Congratulations, you are pregnant!"

Now Winter had violet proof—the clear deep violet of her own eyes—and she wondered if her baby—their baby—would have violet eyes like hers or sapphire ones like Mark's.

Mark frowned as he parked in front of Winter's apartment five hours later. He didn't see Winter's car. She had expected to be home early. By six at the latest, she had said.

She's probably off buying heart-shaped chocolates, Mark decided lovingly as he removed the box of long-stemmed roses from his car.

Thinking about Winter buying Valentine's Day treats filled Mark with joy. Thinking about Winter *always* filled him with joy. Mark saw such sadness, such tragedy, such pathos at the hospital; it tore at his heart, making him weep, but his pain was always blunted by the lovely memory of Winter. Mark loved her so much. He felt so lucky.

Winter's apartment was as dark as the inky black February sky. An icy tremor of worry rippled through him. Where was she?

Making a movie, Mark answered his worry quickly, suddenly realizing how Winter must feel when he would call to say he'd be home in an hour, but by the time he checked the X-rays, wrote the orders, handled a few more details, it would really be two or three hours.

Winter had told Mark how quickly the hours passed on the set. She would think they had been working on a scene for an hour, but suddenly it would be time for the dinner break. Making a movie was like working in the hospital; time wasn't measured by minutes or hours, but by the tasks to be accomplished. A lumbar puncture, two blood cultures, a 14 gauge IV, the car scene, the beach scene, one more close-up . . .

Mark turned on the light in the kitchen, placed the Lalique vase—carved crystal partridges, Winter's birthday present from Allison—by the sink, and opened the gold-foil box of roses. When Mark's eyes fell on a saucepan filled with soup on the stove and the box of saltine crackers on the counter, he frowned. Winter *had* been home and she had left soup, uncovered, on the stove. Winter, who had made a teasing but serious show of refrigerating food promptly ever since he had explained to her about salmonella!

Mark left the kitchen in search of more clues to Winter's whereabouts, never expecting to find *her*. He flicked on the living room lights and saw her purse and coat tossed on a chair. Anxiety increasing, Mark walked to the bedroom. The bedroom door was open. The light from the living room cast a soft beam toward the bed, making a golden halo around the shiny black velvet hair on the pillow.

Mark walked quietly into the bedroom, not wanting to waken her yet worried, wondering why she was asleep. Worry won out. Mark knelt beside the bed and gently kissed her temple.

"Mark." Winter's violet eyes fluttered open and her mind sought anchors. The room—the outside world—was dark and Mark was home. She had just been planning to take a quick nap. Winter had felt so dizzy after her trip to the basement of the apartment building to put the sacks containing the pregnancy kits in the trash. She had decided on a brief nap, then soup, then *after* she would think about what she was going to do.

"Are you all right? Where's your car?"

"At the studio. Peter gave me a ride home."

"Are you sick?" Mark curled the fingers of one hand gently around her wrist, feeling her pulse, and touched her forehead with the other.

"Do I seem sick?"

"Your pulse is a little fast, but you don't feel warm."

That was the physical—heart pounding, because Mark was here, touching her, but no fever, not one that would register on any scale except an emotional one. Winter couldn't give Mark her history. *You see, doctor, I took a crazy chance. It was just one time! One wonderful night of passion with the man I love.*

"What are your symptoms?" Mark asked gently.

Winter looked at his loving, concerned blue eyes and remembered the pain in those same eyes when Mark had told her about his childhood without a father and how he had to be very careful not to make that same mistake. *You didn't make the mistake, Mark. I did.*

"I'm just a little tired. I'll be fine." Winter made a move to get up, swirled, and smiled weakly.

"I'm going to make you some soup." He kissed the tip of her nose. "I'll go turn it on and be right back."

While Winter waited, listening to the distant noise of water running in the kitchen, her swirling thoughts suddenly crystallized; as if, while she had been sleeping, in dreams she didn't remember, her questions had all been answered.

In a month Mark will find out about his residency and he'll—we'll—have to make plans. If Mark's plans include me, if he wants me to be with him in Boston, then I'll tell him about our baby. If not, he will never know. I'll stop seeing him before he notices any changes.

It was so easy! If Mark didn't want her, he could still live his dream, unsullied, unharmed. Winter would never force Mark to repeat the mistake of *his* father. And she wouldn't allow herself to repeat the mistake of *her* mother.

Winter felt the new life inside her—a tiny, swirling hurricane, boldly and dramatically announcing its presence—and wondered what a similar small storm had done to the love of Lawrence Carlyle and Jacqueline Winter. Had Lawrence and Jacqueline been lovers, driven by passion, but not enough in love to marry? Had the creation of their "love-child" precipitated a marriage that should never have happened? Perhaps Jacqueline had loved Lawrence as desperately and as confidently as Winter loved Mark. Perhaps Jacqueline had believed, even though Lawrence didn't love her *enough*, that she could make it work.

But the marriage of Jacqueline Winter and Lawrence Carlyle hadn't worked.

He doesn't want us, Jacqueline had told a six-year-old Winter, bitterly, honestly.

Perhaps Winter had already repeated one of Jacqueline's mistakes—a careless night of passion—but she would make no more. And Winter wouldn't repeat Jacqueline's greatest mistake of all: No matter what, Winter would raise this new little life with love and gentleness and care. Her baby would *never* feel loneliness, rejection, or fear. Winter's baby might not have a daddy, just as she had never had one, but the swirling hurricane would have—already *did* have—a mother who loved her, or him, so very much.

If Mark doesn't want me, if he doesn't love me enough to take the risk, then . . .

But Mark does want me, doesn't he?

Winter's eyes filled with hot tears as Mark returned to the bedroom carrying the vase full of roses.

"Happy Valentine's Day."

"Mark . . ."

"Why are you crying?" Mark put the vase on the dresser, sat beside her on the bed, and snuggled her into his strong arms.

"I just don't want this to ever end."

Mark pulled Winter close but didn't answer. He didn't want their fairy-tale love to ever end, either. Mark would never stop loving Winter, but he couldn't promise that this bliss, this happiness, this *dream* would last forever.

Chapter Twenty

"Allison, it's Peter."

Allison had been expecting Peter's call ever since she had awakened at six A.M. to the sound of torrential rain assaulting her bedroom window. The rainstorm hadn't abated at all in the past three hours, despite the glowers Allison cast at the gray-black sky and despite the fact that she had ironed—ironed!—her jeans and had spent hours planning her outfit. Apparently, the soggy storm simply didn't care.

"Rain," Allison said with a soft sigh.

"Rain."

Allison waited, breath held, in the silence that followed.

"Would you like to go to brunch?" Peter asked.

"Yes."

"I guess the Bel Air Hunt Club has a Sunday brunch that's supposed to be good."

"It's supposed to be the best in Southern California!"

"Shall I still pick you up at ten?"

"Sure." *No, wait. I need time to plan my brunch outfit!*

It didn't matter what Allison wore—except for her smiles and her sparkling eyes—and it didn't matter that the Sunday brunch at the Bel Air Hunt Club was the best in Southern California. All Peter remembered about that gray rainy morning and afternoon were the eyes and the smiles; and her soft voice and joyous laughter; and the way she made him feel.

And Allison remembered the same things about Peter, except for the joyous laughter, which was hers, an old friend that had been lost since the accident. Because of Peter, Allison rediscovered her wonderful lost laugh and the feelings that came with it, sunny feelings of exuberant, boundless, untarnished joy.

And because of Peter, Allison discovered something new, something deep inside her that she had never even known existed.

Allison had felt its periphery—the lovely warmth at the edges, the easy, comfortable warmth she had felt with Dan and with Roger. But Allison hadn't known about its center until Peter. Because of Peter, because his sensuous, dark eyes and soft, seductive voice led her there, Allison discovered a place inside herself where there was fire, a magical place that swirled with hot, powerful, exhilarating feelings.

Peter felt the magnificent fire, too. But for Peter, the powerful, exhilarating feelings weren't new, because he had fallen in love once before. Still, as he gazed at Allison's sparkling eyes and felt his entire being respond with joy and desire, Peter's mind spun, astonished.

It wasn't possible! Peter had known—so surely, so confidently and without bitterness—that he would never fall in love again. Peter had lived his forever love; he would be content to live the rest of his life with the lovely memories of Sara.

But now he was falling in love *again*. Somehow the jade-green eyes and soft voice and joyous laugh had bravely, astonishingly, miraculously penetrated the fortress of memories that surrounded Peter's brain and traversed the treacherous moat of pain that encompassed his heart.

What did Peter and Allison talk about as they sipped vintage champagne and then hot chocolate as the brunch ended and the Club served its traditional Sunday tea? Nothing and everything. The endlessly fascinating raindrops that splashed on the bay window . . . and other things, important things.

"It's so hard to talk to you!" Allison's words were *so* important, and they would have worried Peter very much, except she made the pronouncement with merry eyes, smiling lips, and a voice that sang.

"Hard, Allison? Why?" *It's so easy to talk to you.*

"Because of what you write, the way you write. See? I can't even express my thoughts in complete sentences, much less clearly!"

"How do you know what I write, Allison? Has Winter shown you the screenplay for *Love?*"

"No. I read the book of your plays that was published last year."

"Oh." Peter wanted Allison to tell him what she thought about his plays, but first he had to convince her that it wasn't really hard to talk to him at all. He suggested, "Why don't we review the incredibly eloquent words I have spoken to you since we met last August? OK?"

"OK."

Allison listened, amazed, as Peter repeated their conversations—the August day at Elegance, the December morning on the Windsor trail, Christmas Eve at the Club, Valentine's Day at Elegance. Peter remembered every word, every scene, just as she did!

"You remember."

"Yes. I do," Peter answered quietly. And that was remarkable, astonishing, too. Peter hadn't remembered any other conversations, not the exact words, since Sara. Except, he thought, frowning briefly, the threatening promise made by Rob last December. Peter forced away that memory and smiled at Allison. "Do you remember?"

"Yes." Allison tilted her head. "I thought the line about living in a French Impressionist painting was clever."

"*No*," Peter replied with a smile. "But even if it was a brilliant line—which it wasn't—it glittered all by itself. Perhaps I write eloquent dialogue, Allison, but I certainly don't speak it. The French Impressionist comment *was* honest, though, and that's all that matters, isn't it?"

"I guess." Allison smiled and added honestly, "Yes."

"Good. So, Allison Fitzgerald, tell me honestly, in your own words, what you thought about my plays."

"All right," Allison answered softly. "I thought your plays were sad . . . and complicated . . . and lonely . . . and wonderful."

Sad, complicated, lonely, wonderful. All the things you are, sad, complicated, lonely, wonderful Peter Dalton.

Peter and Allison never left their window table at the Club to sample the lavish buffet. Champagne was served to them in crystal flutes, then hot chocolate in fine china, and at four, a red-coated waiter appeared with a platter of hot raspberry scones.

"It's four?" Peter looked at his watch. "I guess we've been here for a while." *For a wonderful while.* Peter didn't want it to end, ever, but . . . . "I'm—Muffin and I—are having dinner at Steve's at six."

"Muffin, too?"

"Yes. Becky—Steve's nine-year-old daughter—and Muffin have become friends. Becky comes by every afternoon after school to feed Muffin and play with her. I actually think Muffin is a closet Californian. She seems quite at home lounging in the California sunshine, preferably in the kitchen on a designer pillow, and she loves scampering on the beach."

"But has she mastered frisbee-catching?"

"Becky is trying, but there's still a little New York, a little *decorum* left in Muffin."

Allison heard the surprising softness in Peter's voice when he talked about Muffin. Softness and fondness, like the fondness of good friends who had weathered storms together and survived.

"Have you had Muffin a long time?"

"Since she was a puppy." Peter's dark eyes darkened for a moment as he counted the years, drifting back in time to Sara's twenty-first birthday, a year before she died. "Five years." Peter added after a thoughtful moment, "Muffin is a good little dog."

Peter and Allison talked about Muffin, and about a puppy Allison had loved as a little girl, and then another hour was magically gone. Finally, reluctantly, Peter whispered that he should take her home.

Peter hadn't realized the depth of his loneliness! He hadn't allowed himself to realize it. Peter had made certain that his life was frantically busy. When he allowed his thoughts to drift to the past, which he did because he never wanted to forget *her*, Peter's memories were the lovely memories of Sara and of their love, not memories of his own grief at what he had lost.

Peter lived a life of discipline, creativity, and memories.

A life of loneliness.

As Peter drove away from Allison's apartment, the immense magnitude of his loneliness hit him, staggering him. *It was as if he had just lost Sara again.*

Peter drove away from Allison, but it was an act of great discipline. What he wanted — so desperately — was to turn around and ask her to be with him forever.

Allison hadn't even known about loneliness until Peter left. But, *then,* loneliness was there, a powerful new emotion mixed in with the other powerful new emotions of the day. Allison missed Peter, felt empty without him.

Allison wanted more of him, *all of him.*

Peter hadn't even mentioned seeing her again when he left, already late, to get Muffin and go to dinner at Steve's. But Peter *would* see her again, wouldn't he? Sometime, all the time, in the few weeks before he returned to New York?

Allison paced around her apartment — lonely, excited, restless — until her pacing caused angry tremors of pain in her hip. Allison hadn't even explained to Peter about her limp! She would explain next time . . .

Next time?

This magical time had just been a fluke, hadn't it? a distant corner of Allison's mind taunted. Because Winter was ill, and Peter had a free moment and happened to wander into Elegance. And if *she* hadn't rewritten the scene . . .

Quickly, too quickly, the enchanted hours with Peter became a misty dream. Allison gazed at the rain that still catapulted against her apartment windows. The plump raindrops had been part of the day. The raindrops were *real,* but what about all the rest? What about the fire and the magic?

At eight, Allison called Winter to see how she was feeling. Winter said she was better, but Allison heard a soft sigh of fatigue as her friend spoke. Allison hadn't told Winter about Peter — that she would be seeing him today — because . . . And Allison still didn't tell Winter — after she and Peter had spent the day together — because,

because . . .

Because Allison didn't know what to say.

Allison paced restlessly again after her call to Winter. When her hip cried "Enough!" Allison telephoned Emily.

"Hello." Emily's voice was a whisper, small, tentative, almost afraid.

"Emily? It's Allison."

"Hi."

"Are you all right?"

"I'm fine."

"Roger loved the photographs."

"Oh. Good."

"We'll need large prints, larger than what I used for Bellemeade."

"Oh. OK. The ones I did for Bellemeade are as large as I can develop in my darkroom here."

"You told me there is a good photo lab in Century City?"

"Yes. We can have them done there."

"It's probably just as well. Roger wants to use more than we had planned—because they are all so wonderful—and if someone else is doing the enlargements, it won't cut into your time for *Portrait*." Allison waited, wondering if she had lost the connection, and finally asked, "Emily?"

"Yes. I don't work for *Portrait* anymore, Allison."

"What? Emily, since when?" The news was startling. The flatness in Emily's voice was almost terrifying.

"I told Rob on Thursday."

Was that why Rob and Elaina hadn't joined Allison and Roger for the Valentine's Day dinner at Adriano after all? Was Emily's decision to leave *Portrait* the reason for Rob and Elaina's surprising last minute cancellation of dinner plans they had all made in Aspen?

"Emily, what happened? Are you all right?"

"Nothing happened. It just wasn't working out at *Portrait*."

Since when? Allison wondered. In Aspen, Rob's voice had been so gentle when he spoke of Emily. And Emily's voice had been gentle, too—as it always was when she talked about Rob—on Valentine's Day when she had dropped off the photographs for the Chateau Bel Air at Elegance on her way to a meeting with Rob! A meeting at which, apparently, nothing had happened—except that Emily left *Portrait*, Rob and Elaina cancelled dinner plans, and now Emily's voice sounded so flat, so defeated.

"Emily, are you all right?" Allison asked again. "You sound a little—"

"I'm a little tired, but I'm fine, Allison, really."

"I'm sorry about *Portrait*."

"So am I," Emily whispered.

"Do you know what you're going to do?"

"No." Emily looked at the books—*Little Girl Lost* and *Little Girl Found*—that lay on her bedside table. She had read them, over and over and over. That had taken courage, but the next step . . . "I don't know."

"Well, you know I can keep you very busy."

"I may be moving to Paris." Emily had almost flown to Paris Friday night. She had almost thrown the books—already slightly warped because they had been read and reread by Rob—away, gathered all her belongings—a ten-minute task if she did it slowly—and flown to Paris. Escaped to Paris, forever.

"Paris? Emily, do you feel like getting together now?" Allison asked impulsively, her worry about Emily increasing. "We could—"

"It's really not a good time, Allison." After a moment, Emily added softly, "Thank you."

"Let's have lunch sometime this week, or dinner, or a movie, OK?"

"OK." *Maybe.*

When the telephone rang at ten P.M. Allison knew it would be Peter. She had been staring at the phone, *willing* it to ring. Peter would be getting home from dinner at Steve's just about now.

"Hello." *Hello! Hello!*

But it wasn't Peter. It was Roger, calling from Chicago. Roger, with whom Allison had been uneasy and remote at their romantic Valentine's Day dinner; Roger, with whom Allison did not make love Thursday or Friday or Saturday; Roger, who wanted to know what had happened.

"Allison, did you actually meet someone else between our weekend in Aspen and Thursday night? No, I take that back, between the time we spoke Wednesday evening and when I saw you Thursday?"

No, I met him before I met you, Roger. The same day, moments before. And I've been thinking about him ever since.

"Roger . . ."

"*Is* there someone else, Allison?"

"I don't know. I'm not sure." *Yes, for me, Yes. And for Peter?*

"But maybe?"

"Maybe. Roger, I . . ." Allison didn't know what to say. No matter what happened with Peter, a love with Roger could never happen now, could it? Now Allison knew about fire, and even though the fire came with danger and uncertainty and loneliness, it ignited feelings within her — *life* within her — that would never again be content with warmth. "I'm sorry."

Peter and Steve watched the "dailies" from Monday's

291

shoot in the screening room at the studio in Burbank. It was nine P.M. For the rest of the cast and crew, the day had ended two hours ago.

"She's not a hundred percent," Peter said. "She's giving her usual one hundred and ten percent, but she's still ill."

The greenish tinge had left Winter's rich, creamy skin, but her violet eyes were cloudy and uncertain, trying to look deeply in love as she waged a private war against nausea.

"I think we'd better cancel tomorrow's shoot," Peter said.

Steve sighed. *Love* had been going so well! Ahead of schedule, harmony on the set, no ego problems, almost too good to be true, certainly too good to last. Steve knew from years of experience that once a movie started to fall apart, once the balance was disrupted by weather or tempers or rolls of film that mysteriously didn't print, it could unravel quickly and disastrously.

But Winter was ill. It was obvious. Winter wasn't a prima donna. She wasn't playing games. She probably wouldn't even want to cancel another day, but they really had no choice.

"I guess so," Steve agreed reluctantly. "I'll go set the telephone calls to the crew in motion. Do you want to call Winter and Bruce?"

"Sure." Winter and Bruce and Allison. Peter had almost called Allison last night when he'd gotten home from Steve's, but he didn't trust himself. He might have just told Allison Fitzgerald what was in his heart. *I miss you, Allison. I want to see you. Now.*

It was *his* desperation, not hers, *his* years of loneliness erupting like lava from a long dormant volcano—hot, rushing, consuming. *He* was desperate and so confident of his feelings, and *she* was lovely and somehow so innocent and vulnerable. Peter wanted Allison, but he had to be so very careful not to rush her.

Peter called Winter and Bruce before he left the studio. He called Allison from Bellemeade after he finished taking Muffin for a quick, soggy walk.

"Is this too late to call?"

"No." *No time is too late, ever.*

"Winter is still sick, better but still a little wobbly, so we won't be filming at all tomorrow. Would you—?"

"Yes." *Yes to anything.*

"Yes?" Peter laughed softly. "Are you free all day?"

"No," Allison admitted. "But I can be free by mid-afternoon."

"Call me whenever and I'll come get you. I'll be here, making dinner for us, OK?"

"I can drive myself."

"Oh. All right. You don't even need to call first. I'll be here."

Dr. Camden looked at the frightened dark-circled gray eyes that stared at her in proud defiance at eleven Tuesday morning. It was such a familiar look! This pale young woman was here because an instinct deeper than the layers of pain told her to *try*, but she didn't really believe it would help. She believed she would try, and that would cause more pain, and then she would fail.

"You're Emily Rousseau?"

"Yes. I think you know about me. Rob Adamson . . ."

"Rob didn't tell me your name or anything that would identify you."

"Oh, well . . . I read your books. Rob thought—I thought—maybe you could help me."

"I *can* help you, Emily. I can help you find the little girl in you that was joyous and happy and able to trust and love. I can find her with your help. It's hard work, very hard, but it's so worth it."

Dr. Camden looked at the tormented gray eyes and knew the fear she saw wasn't the fear of hard work. Emily's fear was that she would fail—even though others like her had succeeded; and it was fear that she really was unworthy, really somehow to blame for what had happened to her.

Dr. Camden smiled and added confidently, truthfully, "You're going to make it, Emily. I know you are."

Chapter Twenty-one

Allison arrived at Bellemeade at two-thirty Tuesday afternoon. The February sky had been pearl-gray when she left Elegance and gray-black an hour later when she emerged from her apartment dressed in the outfit she had selected last night after Peter called. Allison's carefully selected outfit was an ivory silk blouse, a tailored camel skirt, cocoa-brown suede pumps, and delicate gold earrings.

Understated elegance, Allison hoped, and sophisticated, like the women of New York Peter Dalton must know so well. Sophisticated, modern women who would dress elegantly and drive confidently to his home without bothering to call in advance.

Allison stared at the ominous gray-black clouds as she left her apartment and silently warned, *Don't you dare!* She should have bought an umbrella this morning on Rodeo, but that would have taken time, and the day was already moving in slow motion.

Just as Allison reached Bellemeade the sky opened. As she dashed from the driveway to the front door, Allison was drenched by the incredible cloudburst, a soggy omen that answered, Don't *you* dare pretend to be sophisticated when you really aren't!

Peter was just finishing in the kitchen, the dinner made, the oven timers set, when Allison arrived. He had planned to spend the afternoon in the living room, in front of a fire, watching for her to arrive, greeting her when she did. He had even bought an umbrella in case it was raining.

And now she was here, drenched.

"Hi. Allison, I'm sorry. I was in the kitchen. I didn't see you."

"I'm earlier than I thought I'd be. I don't even own an umbrella. I should have—" As Allison shook her head, raindrops splashed from her red-gold curls to her already-damp and cold cheeks. She fought an ice-cold shiver.

The shivering had started last night, in the warmth of her apartment, moments after Peter called. Her heart had begun to gallop and she had recalled the sudden, unexpected panic that had swept through her just before she rode again. On *that* summer morning Allison had calmed the panic with a mantra, *Trivial, trivial.*

If she panicked now, that mantra wouldn't work, because there was nothing trivial about the powerful feelings that swirled inside her because of Peter.

But she wasn't panicking. She was only shivering and awkward and so aware of her wet hair and face.

And his dark brown eyes.

"Here. Let me take your coat."

"Thank you." Allison somehow unbuttoned the squeaky wet buttons of her unlined Burberry raincoat and searched for something to say.

The obvious topic, other than the weather, was Bellemeade. But Allison couldn't rave about the elegant marble foyer, the Lalique chandelier, the Kentshire antique mirror—no point even looking that way!—or the wallpaper that felt like spring. Allison couldn't say a word about this lovely romantic place, because it was her creation. Allison had made it lovely for Peter, and for all the

296

other women he had brought here.

Say *something,* Allison told herself. And stop shivering. And don't even *think* about the fact that the ivory silk blouse is transparent from the rain, and the sexy romantic lace beneath is *much more* than a misty shadow. And beneath the lace, *completely revealed,* are your breasts, very cold, slightly shivering.

The handsome dark eyes have only to look.

"Where's Muffin?"

"She's asleep in the kitchen, on her designer pillow, recharging her batteries." Peter's eyes didn't leave Allison's, didn't drift at all. "Muffin's had a very busy day."

"Oh?"

"It started early this morning with a posh beauty parlor for dogs in Beverly Hills. Undoubtedly lots of fun. Then she had to be on the alert while I made the casserole, for obvious reasons."

"And she probably helped you put fresh roses in all the vases." From the marble foyer, Allison could see two Lalique vases, filled with beautiful roses artfully arranged by Peter.

"She did." Peter paused. This was silly. Allison was freezing and embarrassed and being a trouper and she really needed to get out of her clothes and into a hot bath. "Allison."

"Yes?"

"Let me get a towel for your hair." Peter disappeared into the powder room and returned with a plush pale pink towel chosen by Allison from the luxurious selections of Pratesi.

Peter didn't give Allison the towel. Instead, so gently, he towelled the sopping red-gold curls tangling her hair, *touching* her for the first time.

"Am I being too rough?"

"No." *No.* So gentle, so tender. Allison looked up at his

297

dark eyes, gentle, sensuous eyes, filled with desire. "Peter."

Allison lifted her face to him, inviting his lips, sending a rich message of desire and welcome.

"Allison."

Her skin was cool from the rain, but just beneath the surface she was warm and soft and alive with passion. Peter felt Allison respond, eager, excited, with a soft laugh of joy, and he felt his own strong, powerful waves of desire.

He wanted her so much! But was he crushing her with the desperate demands of his desire? The tighter Peter held Allison's damp, warm body against his, the deeper his lips explored her mouth, the closer she moved, opening even more to him. But was he hurting her? Was he pushing her too fast?

Peter pulled away. He needed to know what Allison wanted, to know *her* desire, *her* pace, not his. It felt as if Allison wanted him too; now, desperately, all of him, but were his senses consumed by his own passion?

Peter looked at Allison's eyes, a little startled because the kiss had suddenly stopped, and her cheeks, flushed and radiant, and the soft, confident smile on her full lips.

"Allison, I . . ."

"Yes?"

"I don't want to push you."

"Peter," Allison whispered bravely. "I'm the one who arrived with clothes that need to come off."

"They do need to come off, don't they?"

"Yes." *Yes to anything.* "Yours do, too."

Peter was wet from holding her so tightly against him. He smiled, then led her by the hand up the circular staircase that swept to the master suite with its canopied bed, spring meadow walls, and crystal vases blooming with roses.

Peter couldn't make love to her slowly—he wanted her too much—and Allison wanted him, too. She wanted to become part of him, to melt her fire with his, to become one.

"Peter," she whispered to his passionate dark eyes.

"Oh, Allison, I want you."

"I want you, too."

Allison laughed softly as Peter undressed her, peeling away the wet clinging silk and the delicate lace until she was naked in front of him.

"You are so beautiful, Allison."

Dan had told her that—and she had dismissed it with a light laugh—and Roger had told her, too. But now, as Peter whispered the words and caressed her with his appraising, appreciative eyes, Allison at last believed it was true.

I am beautiful for you, Peter. You make me beautiful.

As Peter's eyes drifted to the scars on her lower abdomen, Allison's hands didn't move to hide the ugliness. Her hands had moved the first time, with Dan, even though he knew all about the accident; and her hands would have moved, too, with Roger.

But Allison stood, naked, unashamed, in front of Peter, feeling his desire, feeling so beautiful.

Then they were in bed, touching, whispering, exploring, marvelling in the wonderful discoveries, breathless in their wonder and desire and *need.*

Peter needed to be inside her, and Allison needed him to be. Where he belonged, where she belonged. Fire with fire, closer, hotter, deeper . . . *together.*

"I used to ride all the time." Allison spoke softly as she lay, safe and warm, in the gentle strength of Peter's arms.

Her soft words were the first words spoken since the breathless whispers of their passion. "I had an accident during a show jumping event three and a half years ago. I broke my pelvis. The doctors operated a few times and the bones finally knit, although they're a little uneven. That's why I have the scars. That's why I have a limp."

"Does it hurt?"

"Yes, sometimes, when I overdo."

"Does it hurt when we make love?"

When we make love. Allison felt a rush of joy at Peter's words. They had just made love once, but Peter's question promised other times, many, many other times.

"No." *It will never hurt when we make love.*

"Does it mean you can't have children, Allison?" Peter asked gently after several silent moments.

"No, Peter. I can have children." Allison turned to reassure the gentle, dark eyes. But when her eyes found Peter's Allison wondered if she saw more worry than relief. "Peter . . ."

The bedside phone rang. It sounded with a muted romantic ring, a ring chosen by Allison because, she had decided, important imported talent, like Peter, should have only soft intrusions on their lives. The phone rang softly, but it was an intrusion nonetheless.

As Peter turned away from her to answer it, Allison moved away, too, to get out of the bed. She would wrap herself in a luxurious bath blanket — she knew where they were — and wander downstairs to give Peter privacy.

Peter caught her wrist. "Allison, don't leave."

"Oh. OK." Allison stopped but remained where she was, at the far edge of the bed, distant from him.

"Hello?" Peter answered.

"Hi, Peter. It's Winter."

"Hi, Winter. How are you feeling?"

"Definitely better, but if I could have one more day?"

Winter's nausea wasn't any less, but she was learning to handle it, to *act* through it. She had spent most of today, when she wasn't sleeping, practicing looking well in front of the mirror, training the waves of nausea not to leave ripples of discomfort in her violet eyes. Winter was getting better at concealing the symptom, but it took great effort. By tomorrow night she would have it mastered—for the movie and for Mark.

Winter *had* to learn to hide it from Mark. It would take no time for the top senior medical student at UCLA to correctly diagnose persistent nausea in a "woman of childbearing age."

"Of course you can. I'll call Steve."

"I already have. He says OK, too."

"Are you resting?"

"Yes! I'm doing all the right things."

"Let me know tomorrow how it looks for Thursday."

"I'm sure I'll be fine, but I'll call you."

As soon as Peter replaced the receiver, he turned to Allison and asked, "Why did you start to leave?"

"To give you privacy."

"Who did you think would be calling?"

Allison shrugged, embarrassed, except, *except* handsome, passionate Peter Dalton hadn't just arrived on the planet. Peter was nine years older than Allison, nine years more experienced. Allison wasn't the first woman in Peter's bed. Perhaps she wasn't even the first woman in Peter's bed this week.

"A girlfriend. A lover."

Peter's dark eyes narrowed slightly, amazed, concerned, a little sad. He couldn't believe Allison did this—breathless, intimate, joyous loving—every day, so why would she imagine he did? Didn't Allison know? Couldn't she *tell?*

Peter moved to her, to the far edge of the bed and

301

gently held her face in his hands.

"There isn't anyone, Allison. There isn't anyone but you."

"Oh," she breathed softly.

"Why are you frowning? Does that worry you?"

"No." *No, it's what I want.*

"You're still frowning. Tell me."

"I was just thinking," Allison whispered. "What if Winter hadn't gotten sick?"

"I didn't just happen by Elegance because I suddenly had a free afternoon, Allison."

"You didn't?"

"No. I'd been thinking about you."

"But you left."

"I was just about to turn around when you appeared on Wilshire."

"Really?"

"Really. I was going to ask you if I stood a chance against the sender of red roses."

"I'd been thinking about you, too. I almost bought Muffin a dog toy for Valentine's Day."

Peter smiled and kissed Allison's soft lips.

"I bet Muffin's batteries are recharged by now," Allison whispered seductively between kisses.

"Just Muffin's batteries?"

"Mine, too."

"Allison?"

"Yes?"

"The sender of red roses . . ."

They had been talking between kisses, lips brushing and nibbling as they spoke, but now Allison pulled away and looked thoughtfully at his eyes.

"There isn't anyone but you, Peter." *There never has been.*

* * *

It was seven by the time Peter and Allison left the canopied bed and went to the kitchen, lured by the wine-scented casserole and thoughts of the stranded Muffin. Allison wore Peter's blue terry cloth robe, bulky, cozy, pulled tight around her slender waist, and a pair of his thick woolen socks.

Muffin bounded toward Peter when he opened the kitchen door, then stopped when she saw Allison. Her head tilted and she gazed up at Allison with half-curious, half-diffident brown eyes. Muffin's expression was apprehensive, but her small blond body wiggled with excitement.

Allison laughed softly and leaned over to talk to her. "Hello, Muffin. This is pretty scary, isn't it? I don't blame you. I *do* look frightful. And you are so beautiful, all clean and shiny."

Muffin liked Allison's soft voice and bravely edged forward to Allison's extended hands. Finally, Allison touched the clean, soft fur and there was even more wiggling.

"See? This isn't so bad after all." Allison turned to Peter. "She really is pretty."

"You really are pretty," Peter whispered as he kissed Allison's tangled hair.

Peter patted Muffin, then opened the kitchen door to let her go for a run in the now-crisp, rain-free evening air. He wrapped his arms around Allison while they watched the golden fluff galloping in the yard.

"What are your plans for tomorrow?"

"To work very hard in the office until noon, and then go to my apartment and wait for you to come pick me up. So much for sophistication."

"Was that what that was all about?"

"A modern career woman ought to be able to get herself to a man's home—especially if he's modern enough to be making dinner—without drowning in raindrops,

303

shouldn't she?"

"I guess." Peter laughed. "But let's try it the other way tomorrow. I'm really pretty old-fashioned."

"So am I."

Peter picked Allison up at her apartment the following afternoon and returned her there at dawn the next day on his way to the studio.

After that, it wasn't a question of fashion—old or new—simply one of practicality. If Allison had her car in the garage at Bellemeade, she and Peter could stay in bed a little longer in the morning. They could have a cup of coffee together and kiss a leisurely good-bye. After Peter left, just as the sun was beginning to lighten the eastern sky, Allison could have a second cup of coffee and spend "quality" time with the playful cocker spaniel before getting ready for work.

It was better for Allison to have her own car at Belle-meade for *them,* for their new, wonderful, passionate love; and Bellemeade was also closer to Allison's work. The Chateau Bel Air was only a mile away, and she had two other projects in Bel Air—an estate on Sienna Way and a gatehouse on Stone Canyon Road.

Peter and Allison lived at Bellemeade in a private world of romance and passion and love. Each ventured, alone, into the world beyond Bellemeade, to their successful busy careers, and for the first three weeks they never made that journey together. Allison had dinner with her parents while Peter was viewing the "dailies" with Steve in Burbank, and although Sean and Patricia guessed that a wonderful love had happened in their daughter's life, they assumed it was Roger and waited patiently for Allison to tell them. Allison spoke to Winter on the phone, heard her friend's fond words about Peter,

304

but still didn't tell Winter about *them*.

Peter and Allison's first trip outside Bellemeade, together, was for a trail ride at the Club. The winter rainstorm had long since vanished, but the sky still sparkled clear and bright and freshly washed. As Peter and Allison rode along the Kensington Trail, they were serenaded by a thousand singing birds, gently caressed by a balmy breeze, and enveloped by the fragrances of a just-born spring.

Allison and Peter rode through the lush fragrant paradise for almost three hours. When they returned to the paddock area, the outdoor ring, which had been empty earlier, was filled with colorful, treacherous jumps. Allison stared solemnly at the jumps as they rode past. After they returned their mounts to the stable, she led Peter back to the ring.

Peter watched Allison's eyes as she stared at the jump with the green and white rails. Thoughtful eyes, solemn eyes, determined eyes.

Allison had never told anyone — she didn't dare — but *she* had known for a very long time.

"Someday, I am going to fly over that jump," Allison vowed quietly. As she turned to Peter — the man she loved, the man who made her believe that anything was possible — her eyes sparkled. "Will you be here when I conquer it, Peter? Will you watch me?"

Peter's response was swift and cold

"No."

"No?" Allison echoed weakly.

"No." *I will not watch you die.*

Allison saw the once-familiar, now-almost-forgotten sadness in Peter's eyes. For the past few weeks — their wonderful weeks of love — the dark sadness had almost disappeared. For the past few weeks, there had been great happiness in his eyes . . . almost always. Great happiness . . . and such love, such passion, such desire. There were times, flickering quiet moments, when Allison still saw the sadness, but mostly, Peter's dark eyes told her of his joy.

Mostly, Allison could make Peter happy.

And now her words caused him sadness. *Why?*

Peter and Allison walked in silence to the car and drove in silence to Bellemeade.

"I'm sorry," Peter whispered finally. "But it would be dangerous for you to jump again, wouldn't it?"

Allison had only mentioned her accident once, after she and Peter had first made love. It had been a brief explanation of her scars and her limp, nothing that would make Peter know how dangerous her plan to jump again really was.

"Have you been talking to Winter about me, Peter?"

"No, I haven't told Winter about us at all."

"About us," Allison echoed softly, distracted from the topic of her riding by the gentle way Peter spoke those words.

"Have you told her?"

"No, Peter. I wouldn't know what to say."

"You wouldn't?" *Didn't she know?*

"No."

"I'll give you the line, then." Peter smiled lovingly. "You would say, with feeling, 'Winter, Peter Dalton is very much in love with me.' "

"No, master playwright, I would say, honestly, joyfully, " 'Winter, I am very much in love with Peter Dalton.' "

"I love you, Allison."

"Oh, Peter, I love you."

"How did you know it would be dangerous for me to jump again?" Allison asked two hours later as they lay in

306

bed.

"Your eyes." *How dangerous and how important.*

"Oh." Allison curled up closer to him, remembering *his eyes*, wishing she could tell him she didn't mean it, that it wasn't important to her to conquer that jump. Perhaps Allison could tell Peter that someday. She had to think about it; she would think about it. But, for now, she wanted to shift to a more certain topic. "Did I ever tell you that Winter thinks you're wonderful?"

"No. Does she?" Peter was pleased. "I think Winter's wonderful, too. I assume she has someone."

"Why?" Allison teased. "Are you interested?"

"No!" Peter kissed her. "I just get the impression there is someone important in her life."

"There is. His name is Mark."

Allison told Peter about Mark and Winter.

"I think I won't tell Winter about us," Allison's voice softened lovingly, "until after *Love* is over."

"Which should be Thursday. If you told Winter before then, what would happen?"

"Who knows? She might stop the filming, demand a 'cut and take three hours,' and quiz you about your intentions." Allison smiled, imagining a lively Winter doing that. Her smile faded with more recent memories—over the phone impressions—of her best friend. Winter sounded worried. Allison added thoughtfully, "This is a very important week for Winter. In addition to *Love* wrapping, Mark finds out about his residency."

"Will that be a problem?"

"He'll probably be going to Boston."

"And Winter won't be going with him?"

"I don't know," Allison whispered softly, thinking about Mark and Winter *and* thinking about the other relationship that was about to be separated by a continent. Very soon, Peter would be returning to New York.

"Would *you* like to know my intentions?" Peter asked gently.

"Yes."

"I intend to come back here next November to make a movie of *Merry Go Round*. In the meantime, I intend to see you as much as I possibly can and to talk to you at least once every day." Peter sighed and added apologetically, "Shakespeare on Broadway is going to take a lot of time. We'll probably have to rehearse on Saturdays, which means there would be weekends — many weekends — when I couldn't come here. You could come to New York — any time, all the time. Allison? You have a say in this."

"I say yes." *I love you.*

Chapter Twenty-two

The dean of students at UCLA School of Medicine distributed the results of the residency match to the senior medical students at nine A.M. Wednesday morning. Mark took his unopened envelope, left the auditorium of the Health Sciences Building, and walked outside into the bright March sun. His agile fingers felt clumsy as they pried open the sealed flap, but then there it was: *Internal Medicine - Massachusetts General Hospital - Harvard Affiliated Programs.*

There it was, what he wanted, what he had wanted for four years, a dream come true.

But what about his other dream?

Winter wasn't even a dream. Mark had never dreamed about being so much in love. He had never believed he would need someone as much as he needed her, still, more, *more* every day.

For the past two days, *Love* had been filming on location at UCLA. As she had kissed Mark good-bye and good luck this morning, Winter had told him to come find her — a five-minute walk from the medical school — as soon as he knew his residency results. But Mark had seen the slight worry on her face when she had suggested it — as if he had suggested that she interrupt professor's rounds at the hospital — so he had told her he would arrive in

309

time for the lunch break.

That gave Mark almost three hours, three more restless hours, in which he would ask himself again — as he had for months — if it was simply too selfish to ask Winter to come with him to Boston.

He had so little to offer her. *Just all his love and all his heart.* But Winter would see his love — see *him* — rarely; and he would be tired and distracted, as he had been at Christmas; and the joy would be mostly his — the warm memories of her sustaining him in the long hours in the hospital and the happiness of being with her in the precious moments when he was home.

But what was there for Winter in Boston? Long days and nights, patiently waiting for the rare moments, away from *her* dream — *I want movies, Mark, not theater* — in Hollywood.

Mark believed if he asked Winter to come with him, to marry him, she would say yes. He lay awake at night, holding her in his arms, thinking about the outcomes.

Yes, Mark, I will marry you. Mark's mind could stretch those words into a lifetime of happiness, a lifetime of sparkling violet and joyous laughter and gentle whispers and loving passion. Mark's wonderful visions magically bypassed the years of fatigue and disappointment and apologies. The visions weren't real, simply lovely images of his mind.

Fantasy. Cinderella *before* the stroke of midnight.

The *reality* was, at best, a constant struggle against disappointment; and, at worst, a disaster laced with bitterness, anger, and resentment. Mark and Winter could both try, could both want desperately to make it work, but still it could fail.

Mark was to meet Winter at noon. She wouldn't be looking for him until then. She wouldn't know Mark was one of the many spectators gathered near Pauley Pavilion to watch the filming of the next to last scene of *Love.*

Mark stood in the middle of the crowd. At first he was careful not to stare at her, afraid that his loving gaze might draw her attention. But Winter was totally absorbed in her work, patiently doing the scene over and over, smiling softly as she quietly discussed each take with the dark, handsome man who Mark assumed must be Peter. Winter looked so serious and so *happy*.

On a snowy Christmas Eve, Winter had watched Mark in the Emergency Ward at Massachusetts General Hospital and had realized that he was where he belonged, doing what he was destined to do, happy with his dream. And now, on this sunny day in California, Mark saw Winter living her dream, *loving* it.

And Mark knew what he had to do, just as Winter had known in Boston.

I have to leave her. Mark contrasted the scene he watched now — Winter, the actress, so happy — with a future scene he could imagine — Winter, his wife, alone in their apartment, waiting, fighting disappointment, *withering*.

The greatest loss was his, Mark had told Winter last summer about the father who had lost the great joy of knowing his lovely daughter. *The greatest loss will be mine, Winter,* Mark thought now.

Mark knew that lovely, loving Winter would find other loves, other happiness, other joy.

Mark wasn't sure that he ever would.

Love never broke for lunch because the day's filming was finished by one. Mark waited while Winter changed. Then they walked, hand in hand, across campus to the Sculpture Garden.

They sat on the same sunny patch of grass where the magic had begun nine months before.

Ask me to go with you, Mark. Trust me, trust us, trust our love.

311

I love you so much, Winter. Too much not to let you go.

"Winter," Mark began gently. "Next year, the next *two* years, will be like those days at Christmas."

"Snowy," she whispered hopefully. "Full of Christmas cookies and the ever-present threat of salmonella."

Mark smiled lovingly. *Marry me, Winter Carlyle.*

Winter's heart leapt as she saw the look in Mark's eyes. *You do love me, don't you, Mark? You do want me and our baby!*

Mark fought the powerful emotion that urged him to ask her to marry him with vivid images of Winter, trapped, lonely, not acting, waiting for him.

"It won't work, Winter."

Mark's eyes hardened as he spoke and his voice was harsh. Winter marvelled for a horrible stunned moment at what an actor *he* was. That loving look, so convincing for so long, but all an act.

"I know, Mark," Winter heard herself say. *She* could act, too. Her voice could be calm, even light and breezy, as if she didn't care at all! Mark wouldn't have the slightest clue her heart was breaking. She could give the performance of her life while her anguished heart cried, *He doesn't want you! Did you really believe that he would?*

Mark expected Winter to protest. If she had, could he have resisted? He would have tried—for *her*—but he might have told the suddenly hurt violet eyes the selfish truth: *I love you. I want you. Will you try with me?*

But Winter's lovely eyes weren't hurt, and now she was standing up, about to leave.

"I think it would be best if you moved your things out of my apartment today, Mark. I'll go to the mansion for a while to give you time. Good-bye."

Mark watched in stunned silence as Winter turned and walked away.

He *almost* ran after her. But what was the point? If she was being brave, as he was, because it was the *right* decision and they both knew it, then why spend long, tearful

312

hours saying good-bye? And if she wasn't being brave, if she would have told him "No, I won't marry you, Mark," then so be it.

Perhaps Winter would have said no. In the seven weeks since Mark's return from Boston, their life had been so different than it had been last summer and fall. They were both so busy, and the rested moments together were vanishingly rare. Winter had seemed distant and preoccupied, but Mark had assumed logically that it was the emotional and physical strain of *Love,* and the added strain of her illness in February.

But maybe Winter had decided their love was over and had been only waiting to tell him until he found out about his residency at MGH, until he had a new dream to replace the lost one.

Mark sighed. It was over. It had to be. If it was what Winter really wanted, if it didn't cause her sadness, then that was even better.

Mark watched Winter disappear, vanishing as she had that magical evening last June. As he watched, her fading image became blurred by his tears, and he whispered, "Good-bye, my precious Cinderella."

Winter gave the second best performance of her life the following morning on the beach at Malibu, as they filmed *Love*'s final scene.

"I will love you always," Winter whispered, her violet eyes glistening with a promise of forever. Winter whispered the words over and over, her own heart screaming with pain, as she played Julia, whose heart overflowed with love and joy.

Finally, thankfully, Peter turned to Steve with a smile, "What is that movie expression, Steve? That's a wrap?"

"That's a wonderful wrap," Steve embellished. "Thank you all. Don't forget the party tonight at my house. We begin at six."

Winter didn't move. She sat on the sun-bleached piece of driftwood and gazed at the sea. The swirl of activity around her, the cast and crew preparing to leave, crescendoed, then faded.

Then Winter was alone.

No, Peter was there, sitting beside her as he had done so often in the past ten weeks. And, like all those other times, Peter seemed to be waiting patiently for her to speak.

But there was no scene to discuss. *Love* was over . . . wrapped . . . wonderful.

Finally, Winter turned to him, her eyes spilling tears she couldn't stop and revealing emotions she could no longer hide—pain, sadness, *anger*.

"She—I, Julia—should have died in the end, Peter. Or Sam should have left her. You may have won Tonys and the Pulitzer Prize for your brilliant, insightful writing, but you were *way off* with *Love*. Happy endings are Hollywood, not real life, Peter, don't you know that?"

"I know that, Winter."

Winter saw the sudden pain in his dark eyes. What was she doing lashing out at Peter? She admired Peter. They had worked so well together and he had so gently helped her make wonderful discoveries about her own talent.

She and Peter had had a wonderful professional relationship.

And now it was suddenly personal. And Winter was too raw, too emotional to speak. She needed to get away, to be alone.

"I'm sorry, Peter."

"Let's take a walk."

"No, Peter."

Peter stood, took her hand, and pulled gently, willing her to come with him. His hand was warm and strong, and his eyes were kind and sympathetic, and she had no resistance.

They walked for ten minutes in a silence broken only by the plaintive cries of seagulls overhead and the soft whispers of the sea.

"Something happened with Mark," Peter said finally.

"How do you know about Mark?"

"Allison told me."

Winter heard the softness in Peter's voice when he spoke Allison's name and the expression of love on his handsome face.

"You and Allison?"

"Yes. She was going to tell you tonight at the party."

"And I was planning to skip the party and see if Allison was free. I guess she won't be."

"I think we should all make a brief appearance, together, then if you want to see Allison by yourself . . ."

"I really don't have anything earth-shattering to tell her. Mark's going to Boston by himself and I'm going to stay here to pursue my brilliant career." Winter gave a weak smile. "Very eighties. Love takes a backseat to career."

"That's it?"

"That's it." Winter added softly, "Except my heart is broken. I guess it's your fault. Doing this movie actually had me convinced that it would all end happily, that life would imitate art, but it didn't."

They walked in silence for five minutes, then Peter asked, very quietly, very gently, "Winter, what about the baby?"

"The baby?" How did Peter know? No one else in the entire world knew. Winter hadn't even seen a doctor yet! She had gained a little weight but her sleek body concealed it well, especially in clothes, and even Mark hadn't noticed. Mark would have noticed in another week or two, but not yet. "What do you mean?"

"Aren't you pregnant?"

"How do you know?"

315

I know because you have a glow, a lovely womanliness, a radiance. I know because I saw those changes in Sara long before she told me, only then I had no idea what they meant.

"Pink cheeks, a higher wattage bulb backlighting your eyes, *green* skin a month ago," Peter murmured lightly. He added gently, "Fresh tears in your eyes now. Are you OK?"

"No," Winter admitted with a trembling smile. "But I will be—*we* will be. I just need a little time. Everything is so new right now. Peter, Mark can never know about the baby."

"Is that fair?"

"*Yes.* And please don't tell Allison."

"Do you think Allison would tell Mark?"

"No, of course not. But you know Allison. She would try to make it right. Allison believes in happy endings. Allison would try to convince me to tell Mark, and right now I am too susceptible to that suggestion."

"Maybe it's the right suggestion."

"No, Peter, it's not. Please. I just need a little time. Allison can't know, not yet."

Peter was already troubled by the secrets—*his* secrets—that he kept from Allison. Peter knew he had to tell Allison about Sara and he *would*, but it was still too soon. Their love was so new, so joyous. And Peter knew the tragic story of Sara would fill Allison's lovely jade eyes with tears and her generous loving heart with sadness. Peter hated keeping secrets—his own and now Winter's—from Allison.

"You *will* tell Allison, though, won't you, Winter?"

"Peter, I will have to tell her."

"Have a wonderful flight, Muffin," Allison whispered to the wiggling blond fur in the travel kennel at the airport. "See you late Friday night."

316

Allison stood up as the baggage handler carefully loaded Muffin's kennel onto a cart. She turned to Peter with tears in her eyes. Peter had stayed with her until the very last minute. In the morning, in New York, he would begin rehearsals of *Hamlet*.

It was Sunday afternoon and she would see him Friday night, but still it felt like a forever good-bye.

It *was* a forever good-bye to their private life of love in the romantic sanctuary of Bellemeade.

Allison and Peter's new life promised hours in airports and airplanes and taxis, and late night telephone calls with whispers of longing transmitted three thousand miles, and rare moments when they were together, trying to *love* a week's worth of loneliness into thirty-six precious hours. Allison tried to convince herself that their transcontinental love affair was glamorous and romantic—it was certainly sophisticated and modern—but she spent more time convincing herself *not* to quit her job and go with Peter *now*.

"Allison." Peter's dark eyes glistened, too. He didn't want to leave her, even for five days. Saying good-bye terrified him. He even thought of turning Shakespeare on Broadway over to someone else. But it was *his* incredible project, and he had cancelled his part in a production once before, to be with Sara, until . . . His life with Allison would last forever, Peter told himself. His fear was an ancient emotion, nothing to do with Allison, "This is going to be an adventure."

"It is?" Allison teased, but it helped her tears. "In what way?"

"I don't know. I was just trying to think of something redeeming about it."

"How about being incredibly productive because of unfulfilled passion?"

"I guess I will start writing again."

"Peter, you're going to New York to direct Shakespeare's greatest plays—in record time, with the most distin-

317

guished cast ever assembled. When are you planning to write?"

"At night, after I call you." *When I am awakened by nightmares,* Peter thought. But maybe the nightmares wouldn't return. With Allison in his arms, the nightmares had been driven away. Maybe with Allison in his heart, in his dreams, they would stay away still. "After I call you from my very small, very undecorated apartment."

"You don't have framed posters of your Broadway smashes hung on the walls, or the odd Tony casually displayed on a coffee table?"

"No." Peter frowned as he thought about his dark, barren, austere apartment. He wouldn't even have time, before Friday, to make it better. "Allison, it's really very minimal. I moved there because it was a close walk to the theater district, so I could go home during breaks to take care of Muffin. And it's very quiet for writing, but—"

"Peter! It doesn't matter." After a moment, she added, "It doesn't matter, but if you want me to, I can decorate it for you."

"You *will* decorate it by being there."

"Thank you," she whispered. "I *should* spend some time in the design stores and auction houses in Manhattan, anyway. Without a project, I might just spend every moment with you at your rehearsals."

"That would be fine with me."

"Peter, do you need both hands to direct?"

"What?" Peter laughed softly at the teasing sparkle in her eyes.

"If I could just have one hand, to hold, I would be very happy and very quiet."

Winter bought the copy of *Portrait* magazine's Academy Award issue in late March, but she didn't read it until the middle of April. Between the end of *Love* and the middle of April, Winter had been frantically busy, racing against a not-very-imaginary clock, fighting loneliness and the familiar pain of being left by someone she loved.

Think about your baby, Winter Carlyle, not about yourself.

Thoughts of her baby were wonderful antidotes for Winter's loneliness. She *wasn't* alone, and each day the new little life became more a part of her, a happy, joyful, hopeful part.

So happy, so joyful, that Winter decided it would be safe to read the *Portrait* article about Lawrence Carlyle. Winter studied the photograph first. Lawrence's face was shadowed by a safari hat, protection against the glaring equatorial sun, and he looked as if he had been typecast to play the role of an important director; a king surveying his kingdom. The portrait of Lawrence Carlyle revealed *nothing* of who he was. Emily Rousseau would not have taken such a portrait.

The accompanying article revealed little, too, nothing Winter didn't already know. The article revealed little, but it *concealed* one essential fact. It was a portrait of Winter's father *and she wasn't in it*. There was passing reference to Lawrence's "brief, tumultuous marriage to Jacqueline Winter," but no mention of the "love-child." Winter was an omission. She didn't exist!

Winter imagined a portrait of Dr. Mark Stephens — Chairman of the Department of Internal Medicine at Harvard — twenty years from now. There might be a passing reference to Mark's days at UCLA Medical School — "a charming playboy who nevertheless made top grades and never lost sight of his goals" — but no mention of Winter Carlyle or of their "love-child."

But that was because Mark would never know about his child, not because, like Lawrence, he would pretend his child didn't exist.

Winter closed the copy of *Portrait*. It was a mistake to have read the article, a mistake to have learned that, in

319

the eyes of the great Lawrence Carlyle, *she* had never been born.

A mistake.

You're not a mistake, little one, Winter spoke silently to her unborn baby. I am so excited about you, so proud of you, so eager to get to know you better.

Winter *had* to conceal her baby's existence from Mark, but it was time to share the wonderful joy with her best friend.

"Did you have a nice weekend?" Winter asked when Allison answered her phone moments later. It was Monday night. Allison had just returned from her third weekend in New York.

"Very." *Nice, too short, I miss him already.* "Winter, how are you?"

"Allison, I need your help."

Good. At last. Allison hadn't even *seen* Winter for three weeks. Allison had tried, but Winter had said she was "too busy" and "right in the midst of something" each time. Winter didn't *sound* terrible over the phone and she never mentioned Mark, but she was a very talented actress.

"Anything, Winter," Allison answered quietly. Something in Winter's tone made Allison's thoughts drift to last summer, to the day she had ridden again for the first time. *I need you on my side, Winter,* Allison had told her best friend. And Winter had replied swiftly, *I am on your side, Allison, always.* "Anything."

"Could you come by tomorrow? I'm living at the mansion in Bel Air."

"The mansion? Since when?" *Why?*

"For the past two weeks. I was able to keep the same phone number I had at my apartment." *In case Mark calls.*

"I thought you were planning to sell the mansion, Winter," Allison said gently. *Why do you want to live in a place where the memories are so unhappy? Won't you feel lonely and isolated living there?*

"I was planning to, but for now I've decided to live here. So, can you come by tomorrow? Any time is fine."

"How about early?" *How about now?* "Like on my way to work? Seven-thirty? Eight?"

"Sure. Seven-thirty is fine."

Allison did a double take when she saw Winter's outfit. It was seven-thirty in the morning but Winter looked wide awake; and, Allison realized on closer inspection, it wasn't a bathrobe, anyway. Winter was wearing a silk caftan, elegant, expensive, and quite appropriate for lounging around a mansion in Bel Air, but definitely *not* her style. Winter's clothes always clung to her sleek body, accenting her flawless figure, sending provocative messages of beauty and grace. The silk caftan sent different messages—that it was concealing extra weight, that Winter didn't care.

Allison looked at her friend's face, at the slightly fuller cheeks beneath the beautiful violet eyes. Was Winter miserable and eating? Was she hiding her pain behind the walls of the mansion and her new extra pounds under layers of expensive silk?

"Allison, you're staring at me!"

"I'm sorry. I just . . . what can I do to help you?"

"Follow me."

Winter led the way across the living room, beyond the closed door of the screening room, to the unused wing of the mansion.

"I didn't even realize this was here," Allison said. In high school, on the rare occasions when they had spent time in Winter's eerily silent home instead of Allison's warm, cheery one, Allison and Winter were in the other wing, in the kitchen, by the pool, or in Winter's room.

"As you can see, this wing has been ignored for years, but I think it has potential, don't you? I couldn't see any hope for Bellemeade and look what you did, but even *I* can see new life for these rooms."

"You want me to redecorate for you?" Allison asked, amazed, disappointed. *That's the kind of help you meant, Winter? Professional? What about the emotional help of your best friend?*

"Yes. Allison, I know you're booked until about the year two thousand. I want the whole wing redone sometime, when you have time, but there are two rooms . . . if you could do them soon?"

"Of course." Allison was being *incredibly productive* during the days and nights away from Peter. And she would do whatever she could to help Winter.

"Here." Winter walked into the room with the French doors that opened onto the terrace with the pond of koi. It was the room that would have been hers in a different childhood, a happy childhood with brothers and sisters and love.

"This is lovely." Allison gazed appreciatively at the high ceilings and carved wood moldings and wall of windows.

"This will be my bedroom. I guess I'd like something flowery and cheerful. And I'll need a bed and dresser."

"OK. That's easy. We'll go over samples together." Allison walked toward a doorway, obviously very recently created, that connected the inner wall of Winter's bedroom to another room. "This is the other room?"

"Yes." Winter followed Allison into the smaller but still spacious room.

"What did you want here? Will it be your study?"

"He really hasn't told you, has he?"

"Who? Told me what?"

"Peter."

"Peter?" Worry pulsed through her. Allison knew Peter

had secrets. He had told her *nothing* of his life before he met her, but Allison knew there had been great sadness. She had seen the sadness in his eyes, almost vanquished now by their joyous love, and she had read his tormented plays. She assumed the secret sadnesses of Peter's life belonged to an unhappy, perhaps tragic childhood. Allison hoped that someday Peter would tell her his secrets. She believed, *trusted* that he would.

And now Peter and Winter had a secret, shared by them, *kept* from her!

"This will be the baby's room," Winter said quietly.

"The baby?"

"She's — I think she's a she — due in September. I won't need furniture in here right away because I found my cradle."

Winter had been wandering in the mansion, exploring long-forgotten rooms, and had found her own cradle in a storage room. And in boxes nearby, Winter had found her baby clothes. Why had Jacqueline saved the cradle and carefully folded the tiny clothes? Was it loving sentiment? Or was it merely the same compulsion that had made Jacqueline save and carefully catalogue the magnificent jewels from all her lovers?

"Mark's baby," Allison whispered. *Peter's baby?*

"Yes. Mark's baby," Winter said softly. "Allison, Mark doesn't know. I don't want him ever to know. When I need to, I will tell everyone, including her, that her daddy died."

"Winter . . ."

"Allison! Can't *I* be allowed to make unchallenged decisions, or does that only apply to *you?*"

"What?" Allison was stunned by the emotion — *anger?* — in Winter's voice.

"Sorry." Winter's eyes filled with tears. "I'm still very raw and there are rogue hormones swimming around in my bloodstream making things even harder."

Allison walked to Winter and gave her a hug. *I'm on your side, Winter, always.*

"Let's go down to the kitchen, have some tea or whatever's good for moms-to-be, and talk, OK?"

"OK. My moms-to-be books say tea, in moderation, is all right."

Allison watched as Winter put a kettle on the stove in the kitchen and took two Limoges teacups from a cupboard.

"What did you mean, Winter, about me being the only one allowed to make unchallenged decisions?"

"I meant that a year ago, when you decided not to marry Dan and to work for Claire and to ride again, you simply made the announcements. You didn't ask for help, even from the people who love you."

"Oh." Allison frowned. Winter was right, of course. Allison hadn't talked to Dan as she made the momentous decision about *their* marriage. And she hadn't talked to Winter, Patricia, or Sean—the people who were with her, loving her, helping her survive after the accident—about her decision to ride again. Was that selfish? What if Allison had asked their advice and they had said no? Now there was another momentous decision—to jump the green and white railed jump—and she had shared it with Peter, and he had said no. Jumping the jump was something Allison needed, for *herself*, but was her need more important than erasing the worry from the eyes of the man she loved?

"Allison, I didn't mean to hurt your feelings," Winter whispered softly, apologizing for her earlier harshness. She added, smiling, and without resentment, "Besides, so far your momentous decisions have been pure gold."

"And yours isn't?"

"My decision to keep her is," Winter answered quietly. *That* hadn't even been a decision. Winter felt as if she had been given a precious little gift to love, a precious little

324

gift *of* love.

"Winter, what horrible thing would happen if you told Mark?"

"He would marry me."

"And that's horrible?"

"Allison," Winter's voice faltered and new tears dampened her eyes, "Mark didn't want me."

"I just can't believe that."

"It's what happened." Winter gave a wobbly smile. "So, here I am, in this mansion for the duration. You've heard of confinement?"

"You're not going out at all?"

"Only to see my doctor at Cedars, for which I will wear a large straw hat and a blond wig. As soon as the prerelease ads for *Love* start appearing, I will be recognized. Maybe it doesn't matter. By then Mark will be in Boston, completely involved in his residency, but I just can't take the risk of him finding out."

"What about food? Clothes?"

"I've spent the past few weeks — I've only just gotten really pregnant-looking — stocking up. I have canned goods and frozen food, all very healthy stuff, to last until about Christmas. I bought a few maternity dresses, which you and Peter will get to see. Nothing very glamorous."

Allison frowned at the mention of Peter's name.

"Why did you tell Peter, Winter, and not tell me?"

"I didn't tell him, Allison. He *guessed*. I have no idea how he knew. It was a month ago, the day we finished *Love*. You saw me that night. Did you think I looked pregnant?"

"No." Allison remembered that night very clearly. She had watched Winter closely, worrying about her. Winter had looked sad, exhausted, devastated, but not *pregnant*. "What did Peter say?"

"Something poetic about the color of my cheeks. I'm sorry I asked him to keep it from you, Allison. It wasn't fair to either of you. I just needed a little time. So now you both know and no one else needs to."

"Except my mother."

"No, Allison."

"She has to know, Winter, because I am not going off to New York every weekend unless I know you have someone to call if you need anything."

"I won't need anything."

"And there may be times that I can't be here to answer the door for the wallpaperers and painters and furniture deliveries."

"I was just planning to leave the front door unlocked. Allison, you don't have to be here."

"I *want* to be. And I want Mother to be able to be, too. She loves you, Winter. She's not going to be judgmental." Allison smiled. "She's an expert at not challenging momentous decisions. And she's getting very good at keeping secrets."

"Such as?"

"Me and Peter." Allison had told Sean and Patricia, finally, about Peter. Before Peter returned to New York, Sean and Patricia met and *liked* the man who had brought such great joy to their precious daughter.

"You and Peter are a secret?"

"Not *really*. It's just that we have so little time together that we're trying to keep it private. Mother hasn't told anyone, including Vanessa."

"Vanessa wouldn't print anything about you that you didn't want her to. With anyone else in this town, she wouldn't hesitate, but she cares about you."

"I'm sure you're right. But Vanessa's such a fan of Peter's work. She would think it was wonderful that Peter and I are together."

"It is wonderful."

"Yes." Allison smiled.

"Too wonderful to share."

"Except with you and my parents." Allison paused, then added, "And Emily knows. She just did five photographs — her best work ever — for Peter's apartment in New York."

"How is Emily?"

"Winter," Allison looked meaningfully at her friend. They had already strayed from the important topic and now Winter was meandering off on another path. "May I tell Mother, please?"

Winter hesitated a moment, then, with a grateful smile, whispered, "Yes."

"Good. And can she and I come over, like every day, with fresh fruit?"

"Yes," Winter answered softly. "Allison, thank you."

"Don't mention it! Now, would you like to hear about Emily? I don't really know very much. I'm not sure what work she's doing, if any, other than photographs for me. She's definitely moving to Paris in June."

"You still think something happened between Emily and Rob?"

"Something must have, although I have no idea what."

"Have you seen him?"

"No," Allison answered thoughtfully. She hadn't even seen Rob from a distance, not even a friendly wave in a check-out line at the grocery. She hadn't seen Rob, Allison realized, since that snowy weekend in Aspen. Since then, Allison and Peter had been living in their private world of love.

"Things change, don't they?" Winter asked, as if reading Allison's thoughts. "The other day, I was thinking about the Diet Pepsi toasts we made last fall at the Acapulco. Except for your success with Bellemeade, it didn't quite work out the way we planned, did it?" Winter sighed softly, sadly. "Something happened that made Emily leave *Portrait*. And Mark and I —"

Winter's *love* without the capital *L*, the private love, the important love, had failed.

"But the movie, Winter. Peter said you were wonderful."

"Well, we'll see when *Love* is edited. Do you know when that will be? I assume Peter will be coming out to see it."

"Peter will be here for an entire week," Allison answered, smiling, "the first week of June."

Chapter Twenty-three

Burbank, California
June, 1985

Steve watched Peter as the final credits appeared on the edited, sound-tracked, *completed* version of *Love*. To Steve's critical, experienced, savvy movie eyes, *Love* was a masterpiece, virtually flawless. But Steve still worried that Peter might not agree. Peter might have artistic differences, prejudices of style that could mire *Love* in the kind of conflict that so far had been remarkably absent.

But Peter didn't have artistic differences.

"It's everything I hoped it would be, Steve," he said quietly.

"Good."

"When will it be released?"

Steve arched an eyebrow, surprised by Peter's question. Peter had made it crystal clear from the beginning that his involvement would end with final approval of the movie. Steve and Peter had agreed, in writing, that Peter wouldn't make promotional appearances or grant interviews. But now Peter was asking about the commercial aspects of *Love* and his curiosity seemed more than idle.

"*Love* will open in theaters nationwide during the second weekend in August," Steve answered. "I've arranged private showings for the press and film critics in New York, Dallas, Chicago, San Francisco, and here in late July."

"What about the Los Angeles premiere?"

"That will be on August second. It's a Friday night. We have both the Westwood Village and Bruin theaters—they're across the street from each other—and Broxton Avenue will be ours, too, for the reception immediately following. Why, Peter? Are you thinking about coming?"

"I open *Romeo and Juliet* on Broadway the following night." Peter gave a wry smile. *Juliet* and *Julia*, heroines of two very different stories of love. "Would you like me to be at the premiere, Steve?"

"Of course I would like it, Peter, but it's not essential. Premieres are star and media events. Our celebrity guests will come to be *seen*, to be photographed by the paparazzi, and to offer their professional opinions about *Love*. The cameras and attention will be on our actor and actress guests, and, of course, on Winter and Bruce. You and I aren't nearly as interesting, Peter, although a show of solidarity is always nice."

"Where else do you plan to have Winter and Bruce appear?"

"Everywhere. *Good Morning America, The Today Show, The Morning Show,* Phil, Oprah, local talk shows in big cities. All the big shows are holding space for us already—everyone is very interested in *Love*—and now that I know you're happy with the finished version, I will contact Winter and Bruce and set firm dates."

"Steve, you and Winter and I need to meet."

"We do?"

"Yes, we do. Without Bruce. Is tomorrow afternoon convenient for you?"

"Sure," Steve answered, curious, worried, but sensing he would simply have to wait until tomorrow to find out why they needed to meet.

"Winter lives in Bel Air, in the house where she lived

with her mother. Do you know it?"

"Oh, yes."

If there had been a rift between Winter and Bruce during the filming of *Love*, they had certainly kept it to themselves, Steve thought for the fiftieth time in the past twenty-four hours.

If this meeting was simply because Winter wanted to make appearances by herself, without her costar, that was fine. Separate appearances by Winter and Bruce would mean twice as much publicity for *Love*. Steve had considered calling her and telling her that—"You can fly solo on every show, Winter"—but perhaps Winter's battle was with Peter, not Bruce. In that case, Steve needed to be there to mediate. Besides, Steve was a little curious about visiting the mansion again after all these years.

Steve pressed the doorbell and let his thoughts travel to a time when the chimes were a melodic signal to Jacqueline that he had arrived. Steve was lost in that remote romantic memory when Winter opened the door. For a moment he was confused by the violet eyes, not Jacqueline's sapphire ones, and the black velvet hair, not Jacqueline's platinum blond.

Steve was pulled unceremoniously to the present, however, when he realized he was looking at a very pregnant Winter Carlyle.

"Terrific."

"Thank you, Steve," Winter replied sweetly.

"This is why Winter and I thought it would be best for us to meet without Bruce," Peter explained as he and Steve and Winter moved to the living room.

"Is Bruce the father?"

"No," Peter and Winter responded in unison.

"Are you?" Steve asked Peter.

"No," Winter asked solemnly. "The baby's father is dead."

331

Steve tilted his head thoughtfully and said to Winter, "You're a helluva an actress—I think you have a very good shot at this year's Oscar—but that last line didn't convince me." Steve saw such worry in Winter's eyes—genuine, unscripted worry—that he added gently, "If he's really dead, I'm very sorry. If not, it doesn't matter, none of my business. But I am to assume that secrecy is important?"

"Yes. I can't appear publicly, Steve. After the baby's born, I can, but not before."

"And you're due, let me guess, the night of the premiere?"

"No, even worse. Early September," Winter smiled wryly. It meant she wouldn't be available for public appearances until at least six weeks after *Love* was released. "Steve, I'm sorry."

Steve shrugged and smiled. He liked Winter very much. She had been such a trouper, such a professional. Steve knew this couldn't be easy for her—not now, not a year from now.

"It's OK. Bruce thrives in limelight. I'm sure he'll be delighted to hear that you're involved in 'another project.'"

"I would be very happy to make appearances," Peter offered.

"Peter's going to win Best Screenplay and Best Director, of course, but he's going to get a special Oscar for being so nice." Winter smiled at the nice handsome man who she guessed *hated* the thought of public appearances—queries about why he wrote what he wrote, questions about his private life—but had offered anyway simply to help *her*.

"Bruce and I can make the rounds in August and September," Steve said. "*Love* isn't going to vanish by October. After your baby's born, Winter, and once you look the way you want to in front of a camera, perhaps you could appear on the morning network shows?"

"Yes, of course. That would be fine. I could do them from LA, couldn't I?"

"Sure." Steve turned to Peter. "I think we're all right for the television spots, Peter, but—"

"The premiere?" Peter guessed with a smile.

"I'm afraid so. Even though the press isn't nearly as interested in you or me as they are in the stars."

"The show of solidarity is suddenly a little more critical."

"Yes."

"I'll be there, Steve."

"And back in New York twenty-four hours later for *Romeo and Juliet?*"

"It won't be any problem."

As Steve stood up to leave, he had a vivid memory of young violet eyes peering around a corner, uncertain, afraid. Steve looked at the violet eyes now, at what they had become, and still saw uncertainty.

"When are you going to see the masterpiece, Winter?"

"When it comes to cable."

"Don't you want to see it?"

"I really don't know, Steve."

"Well, you're magnificent. I'm sure Peter told you."

Winter smiled softly and nodded. Peter *had* told her.

"You have a screening room here, don't you?" Steve asked.

"Yes."

"Then I'll get a print of *Love* for you, just in case, OK?"

"OK. Thank you."

As Steve stood to leave, he thought about Lawrence Carlyle, the ghost that haunted this mansion, the ghost that might haunt the film. The issue of Lawrence Carlyle could wait for another time, Steve decided. The estrangement of Lawrence and Winter *had* to be addressed and handled, but there was still time. Winter had other worries to deal with now.

"Winter, if there's anything you need. I'm here."

"Thank you, Steve."

After Steve left, Winter said to Peter, "That wasn't too

bad, thanks to you."

"Steve's a reasonable man."

"Did I really say it would be *fine* to be at a television studio downtown at four A.M., trying to look bright-eyed and bushy-tailed for the wide-awake East Coast?"

"You did, Winter." Peter smiled. "Had I been directing the scene, I wouldn't have even asked you to do a second take. Your enthusiasm was really very convincing."

"I guess I was just relieved that—"

The phone rang, stopping Winter mid-sentence. The only people who ever called were Allison, Peter, and Patricia. Peter was here. Allison was on her way to take Emily to the airport. Perhaps it was Patricia, but . . .

It could be Mark. Tomorrow or the next day or the next, Mark would be leaving for Boston. Maybe he was calling to ask, *Do I have to go to Boston alone?*

"Hello?"

"Hi."

"Allison."

"Is Peter still there?"

"Yes. Sure." Winter handed the receiver to Peter and sat down on the sofa a little defeated, mostly annoyed at herself for still fantasizing.

"Hi. Are you at Emily's?"

"No. I'm on the Pasadena Freeway. Actually, I'm at a roadside café near the Pasadena Freeway."

"Are you all right?"

"I'm fine. A truck jackknifed somewhere between here and where I want to be. There's oil or honey—something gooey—all over the freeway and the road is now impassable and it's going to be at least an hour."

"And you're supposed to get Emily in"—Peter glanced at his watch—"twenty minutes."

"Yes. I tried to call her, but her phone has already been disconnected, so—"

"So give me her address."

334

"You don't mind?"

"Of course not. It will give me a chance to meet her even if it's only to wish her *au revoir*."

"Thank you." Allison gave Peter Emily's address. "I hate these freeways! So, how was the meeting with Steve?"

"It was fine. You and I are making an appearance at the premiere in August—more to give Winter the report than anything else, I think—and then how do you feel about doing some three A.M. babysitting in October?"

"Can't wait." Allison laughed. "Oh, speaking of waiting, there's a line forming at this phone booth."

"I should leave soon to get Emily anyway."

"Peter, I was going to give Emily the phone number and address of your apartment in New York."

"*Our* apartment."

"Our apartment," Allison echoed softly.

Emily sat on the narrow bed in her basement apartment on Montana Avenue. Allison would be here in ten minutes. Emily was ready.

The apartment looked exactly as it had when Emily had moved in six years ago—Spartan, sterile, dark. The dresser drawers and closets were empty, and the corner that had been Emily's darkroom was open again, the black curtains gone, the chemicals and pans discarded.

Emily was taking very little with her to Paris. Her camera, of course, and a small suitcase. The suitcase contained the picture she had taken of Robert Jeffrey Adamson—she didn't know his name then, only his gentle blue eyes—at Meg's wedding; the two very important books—*Little Girl Lost* and *Little Girl Found*—given to her by the man with the gentle blue eyes; a new soft cotton nightgown; a fluffy bathrobe; a change of lacy underclothes; and the letters.

The letters. One letter was written to the man Emily

hated, and the other letter was written to the man she loved. Neither man would ever read the letters; but Emily had needed to write them, to give voice to the powerful emotions. She needed to *face* the hatred and to *admit* the love.

The letter to the man Emily hated, the evil man who had stolen her innocence and her trust and her hope, was a letter of rage, not forgiveness.

"Do you want to forgive him, Emily?" Dr. Camden had asked.

"No. He knew what he was doing, didn't he?"

"I think so," Beverly Camden had answered evenly, although her own feeling on the issue was strong. A man who would knowingly cause such harm to a defenseless child—a man who would steal trust and the hope of love *for a lifetime*—deserved no forgiveness, no pardon.

Emily told Dr. Camden she had written the letter of hatred and rage to her stepfather, but she never mentioned the letter written to the man she loved. If Emily had been stronger, she might have thanked Rob in person. Perhaps she might even have gone back to work at *Portrait*, met with Rob once a week, taken pictures at his wedding.

I hope you'll photograph our wedding, Emily. I know Rob would want you to, Elaina had said. *We'll probably be married in June, at the Club.*

If Emily had been stronger . . .

But maybe it was really a sign of *great strength*. Four months ago, Emily had been willing, *happy*, to spend her life meeting with Rob for an hour a week *if she was lucky*. Emily never imagined there could be more for her; she believed she didn't deserve more.

Emily was stronger now. She wanted *more* for herself and for her life. Emily wanted love. She had a right to love and be loved, *didn't she?* For now, Emily's belief was only a leap of faith. In time, if she was lucky, there would be new *good* experiences to counterbalance the bad. Emily already knew that Rob Adamson existed. There were other men like Rob, weren't there? Somewhere in the world? Maybe?

Finding love with a man was a very long way off. Emily was still learning to love herself, to believe in herself, to *trust* herself. But, someday, there would be love.

Emily's old clothes—cleaned and ironed and baggy—were going to the Goodwill. They were neatly folded in a cardboard box outside the basement door.

For her flight to Paris—for her *arrival* in her new home—Emily was wearing a new, brave look. Her outfit, purchased at Bullock's-Wilshire, was a little denim, but not at all drab. The ivory blouse was soft and silky and feminine. The calf-length skirt was designer denim, tight at her small waist, stylishly flared, not baggy. Emily wore lapis earrings, and they could be seen because her long golden hair was swept gently off her face with barrettes and braided into a thick, shiny rope.

The knock at the door startled her. Allison was early. Emily had planned to be at the curb, waiting.

"Allison, I—" But it wasn't Allison! It was a man, dark, handsome, smiling, curious.

Emily fought the instinct to reach for the barrettes that held her hair, leaving her face exposed, vulnerable, naked. *Courage,* Emily told herself. Besides, loosening the barrettes would accomplish nothing; the familiar, protective golden curtain was tightly woven into a long, silky braid.

"Hi, Emily? I'm Peter Dalton. Allison is stuck in traffic across town, so I get to drive you to the airport."

"Oh, that's not necessary. I can call a cab."

"*That's* not necessary. I want to give you a ride, Emily. I've wanted to meet you. I'm a great admirer of your work."

"Oh. Thank you."

"Is this all your luggage?" Peter asked as he reached for the small suitcase that stood beside her purse and her camera case.

"Yes." *I'm starting over, you see, in Paris. I'm just taking a photograph of the man I love, two very important letters, and the guide books for the rest of my life.*

Peter put Emily's suitcase in the trunk of the car and held the door open for her.

"Thank you."

"You're welcome." Peter smiled, a warm smile for a beautiful woman. Emily was quite different from what Peter had expected from Allison's gentle, concerned descriptions of her friend.

"Oh, before I forget." Peter removed a notecard from his shirt pocket. "Here's our address and phone number in New York. For the foreseeable future, that's where Allison and I will be on weekends."

"Thank you. I'll send my address and phone number as soon as I have them."

"Good. Allison says you'll be working for *Paris Match*."

"Just free-lance to begin with." When Emily contacted *Paris Match*, they had been eager to sign the already-famous photographer from *Portrait* to their full-time staff, but she had said no. It had more to do with *choice* than business—choice and control over her life. And the other thing, the haunting thing: Signing with another magazine seemed like a betrayal to Rob. Rob, who had never betrayed her, even though she had angrily accused him of it.

"I'm sure you'll be in great demand."

As they neared Los Angeles International Airport, Peter sensed Emily's tension. The pink-flush left her cheeks and her body stiffened beneath the soft folds of silk.

"I'll come in with you, Emily, if you don't mind. I'd like to see the new international terminal."

"Oh, all right."

Peter and Emily drew stares—the dark handsome man, the beautiful blond woman. The stares would have terrified Emily if she had been alone. But she wasn't alone. Peter was right beside her. After a while, Emily courageously met the stares of the men who passed her, *and they weren't menacing, only appreciative.*

Just as Peter's dark eyes smiled appreciatively at her. Appreciatively, gently, supportively, as if Peter somehow knew this was a huge step for her and he was here to make sure she didn't lose her fragile footing.

Emily's courage *might* have faltered without Peter. She might have forgotten the months of hard work, her new strength, her belief in herself. She might have unbraided her golden hair, pulled the silky blouse loose from the waistband, and gone into familiar, comfortable, *horrible* hiding.

But Peter *was* there, smiling and somehow wise. Emily made the giant, all-important step, and she would never forget Peter's kindness.

Now the balance of Emily's experience with men was shifted a little more to the good. Now she knew there were two kind, gentle men in the world: Rob Adamson and Peter Dalton.

"Please wish Allison good luck with the opening of the Chateau Bel Air," Emily said to Peter before she boarded the Air France flight to Paris.

"I will, but I know for a fact Allison thinks she could open with unpainted walls and bare floors littered with sawdust, and as long as your photographs were on display, it would still be a hit."

The private opening of the Chateau Bel Air was held on a Thursday evening in early July. The invited guests wore tuxedos, designer gowns and jewels, and expressions of obvious approval as they wandered through the elegant hotel during the champagne reception that preceded the gourmet dinner in the splendid Versailles Room. The invited guests were rich, powerful, famous, and discerning. They needed to know about the best hotels in Los Angeles, hotels with spacious conference rooms for hammering out multimillion dollar deals, and hotels with luxurious suites for intimate weekends of romance.

As the rich and powerful guests strolled through the magnificent Chateau Bel Air, they made vows to use this grand place—for business, *and* for those very special, very private, very discreet weekends of love.

"Rob, how nice of you to come!" Allison smiled at the ocean-blue eyes she hadn't seen since February in Aspen. She felt a moment of nostalgia, sorry that it had been so long, afraid that . . . No, the special bond, the special warmth, was still there.

"I wouldn't have missed it, Allison. This is an absolute masterpiece."

"Thank you, Rob. Of course, the photographs," Allison began automatically. It was the way Allison had answered every compliment throughout the evening: *Of course, the photographs by Emily Rousseau are what really make it work!*

"Is she here?" Rob asked.

"Emily? No. She moved to Paris a month ago."

"I see."

Allison saw sadness in Rob's eyes and strain on his handsome face. *Something happened between Rob and Emily. Something that left them both so sad.* Rob had come this evening to see Allison's triumph, but he had come, too, in hopes of seeing Emily.

"Did you see Emily before she left, Allison?"

"Yes."

"How was she?"

"She seemed sad—a little lost—after she left *Portrait*," Allison told the dark blue eyes that obviously cared so much.

"Lost," Rob echoed quietly. *Little Girl Lost.*

"But, then . . ."

"Then?"

"Then . . . I don't know. In a way that I can't really define—just a feeling, I guess—Emily seemed to get better."

"Better?"

"Yes. Better." Allison frowned slightly, wishing she could be more specific, wishing she had something to say that would erase the obvious concern and worry in Rob's eyes. Allison believed Emily was better, stronger, more confident, but it was just a *feeling.* I've gotten a few postcards from her from Paris. She's busy—naturally—and I think she feels very much at home in Paris."

Rob and Allison were interrupted briefly by someone who wanted to congratulate Allison.

"Is Elaina with you?" Allison asked Rob when they were alone again.

"No. I'm here by myself. What about you? Roger, brokenhearted Roger, says there is someone new in your life. Is *he* here?"

"Roger's not brokenhearted! But he *is* right. There is someone. He couldn't be here tonight," Allison answered softly. Peter was in New York at the final dress rehearsal of *Hamlet.*

"He sounds very important to you," Rob said with a smile.

"Yes, he is very important to me," Allison answered quietly. She smiled into Rob's dark blue eyes. "I would like you to meet him, Rob. I know you would like him and he would like you."

"I would like to meet him, Allison. Will that ever happen?"

"Yes." Allison *knew* Rob and Peter would meet sometime. Peter would certainly be in *Portrait's* Academy Award issue, if not before. Allison and Peter's love was still very private, a lovely secret known only to a trusted few. Allison suddenly wanted to share her wonderful secret with Rob. "In fact, Rob . . ."

341

This time Rob and Allison's conversation was interrupted by someone who wanted to speak to Rob. Then someone, and someone else, and someone *else* wanted to speak to her. By the time Allison was free and she looked for Rob again, he was gone.

Allison was going to say, "In fact, Rob, you'll meet him next month at the premiere of *Love*."

Rob Adamson certainly would be among the celebrities who received engraved invitations to the gala premiere of *Love*. Rob would be there, and Allison would proudly, happily, *joyfully* introduce her dear friend Rob to her beloved Peter.

Chapter Twenty-four

Bel Air, California
August, 1985

Allison arrived at Winter's mansion at seven P.M. on the first of August, twenty-four hours before the Los Angeles premiere of *Love*.

"I bought you a dress for the premiere." Allison handed the pale blue box tied in a gold ribbon to her surprised friend. "Or at least for our private premiere after-party. I got it at a maternity boutique on Dayton, very upscale, for pregnant actresses and Hollywood wives, I guess. No one recognized me, of course, or seemed the least bit interested in why I was buying a glamorous maternity gown. I was actually a little disappointed because I had prepared about ten plausible reasons." Allison's eyes sparkled conspiratorially, "Anyway, I *did* pay in cash and made sure I wasn't followed!"

"Allison," Winter whispered softly as she opened the pale blue box. Tears filled her eyes as she removed the lavender and ivory silk gown. The maternity clothes Winter had bought in March and early April, to last throughout her pregnancy, were uninspired, *something* to wear during the long months in the mansion. "It's beautiful."

"It is, isn't it?" Allison smiled.

"This is going to be such fun. What are you wearing?"

"For *Love,* I'm wearing pastel chiffon." *So romantic,* Allison had decided when she bought the dress last week at Gorgissima.

"And for *Romeo and Juliet?*"

"Gold lamé, very sleek, very Fifth Avenue. Peter has tuxedos rented on both coasts."

"Talk about a whirlwind weekend. *Love* in Westwood, *Romeo and Juliet* in Manhattan. Saturday night you'll be at the Tavern on the Green, drinking champagne till dawn, waiting to read the reviews."

"The part of the weekend Peter and I are looking forward to the most is dinner with you tomorrow night after the premiere. We'll stop by with the food about six."

"You two look so glamorous!" Winter exclaimed when Allison and Peter arrived the following evening. "Allison, that dress. Peter, gorgeous in a tuxedo."

"You look pretty glamorous yourself, Winter Carlyle," Peter said.

"I love my upscale maternity gown."

Allison and Winter followed Peter as he carried boxes of gourmet food, prepared at the Club, into the kitchen.

"Do you think we have enough food?" Winter laughed. "Just figuring out *what* we have will keep me busy until you return!"

"Why don't you wait, Winter?" Allison suggested. "Just leave everything in the refrigerator, and we'll set out plates and fire up the microwave when we get back."

"Allison, I may be almost eight months pregnant—God knows I look it—but I'm quite healthy."

"Just don't overdo."

"I won't."

"Are you going to watch the movie tonight?"

"I don't think so," Winter said. As promised, Steve had given her a print of *Love. Someday* she would settle into the

344

cushiony chairs in the screening room and watch her performance as the heroine of the romantic film of the decade, but not yet.

"We'd better go, Allison," Peter said quietly.

"OK." Allison smiled thoughtfully at Winter. "I really hate leaving you alone, Winter."

"I'm not alone, Allison." *I have my lively little baby frolicking happily inside me.*

Allison didn't remember when it happened, or whether Peter withdrew his hand from hers or she from his, but she became aware that her hands were alone, clasped tightly in her lap. The unsettling realization that her fingers were no longer entwined with Peter's was just a tiny ripple in the storm-tossed sea of confusion and fear that raged inside her as she watched *Love.*

Who is Julia? The bewildering question came with a swift, confident answer: *Julia is the woman Peter loves.*

But where is Julia? No longer, apparently, in Peter's life, but still, *so obviously,* in Peter's heart.

Did Peter write Love *for Julia? Was* Love *Peter's gentle and so-eloquent plea to his beloved Julia to return to him?*

Yes. Of course. What other explanation could there be?

The devastating questions with their heart-stopping answers thundered in Allison's mind as she watched *Love.* They thundered still even after the movie ended and the theater fell silent.

The silence lasted for several moments. Every man and woman in the audience needed a little private time in the still-dark theater to reflect on the magnificence of what they had seen; time to brush tears from eyes and clear emotion from throats; time to wonder sadly how such a perfect love had eluded their lives; time to make vows to find such a love or to gently nurture a once-cherished-now-neglected one.

The reverent, reflective silence was finally broken by a

single clap. The clap broke the silence and with it the magical spell that had been cast on them all. The audience had to leave the enchanted world of Julia and Sam, but they weren't leaving empty-handed. They left with the gifts Peter had given them, together with their own solemn vows to treasure and nurture whatever love existed in their lives.

The clapping became a roar and the audience stood. Allison stood, too, and somehow unclasped her numb hands to join the applause.

Allison didn't look at Peter—she *couldn't*—not during the seemingly endless applause and not when he leaned *so close* and whispered to her that he and Steve were leaving to have "a word with the press." After Peter and Steve disappeared, Allison moved with the river of rich and famous that flowed from the sanctuary of the dark theater into the bright lights of the gala reception, where champagne splashed and celebrities mingled and the only topic of conversation was astonished praise for *Love*.

"The script was brilliant, poetry really."

"Winter Carlyle, what a debut!"

"*Love* will sweep the Academy Awards."

"Vanessa Gold certainly was right about Peter Dalton. His is truly a six octave talent, from despair and hopelessness—did you ever see *Say Good-bye?*—to this! Absolutely amazing."

"What a gift!"

"What an imagination."

Imagination? Allison's reeling mind focused for a moment. Didn't they see it? Couldn't they tell *Love* was real? Apparently not! Maybe *she* was wrong. The thought came with a flickering hope, but it faded quickly.

Allison wove through the crowd to a far corner where the lights weren't so bright and where she would have to speak to no one. She spotted Vanessa in the distance, prayed that the columnist hadn't seen her sitting beside Peter, and was suddenly so glad that no one knew about

346

them.

Because there was nothing to know. Peter and Allison weren't in love, not really, because, *because* Peter had another love.

Tears threatened. Allison wanted, needed, to escape, to find a private place where she could be alone with her swirling thoughts. Once before, Allison had escaped from a grand celebration because tears threatened and she needed privacy to think about shocking revelations. On that beautiful June day Allison had escaped to a fragrant alcove of lilacs, and she had been alone until a handsome man with smiling blue eyes had found her.

Find me now, Rob. Help me get away from here.

From her vantage point in the shadows, Allison scanned the crowd for him, recalling sadly that this was the night she had planned to proudly, happily, *joyfully* introduce her good friend Rob to her beloved Peter. Allison searched for Rob, knowing that she wouldn't tell him anything or ask him to help her flee, but needing to see his kind eyes and hoping the warmth of his smile would melt the shivers of icy fear that pulsed through her.

But Rob Adamson was not in the celebrity crowd that had gathered to celebrate Peter Dalton's magnificent triumph.

Peter's magnificent triumph. Peter's and Winter's and Steve's and Bruce's.

And Julia's. Whoever Julia was, wherever she was.

On an August day, just a year ago, Allison had stood in a bustling paddock surrounded by haunting memories of her shattered dreams and had realized *I don't belong here.* Allison had rushed away from the paddock to Elegance, to explore her wonderful new talents and find wonderful new dreams. She had begun her new career that day. And, that day, she had met Peter.

Because of Peter, Allison had discovered the fire and passion and love that lived in her soul. And, because of Peter, Allison had discovered a dream she had never even known to dream.

And now Allison felt this dream — the dream of love —

347

shattering, too, and the haunting words came to her again: *I don't belong here.*

"Allison. Here you are. Are you ready to leave?"

Allison couldn't meet Peter's dark eyes, but she felt them, staring at her, intense, curious, demanding.

"Yes," she whispered.

Peter and Allison didn't speak as he drove from Westwood to Bel Air, toward Winter's mansion and the festive late night dinner that was going to be such fun.

Peter didn't slow down as they neared the entrance to the mansion on Bellagio. He drove past, a half mile further, finally stopping the car in a distant corner of a parking lot at the Club. The remote corner would have been dark, but the full summer moon cast a soft, golden glow.

"Allison, what's wrong?"

"Please tell me, Peter."

"Tell you what, darling?"

"Tell me about Julia."

Allison spoke bravely to the dark eyes whose gaze she had avoided since the movie ended. Now Allison wanted, *needed*, to see Peter's eyes. Her jade eyes were illuminated by the moonlight, fully exposed, but the moon was behind Peter, casting shadows on his handsome face, concealing the message of his dark eyes. Allison couldn't see Peter's eyes, but she sensed the effect of her words on him, stunning him, as if she had inflicted a blow.

And Allison knew she had not been wrong . . . *Julia was real.*

Peter didn't answer right away, and in moments that seemed like forever, the summer night became eerily still, soundless, as if waiting in breath-held silence for his reply. Allison thought she heard a distant whinny, but maybe it was just her imagination. Or maybe it was a ghostly reminder of the *other* dream that had died.

"Allison." When Peter spoke at last, his voice was soft and gentle. "Julia is a fictional name and the story is fiction."

Peter paused, and in that new endless moment, Allison's heart cried, *Oh, Peter, please don't lie to me! Please don't pretend that the passion and emotion for Julia flowed from your brilliant, creative mind, not from your loving heart. I know it isn't true!*

Peter didn't lie to Allison.

"But," he continued very quietly, "she is based on a woman I knew."

"And loved." *And still love!*

"Yes." Peter reached for her hands, to hold her while he told her the rest, but Allison wouldn't let him have them. "Allison . . ."

"Please tell me, Peter. What woman?"

"My wife."

"Your wife?" Allison echoed weakly. Allison had prepared herself, *steeled* her trembling body as well as she could, to hear her beloved Peter confess to another love, a passionate affair that had ended badly and still lingered in his heart, its smoldering embers ever ready to burst into new flames. *She had not imagined a marriage.*

"We were married eight years ago. We were together for four years before she died."

"Died?" It was a whisper of pain.

"Yes. I wrote *Love* just before her death. She wanted me to write a happy love story. I promised her that I would make *Love* into a movie and that I wouldn't change the ending."

"Even though . . ."

"Even though."

Peter had given Allison the truth, the essential facts, as succinctly and unemotionally as he could, but the effect on her lovely eyes was still devastating. Peter helplessly watched the array of emotion — fear, surprise, sadness, confusion.

"Why didn't you tell me before, Peter?"

"Because of these." His hands trembled as he so gently touched the hot tears that fell onto her cheeks. "I didn't want to make you cry."

"Don't touch me!" Allison's words and the harshness of her voice startled them both. In the wonderful months of their love, Allison had longed for Peter's gentle touch, welcoming him always and with such joy. *And now Peter's gentle touch caused pain.* Bewildered, Allison added softly, "Please."

"All right, darling." Peter reluctantly withdrew his hands from her tear-damp cheeks. "Allison, I was going to tell you."

"You should have told me a long time ago." *Why didn't you tell me, Peter? Why did you hide something this important from me?*

"Yes, I guess I should have," Peter agreed softly. He had only wanted to protect his precious Allison from sadness, and instead he had hurt her so deeply. He needed to explain, to make her understand. He continued gently, "But when should I have told you, darling? In those few enchanted weeks we had together at Bellemeade, when the delicate roots of our new love needed joyous nurturing? Or in the past few months when we've had rare, desperate moments together and we have wanted to fill them only with happiness? I knew it would make you sad, Allison. I couldn't—didn't want to—do that to you."

"So you just let me be emotionally ambushed."

"I guess I foolishly hoped . . ." Peter couldn't finish the sentence, because suddenly the hope that Allison would see *Love* as the world would see it—a celebration of the gifts of love created by a gifted writer—was *so foolish.*

For the past few weeks, alone in his apartment in New York, Peter had been driven from sleep not by nightmares but by worry. Did he need to tell Allison about Sara before the premiere? he had asked himself over and over again in the darkness. No, he had decided finally. It wasn't necessary. He didn't have to put sadness in the joyful heart of his lovely Allison—not yet.

Love was about Sara, not him, he reminded himself. *Love* was about Sara's loveliness, Sara's innocence, Sara's courage. Only the people who loved Sara—Peter, her parents, and Rob—would see Sara in Julia.

Love was about Sara. But *Love* was also Peter's lovesong to Sara. And Allison, the woman who loved him, would know the words flowed from his heart.

So foolish. He should have known. He should have told her. He should have caused her tears then instead of now, because now there was doubt in the jade-green eyes that before had glowed only with joyous, untarnished confidence in him and in his love. Doubt where there should be none, ever.

How much harm had he done in the name of love? Peter gazed at her hurt, bewildered eyes and had his grim answer: *So much.*

Peter desperately needed to undo the harm, to restore her radiant confidence, but Allison was so wounded, so wary, *so far away.*

"I was very wrong, Allison. I should have told you before." *I should have held you in my arms and told you and kissed your tears until they were vanquished. Let me hold you now! Let me kiss your tears!*

But Allison didn't want him to touch her.

"Yes, you should have." *How could you have kept something this important from me? What other monsters are lurking in the darkness, waiting to devour my heart and my dreams?* "What other secrets, Peter?"

"No other secrets, Allison. I promise you, darling, there never will be."

Allison started to speak, but she couldn't find coherent words for her swirling thoughts and emotions. Suddenly, she felt so tired, so defeated. Instead of speaking, she sighed softly and slowly shook her red-gold head.

"What, darling? What are you thinking? Tell me."

"I feel so lost, Peter," Allison answered finally. "I thought I knew about you and us." *I believe in us. I trusted us . . . you.*

"You do know about us, Allison. Please don't feel lost." *Lost.* That was how he had felt when Sara died, how he had felt until he found Allison. Peter didn't want Allison to feel lost, not ever; there was no reason. "Allison, don't you know how I feel about you?"

"Tell me how you feel about her."

"Allison . . ."

"Honest words, Peter, *please.*"

"All right, darling," Peter agreed softly. *The truth.* "I loved her very much. After she died . . . That was a very difficult time for me, Allison."

"That was when you wrote *Say Good-bye,*" Allison whispered quietly. She had read Peter's plays last December, before their love. She had wept at the sadness in the beautiful words and had wondered about the talented writer whose life had obviously not been so happy. *Say Good-bye* had been the most tormented and most magnificent of the plays she had read. *Now she knew why.* As with *Love,* the words and emotions in *Say Good-bye* had flowed from Peter's heart. *Love* was the joyous celebration of a forever love, and *Say Good-bye* was its dark twin, the anguished farewell to that forever love when it died.

"Yes. I started writing again and directing. I immersed myself in my work and planned to let it consume me for the rest of my life." Peter paused, then whispered gently, "But, one day, something incredible happened."

It was then that Peter realized Allison couldn't see him. Her lovely anguished face was illuminated by golden moonlight, but the moon was behind him, a halo he didn't deserve, casting shadows and doubt where he wanted none. Peter moved a little, not toward her, because Allison didn't want that, but enough so that she could see the love in his eyes.

Please see my love, Allison!

Peter gazed at her, waiting for even a slight acknowledgement of the *something incredible* that had happened, but Allison's confusion only seemed to deepen when she saw the familiar look of love and tenderness on his handsome face. Didn't she know?

"Allison," Peter whispered urgently, "the *something incredible* that happened was that I fell in love with you."

"Oh!"

"Yes," Peter lovingly told the startled eyes. "*Oh!* Allison, I always believed that love—if love even existed—would never touch my life. When I fell in love eight years ago, it was such an astonishing and unexpected gift. After she died, I knew I would never love again. I sealed myself off from the possibility. I was immune, impenetrable, surrounded by a wall of memories and without a breath of desire. I wasn't looking for a new love, but one day I innocently walked into Elegance, and . . . well, speaking of being emotionally ambushed . . ."

That brought a trembling smile to Allison's lips and a sudden mist of hope to Peter's eyes.

"I love you, Allison, with all my heart."

"I love you, too, Peter," Allison replied quietly. *I love you with all my heart, too. But this secret was so important. It terrifies me that you didn't tell me.* "But I need time. I have to think about what you have told me and I have to try to understand why you kept this secret from me."

"I told you why, Allison. I wanted to protect you from sadness and it backfired. I was very foolish and I am so sorry." *And so afraid.* "May I hold you, please, just for a moment?"

Allison listened to Peter's gentle apology and saw the love in his eyes and *wished* that his loving arms could protect her from the terrible hurt. But he had caused the hurt, and Allison had already learned—a horrible, bewildering discovery—that tonight Peter's gentle touch caused her even more pain.

Allison wished she could go to him, as she always had, so joyfully, so confidently. *But she couldn't.* It had been a night of truth and secrets, of golden moonlight and dark shadows, and she needed time to think about what she had learned, the *truth* about Peter's forever love and the *secret* he had kept from her in the name of love. Time to think, time to understand, time to forgive, time to *heal*.

"Peter, no. It's too soon."

Earlier, when Peter's face had been in shadows, Allison had only sensed the effect of her words — "Tell me about Julia" — on him. Now she saw the effect of what she had just told him — *I can't let you hold me, Peter, not even for a moment* — in his dark eyes. Another stunning blow, and such pain!

Allison didn't want to punish Peter, or herself, but she had no choice. She was too raw, too wounded, too shaken. A deep instinct warned her to stay away until she was stronger. She *would* be strong again. Their love would be strong again. It *had* to be.

"All right, darling," Peter whispered softly. Then he asked, a gentle, uncertain plea, "But will it — we — be all right?"

Allison looked at his worried, loving eyes and answered with a promise from her heart, "Yes, Peter, we will be all right. I just need a little time. Right now, we should go to Winter's. I'm sure she's wondering where we are."

"OK," Peter whispered quietly, aching with fear and churning with anger at himself for his foolishness. *Take all the time you need, my darling Allison, but please, don't let this hurt us. I love you so much.*

Chapter Twenty-five

"How was it?" Winter asked eagerly when Peter and Allison arrived at the mansion ten minutes later. Her smile faded as she saw their strained smiles and troubled eyes.

"Wonderful," Allison said. She added, to make it the truth, "You were wonderful, Winter, really sensational. *Everyone* raved about you."

"What's wrong?"

"Nothing," Allison answered swiftly. That was the truth, too, wasn't it? *Yes*. She just needed time to believe it was true. Someday, when she was confident again of their love, Allison would ask Peter more about his wife, who she was and how she had died. Some faraway day Allison would ask Peter those questions.

"Peter?" Winter persisted.

"Nothing's wrong, Winter."

"I think we're still just a little stunned." Allison forced a smile for her friend. This wasn't fair to Winter! Winter had worked so hard, *Love* meant so much to her, and her performance had been magnificent. "The movie was stunning, *you* were stunning. You should really see it sometime."

"Sometime I will. So, we're not closing before we open?"

"No," Peter found a soft laugh. "Not at all. Speaking of opening, how about a little champagne? Or, for the pregnant star, chilled ginger ale?"

Winter had both champagne and ginger ale chilling in silver bowls in the living room. Peter opened the bottles and filled the crystal champagne flutes. When each held a glass of honey-colored liquid, they softly touched crystal to crystal, wordlessly toasting the magnificent movie.

"What time is your plane for New York?" Winter asked.

"Eight-thirty."

"That means we should start on the gourmet crab puffs I spent all day making, before we have the gourmet dinner I spent all day making!" Winter made a move toward the kitchen, but Allison stopped her.

"Winter!" This was Winter's night—or should have been—a night to celebrate with two people who loved her very much, a small oasis in her lonely, isolated life. Not that Winter ever gave a hint that she was lonely, or that she missed Mark desperately, or that she was so afraid of what lay ahead. Winter, the remarkable actress, hid it all. But Allison knew. "Peter and I can sleep on the plane. We're not in any hurry. Sit."

"And stay?" Winter's words took her back to the day in December, when it was Allison who had given the command: "Winter! Sit and stay!" That distant day, the night of love, the tiny new life created from that loving . . . Winter's eyes clouded briefly at the memory.

"I have a toast," Peter said quietly. "To Winter, who gave so much love and loveliness to the movie and will give so much of both to her baby."

"Peter. Thank you." Tears threatened. Winter smiled a wobbly smile, stood up, and announced firmly, "That's it. Time for crab puffs."

"Let me help you."

"No, Allison, you really have to banish the invalid concept from your mind. You sit and stay with Peter. I'll be right back."

Winter disappeared beyond the crystal and flowers on the dining room table through the door that swung into the kitchen. Allison sat on the edge of a chair across from Peter, eyes downcast, suddenly uncomfortable at being alone with

356

him in lights that were brighter, more probing, than the soft gold of the August moon. Allison's thoughts drifted to Peter's wife—his *wife*—and to the love that had died four years ago but had been enough, Peter believed, to last him a lifetime.

"I have a toast for you, for us, too," Peter began. He saw the sad eyes as she looked up when he spoke and pleaded softly, "Allison, don't do this."

"I can't help it."

"I'm so sorry. I don't want you to be sad or worried *ever*. There is no reason for you to be."

"I can't just turn it off, Peter. I need to work through my feelings."

"We'll do that together, OK? This weekend, every night on the phone, next weekend."

Allison heard the edge of panic in Peter's voice and saw his fear. *Fear?* What did Peter fear? Was he afraid of losing her? Didn't he know that could never happen?

"Peter . . ." Allison stopped because suddenly Peter's gaze shifted beyond her and the fear in his eyes became terror.

Winter stood at the top of the stairs that led from the dining room to the living room. She leaned against the wall, her violet eyes bewildered.

"Winter!"

"Something's wrong," Winter whispered. "Something's happening."

Winter didn't feel pain. She just felt a strange emptiness—an eerie feeling of doom—followed by a hot dampness on her legs.

The hot dampness was blood. Winter didn't see the blood, but Allison and Peter did.

"Winter, it's time to go to the hospital," Peter said, moving swiftly beside her, uttering the ominous words Sara had spoken to him four years before.

"No," Winter said as Peter lifted her in his arms. "It's too soon. Peter, it's too soon!"

"It will be all right, honey," Peter murmured mechanically, shifted in time, reliving the most horrible night of his life, placed here again by some demonic force bent on his de-

357

struction and the destruction of those he loved. "Allison, you drive. The keys are in my right-hand pocket. Let's go."

The sound of her name jerked Allison into action. Until then she had stared, immobile, terrified by how Winter looked and even more terrified by Peter. His dark eyes had filled with hopelessness and a heart-stopping wisdom.

As if he knew what was going to happen. As if he had seen it all before.

And there was something else in Peter's stricken eyes . . . *blame.*

As if whatever horror was about to unfold was his fault.

Allison drove. Peter was in the backseat with Winter, cradling her, whispering reassurances to her. His voice was soft and low and gentle, but the promises he made to Winter— "You'll be fine, honey, and so will the baby"—sounded false, as if he were an actor who had perfectly memorized his lines but hadn't bothered to study his character's motivation.

Peter's reassurances lacked conviction, but his hopelessness seemed to give Winter strength. She countered defiantly, "I *am* all right, Peter! My baby *is* fine!"

They reached the Emergency Room at UCLA three minutes after leaving the mansion on Bellagio. Peter carried Winter inside. They were instantly surrounded by an ER staff that was stirred into prompt action by the sight of blood. In moments, Winter was on a stretcher being wheeled into a "trauma room" as one nurse took vital signs, another searched for veins, and a doctor asked a few pithy questions.

Allison and Peter followed the procession into the room, but once inside they were separated from Winter by a wall of doctors and nurses.

The doctor asked questions: "When are you due?" "When did the bleeding start?" "Is there pain?" "Did your doctor do an ultrasound?" "Have there been any problems with your pregnancy?"

And Winter answered, her voice still strong and defiant despite the blood loss and the chilling pallor of her face: "In September." "*What* bleeding?" "No pain, just a queasiness, a little cramping like a period." "No ultrasound, no problems. I'm fine, healthy, and so is my baby!"

The nurse announced the vital signs as the doctor took the history and felt Winter's abdomen: "Pressure eighty over fifty, pulse one twenty-eight."

"We need two lines," the doctor said. "Fourteen gauge. Type and cross for five units. The usual blood work plus a coag screen. Have you paged OB?"

"Stat-paged," the nurse answered, then turned her head slightly as she heard the distinctive sound of paper footsteps running on linoleum.

The OB team appeared, clothed in operating room attire, including once-sterile paper galoshes.

"You have some business for us?" the chief resident asked, quickly assessing the situation, relieved that Winter was conscious, frowning as he noticed the blood.

"Yes. She's about eight months, followed at Cedars, uncomplicated until now, developed painless bleeding fifteen minutes ago. Her blood pressure is dropping."

"Baby?"

"I hear heartbeats."

"Good. Sounds like a previa."

"I think so."

"OK. Lines in? Great. We'll take her upstairs right now. Call L&D and let them know we need a double setup. Thanks." The chief resident moved to the head of the stretcher, smiled at the most beautiful violet eyes he had ever seen, and said, "Hi. I'm Dr. Johnson. We think your placenta is blocking the outlet of your uterus and it's bleeding. I need to take a look, but if that's what you have, we'll need to do a Caesarean section."

Dr. Johnson talked as he and the OB team wheeled Winter's stretcher out of the ER to a waiting elevator. Allison and Peter started to follow but were stopped by a nurse.

"Are you family?" she asked, then, looking at Peter, she added, "Are you her husband or the baby's father?"

Allison watched Peter for a horrible breath-held moment. *No more secrets, Allison,* he had promised, but her confidence in him and their love was still shaken. From a deep instinct for self-preservation, more than from conscious thought, Allison steeled herself for another dark, destructive secret. She waited, fearing that Peter was going to say, "Yes, I'm the baby's father." He looked so confused by the nurse's question, so frantic that the stretcher was disappearing and he wasn't with Winter. After a long, bewildered silence, Peter finally whispered, "No. No to both."

"Then you'll need to wait in the Labor and Delivery Waiting Room. This elevator goes directly to the Delivery Room. You'll need to take another one. Just follow the blue line on the wall."

"I can't be with her?" Peter asked numbly.

"No."

Allison saw more confusion on his handsome face. Confusion, and such pain!

Once in the Waiting Room, Allison tried to erase Peter's pain. Winter is strong and healthy, she reminded him. And this was a hospital of miracles. Allison had been saved here. Winter would be saved, too. Winter will be fine, Allison gently assured Peter. And Winter's baby will be fine.

But Peter didn't seem to hear her reassurances. His dark eyes gazed beyond her to a horrible, distant memory.

Peter has been here before, Allison realized finally. *He is reliving a nightmare.*

Was this how Peter had lost his wife? And his unborn child? *Yes,* it must have been. This was why Peter had asked Allison if her accident meant that she couldn't have children, and why he had looked worried, not relieved, when Allison had said no. And this was why he was able to tell before anyone else that Winter was pregnant.

Oh, Peter, Allison thought as she helplessly watched his terrible torment.

The chief resident appeared, finally, an hour later. He was smiling.

"Winter is all right."

"And the baby?" Allison asked.

"She's fine, too. She's premature, so we've put her in the

neonatal ICU to watch her carefully, but so far her lungs are strong and she's doing well."

"Winter's really OK?" Allison pressed.

"Yes. She had a placenta previa—that was why she was bleeding—so we did a Caesarean. She's in the Recovery Room now, groggy but awake." Dr. Johnson saw Allison's concern and relief and decided he was talking to a loving friend of the astonishing violet eyes. "Winter's going to be very weak for a while. She lost quite a bit of blood. In the old days, we would have given her transfusions, but now, if the blood count isn't dangerously low, we prefer to give iron and let the body rebuild its own blood supply."

"Because of AIDS," Allison said.

"Yes. Winter will be fine, but for the next few weeks she'll be quite weak and wobbly. Does she have someone who can help her?" The doctor guessed he was looking at that someone.

"Oh, yes." Allison smiled. Helping Winter until her boundless energy and exuberant health returned would be a tiny, *tiny* repayment for the long, patient months her friend had sat by Allison's bed and taught her how to read again, and write, and remember. A repayment you don't owe, Allison! Winter would exclaim, her violet eyes hurt by the suggestion. *But I want to help, Winter! Just like you wanted to help. I'm on your side, Winter, always.* "Can we see her and the baby?"

"Not now. The nurses are still getting them settled in. It's best not to disrupt that process." Dr. Johnson correctly interpreted the flicker of worry in Allison's eyes and added, "Really, both Mom and baby are fine. It's time for everybody to get some rest. Why don't you come back at eleven this morning, during visiting hours?"

"All right. Give her our love, though, OK?"

"OK."

After the doctor left, Allison turned to Peter. He hadn't spoken at all during Allison's conversation with Dr. Johnson. In fact, Peter hadn't even moved from the corner of the room where he had stood, stiff, waiting, bracing himself for the inevitable news of the death of the mother and her child.

But Peter had heard the doctor's words. Allison saw it on his handsome face as he tried to reconcile this ending—a happy one—with the ending four years before, the one that had almost ended his life. Peter tried to find joy in the fact that Winter and her baby were fine, but part of him was lost in the grim memory of a woman and baby who had died.

Earlier in the evening, Peter's secret had caused a distance between them, and Allison had kept them apart because she needed time. When Peter had asked her so gently if he could touch her, hold her, *just for a moment,* she had said no. She had been too wounded, not strong enough or confident enough to forgive him swiftly and return to his loving arms.

But now Allison gazed at Peter's tormented face and his bloodied arms and clothes, and she suddenly felt very strong and very confident. She didn't need time. Allison and Peter didn't need to spend the next hours, days, and weeks of their love reliving his past and finding loving ways to reassure her. Allison didn't need to be reassured of Peter's love, and she *wouldn't* put him through the painful memories.

They wouldn't talk about it at all, unless *Peter* needed to.

Allison would just love him, as she already did, with all her heart.

Allison walked across the room to him. When she stood in front of Peter, she looked up into his dark eyes and smiled softly at him.

"I need a hug, Peter," she whispered gently. *You need a hug.*

Without speaking, Peter circled her with his strong arms and so tenderly, so gratefully, drew her to him. Allison felt the taut emotion that stiffened his body. And then she felt it flow out, a river of grief and pain.

In the few hours left before dawn, Peter and Allison showered together and lay together, awake, touching, loving. As the pale yellow of a new summer day crept into the bedroom window, Allison gently kissed a circle around his lips. *Goodbye kisses. Peter recognized them.*

"I'm not going, either," he said.

"It's opening night of the greatest production of *Romeo and Juliet* in history. Your production. You have to be there." Allison added softly, "And I have to be with Winter."

"I know that, darling. And I have to be with you."

Allison shook her head and gazed lovingly into his eyes. She was going to spend today, the weekend, next week, getting Winter's home ready for the baby. She and Winter hadn't done that yet—gotten baby supplies!—because there had still been time. They had laughed about doing it and had decided they would rely heavily on Allison's mother, whom they both loved, who had kept Winter's secret a secret, and for whom this baby would be like a grandchild. After Allison visited Winter this morning, she would go to her parents and tell them the wonderful news. Then she and her mother would go shopping.

Peter could be part of it—Allison didn't want him to leave!—but maybe he was an expert on baby supplies, and maybe it would tear him apart with sadness.

Allison wanted no more pain for Peter.

"I'll just get a phone at my table at the Tavern on the Green and we'll talk all night while we're waiting for the reviews."

"Good. But you'll call me before then, won't you? As soon as you arrive in New York?"

"And before I leave for the theater and during intermission," Peter teased gently. Then his eyes grew serious. "I hate to leave you now. I promised that we would talk and that I would help you understand."

"All I need to know is that you love me."

"I do love you, Allison, more than anything in the world."

"Then we've had our talk." Allison kissed him, pulling away reluctantly after a long, hungry moment. "You have to get ready or you'll miss your plane."

"I was thinking about next weekend," Peter said, reaching for the curve at the back of her neck, his strong fingers caressing.

"Oh." Allison bit her lip. She had planned to go to New

York next weekend, but now she needed to be with Winter. She needed to be with Winter and she needed to be with Peter.

"I would like to spend four days—and four nights—in an elegant suite at a luxury hotel. I hear they have a very nice one nearby. The Chateau Bel Air, I believe it's called. Stunning interior design, conveniently located to Bellagio, and yet private, romantic." Peter smiled lovingly.

"You'll come back next weekend? You can get away?"

"I *will* get away. I don't know, Allison, but it seems that if you've just written and directed a movie that the movie critics *already* love, and directed a play that, modesty aside, the theater critics *will* love, at some point you can do what you want, play hooky, be with the woman you love. What do you think?"

"I love you."

"Winter!" Allison had approached Winter's hospital room with trepidation, preparing herself for a ghostly, fatigued version of her best friend, reminding herself what she must have looked like in those most critical days in the ICU after her accident.

Winter looked pale—her rich creamy skin was translucent—but she was sitting up, propped against pillows, her violet eyes clear and sparkling as she wrote on a notepad that lay on her lap.

"Hi!"

"You look wonderful, glamorous as always."

"I'm a little wobbly, but I'm fine." Winter's voice softened, "Thanks to you and Peter. You saved my life."

"No," Allison countered swiftly, but she wondered. Perhaps Peter *had* saved Winter's life. Perhaps the horror of the other time—when he had tried desperately and unsuccessfully to save a life—had made Peter act as quickly and as surely as he had last night.

"*Yes.* Thank you." Winter noticed Allison's frown and shifted happily to a wonderful topic. "Have you seen her?"

"Not yet."

"Oh, Allison, she is such a miracle! She has tiny delicate little hands and feet, and her mouth is so pink, and she is so soft."

"The nurses say she is beautiful," Allison said. The nurses had spontaneously offered that bit of information when Allison arrived on the ward looking for Winter's room. "They say that most babies aren't really beautiful, and that premature babies never are, but she is."

"It doesn't matter," Winter murmured distantly. Part of her, she realized, had assumed that her baby would be like she had been—gawky, awkward, clumsy, *ugly*. Winter would atone for what had been done to her. She would love her little girl so much! Was she disappointed that her daughter was already beautiful? No, of course not. Not if it would make her precious baby's life even easier.

"Have you decided about her name?" Allison asked after a few moments. Winter had been so certain that her baby would be a girl, but she had never mentioned a name.

"I've been working on it. Here." Winter handed Allison the notepad. "See what you think."

"OK." Allison read aloud from the top of the long list, "Marcia Lauren . . . Lauren Marcia . . . Marky . . . Laura . . ."

"I've decided against those," Winter interjected. *I've decided not to name her after the men who didn't want me.* "You can skip down past all the feminine forms of Lawrence or Mark."

"All right. Let's see. Autumn . . . Spring . . . Summer." Allison tilted her head thoughtfully. "Winter?"

"I think that's what's left of the anesthetic making me goofy. No seasons. Read on."

"Allison . . . Jacqueline . . . Patricia . . . Julia." Winter's best friend . . . Winter's tragic mother . . . Allison's loving mother . . . the role Winter played in Peter's movie, an imaginary role based on the woman Peter had loved and lost. Allison suppressed a frown. This was Winter's decision, not hers.

"It's none of those, either." Winter retrieved the notepad

from Allison, turned to the next page, wrote three words, and handed the notepad back to Allison. "This is her name."

"Roberta Allison Carlyle."

"Roberta is Mark's mother," Winter said softly, remembering the kind woman whose children teased her about "grandbaby lust." Roberta Stephens would never see her granddaughter. Or would she? a mysterious voice within Winter asked. Was it a voice driven by anesthetic goofiness? Or was it the voice of a new mother who wondered if she could really hide this miracle from the man she loved?

"It's a beautiful name, Winter."

"Yes." Winter smiled. "I think we should call her Bobbi."

Part Three

Chapter Twenty-six

Paris, France
September, 1985

Emily emerged from the darkroom of her spacious apartment on Rue de Bourgogne and glanced at her full-to-overflowing appointment calendar to confirm the time of her afternoon appointments. She frowned slightly as she realized the date: September seventeenth. One year ago today she had started to work for *Portrait*, for Rob. One year ago today . . .

Now Emily worked for herself. Now she cared about herself. Now she believed in joy and happiness and love.

Her new life, her new hope, had begun a year ago today *because of Rob*.

Emily looked up from the appointment calendar and saw her image in the mirror above her desk. It was one of many mirrors in her cheery apartment, mirrors that demanded Emily notice herself, demanded that she smile at her own image.

Emily smiled now, softly, thoughtfully, approving the cover of the book—her long golden hair swept off her face and twisted into a soft chignon, the cashmere heather-gray sweater, the mauve silk scarf—but knowing the real change, the real *beauty*, was deep inside.

The phone rang. Emily took the appointment calendar with her as she moved to answer it.

"Emily, love, it's Brian, calling from foggy London."

"Hello, Brian." Brian was a free-lance journalist. He and

Emily had done five feature stories together, he writing, she photographing.

"Emily, I'm really in a jam. When are you taking the pictures of Monique LaCoste?"

"This afternoon."

"Great. Listen, I cannot get out of London, not by plane or boat. The entire country is shrouded in an impenetrable fog. Could you do the interview?"

"I'm not a journalist, Brian."

"I can tell you exactly what questions to ask. All you have to do is get the answers and I'll write the story. It's very easy, Emily, but don't tell anyone I said so. Monique LaCoste is a top movie star, so you just run down the usual movie star questions."

"The usual movie star questions?"

"Right. You ask who she's in love with now, and why she made her last picture — her *motivation* — and has she ever been raped or was she sexually abused as a child."

"What?" Emily asked softly.

"That's very *in* now, Emily. A few years ago it was bulimia and anorexia — all the big stars had one or the other — then alcoholism, then cocaine addiction. Now it's rape and —"

"I can't do it, Brian."

"Surely you establish rapport while you're taking those incredible portraits," Brian pressed.

"I just can't do the interview, Brian."

There was still something about saying no that frightened her. For so much of Emily's life, her no's to men had been received with mean laughter, followed by force and violence. Now she said no, waited for the violence, and when it didn't come, her eyes misted with grateful tears of relief. Emily didn't date — it was much too soon — but she established professional relationships with men throughout Europe, repelled their occasional advances with fear and grace, and wondered what had happened to the kind of mean men who had terrorized her life for so many years. As Emily became stronger, they seemed to have vanished.

Still, Emily couldn't let down her guard. She had to be

wary.

"That's a definite no, Emily?"

"It really is, Brian. Sorry."

"Well. You were my first choice. I'll give Bernard a call. I understand you are photographing the new Canadian Ambassador for *Dominion?*"

"Yes. On Friday."

"I did my interview with him when he was in London last week. Nice man. These interviews are such a wonderful—"

"No," Emily interjected sharply. She tried to soften it a little as she repeated, "No."

"OK. You have your reasons. Lunch next week if I ever get out of soupy England?"

"Sure." *Thank you.*

Before she left her apartment to meet Monique LaCoste at a portrait studio on Rue du Faubourg Saint-Honoré, Emily checked the movie theater schedules in *Le Journale. Love* had just opened in Paris and was playing on the Champs-Elysées. The theater lines would be long, but Emily didn't mind. She had been looking forward to seeing *Love* very much.

"This is the worst fog I've ever seen," Margaret Reilly Carlyle murmured quietly, ominously, as she and Lawrence drove slowly through the opaqued streets of London.

"A night for a good murder," Lawrence observed, trying to lighten the somber mood and the treachery of the drive.

"No doubt nights like this inspired Doyle, not to mention Jack the Ripper."

"And Margaret Carlyle?"

"I'm inspired to find the nearest hotel and hole up for the night."

"We're very near the theater."

"How do you know?"

"There," Lawrence announced with triumph and surprise as a brightly lit marquee appeared behind a veil of smoky fog.

"Luck!" Margaret exclaimed, laughing, relieved.

Margaret and Lawrence Carlyle were not alone in the theater. *Love* had lured many Londoners into the cold, somber, misty evening. A love story with a happy ending was a perfect counterbalance to the heaviness that enveloped London.

Lawrence Carlyle hadn't braved the fog in search of a love story with a happy ending. Or *had* he?

Lawrence realized, as he watched, that he *had* been hoping to see a happy ending, hoping to see that life was happy for the little girl with violet eyes. Lawrence watched Winter through a blur of tears, so happy for her, so sad for him.

The following afternoon, Nigel March, the press agent for Carlyle Productions, arrived at Laurelhurst with a face to match the grim grayness of the autumn fog. Margaret and Lawrence ushered him into the sitting room, cheerily lit and warmed by a crackling fire, and served him tea before addressing the issue at hand.

"Fleet Street is going crazy," Nigel said finally. "They are really going to have a go at us with this one, Lawrence."

"Did you get a copy of Vanessa Gold's column?"

"Of course. It's been reprinted in all the local rags. Which do you prefer?" Nigel asked as he opened his briefcase. "*The Sun? The Daily Mirror?*"

"Just give me a copy and Margaret a copy," Lawrence commanded irritably.

Lawrence's irritation increased as he read Vanessa Gold's *All That Glitters* column published three days before in Los Angeles.

The recent release of *Empress*, Lawrence Carlyle's epic saga of the French Revolution, creates a real-life drama that surpasses even the glittering imaginings of Hollywood's best writers. There is no doubt that *Empress* will receive Academy Award nominations in the top categories: Best Picture, Best Original Screenplay, Best Director, Best Actress, and Best Actor. The main competition — indeed the only competition as far as this writer is concerned—is *Love,* which will compete, perhaps successfully, in every category.

On the face of it, the match-up is between the incredible gifts of Lawrence Carlyle and those of Peter Dalton, but the real drama is an ancient one between father and daughter.

Lawrence Carlyle vanished from his infant daughter's life over twenty years ago. Although the stunning star of *Love,* Winter Carlyle, has been unavailable for comment, she is scheduled to appear on *Good Morning America* and *The Today Show* early next week. Undoubtedly, the question of the estrangement of talented father and talented daughter will arise. One wonders how Winter, the abandoned child, will answer it. One wonders, even more, what Lawrence Carlyle will have to say.

"Jesus Christ," Lawrence whispered.

"*The Daily Mail* has a lovely portrait of you and Margaret and your sons, to which they have convincingly grafted a picture of Winter. Quite a family photo. It will appear in tomorrow's edition." Nigel March arched a critical eyebrow. Lawrence Carlyle should have told him about this months—years!—ago. Why hadn't he?

"Oh, no," Margaret breathed.

"Margaret, we need to call the school and get the boys home *now.* Nigel, you're going to have to keep Fleet Street at bay for a few days."

"What are you going to do, Lawrence?"

"I'm going to talk to her."

"To reconcile?" Nigel asked hopefully.

"Lawrence, can't you just let the attorneys handle it?" Margaret asked.

"If I find that she's doing it for publicity, I'll send an army of attorneys against her. But, Margaret, what if she doesn't know?" Lawrence cringed at his own question. *What if the little girl with the violet eyes had spent her life hating him?*

"But you told me you discussed it with Jacqueline on a

number of occasions."

"I did, but remember what an actress she was. Nigel, please get Steve Gannon for me. He'll know where Winter is."

"I don't want to see him, Steve!"

"You have to, Winter."

"Sometime, I know. But not now, not yet." Winter's mind drifted to the fantasy she had created a year ago as she watched *Hong Kong* with Allison and Emily. In that lovely fantasy, when Winter finally met Lawrence Carlyle, Mark would be there, and Allison, and Emily armed with a camera and a box of Milk Duds. But that was a fantasy, and now Allison would be in New York with Peter, and Emily was in Paris, and Mark was gone.

Now Winter was alone.

No, Winter's heart corrected swiftly. She wasn't alone. Bobbi was with her.

"Winter, the press is going crazy with this now. It will only get worse. It's all they'll ask you about next week on the shows."

"He's planning to be here tomorrow?"

"Yes. Winter, I'll be right beside you the entire time."

"No, Steve." *Bobbi and I will manage.* "That's not necessary. Tell him to come here, to this house, at noon."

"I think I should be there."

"No. Thank you. He's not an axe-murderer, is he?"

"No," Steve said, then asked quietly, "Are you?"

"No." *I'm a mother who can't imagine how a father could ever leave his baby. I need to look him in the eye and ask him what kind of man he is to have done that to me.*

After Steve hung up, Winter held Bobbi close to her, nuzzling her dark black, silky hair, gently kissing her daughter's soft cheeks, silently renewing the promises she had made the moment she knew she was pregnant. *I will love you, precious little one, and protect you, always.*

It was such an easy promise to keep! Loving Bobbi was instinctive for Winter, effortless and strong and good, like the way she had loved Mark, like the way she had once loved her own father.

Winter barely slept that night. She wandered quietly, restlessly, around the mansion, reliving the pain and loneliness and fears of her childhood.

In the morning, Winter dressed in a beautiful pale blue silk sheath. She decided to wear the sapphire earrings that Lawrence had given Jacqueline hours before Winter's birth and that Jacqueline had given Winter hours before her death. Winter remembered that Jacqueline had mentioned a matching necklace. Winter decided she would wear that, too.

Winter went to Jacqueline's bedroom, in the wing of the mansion where she and Bobbi didn't live, and opened the velvet boxes of jewels in the safe until she found the one containing the long strand of flawless sapphires and a note, in Jacqueline's elegant script: *From Lawrence, December 31, 1960.*

At eleven-thirty, Winter gently put Bobbi in her cradle, wound the key to the music box Mark had given her, lifted the carved thatched roof, and softly sang the lyrics, as she always did when she watched her precious daughter fall asleep.

By eleven-forty-five, Winter was in the living room, waiting. She paced — despite dizziness from her sleepless night and a blood count that had still not returned to normal — during the fifteen-minute eternity. As she paced, Winter rehearsed her opening line.

Lawrence Carlyle arrived at precisely noon.

"Hello, Daddy." Winter's delivery was perfect — just as she had practiced — ice-cold, bitter, defiant. But, as she saw the living form of the man whose photographs had meant everything to her as a child, filling her scrapbooks and her dreams, Winter's eyes filled with sudden, surprising tears. Perhaps, if Emily Rousseau had ever taken a portrait of this man, Winter would have been prepared for the sensitive eyes, the quiet shyness, the *uncertainty* she had never imagined in the great Lawrence Carlyle.

"Winter." Lawrence had prepared his lines, too, an eloquent articulation of the rage he felt toward the young woman who was using him, just as her mother had used him. But Lawrence heard Winter whisper "Daddy," saw sad, brave, shimmering violet, and his own eyes became moist as he whispered hoarsely, "My God, you really don't know, do you?"

"Don't know what?" Winter asked, stunned by his emotion, worried by his words.

"May I come in?"

She stood aside and watched Lawrence enter with trepidation that reminded Winter of her own fear about returning to the mansion after five years. Hers had been the fear of the lurking monsters.

Were there dark monsters lurking here for Lawrence Carlyle, too?

"I don't know what?" Winter repeated weakly, sensing danger.

"You don't know that I'm not your father."

Winter swayed, unsteady, weak. Lawrence caught her and guided her to the living room, gently settling her into a chair, then sitting across from her, finding her eyes, not letting them go.

"I'm not your father, Winter."

"I don't understand."

"Jacqueline and I met during the filming of *Marakesh*. We had a brief affair, very stormy, very emotional. We weren't good for each other. When we saw each other again at the Academy Awards the following spring, we exchanged civil hellos, nothing more. Then, in May, while I was filming *Destiny* in Montana, Jacqueline simply appeared. Our affair resumed, and two months later Jacqueline told me she was pregnant with my child."

"With me."

"Yes, but you weren't mine. Jacqueline was already pregnant—and she knew it—when she came to Montana in May. She wanted me—or thought she did. Our marriage was a disaster. I was too quiet for her, too serious, not very exciting."

"So was I."

"Jacqueline knew our marriage wasn't working, but I was the one who made the move to get out and that infuriated her. She matched my desperation to get away with desperation not to let me, or to harm me if I wouldn't stay." Lawrence paused.

He smiled gently as he continued, "My marriage was a disaster, but I had a lovely little daughter who was my life. When I told Jacqueline I wanted a divorce, I also told her I wanted custody of you. I had already discussed this with my attorneys and they thought we could prove that she wasn't—"

"—a terribly good mother."

"Yes, that she wasn't a terribly good mother. But Jacqueline had a trump card I knew nothing about until it was too late. She knew you weren't my child. I didn't believe it. I hated having them get blood from you, hurting you for even those few seconds, but we did all the blood tests, more than once. I wanted so badly to prove that you were mine, but the tests proved, quite conclusively, that you couldn't be. I brought all the documents, if you want to see them." Lawrence gestured to the briefcase he had dropped in the foyer when he'd caught Winter as she swayed. "I tried to get custody of you, anyway, but it wasn't possible. The more I wanted you, the more Jacqueline was determined to punish me by preventing me from even seeing you. I fought it for a very long time, Winter, but I finally realized it would be worse for you to be caught between us, and the attorneys convinced me I would never win."

"But you paid child support."

"It wasn't child support and I wasn't required to pay it. I just wanted to be sure you had money in case something happened to Jacqueline. I had no rights and no obligations. I agreed never to contact you. Jacqueline agreed—*in writing, under oath*—to tell you, when you were old enough, that I was not your father. I saw her in Cannes when you were six. She told me all about telling you. She said she told you that your father had died, that I had married her as a favor, and that we had parted as friends. It was an elaborate story, very convincing. I had her repeat it to me each time I saw her over the next ten years, and it was always the same."

"She never told me. She just said you left because you didn't want us."

"I wanted you."

"You loved me?"

"I loved you very much, Winter."

377

"I never knew," Winter whispered. Then, very quietly, she added, "Maybe I did know. Maybe that's why I was so lonely, because there had been love and then it was gone."

"Oh, Winter, I am so sorry."

"I waited for you to come to me after she died."

"I would have come if I had known—even imagined—that you were waiting. But I believed you knew. I thought I was nothing at all to you, a face and a voice that you were too young to even remember."

"I missed you all those years."

"I missed you, too . . . all those years."

Winter heard the soft sound, a vibration that only a mother would hear, but when she looked up she realized Lawrence heard it, too.

"I have to—"

"May I come with you?"

"Yes." Winter led the way to the wing of the mansion where she and Bobbi lived in the wonderful rooms decorated by Allison.

"This was always my favorite part of the mansion," Lawrence said.

Winter stared at the serious, sensitive man who wasn't her father but was so much like her!

"Mine, too."

Bobbi was awake and cooing, wanting Winter, wondering at her mother's surprising absence.

"Oh," Lawrence breathed. He looked questioningly at Winter—May I pick her up?—then gently lifted the baby out of the cradle from which he had lifted Winter so many times. "Who are you?"

"She's Bobbi."

"Hello, Bobbi. You look just like your mother looked at your age."

"No. I was an ugly baby, an ugly child," Winter reminded him.

"You were? I don't remember that. I thought you were very beautiful." Lawrence's words were causing pain, fresh wounds for both of them, so he carried Bobbi to the French doors that

378

opened onto the terrace surrounding the pond of koi. "We used to spend hours here, Winter, you and I. You loved watching the fish."

"I did?" No wonder this place had been her sanctuary! In this place, for the first year of her life, she had been safe and happy and *loved*.

"You laughed when they splashed and giggled when they ate out of your tiny hands."

Lawrence and Winter sat at the edge of the pond in the warm autumn air. Lawrence held Bobbi, gently, lovingly, as he must once have held Winter. Bobbi was intrigued with the deep voice and strong arms and warmth, but she was hungry, too.

"Are you starving?" Winter asked gently as she took her suddenly fussy daughter from Lawrence's arms. "I—I have to nurse her."

Lawrence stood up.

"I'll . . ."

"Don't go. I mean . . ."

"I'll wait downstairs. I won't leave, Winter. I don't want to leave. Take your time feeding this hungry little girl. I'll still be here."

Lawrence waited for Winter and Bobbi in the screening room. After thirty minutes, they joined him in the peach room with the cushiony chairs.

"I used to spend hours in this room watching the movies," Winter told him.

"So did I, with you on my lap."

"You cared about all these treasures more than she did, didn't you?"

"Yes," Lawrence answered softly and looked at Winter gently. *These treasures, and the greatest treasure . . . you.*

Winter smiled at him through fresh tears.

"Do you have a screening room at Laurelhurst?" she asked finally.

"Yes," Lawrence answered casually, not suspecting until he

saw the sudden sparkle in the glistening violet. "Winter . . ."

"They belong to you. You should have taken them with you when you left." *Just like you should have taken me!*

"No, Winter."

"Yes!" Winter laughed. "I'm shipping them to you whether you like it or not! It will take me a little while to find the best movers and arrange for insurance."

"You have other things to do."

"Not really. Bobbi and I have lots of fun making telephone calls. She loves tugging on the cord! Really. It's settled."

"Thank you."

Winter, Bobbi, and Lawrence spent an hour in the screening room, then walked to the kitchen for tea.

"You haven't asked me about your real father, Winter."

"No, I . . ." *You are my real father!*

"I don't know who he is. I don't think Jacqueline knew, either."

Winter nodded solemnly.

"I loved her, even though she wasn't a terribly good mother," Winter whispered after a few moments.

"I loved her, too, Winter. I wished I could make life happy for her, but what I had to give wasn't enough for her. Jacqueline was always searching for something more — more magic, more enchantment, more love. I think she found it, in brief spurts, in the films she made, when she could be someone else for a while, but then the letdown of returning to her own life was devastating."

Lawrence held Bobbi while Winter made the tea.

"Tell me about Bobbi's father, Winter."

"He didn't want me. He didn't love me enough."

"You spent your life believing that about me and you were wrong. Are you sure about him?"

"Yes." *It is dangerous to care. People leave you.* Lawrence, Jacqueline, Mark. But she *had* been wrong about Lawrence! And Mark? Winter relived the scene — such a brief good-bye scene! — in the Sculpture Garden over and over. She was acting, pretending it didn't matter, rushing to get away from Mark before he saw that her heart was breaking. What if

Mark had been acting, too?

"Winter?"

"Maybe I'm not sure," she whispered quietly.

Lawrence and Winter drank tea and played with Bobbi, and, in little bits, Winter told Lawrence the fears and secrets she had always planned to tell him when they were reunited.

"And I had a dream that I would be a wonderful actress and I would star in one of your films."

"In the briefcase, beneath all the legal documents, is a script for a movie I'm going to film on my estate in England next spring. When I saw you as Julia, I knew you were perfect for the lead. I was going to call you — thinking I'd need to remind you who I was — and then the *All That Glitters* column appeared."

"I'm not going to act for a while. I want to be with Bobbi."

"Bobbi is very lucky to have you as her mother," Lawrence said quietly. "If you wanted to be in the movie, Winter, Bobbi could be with you. I would want both of you to live with me and my family at Laurelhurst during the filming. My wife, Margaret, will love you and Bobbi. And my sons will be enchanted with you both. My twelve-year-old will demand more blood tests because he'll want you to be his sister. And my sixteen-year-old will demand them, too, to prove that you aren't, so he can marry you."

Winter laughed lightly, but Lawrence saw the soft hope in her eyes.

"I'm not your father, Winter," Lawrence reminded her gently, sadly. "The tests really are conclusive."

"But we are so much alike!"

"Yes. And we loved each other very much." Lawrence added softly, something he had never told anyone, "When Margaret was pregnant, I secretly hoped we wouldn't have a daughter. As far as I was concerned, you were my daughter. I didn't want to replace you."

Lawrence and Winter and Bobbi spent the afternoon together. As twilight began to fall over the autumn sky, Winter agreed that she and Bobbi would spend Christmas at Laurelhurst. She also decided to read the movie script Lawrence had brought with him.

"We will make other movies together, Winter," Lawrence assured her. "But take a look at this role and know that you wouldn't really be away from Bobbi during the filming."

"All right. Thank you." Winter frowned briefly. "What shall we do about the press?"

"I think we should tell them the truth."

"Do you want to give the story to Vanessa Gold, or are you angry with her?" Winter asked.

"I'm not angry anymore, are you? Vanessa's words were simply righteous indignation for an abandoned little girl. Did you know that she came to the hospital the night you were born?"

"No."

"Maybe that's why she was so surprised—and outraged—that I vanished from your life. When I talked to her that night, I'm sure she saw how much I loved you. It's fine with me to give Vanessa the story."

Winter made two phone calls. The first was to a thrilled and amazed Vanessa Gold. Winter gave Vanessa no details over the phone, saying simply that she and Lawrence would like to meet with her, to *explain*. Vanessa replied simply, "Fine. Wherever. Whenever."

Winter's second call was to Patricia Fitzgerald, because Allison was probably just landing in New York and because Bobbi was still a secret. Patricia said she would be delighted to babysit her surrogate granddaughter.

After she finished the two calls, Winter thought about Bobbi's real grandmothers: Roberta Stephens, whose merry eyes twinkled when she talked about grandbabies, and Jacqueline, who had had magic and love—Winter's love, Lawrence's love—but had frantically searched for more.

Lawrence watched Winter's beautiful face become very sad as she thought about Jacqueline.

"Winter?"

"I don't want Mother to seem like the villain in all this. Perhaps she *is,* but I did love her. Sometimes I think she was trying very hard."

Lawrence nodded thoughtfully.

"All right, Winter," Lawrence said quietly, marvelling at her lovely generosity despite the pain she had suffered because of Jacqueline. "I don't want that, either. We'll tell Vanessa it was a terrible misunderstanding."

"It *was* a terrible misunderstanding. And . . ." Emotion swept through Winter as she remembered the words, *Mark's words about Lawrence.* But she and Lawrence had another chance. She and Lawrence were the lucky ones. And Jacqueline?

"And?" Lawrence asked gently.

"The greatest loss was hers."

Chapter Twenty-seven

"Hello, Muffin," Allison greeted the excited blond fluff as she let herself into Peter's apartment at ten P.M. Friday night. Peter was at the theater. Allison had taken a cab from LaGuardia into Manhattan. "How are you? Come help me unpack."

Unpacking was a quick process. Allison had clothes in New York, just as Peter had clothes in Los Angeles. Only six weeks until November, Allison thought with a smile. "In six weeks, Muffin, you'll be a California girl again. How does that sound?"

If wiggling were a measure, it sounded very good to Muffin.

"It sounds good to me, too." Allison laughed. "How about a cup of tea?"

After she made the tea, Allison sank down into a dark couch made soft and bright with plush pastel accent pillows. Muffin curled up at her feet, on her own pillow, and Allison turned on the television to watch the news while she waited for Peter.

"*Terror struck in Paris today as seven armed men seized the Canadian Embassy. No group has yet claimed responsibility for the act of terrorism, however four hostages are being held at this time. Three of the hostages are Canadian, all members of the military. The fourth hostage, pictured here in a passport picture released to the press by the terrorists, is an American citizen. Emily Rousseau is a free-lance photographer living in Paris.*"

"Oh, no!" Allison gasped as she saw the photograph of Emily. "*Emily.*"

The news was sketchy. Allison checked all channels, but there were few details. Emily had been in the embassy doing a

384

photograph of the new Canadian Ambassador to France. For unknown reasons, she had not been released with the embassy staff and the other women who were in the embassy at the time of the takeover. One newscast commented on this, wondering if it was because Emily was an American, a valuable prize, but noted that several American men *had* been released.

The information was frustratingly meager. Allison was seized with helplessness and an overwhelming need to do something, or find someone who *could*.

Rob could do something. Rob had journalistic connections, and he cared very much about Emily.

It was seven-thirty in Los Angeles. Allison called Directory Assistance. The number provided for Rob Adamson, Allison realized as she wrote it down, was his office number at *Portrait*. Rob's home phone number was unlisted.

But Elaina Kingsley was listed. Allison reached Elaina at home.

"Elaina. It's Allison Fitzgerald. Is Rob with you?"

"Rob? No." *Rob hasn't been with me for months,* Elaina thought sadly. She was still bewildered by what had happened. Elaina didn't *know* what had happened, why it had all just fizzled out. Rob had been quiet, apologetic, firm—"It's over, Elaina. I'm sorry"—but almost as bewildered as she.

"Are you expecting him?"

"No." *But every time the phone rings, I hope it will be him.*

"Elaina, I need to speak with Rob. Could you give me his home telephone number?"

Allison reached Rob's answering machine and left a message.

"Rob, this is Allison Fitzgerald. Would you please call me as soon as you get this message—no matter what time. I'm at a number in New York, area code 212 . . ."

Allison watched the twenty-four-hour news channel. The hostage situation at the Canadian Embassy in Paris was mentioned twice every thirty minutes, but each report was the same. The embassy was under siege, hostages had been taken, the authorities were awaiting demands from the terrorists.

Peter returned to the apartment from the theater at eleven-thirty.

"Peter!"

"Hello, darling. Allison, what's wrong?"

"Oh, Peter . . ."

The phone rang and Peter answered it.

"Hello?"

"Hello. This is Rob Adamson returning Allison Fitzgerald's call."

Peter's heart raced at Rob's *name,* at the sound of Rob's voice, and at the stunning fact that Rob was calling for Allison. Allison knew Rob? Allison knew Rob and something was wrong and . . .

"It's Rob Adamson," Peter said quietly.

"Oh, good." Allison took the receiver and Peter held his breath "Rob?"

"Hi," Rob answered tentatively. Rob hadn't seen or spoken to her since the opening of the Chateau Bel Air. Allison's voice told him she wasn't calling out of the blue on a Friday night from New York to say merrily, The interior designer *extraordinaire* is ready to be in *Portrait.* "Allison, what's wrong?"

"I was calling about Emily, to see if you knew anything."

"What about Emily?" Rob asked anxiously.

"Oh, you don't know!"

"Know what, Allison?"

"Rob, Emily is being held hostage in the Canadian Embassy in Paris. It's on the news. I thought you would have heard."

"I just walked in," Rob murmured, stunned, seized with fear.

"I thought you might be able to find out more, or that you might know someone who could."

"Yes. I do. I will. I—I'll leave for Paris tonight." Rob was supposed to take the eleven P.M. Qantas flight to Australia. His bags were already packed. He had just been for a long run on the beach before getting ready to leave. He would go to Paris instead. "I'd better get going."

"Will you let me know, Rob? I'll be at this number until Sunday, then back in LA."

"Yes, I will."

Rob hung up without a good-bye or a thank-you. Allison returned the receiver to its cradle and fell into Peter's arms.

"Peter, I'm so afraid for her."

"She'll be all right, darling."

Peter's heart and mind were caught in the midst of two horrors: the horror of what was happening to Emily, and the horror of what *might* happen to his love. The angry promise Rob had made last December—the promise to destroy a love if Peter ever found one—thundered in his mind. *If I can hurt you, Peter, if I can make you ache until you want to die because the loss is so great, I will do it. That is my promise to you.*

"You called Rob Adamson, Allison," Peter whispered as calmly as he could, given that his mind screamed, *Why?* "He owns *Portrait* magazine, doesn't he?"

"Yes. Rob knows Emily, of course, and I thought he might have connections."

"Do you know him?" Maybe Allison didn't actually know Rob. Maybe she just knew his name and knew about him through Emily.

"What? Oh, yes."

"Is he—?" Peter paused. He needed to absorb this—*Allison knows Rob Adamson*—and to force control into a voice that threatened to betray his fear. Had Rob been Allison's lover? Was he the mysterious sender of red roses on Valentine's Day? *Oh, Allison, have you made love with this man who would happily destroy me and us?* "Did you date him?"

"What? Oh, no." Allison pulled away from the strong arms that held her so securely just enough to see his face. He looked so worried, so *afraid!* She found a trembling smile and whispered gently, "Peter, Rob is a friend."

"Oh." Peter pressed his lips against her red-gold curls and drew her close to him again.

No more secrets, he had promised her on that moonlit night last August. That night he learned that he had kept the secret of Sara for too long. His foolish hope to spare Allison sadness had backfired. The revelation that night had caused more than sadness; it had *threatened their love.*

Since that night, after Bobbi was born, Peter and Allison

had so gently, so tenderly, so lovingly repaired the damage he had caused, restoring the trust and the joy and the love. Now their love was whole again, stronger even, and more confident.

And now there was a new secret that threatened to destroy.

Since that moonlit August night, Peter and Allison hadn't spoken of Sara, or of his past, again. Now Peter would have to journey back to that time, and he would have to take his lovely Allison on that painful voyage. He would have to cause her merry eyes to sadden with bewildered tears again.

Rob was Allison's friend, but she obviously hadn't told him about *them,* not yet, because in these months when she and Peter were mostly a continent apart, they had protected the rare moments together by keeping their love hidden. Peter knew Allison wouldn't tell Rob about their private love before November, when he and Allison would be together always, forever. Then Peter would tell Allison everything—how he blamed himself for Sara's death, just as Rob blamed him for causing it.

Peter wanted to be the one to tell Allison—he *would* be—but even if she heard the story from Rob, the truth would be the same no matter who spoke it.

The truth was the same, and Peter's only defense against Rob's rage, Rob's attempt to destroy their love, would be so painful for Allison to hear.

The truth was, simply, that Peter's great crime—his only crime—was that he had loved Sara Adamson Dalton *too much.*

I'll tell Allison everything in November, Peter decided. *I will hold her and love her and tell her the simple, painful truth.*

Peter would keep this final secret until November, only six weeks away. Only six weeks until their forever . . .

"Robert Jeffrey Adamson," the distinguished white-haired United States Ambassador to France read the name on Rob's passport. Rob presented the passport to the guard at the embassy entrance. Security had been increased in all embassies in Paris in the past twenty-four hours.

"Rob."

"And your relationship to Emily Rousseau, Rob, is what?"

"A friend."

"Do you know her family? The permanent address on her passport is a house in Santa Monica where she apparently rented a room for the past six years. The owners don't know how to reach her family, and despite the publicity no one has come forward."

"No one will. Emily left her family years ago."

"You are, I believe, the owner and publisher of *Portrait* magazine."

"I'm not here for a story. I'm here to help Emily."

"Help?"

"Whatever I can do."

"Frankly," the Ambassador said with a sigh, deciding the worried blue eyes and strained face really cared about the young woman hostage, "we're all feeling a little helpless. The French police and an international terrorist unit and a special team from the U.S. are working together, but I'm sure you've heard the demands—outrageous demands for release of so-called political prisoners."

"There are no plans to meet the demands?" Until this moment, Rob had firmly believed in the policy of not negotiating with terrorists, no concessions whatsoever. It made sense—reasonable, rational.

But this was emotional, this was *Emily*.

"No. Paris has become a war zone in the past few months—car bombings, hostage-taking, *plastique* exploding in cafeterias and department stores. It's a war that the French government has no intention of losing."

"So what are they doing to get her—them—out?"

"Talking. Plans beyond that, if there are any, are top secret."

"I see. You know, I might be a much more valuable hostage than Emily. I *would* be. I have a great deal of money, and even though we don't believe in concessions to hostages, from the terrorists' standpoint, I would be a good bargaining chip because there are many influential people who would put pressure on the authorities to get me released."

"You want to trade yourself for Emily?"

"Yes." Rob repeated quietly, firmly, "Yes."

"I don't think that's possible."

"Will you at least tell the negotiators, or let me tell them?"

"I will tell them. I think the terrorists might be happy to have you, too, but they wouldn't necessarily release Emily."

But at least I could be with her!

"Besides, it's very likely that Emily will be released anyway. Terrorists rarely hold women hostages for very long. It's a bit of a mystery why she is being held at all. She seems to have no political ties that would be of value to them, except that she is American, but there were American men in the embassy who were released. Do you have any idea?"

Rob had an idea, but it was unspeakable. It filled every corner of his heart and his mind, tormenting him, making his desperation to free her, or be with her, almost frantic.

Rob shook his head but his mind screamed, *Because evil men sense Emily's vulnerability and want to harm her!*

"You will tell them that I am offering myself in trade," Rob said, giving an order, barely maintaining control.

"I will."

"I'm staying at the Ritz. Will you call me if there is any news?" The command became a plea as the reality of his helplessness — the helplessness of all of them — settled in.

"Yes. I will call you."

The Ambassador called the next day to say that Rob's proposal had been rejected and to report that there was no news. For the next five days, the telephone in Rob's room was silent. Rob used the phone twice, shortly after he arrived, to leave messages on Fran's answering machine at his office and on Allison's machine in Santa Monica. He told Fran to reach the people he was supposed to meet in Sydney, Auckland, Bangkok, Hong Kong, and Tokyo, to cancel, and to say that he would be in touch. Rob didn't tell Fran where he was. Rob's message to Allison was that he was in Paris and he would call her if there was news.

For five days and nights after Rob arrived — six days and nights after Emily had been taken — the phone was silent and there were no messages for him when he returned from his daily pilgrimage to the cordoned-off area in front of the besieged Canadian Embassy on Avenue Montaigne.

Rob paced between the hotel and the embassy, restless to be away from either place too long, tormented by the silence of the room and by the ineffectual hubbub of the reporters and onlookers who hovered outside the embassy. A crowd kept vigil, waiting, expectant, hoping for drama.

The Canadian Embassy had become another tourist attraction in the City of Light, another place to spend part of a gorgeous autumn day. The September sun bathed Paris in unseasonable warmth and the city responded gaily, pulsing with laughter and energy, forgetting even the recent reigns of terror that had plagued its streets during the too-hot summer.

In most parts of Paris everything was sunny and vibrant. But on the Avenue Montaigne was a small island of terror, a zone of war. Emily's girlhood home had probably been just like this. From the quiet street, Emily's house probably looked like any other house. Outside, children laughed and played, and there was an eerie illusion of normalcy. But inside, there had been terror, assaults on bright sunny days and moonlit nights, in defiance of all that was good and lovely.

The entire block around the Canadian Embassy, a majestic structure of once-white marble, was roped off. Helmeted, armed, uniformed guards were posted at frequent intervals. In the center of the empty street was a van, equipped with electronic equipment, which served as the command post for the small war that was being waged in the center of Paris.

Rob stared at the gray-white walls of the fortress — Emily's prison, her latest prison — and sent screaming messages from his heart.

I'm here, Emily. I'm here and I care so much. Please hear me, please know.

The call from the United States Ambassador came at

eleven-twenty on Rob's sixth night in Paris. Rob stared for a moment at the phone, the strident noise piercing the darkness, and his mind took him unwillingly, horribly, to a late night call years before, the night Sara had died.

"An antiterrorist team stormed the embassy an hour ago. Emily is here."

Emily? Emily's body?

"She's alive?"

"Yes."

"How is she?"

Rob heard the hesitation in the Ambassador's voice, and then the grimness as he answered, "She's very bad. In shock, I think. She refused to go to the hospital, so the French police brought her here. So far, the press hasn't discovered she's not with the other hostages."

"I'm on my way." Rob started to add, *Please tell her I am on my way and I will help her,* but he didn't. He had tried to help Emily once before and all she had felt was betrayal.

The street in front of the United States Embassy was empty, a gray ribbon illuminated by streetlights and the full autumn moon. Rob asked the taxi driver to wait and dashed to the front door.

When he saw the Ambassador's grim face, Rob's heart wept. *No! Emily, you were supposed to wait. I was on my way.*

"She's alive," the Ambassador answered Rob's fear swiftly. "Barely."

"Where is she?"

"In my office."

Emily was curled up, a tiny embryo wishing she had never been born, on a huge leather couch. Her golden hair was snarled, her clothes dirty and torn. She didn't move; the slightest undulation of her chest was the only clue to life.

Rob knelt beside her.

"Emily," he whispered softly to the tangled gold, the incredible beacon that shone above the wreckage. "It's Rob. Honey . . ."

Rob could tell that Emily heard him. Something rustled beneath the gold, but he couldn't see her face. What if his voice, his name, caused more fear? What if it was the lethal shock, the final betrayal?

"Emily, I won't hurt you. I want to help you. I know you may not believe that, but it's true. May I look at your face, Emily? May I move your hair so I can see your eyes?"

Rob held his breath, fearing more withdrawal.

But Emily nodded slightly, and, *so gently,* Rob parted the tangled hair until he saw her face. Her skin was deathly pale and her gray eyes were cloudy, beyond fear, beyond hope, almost beyond life.

"Rob?"

Rob's heart leapt as the gray flickered a little, a sign of life, not fear. *Good, darling, know that I care about you.*

"You're safe, Emily. I'm here. I will take care of you. Honey, I think you need to go to the hospital."

"No, please, Rob. Just take me away." Emily's eyes met his. Her plea tore at his already-weeping heart, but her voice gave him hope, a spirit not quite dead.

Going to the hospital might kill her, Rob realized. The intimate examination by strangers, studying her, poking, prodding, invading, might be too much. If Emily didn't go, she might die, too. She would die in his arms. Rob fought his own fear and said gently, "OK. No hospital. We'll go somewhere else. I'll carry you."

To Rob's amazement, Emily slowly pushed herself up.

"I can walk."

Rob put his tweed jacket over her frail shoulders, draping her torn clothes and protecting her against the coolness of the autumn night. He put his arm around her and was stunned by how light she was, how little there was of her, how gratefully the delicate, trembling body fell against his. Rob grabbed her camera and her purse from where they lay on the floor. Very slowly, Rob and Emily walked across the office to the door and toward the taxi that waited outside.

"Thank you," Rob murmured to the Ambassador. "One more favor. We'll be at the Ritz. If you need to talk to me or if the authorities need to talk to her, that's fine, but I would appreciate it if the press didn't know."

The Ambassador nodded, then frowned and whispered, "She needs to see a doctor."

"I know that, but she needs privacy even more."

Rob planned to leave Emily in the taxi in the circular drive at the Ritz while he arranged for a room, but as he moved to get out, Emily moved with him. Rob sheltered her with his arm and she turned her face against his chest.

"Monsieur Adamson. How may I be of help?" The concierge asked when Rob and Emily stopped at the reception desk.

"I need another room, a suite."

"*Mais oui.*" The concierge looked briefly at Emily and promptly deduced that she was an actress or a rock star, *certainly* on drugs. "You would like the bridal suite?"

"A two-bedroom suite."

"Yes, of course. And your other room?"

"I'll keep it, too, for a while."

"*Certainement.* Pierre will show you to the suite."

"If you'll just give me the keys," Rob said impatiently. He felt Emily slipping, her weightless body becoming heavy as she no longer had the strength even to resist the pull of gravity.

Emily stayed pressed against him, needing his strength.

When they entered the elegant suite, Rob guided her toward one of the bedrooms, talking to her, reassuring her, "You need to rest, Emily, to sleep, and you need food, and—"

"A shower."

"Are you strong enough for that?" *I can help you. I can remove your torn clothes and bathe you, but I know that would terrify you.*

He had to walk such a careful line! He wanted to take control, as he had wanted to take her to a snowbound suite in Aspen, lock the doors against all the outside storms, and talk to her, cry with her, hold her if she would let him, until the demons were purged and she believed in herself and happiness. But control and power and strength over her weakness were her greatest enemies, her greatest oppressors.

"I think I am."

"OK." Rob guided her to the bathroom door. "I'll be in the other room if you need me. Emily?"

"Yes?"

"Honey, you can trust me. I know you don't believe that, but it's true."

Emily gazed at him and her gray eyes softened with a faint happiness, a distant memory.

"I do know that. I do trust you, Rob."

Emily withdrew and closed the door, and Rob held his breath, praying she wouldn't throw the lock. She didn't. After a moment, Rob returned to the suite's living room and paced, worried, restless, *elated* — "I do trust you, Rob" — until finally the sound of water splashing against marble stopped and there was silence.

Silence, and it went on forever. Rob envisioned Emily on the shower floor, her fragile skull cracked as she fell. Finally, he returned to her bedroom.

"Emily?" he called softly, and when she didn't answer, he called more loudly, more urgently, "Emily?"

The bathroom door opened. Emily's face wasn't flushed from the heat of the shower, but more pale, more gray, more near death. The circles under her gray eyes were deep and black. She probably hadn't slept — or maybe there had been brief dreams between the nightmare she was living — much in the past seven days. Hadn't slept, hadn't eaten.

Rob wondered if he should just take her to the hospital. *Against her will?* No, never.

"Why don't you get into bed and I'll order some food."

"No food." Emily walked into the bedroom barefooted, wrapped in the plush terry cloth robe provided by the hotel, bulky and baggy against her small frame.

Her gait was unsteady and wobbly as she made her way to the bed. Rob pulled back the heavy covers, opened to the cool clean sheets, and Emily crawled in, carefully, modestly, in the bulkiness of the robe. When she was lying down, Rob tucked the covers over her and sat in a chair beside the bed.

"Shall I tell you a bedtime story?" he asked.

Rob thought he saw a faint, dreamy smile on her lips.

"OK. Once upon a time there was a beautiful princess. She had long golden hair and eyes the color of the morning mist. . . ."

Emily fell asleep in moments, but Rob stayed beside her for another hour, watching the gentle rise and fall of the covers as she breathed. Finally, he went to his bedroom, but he couldn't sleep. He sat in the living room of the suite all night, every few minutes walking to the open door of her room, making sure the covers still rose and fell.

Chapter Twenty-eight

Emily slept through the night and in the morning, when the bright autumn sun streamed through the bedroom curtains Rob had forgotten to close, he drew them quietly and she slept still.

Rob left the suite twice, leaving notes for Emily each time. The first trip was a brief one, to his other room in the Ritz, to get his things. The second trip, mid-morning, taken when Rob saw that she hadn't stirred and perhaps wouldn't awaken all day, was shopping at the *Bon Marché*.

Emily would need clothes when she awakened. Clean, fresh, new clothes that bore no memory of her ordeal of horror. Rob bought jeans, a cotton blouse, a V-neck sweater, and a warm jacket for her, and a casual outfit for himself, too, because all he had packed in the luggage for his trip to Australia and the Orient was formal.

Rob bought what he thought would be comfortable for Emily — a loose, concealing outfit in subdued colors — although he had a vague memory that the torn and dirty clothes she was wearing last night had been colorful.

Rob bought Emily a pale blue nightgown, too, made of soft flannel, with a ruffled collar and long sleeves, modest and innocent and warm.

When Rob returned to the suite after shopping, Emily was still asleep. He went to his bedroom, lay on the bed, fully clothed, with the door open, and fell asleep.

Five hours later, Rob was awakened by Emily's screams. The suite was dark, shadowy. The bedside clock told him it was eight o'clock. He rushed into Emily's room. She was sitting up in bed, gasping, sobbing.

"Emily!" Rob knelt beside her and saw confusion in her frightened eyes. Had Emily forgotten he was here? Was she so ill last night that she didn't even remember? Had she forgotten what she'd said? *I do trust you, Rob.*

"Rob," Emily whispered, and her gray eyes flickered with hope.

"This is going to be bright," Rob warned gently as he reached for the bedside lamp. He wanted to drive away the darkness and its demons as quickly as possible.

"Yes." Emily squinted, but her lips curled into a soft smile.

"I think you had a nightmare."

Emily nodded.

"Why don't I call room service and we'll have a nice dinner in the living room. OK?"

"Yes. OK."

"Oh, I got you some clothes. I'll be right back."

Rob returned in moments with the packages from the department store. Then he left to order dinner, while Emily dressed.

Tears filled Emily's eyes when she saw the baggy jeans, symbols of her old life, symbols of the only way Rob had ever known her.

The only way he will ever know me, Emily thought sadly. She *believed* she had made such progress! But those evil men had seen through her delicate facade of strength and courage. They knew she was a victim and always would be.

Emily had had such lovely fantasies of seeing Rob again. He would be in Paris, doing a portrait, and they would pass on the Champs-Elysées. Rob would do a double take, then whisper, his dark blue eyes smiling appreciatively, "Emily, is that you? You look wonderful!" And she would smile, a beautiful, confident smile, and answer softly, "I am wonderful, Rob. Thanks to you."

But now . . . Emily looked at the baggy jeans and tears spilled from her eyes. Finally, she put on the lovely nightgown, under the bulky robe, and walked into the living room.

As they ate the gourmet dinner, Rob cast careful glances at Emily, trying to assess but not stare. His horrible fears that she might die in her sleep were eased. Emily still looked pale, ravaged, exhausted, but she was stronger. She would be even better with more sleep, if her nightmares didn't conspire to prevent the necessary rest.

Here, in the City of Light, on a dark night in January, Rob had urged Emily to talk about her demons, hoping that talking might help vanquish them. Would it help for Emily to talk now? If she could speak of the horrible ordeal in the embassy, would the nightmares be quieted?

"Emily?"

"Yes, Rob?"

Rob's heart ached. He didn't want to hear about it, but, for her, if it could help . . .

"Do you want to tell me what they did to you?" he asked gently.

Emily saw the worry in his blue eyes and smiled softly.

"They did nothing, Rob."

"Nothing?" Was Emily denying what had happened? Was the horrible memory banished to her dreams, a torment that would awaken her for years to come? Was she trying to spare *him?* "They didn't touch you?"

"No, Rob," Emily answered truthfully. "They were planning to, after it was over, as a reward." Emily frowned at the terrifying memory of their taunts, their wicked promises, their evil laughs, the pleasure they took in her fear. "They made threats, that was all."

Thank God, Rob thought. If they had touched her, if they had carried out their threats, he wondered if Emily would still be alive, or if she would have found a way to die.

The rich gourmet food and her week of sleepless terror made Emily's gray eyes grow weary long before the meal was over.

"Back to bed," Rob said gently.

"OK."

Rob followed Emily into her bedroom. She looked at him shyly but without fear as she removed the bulky bathrobe, revealing the modest nightgown, before crawling into bed. When she was in, Rob tucked the plush satin covers around her.

He was about to ask if she wanted to fall asleep to a bedtime story, when *she* asked a question.

"Why were you here, Rob? Why were you in Paris?" *Would I have seen you on the Champs-Elysées if this hadn't happened? Was I that close to my fantasy?*

"I was here because of what happened to you, Emily. I came as soon as I heard."

"You did?"

"Yes, of course," Rob told the astonished gray eyes.

"When was that? How long ago?" *How long was I in that hell?*

"A week ago."

"A week?" Emily whispered softly, sadly, "Then you need to go back soon."

"I do? Why?"

"Because of *Portrait*." Emily frowned slightly. "And because of Elaina."

"*Portrait* will survive. And I don't see Elaina any more."

"You didn't marry Elaina?"

"Marry? No." Rob gently moved a strand of golden silk that had fallen into her eyes. Emily didn't stiffen at his touch, and Rob saw no fear. "I couldn't marry Elaina, because I am in love with someone else."

"Oh. Well, you need to get back to her then."

"Emily, I am with her. I am with the woman I love."

Rob watched her lovely gray eyes fill with tears as she understood the meaning of his words.

"I love you, Emily."

Emily's tears spilled, like a gentle, nourishing spring rain, without clouds, without doubt, without fear.

"I love you, too, Rob."

"You do?"

"Yes," she whispered. *I have loved you for a very long time.*

Emily wanted to gaze into his loving ocean-blue eyes forever and to lose herself in his gentle voice. But her exhausted-trying-to-heal body fought the lovely wishes of her heart, demanding sleep.

"Sleep now, darling Emily," Rob whispered as he watched her valiant struggle to stay awake, his own heart filled with immeasurable joy. "I'll be right here when you awaken. Tonight I think I'll tell you a story about a man—we'll pretend he's a prince—and how he fell very much in love with the golden-haired princess. It all began at a magnificent wedding in a rose garden. . . ."

In the morning, while Emily was still sleeping, Rob made calls to Fran and Allison. Rob told Fran he would be away a little longer, perhaps much longer, and he would call her later with details.

Rob apologized to Allison for not calling the minute Emily was freed. He didn't explain the delay—"I was so afraid she was going to die, Allison"—and Allison just asked Rob to give Emily her love. Allison didn't tell Rob about the postcard she had received from Emily. It had been mailed from Paris two days before the embassy was seized and had arrived in Santa Monica while Emily was still being held hostage. Emily had written, *Dear Allison and Peter, I saw* Love *last night—twice!—at a theater on the Champs-Elysées.* Love *was wonderful, something to remember when the moments of one's life are not so joyous. Your movie is a gift, Peter, a generous loving gift.*

While Emily slept, Rob paced quietly in the suite, thinking, planning. At ten A.M. he wrote her a note—*I'll be back soon. I love you*—and walked out of the Ritz and across the Place Vendome to Van Cleef and Arpels. Rob had decided to simply order the ring today, with a request—a demand—that it be rushed. But the ring was there, already set, a flawless two-carat emerald-cut diamond set between delicate rows of glittering baguettes. It was exactly what Rob wanted, beautiful and perfect, like Emily.

"Flawless, *oui monsieur,*" the jeweler assured. "Of course, it may need to be sized. This ring will only fit a very slender finger."

"If it needs to be sized, you can do that in less than a day, can't you?"

"*Mais oui.*"

Emily was awake, dressed in the baggy jeans, cotton blouse, and V-neck sweater, when Rob returned to the suite.

"Good morning."

"Hi." Emily smiled shyly. Last night would all have been a dream if she didn't have Rob's note. Last night, Rob had spoken the words and this morning he had written them, and now his blue eyes were telling her all over again.

"I got something for you." Rob smiled and added uncertainly, "I hope you like it. If not, I can take it back."

Rob removed the small blue velvet box from his jacket pocket. His hands trembled as he handed it to her, and Emily's trembled as she opened it.

"Rob." Emotion stopped her words. After a moment, she whispered, "I don't understand."

"It's an engagement ring. Emily, will you marry me?"

"Why wouldn't I like it?" Emily asked, not answering his question, fearing his answer to her own.

"Because—" Rob answered gently, "because part of you believes you don't deserve beautiful things. Emily, if this makes you uncomfortable, we can have simple gold bands, or no bands at all. All I really care about is marrying you. I don't want you to change, darling. I only thought you could be happier."

I was happier, Rob! You never knew me the way I could be—strong and happy and full of hope.

Emily frowned as dark fear from the old Emily Rousseau—the Emily with no self-confidence, no belief in herself—

taunted her. *What if Rob doesn't love the new Emily?*

No! He must. He will. Rob was the one who knew to search for the loving, beautiful part of you! He knew your life could be happier. He wanted that for you.

"Emily?" Rob saw her fear and uncertainty, fear and uncertainty caused by *him*. "Darling, I'm sorry. I'll take the ring back."

"No, Rob. Don't take it back, but give it to me later. Ask me again, later, to marry you." *If you still want me.* "Tonight, at dinner, at the Tour d'Argent. OK?"

"OK," Rob answered uneasily. His anxiety increased as Emily gathered her purse and the jacket he had bought for her. "Emily, where are you going?"

"I can't wear jeans to the Tour d'Argent, can I?"

"*Yes.* Emily, as far as I'm concerned, you can always wear jeans."

Emily wrote an address and phone number on a piece of paper and handed it to Rob.

"This is the address of my apartment. I'll be ready at seven-thirty."

"Emily, please don't go!"

"Rob, why not?"

"I'm afraid you won't come back."

Emily's surprised, lovely smile reassured him a little.

"With all the collateral you have?" she asked softly.

"What collateral?" *The ring, which you don't want? The cotton nightgown?* Rob asked sadly, "What? Are you leaving your camera?"

"No, Rob. I'm leaving my heart."

Emily did a portrait of the fashion designer at Givenchy soon after she'd arrived in Paris. The designer made Emily the same offer the designers at LaCroix, Dior, Chanel, and St. Laurent had made in January, an offer to clothe her in his finest silks and satins—the smooth, feminine Givenchy lines—as a gift. Although by June Emily Rousseau already looked more stylish, the designer knew he could make her look sensational.

Emily took a taxi from the Ritz to Givenchy.

"*Bonjour.*"

The designer gazed at the young woman with the brilliant flowing golden hair, baggy jeans, and bulky jacket without recognition. Emily swept her hair off her face. "*C'est moi.*"

"*Emily.* Are you all right?"

"*Oui. Merci.*" Emily smiled. She didn't want to talk about the ordeal in the embassy. "You told me once you could make me look beautiful."

"You are beautiful. But I can dress you in something that will make you look exquisite."

"Something soft and feminine? Something for being in love?"

"*Certainement.*"

The dress was chiffon, soft layers of pastel, like a spring garden. The designer told Emily to sweep her golden hair off her face and gave her pastel satin ribbons to weave in with the gold.

"Just a single strand, a ray of sunshine mixed in with the flowers," he suggested. "Then let the rest of your magnificent hair fall free, like a golden waterfall cascading down your back."

Emily arrived at her apartment building on Rue de Bourgogne at three o'clock. After reassuring her landlady that she was fine, Emily went to her bright, spacious apartment. Without hesitation—she had already decided—Emily removed the letter she had written to Rob last spring from a locked drawer in her desk. Emily didn't reread the letter. She knew its words—her love for Rob, her gratitude, the news that she had seen Dr. Camden and had worked very hard and was better. Emily didn't reread the letter. She just sent it to him, by messenger.

* * *

Rob's heart pounded anxiously when Emily's letter arrived. He recognized her handwriting immediately and feared what he had feared ever since she left . . . that she wasn't coming back, that he had frightened her away again.

Rob read the letter and tears spilled from his eyes. When he could speak, he dialed the telephone number Emily had left for him.

"I miss you, Emily."

"Did you get my letter?"

"Yes. I miss you. I love you. May I come over now?"

"Yes." Emily was ready—it would take only a moment to slip into the dress and do her hair—and she missed him, too. *Please let this be all right.*

Emily was so beautiful and so uncertain, as if she really didn't *believe* he would love her this way, too.

"Emily." Rob reached into his pocket as he walked toward her, removing the blue velvet box. "Will you marry me? I can't wait until our champagne dinner to ask you."

"Yes. I will marry you, Rob."

Rob slipped the diamond ring on her trembling finger. It fit perfectly.

"My nails . . ." The long, tapered nails had fallen victim, as she had, to the terror in the embassy.

"They'll grow back, Emily. While we're on our honeymoon."

"Our honeymoon?"

"Oh, Emily, this afternoon I was so afraid I would lose you again. I kept myself busy by making wonderful plans for us. I spoke to the U.S. Ambassador. He can arrange for us to be married—very soon—right here, if you want."

"I want."

"Then, if you want, we can wander around Europe for three or four weeks."

"I want that, too."

Rob stood in front of her, gently took her hands in his, and smiled.

"I love you, Emily."

"I love you, Rob."

Rob and Emily had never kissed. They had barely even *touched*. Rob would marry her, spend his life with her, even if they never could kiss, even if that was still too great a terror for her.

Emily saw the love and uncertainty in his dark blue eyes, and read his thoughts.

"Rob, I have never been kissed by a man who loves me."

Rob and Emily made love for the first time on their wedding night. They made love gently, tenderly, in the darkness. Emily didn't stiffen with fear as Rob worried she might, and he could feel her *relief,* but for Emily, there was no pleasure and no joy.

There was no pleasure for her the next night, or the next, or the next, even though it was Emily who wanted to make love, Emily who desperately wanted their love to be whole. Each night she would remove her modest nightgown and curl up quietly in bed beside him. They would make love in the darkness, silently, swiftly, joylessly.

Afterwards, Emily would put on her nightgown again and Rob would put on his pajamas, and, still silent, she would fall asleep.

Emily would fall asleep and Rob would lie awake rehearsing the gentle words he would speak to her lovely gray eyes in the daylight. "Darling, maybe it's too soon for you to make love," he would plan to say. But what if those gentle words caused her pain? What if her gray eyes became cloudy and she asked, hurt, worried, as she had asked once before when Rob had only wanted to find happiness for her, "You think there's something wrong with me, don't you, Rob?" Or, so softly, with tears in her eyes, "Don't you want to make love with me, Rob?"

Rob wanted to *make love* with Emily. He had wanted that for a very long time. His desire for her was so strong. Rob had to be so careful, so controlled, for fear that the power of his desire might feel, to Emily, like familiar violence. Rob wanted to *love* Emily, to share the wonderful pleasures of their love and their loving.

Rob hated the silent, joyless sex.

Rob rehearsed the words but he never spoke them, because, in the morning, Emily's lovely gray eyes would look at him with such hope. *Was I all right, Rob? Do you still love me?*

Rob didn't speak the words, because they would hurt her, and because the joy and love that filled their days was so magnificent. Rob loved Emily more — even *more* — every second of every day. Rob and Emily *touched* in the bright, sunny daylight — holding hands, sharing gentle caresses of affection and warmth, not sex — as they smiled and laughed and talked and loved.

Their days were perfect, golden crescendos of joy and love and happiness that should have led to nights of breathless passion.

But the nights were all the same . . . silent, dark, joyless. Rob knew that for Emily making love without terror, without the fortification of drugs, was a monumental triumph, a symbol of her great trust in him. In some ways, Emily was like a virgin, modest and shy. But, Rob realized sadly, Emily had the modesty and shyness of a virgin, but none of the wonder, none of the innocence, none of the *hope*.

Rob lay awake, rehearsing lines he never spoke, loving Emily with all his heart, hoping that one bright, sunny day they could talk about this without causing her pain.

Eleven days after Emily married Rob, she made an astonishing discovery about herself.

They were in Salzburg at the castle. Emily had left Rob to take a photograph of the valley and lake below. When she returned, she looked up as she approached him and suddenly stopped, stunned.

It was as if she were seeing Rob for the first time ever.

Rob leaned against the stone wall of the castle, his body lean and strong and taut, his handsome face lifted toward the autumn sun, his dark brown hair softly tousled by the breeze, a slight smile on his lips. Emily gazed at Rob—the man she loved with all her heart—and realized that she had *never really looked at him.*

To Emily, Rob was, had always been, *gentleness.* When she thought about him, she thought about his kind, smiling blue eyes, his gentle smile, his soft voice, and his loving heart. She never thought about his *looks.*

Rob's looks were sensational. He was a stunningly handsome man—handsome, sensual, *sexy.* Other women noticed, appreciated, and *wanted* Rob. But until now, Emily had never really noticed her beloved Rob's alluring sexuality, because for her sex had always meant violence, not gentleness, not love.

Until now . . .

Powerful, unfamiliar, *exciting* feelings pulsed through Emily as she stared at him. Rob Adamson, the handsome man who so proudly, so happily wore the gold wedding band she had given him. Rob Adamson, her *husband,* the wonderful, sensual man who loved her and wanted her. Rob Adamson, the man whom she loved, *the man whom she wanted.*

The powerful feelings—Emily's desire for Rob—brought with them a wonderful confidence and a soft, seductive smile.

"Hi, Rob."

"Hi." Rob returned Emily's smile with a look of surprise. Her beautiful pale gray eyes sent a bewitching message—bewitching, provocative, beckoning. He asked with a soft laugh, "What?"

"Come with me."

"All right. Where are we going?"

"Back to our room."

"Are you all right?"

"Yes." *Oh, yes.*

When Rob and Emily were inside their sunny, charming

Austrian hotel, with its brocade chairs, lace doilies, and wood-frame bed topped with a downy puff, Emily gazed bravely into his ocean-blue eyes and whispered, "I want you."

"You do?" Rob asked softly as his heart raced with joy. *You do, my beloved Emily?*

"Yes. Rob, show me how to make love."

Rob didn't show Emily how to make love . . . *they showed each other,* learning, discovering, marvelling together. As Emily learned about the wonder and beauty of her desire for Rob, he learned new things about the astonishing intensity of his love for her and new things about his own capacity for tenderness.

Rob and Emily made love in the gentle light of a golden autumn sun that filtered through lace curtains. They made love with open eyes and gentle hands and tender lips and loving words whispered softly.

"Rob? What are you doing?"

"I'm loving you, Emily. Let me love you. Trust me."

"I do trust you, Rob."

Emily showed him her trust. And Rob showed her the gentleness of his love.

"Emily, are you cold, darling?" Rob asked moments later as he felt her trembling beneath his lips.

"No."

"Are you afraid, honey?" *Please don't be afraid!*

"No, not afraid. Rob?"

"Yes?"

"Don't stop, please. Rob?"

"Yes, darling?"

"I need you. I need all of you."

"Oh, Emily," Rob whispered as she welcomed him and he smiled into her glowing gray eyes. "I love you so much."

"I love you so much, too."

Afterwards, they lay together, caressing gently, silently marvelling at the wonder of their love and of their loving. Rob pulled away, just a little, because he wanted to see her eyes.

Tears spilled softly from the lovely gray, tears of happiness and joy.

As Rob gently kissed Emily's tears, he felt a sudden mist of emotion in his own eyes.

"My lovely Emily, why are you crying?"

Emily smiled a loving smile and gently touched the joyous tears that now fell from the dark ocean-blue.

"I don't know, my darling Rob," Emily whispered. "Why are you?"

Chapter Twenty-nine

Bel Air, California
October, 1985

"Winter, are you OK?" Allison asked as soon as her friend answered the phone. Winter's voice was so flat.

"I have *something*—a virus of some sort. Actually, I'm a total mess. I'm just finishing my period. I have a virus. I can't even do my stupid sit-ups because, in addition to being tired, for some reason all my muscles ache. So, I'm a mess. How are you? How was your weekend in New York?"

"Short. Wonderful. Winter, why don't I come over and babysit my favorite baby in the world so you can get some rest?"

"No, Allison. Thank you. Bobbi senses that her mommy is under the weather so we're just playing quiet smiling games." The flatness in Winter's voice vanished as she spoke of her daughter. Winter loved Bobbi so much! "She is such a miracle, Allison. Every second of every day."

"I know. That's why I'd love to come see her."

"We're fine, really. Tell me about you and Peter. November is only two weeks away. T minus fourteen and counting."

"But who's counting?" Allison laughed.

"Are you still both planning to take off all of November?"

411

"That's the plan. Peter doesn't begin work on *Merry Go Round* until December. Steve's daughter is very eager to take care of Muffin, so Peter and I may even go away for a while."

"How nice. A love story with a happy ending."

Allison hesitated, thinking about another love story, one that *should* have ended happily.

"Have you thought any more about Mark?" Allison asked.

"I think about Mark all the time, Allison," Winter admitted softly, too tired even to deny it. "But I should never have told you I wondered if I could go a lifetime without telling him about Bobbi. Those words were said during my postpartum euphoria."

"You're still euphoric about Bobbi."

"Euphoric about Bobbi, realistic about Mark." *Realistic*, but . . . "Allison, I'd better go. Bobbi is napping and I should be, too."

"Are you sure I can't babysit?"

"Yes, I'm sure. Thank you. As soon as I'm well, would you like to come over and play with us?"

"I'd love to. Let me know if there's anything I can do."

"I will. Thanks, Allison."

When Allison's phone rang two minutes later, she assumed it would be Winter. It was too early for Peter's nightly call from New York, still only halfway through the second act of *Macbeth*.

"I'm on my way!"

"Allison? It's Meg."

"Meg! Hi. Are you in town?"

"No. I'm calling from Greenwich. Cam's at a board meeting in the city. I thought it would be nice to catch up."

Allison felt a twinge of guilt. In her many, many trips to

412

New York in the past six months, she had never called Meg and Cam. A call to Meg and Cam would have meant dinner, at least, a waste of precious moments when she and Peter could be alone.

"How are you, Meg?"

"Fine . . . wonderful . . . *pregnant.*"

"Congratulations."

"Thanks!"

"When are you due?"

"In February. We're very excited." Meg paused briefly, then asked, "Allison, how's Winter?"

"She's fine," Allison answered carefully. The question about Winter followed *too closely* on the heels of Meg's announcement about her own pregnancy. Bobbi was already two and a half months old, but her existence was known to just a trusted few.

Surely Meg didn't know about Bobbi, and yet her voice carried the promise of something dramatic, a delicious secret.

"Why?" Allison asked.

"Oh, I just hoped that Winter hadn't gotten involved with Peter Dalton."

Allison knew Meg and her love of drama, but still her heart began to race and icy shivers of fear pulsed through her.

"Peter Dalton directed *Love,* so of course Winter knew him," Allison said quietly, forcing calm, as if *her* calm would tranquilize Meg and her dramatic news. "Meg, why would you hope that he and Winter hadn't gotten involved?"

"Because Winter is Peter Dalton's type—a beautiful young heiress. Of course, Winter may not be *blue-blooded* enough for his taste. I don't really know about the branches of Winter's family tree. And she's probably not innocent enough, either." Meg took a breath, then confided ominously, "Actually, Allison, *you* are more Peter Dalton's type."

"Meg. What are you talking about?"

"I'm talking about Peter Dalton. Allison, he's the man I told you about at my wedding."

"What man?"

"The man who murdered Sara Adamson. Peter Dalton is the fortune hunter who committed the perfect crime." Meg paused, waited, then finally, taking the stunned silence to be a signal that Allison wanted to hear more, continued, "Sara's mother told Cam's mother. The attorneys told Sheila Adamson not to tell anyone, but she did. Cam's mother told me this weekend. She had to, of course, because I'd been talking about seeing *Love,* and she kept telling me not to without giving a reason. So, I paid careful attention because I knew you'd be interested, given that you knew Sara and know Winter. It's really an incredible coincidence, isn't it? Allison?"

"Yes?"

"Do you want to hear about it?"

"Yes." *No!*

Somehow Meg's breathless words registered above the thundering of the blood in Allison's brain and the screaming of her heart.

"Peter's family was very poor. He and his father hated the wealthy patricians of Greenwich. Maybe Peter wanted Sara's money, but *maybe* he just wanted to harm her for who she was—rich, privileged, born with a silver spoon. Just like us, Allison."

"But, Meg, you said Sara was dying." The words came from Allison's trembling heart, a defiant heart that refused to even *consider* that what Meg was telling her could be true.

"She *was* dying. It was just a matter of time—a very *short* time—before all her fortune would have been his,

414

anyway. That shows how evil he really is, doesn't it? He was too greedy to spend even a penny of the money he would inherit on expensive medical techniques that might have kept her alive a little longer. Or, maybe, he just wanted privileged Sara Adamson to suffer."

No! It's not true! I don't, won't, can't believe it!

"Does Rob believe Peter murdered Sara?" Allison asked, finally breaking the silence that had fallen after Meg finished her devastating story.

"I imagine so. Apparently, there was an angry, almost *violent* scene between Rob and Peter. Peter actually had the nerve to show up at the Adamsons' estate a few days after Sara died."

"So Peter knows how Rob feels about him."

"Yes, of course. Well, Allison, I'd better go. I need extra sleep these days because of the baby. I just thought you'd want to know. I'm so glad Peter and Winter weren't involved."

Peter and Winter weren't involved, but there was another innocent young heiress . . .

In the three hours between the time the conversation with Meg ended and Peter made his nightly call, Allison replayed her friend's words a hundred times, a thousand times, and she replayed, too, every scene of her love with Peter. There were some scenes that Allison wanted to change, just a little, but this time the mind that had urged her, *warned* her, not to run after Peter on Valentine's Day — changing that scene and her life forever — wouldn't permit *any* changes.

Allison *wanted* to forget that Peter had kept the secret of Sara until he was *forced* to tell her because of *Love*.

She *wanted* to forget the horrible fear in Peter's dark eyes after Rob had called the night Emily had been taken hostage, when Peter had asked so innocently, "He owns *Portrait* magazine, doesn't he?" As if he didn't *know* Rob, as if they hadn't been *brothers-in-law* for four years.

She *wanted* to forget that Peter didn't read *Portrait* and that Rob hadn't been at the premiere of *Love*.

And she *wanted* to forget that Peter had promised *no more secrets*.

Allison wanted to forget all those moments, *but she couldn't*.

The greatest battle of Allison's life had been her fight to heal her injured brain so that she would be able to *make new memories*. Allison had fought that battle like a champion, with courage and determination and a spirit that wouldn't lose. She had fought . . . and she had won. Now her healthy mind faithfully recorded all the memories with Peter, every second of their enchanted love.

And now some of those memories threatened to destroy.

The autumn night was moonless. As darkness fell, Allison's apartment became a somber place of silent shadows. Allison sat, numb and immobile while a war raged inside her, a war between her heart and her mind.

There has to be a simple, logical explanation, her heart offered bravely, remembering Peter's reason for not having told her sooner about his wife and his marriage. Peter had wanted to protect her from the sadness. A simple, logical explanation . . . *a loving explanation*. Surely there would be a loving explanation this time!

Such as? came the taunt from her mind.

Well, maybe Sheila Adamson, devastated by the death of her daughter and wanting to place blame for the blameless, had gone a little crazy. Perhaps she made up stories because she couldn't face the tragic reality of Sara's fatal illness. And maybe Peter and Rob had really been like brothers when Sara was alive, but the sadness of her death had made it too painful for them to see each other. Maybe Peter didn't tell me he knew Rob because he wanted to talk to Rob

416

first. Maybe . . .

Make-believe! You're rewriting endings again. Won't it be interesting to see what the master playwright has to say for himself?

Peter will tell me the truth. I know he will. I know that somehow, somehow, this will be all right.

You don't know that! You are scared to death that this ominous dark black cloud won't have a silver lining no matter how much you want it to.

The war raged inside her, confusing her, exhausting her. Allison wondered if she would have the strength to talk to Peter when he called. She prayed that swiftly, so swiftly, he would gently provide the answers—answers she couldn't even imagine—that would make their love safe.

"Hello?"

"Hello, darling. I have such a wonderful surprise for you." Peter's voice was so excited, so happy. "I hope you like it. Allison?"

"Please tell me about Sara Adamson, Peter."

A distant corner of Allison's mind—the corner that would remind her unmercilessly of this conversation—counted the agonizing seconds of silence before Peter spoke.

"I told you about Sara, Allison," Peter answered finally, quietly, as his mind swirled. Rob had gotten to her! But how? When? Peter had worried about waiting until November to tell Allison all the truths about Sara. He had considered telling her sooner, even though he wanted to wait until they had all the time and all the privacy in the world. Then he'd learned that Rob would be in Europe, on his honeymoon, until November, and he knew it was safe to wait. By the time Rob and Emily returned, he and Allison would be far away, on a white sand beach in the South Pacific or in a cozy cabin in the mountains. But

Rob had gotten to her. *Damn him!* "Whatever Rob has told you—"

"I haven't spoken to Rob. It was someone else." Allison heard the anger, laced with fear, in Peter's voice, and she felt her hopes and dreams begin to die. Peter wasn't going to swiftly, tenderly, gently tell her about a mother-in-law whose grief had led to horrible falsehoods, or about a man who was like his brother until the pain of a shared loss made it easier for them not to see each other any longer. Peter wasn't going to make it right. He *couldn't.* Allison asked sadly, "Does it matter who told me, Peter?"

"It matters what you were told."

"I was told the truth. You were married to Sara, the sister of a man you knew to be my friend but whom you pretended not to know."

"I was going to tell you, Allison."

I was going to tell you, Allison. Peter had whispered those same words to her the night he was forced to reveal the secret of his marriage because of *Love.* Allison had believed those words then, and Peter's words of love, and Peter's promise that there would be *no more secrets.*

Now those words, *all Peter's words,* seemed so meaningless, so empty.

Empty. But as Allison felt her dreams of love shatter and die, she didn't feel the emptiness that had accompanied the death of her dreams of blue satin ribbons and Olympic gold. Allison was *full* now, not empty, *full* of powerful and unfamiliar emotions. The new, powerful emotions were terrifying in their strength. And they were beyond her control, *controlling her.*

When Allison finally spoke it was with a voice she didn't recognize, a voice that hurled accusations with a soft hiss, a voice fueled by the immense power of her shattering dreams. At first the voice startled her. The voice with which she had always spoken to Peter—a soft, loving voice laced with joy, a voice just for Peter—was gone. But so was Peter, *her* Peter. And this new voice, this voice of venom, would be understood by the *real* Peter, the evil Harlequin of Allison's nightmares, the man who cut the girth of Sara's saddle with a bloody knife and burst into raucous laughter as he watched fragile, innocent Sara die.

"When were you going to tell me, Peter?" the new voice demanded. "Certainly not *before* you encouraged me to jump the green and white railed fence. That was your plan, wasn't it, Peter? You even *pretended* that you didn't want me to jump again. But you were going to relent, weren't you, Peter? Yes, Allison, you would say. I will watch you. Go ahead, Allison, jump the jump, one last time! One last time, and then I would be dead, too, *just like Sara.* Another heiress whose blue blood you spilled with such joy."

"My God, Allison, what the hell are you talking about?"

"You told me your wife died, Peter. But you *forgot* a few tiny details. That's strange, isn't it? Peter Dalton is so famous for carving the finest point on a thought or an emotion. Yet, you forgot to tell me who she was. And you forgot to tell me why she died."

"Why she died?" *Why had Sara died?* Why couldn't Sara have lived a long, happy life of love? Why couldn't she have been blessed with children and grandchildren and the magnificent privilege of growing old? Why couldn't there have been no pain for lovely Sara? Why? Why? Why? Peter had no answer to such tormenting questions. That was why he wrote. Something deep inside drove him to search the mysterious questions of life. Peter explored the questions, but he had no answers. Peter said sadly, quietly, truthfully, "I don't know why Sara died, Allison."

"Oh, but you do know, Peter! Sara died because you *wanted* her to die."

"*What?*"

"She died because you killed her."

This time the silent seconds were measured by the anguished screams of loving hearts, betrayed, broken, dying.

"Is that what Rob believes?" Peter asked finally, his voice a whisper of despair.

"That's what the Adamsons believe."

"And what about you, Allison? Is that what *you* believe?"

Yes, Peter realized, and with this staggering realization came the beginning of the horrible emptiness that would live with him for the rest of his life, the excruciating pain of the great loss of this love. The loss was even worse this time, because this time it was more than the tragic loss of a joyous, wondrous love. This time, there was the agonizing *betrayal* of that love.

Peter's pain would be everything Rob had promised.

Rob had won.

Allison never answered Peter's question. Sometime in the horrible silence that followed, her trembling hands returned the telephone's receiver to it cradle.

Allison wasn't numb anymore. She remembered the venom of her words and the emotion that gave life to her unspeakable thoughts. Allison had learned new emotions because of Peter Dalton. Because of Peter, Allison had learned about love and fire and passion.

And tonight, because of Peter, Allison learned about hate.

Allison's telephone rang again, four hours later, at one A.M. Allison was awake, sitting in the cold darkness. The harsh noise didn't even startle her. Allison had been surrounded with harshness for hours, the thundering sound of her heart, the piercing cries of her mind. *Peter murdered Sara. Peter is the evil Harlequin. Peter is the one you were going to trap into a confession.*

Had she trapped Peter into a confession? *No.* In fact, if Allison allowed herself to remember Peter's voice, there had been such despair, such hopelessness.

Peter is the evil Harlequin, she reminded herself.

The ringing phone was just another strident noise in the night.

Peter, leave me alone! I can't ever hear your voice ever again. I can't.

Strident, persistent. Allison knew Peter wouldn't hang up.

"Peter, leave me—"

"Allison, help me!"

"Winter?"

"Help me . . . please . . . so sick . . ." Winter's breath came in gasps.

"Winter, I'll call the medics and be right there, OK? Winter, honey, hang up the phone."

It took Winter a moment to respond. Then Allison heard the receiver hitting the phone, close to the cradle, missing it. Then, finally, silence.

The October night was filled with more strident noises—the ambulance sirens and the sound of the alarm at the mansion as the paramedics crashed through the front door. The Bel Air Patrol arrived just as Allison did and quickly silenced the alarm.

Allison rushed to Winter's bedroom. The medics were there, crouched over Winter who lay on the floor. The medics started IVs and oxygen. Their trained eyes reflected worry as they worked on the barely conscious woman who was gasping and in shock.

Allison caught a brief, terrifying glimpse of Winter. She didn't even look like Winter! Her rich creamy skin was angry red and her full pink lips were icy blue. Allison

421

bundled an awake, but strangely quiet and subdued Bobbi in a soft blanket as the medics disappeared with Winter, sirens screaming. The Bel Air Patrol officer offered to drive Allison and Bobbi to the UCLA Emergency Room. Allison gratefully accepted the offer.

Déjà vu. The unsummoned thought settled in Allison's mind as she recalled the other middle-of-the-night rush to UCLA to save Winter's life. But this time Peter wasn't here, *directing a scene he had written so carefully, so evilly,* a scene in which the pregnant mother and her unborn child were destined to die. Allison recalled the terror in Peter's eyes that night. Had it been remembered terror, *remorse* for what he had done to Sara? Or had it simply been rage that he was being forced to face his crime again? Had Allison ever accurately read the messages of Peter's dark eyes? Had there been arrogance—icy contempt for her wealth and privilege—from the very beginning? Was the sadness just a facade, just the Harlequin's sinister disguise worn to lure *her* into his trap?

That August night Winter had fought Peter's fear, the assurances that sounded *false*—were false!—with strength and defiance. I'm fine, Peter! My baby is fine!

The night Bobbi was born, Peter could not will Winter to die, as he had willed Sara to die on another night.

But tonight, Winter was quiet. Tonight, Winter had no strength to fight.

Finally, thankfully, the Bel Air Patrol pulled to a stop at the brightly lighted Emergency Room entrance. Allison pulled herself gratefully from her dark thoughts and rushed inside to be with Winter. She cuddled Bobbi and told the senior on-call resident what she knew about her friend's illness, while a junior resident and two nurses were in a curtained room with Winter.

"She said it was a virus."

"What were her symptoms?"

"She didn't really say, except that she was tired and hadn't been doing sit-ups because her muscles ached."

"Aching muscles?"

"Yes."

"Anything else, Allison, anything at all?"

Allison tugged briefly at her lip. It seemed irrelevant, private. In fact, she was surprised Winter had even mentioned it to her.

"Winter said she was just finishing her period."

At that moment, the junior resident appeared from behind the curtain.

"Her shock is responding to fluids and pressors. The room air blood gasses are pending, but I put her back on oxygen because she was cyanotic."

"OK. Good. This is her friend."

The junior resident turned to Allison.

"Was she lying in the sun today?"

"I'm sure she wasn't. Winter never lies in the sun."

"Allison says Winter just finished her period."

The two men looked at each other and exchanged knowing nods. Allison guessed that the answers she had given were simply the final pieces in a jigsaw puzzle for which the picture was already clear.

"You think it's T.S.S.," the senior resident said to the junior resident.

"It all fits."

"T.S.S.?" Allison asked.

"Toxic Shock Syndrome," the senior resident replied. "We're going to take Winter upstairs now, Allison. She'll be in the Medical ICU."

The residents disappeared behind the curtain with Winter, where they needed to be. Allison remained in the corridor and was soon approached by the E.R. administrator, who needed her help to complete the paperwork. The administrator led Allison to a cubicle near the entrance of the Emergency Room.

"Who is to be listed as her Legal Next of Kin?"

In August, on the night Bobbi was born, Allison had provided that information without hesitation: Lawrence Carlyle.

But now?

Now Allison was *holding* Winter's Legal Next of Kin in her arms. Allison kissed Bobbi's silky black hair. *Oh, little Bobbi!*

After the paperwork was complete, Allison asked directions to the Medical ICU.

"The baby can't go upstairs."

"Oh! All right."

Allison called her parents. In fifteen minutes, Sean and Patricia arrived at the Emergency Room parking lot to collect the quiet, precious bundle.

"How is Winter?"

"I haven't been able to go upstairs. I'm really afraid—"

"She'll be all right, Allison," Patricia Fitzgerald interjected firmly. "We'll get Bobbi tucked in, then one of us will be back."

"OK. Mother, I think Bobbi only nurses."

"Allison, your father and I can handle this." Patricia smiled lovingly, remembering for a moment how much she and Sean had loved caring for their own infant daughter. Patricia looked into that beloved daughter's jade-green eyes now and saw such heart-stopping worry, such strain, such confusion. She added gently, "One of us will be back to be with you, Allison. In the meantime, you should think about who needs to be called. Peter, of course. And maybe Lawrence?"

After her parents left with Bobbi, Allison went to the Medical ICU. The senior resident told her that Winter's condition was guarded. He, too, asked ominously if there was anyone who should be notified.

Allison sat in the Waiting Room and considered the question. Who needed to know?

Peter? Peter, who cared about Winter. Peter, who had gently helped Winter discover her remarkable talent and had carefully kept the secret about her pregnancy and who, perhaps, had even saved her life. No, *that* Peter did not exist. He never had.

Lawrence? Winter had told Allison that Lawrence and Margaret and "the boys"—as Winter fondly called them— were in a remote corner of India making another block-buster. Allison didn't have the energy to begin the long search for Lawrence tonight. Perhaps tomorrow. Perhaps— *yes!*—it wouldn't be necessary to reach Lawrence at all, because Winter would be fine.

Mark? Mark needed to know. Allison didn't even question the decision. Tonight her own world of love had been brutally shattered. With every ounce of her being, with all of her heart, Allison had believed in her magical love with Peter, but now she knew she was wrong; it had all been merely a horrible illusion. Mark and Winter believed their magical love had been just an illusion, but wasn't that *wrong,* too?

On a night when everything else was *so wrong* and *so evil,* calling Mark because of Winter felt *so right* and *so good.*

Allison dialed Directory Assistance in Boston. When Mark didn't answer his home phone number, she called the operator at Massachusetts General Hospital. Yes, Dr. Stephens was on call, in the Emergency Ward. She would connect the call.

Mark glanced at the institutional clock in the E.W. nurses' station. It was six A.M. His twenty-four-hour shift would end in one hour. The E.W. was quiet now, at last, and Mark had only one more chart to complete.

Mark sighed softly. He was very tired.

"Long night, Mark." Jill, one of the three night shift nurses, smiled and gently touched his shoulder.

Mark returned the smile but not the touch.

"Dr. Stephens, call on line one," a voice announced over the intercom that linked the nurses' station to the triage desk.

"Maybe the long night's not over yet," Mark said as he depressed the blinking button of the phone beside him. "This is Dr. Stephens."

"Mark, it's Allison Fitzgerald."

"Allison, what's wrong?"

"Winter was just admitted to UCLA. They think she has Toxic Shock Syndrome."

A thousand questions bombarded Mark's mind, instinctive medical questions, sophisticated clues to the severity of Winter's illness. What is her blood pressure? Her platelet count? Her BUN? Her arterial oxygen content? Her protime? Those were medical questions Allison couldn't answer. But there was one question Allison could answer, and it would tell Mark what he needed to know.

"Did Winter ask you to call me?" *Please. Please have her be well enough to have asked!*

"No, Mark, she didn't. She's too sick."

"I'll be there, Allison. I'm on my way. Please tell her that. And, Allison, please tell her that I love her."

Chapter Thirty

Seven hours later, Mark told Winter himself. He whispered the words against her feverish temple as a chorus of beeps played in the background.

"I love you, Winter. I wanted to ask you to marry me last March, but it seemed so selfish and you seemed . . . But were you acting? Were you *playing* with me the one time it really mattered not to play? Yes, I was playing, too, pretending it was best. But it *wasn't* best. At least, it hasn't been best for me."

Mark gazed at Winter's motionless body, her closed eyes and long black eyelashes that didn't even flicker. Could she hear him? *Please* . . .

"Would you like to hear my plan?" Mark asked hopefully. Winter's lifeless body gave no reply, but he continued as if she heard every loving word, "OK, here it is. I have survived the past few months by promising myself a wonderful reward on New Year's Day—a gift to me on your birthday. I was going to call you then—find you, wherever you were filming—and ask if we could spend my vacation, two weeks in February, together. If you said yes, I might have even asked you then and there—because I couldn't wait—if you would spend more than my vacation with me, if you would spend your life. Winter, darling, I can finish my residency here, in LA, and you can do your movies. I don't think my parents ever had as much love as we have. I don't think *anyone* ever has, do you? I know we can make it work, if it's what you want, too. So, you didn't have to get sick to get my attention, you've always had it. Oh, Winter, my darling Winter."

Winter's eyes fluttered. Her long dark lashes trembled and her violet eyes opened briefly.

"Mark. You need to know about Bobbi." Winter's whisper ended in a gasp, frantic gulps for air, and her pink lips quickly turned deep blue.

The residents and nurses rushed in, signalled by the heart rate monitor that started racing as Winter's breathing failed.

"It could be fluid overload."

"Or ARDS. She was hypoxemic on room air on admission, but her saturation has been fine on nasal prongs."

"It's not fine anymore. Whatever the cause, she needs to be intubated *now.*"

Mark listened but didn't participate. He knew the words of his colleagues were correct and that their plan — to put a tube in Winter's throat and allow a ventilator to breathe for her — was necessary and appropriate.

All Mark could think was *Please help her. Please care for her as you would care for someone you love. She is who I love . . . so very much.*

Mark held Winter's hand during the intubation. Her hand was lifeless, because she had been given curare to paralyze her temporarily, so that she couldn't struggle as the cold steel blade of the laryngoscope pressed against the delicate tissues of her throat.

Don't hurt her! Mark watched in horror as the steel blade arched Winter's long, lovely neck to allow passage of the endotracheal tube into her larynx. The doctors were doing everything correctly, but *still.*

As Mark watched, he fought the facts that bombarded his brain, facts about Toxic Shock Syndrome, facts he had learned, memorized, always got *right* on the big tests. Young women—young *healthy* women—die of Toxic Shock. The ones who die are like Winter, ones whose illness was caught too late, after the lungs and kidneys and liver and bone marrow had been assaulted by the toxin for too long.

The hope—the only hope—was *aggressive* support. Aggressive . . . cold steel in her lovely throat, machines to control her breathing, needles in her veins dripping in medicines to keep her out of shock, all that modern medicine had to offer.

What could Mark offer?

Only his love.

When Mark left Winter's room to give the ICU nurses a chance to perform their many tasks, he found Allison in the waiting room.

"How is she, Mark?"

"She's on a ventilator, which is probably better for her. This way, she can get more rest, not expend energy struggling to breathe."

Allison nodded.

Mark and Allison were alone in the waiting room. Mark thought someone else, someone whose name Winter had made such an effort to speak, would be there, too.

"Where is Bob, Allison?" Mark asked finally.

"Bob?"

"Winter just spoke his name. I assume he is her new love." *I assume Winter heard my words of love and wanted to give me her answer: Mark, there is someone else.*

"Mark, what exactly did Winter say?"

"She said, 'You need to know about Bob—Bobby.' "

"You do need to know, Mark."

429

"Can you tell me?"

"I think you and Bobbi should meet. Come with me."

"I don't want to leave Winter."

"We won't be far, just at my parents' house in Bel Air. We can leave the number. It's important, Mark."

"Hello, Mark," Patricia Fitzgerald smiled warmly, trying to ease the heart-stopping worry in his tired eyes. "How is Winter?"

Patricia would have been at the hospital every minute with Winter, but she had a precious little life to care for here.

"Stable," Mark answered, instinctively trying to reassure. But his mind taunted, *Stable?* Not really. The emergency intubation was a huge setback.

"Mother, we're here to see Bobbi."

Good, Patricia thought.

"In your bedroom, sleeping."

Allison led the way. When they reached the open door, Allison stood aside to let Mark enter. Bobbi was lying on her stomach on the bed, in a soft cradle of feather pillows, sleeping peacefully, beautifully, her tiny delicate lips curled in a soft smile.

"Allison?" Tears filled Mark's eyes as he asked the question.

"We call her Bobbi, but her real name is Roberta, after her grandmother." Allison's voice broke as her own tears spilled.

Mark awakened Bobbi gently and held her close against his heaving chest. Bobbi cooed, intrigued with his warmth and his eyes, unconcerned about the hot tears that splashed on her head as he nuzzled against her.

Allison withdrew to give Mark privacy for his tears and joined her mother in the kitchen. When Mark finally reappeared, he was carrying Bobbi.

Patricia smiled and teased very gently, "Mark, it took me an hour to convince Bobbi to close her sapphire eyes."

"It's very nice of you to have taken care of her," Mark murmured. Bobbi was his daughter, his responsibility now. Mark needed to assume care of Bobbi, and he needed to be with Winter. His tired mind had not yet decided how he would manage both.

Patricia looked at Mark's exhausted, worried eyes.

"Mark, leave Bobbi with me. I love taking care of her. Why don't you plan to stay here, too?"

"I can call my mother."

"Fine. I would love to meet her. Please tell her that she'll stay here, too. That way, she and I can take turns watching Bobbi and visiting Winter, OK?" Patricia was planning to insist no matter what the fatigued sapphire eyes replied.

"Yes. Thank you," Mark whispered. "Thank you."

On the third day, Winter squeezed the strong hand that had held hers almost without pause; on the fourth day, her blood pressure maintained itself without medications; on the fifth day, the tube came out of her throat and she began to give Mark the answers to all his questions, to whisper to him all the loving words he had whispered to her, over and over, for the past five days.

"I love you, Mark."

"Do you know how angry I am with you?" Mark asked lovingly.

"Yes, you've been telling me." Winter smiled. Mark had scolded, as Winter had scolded Allison years before when she lay in the coma, loving, frightened scolding. *Don't you dare leave me, Winter! How could you imagine I didn't love you or want you? Were you ever going to tell me about Bobbi?* "I probably would have lasted until about my birthday, too. Then I

431

would have called you. I thought about it all the time, wondering—"

Mark stopped her words with his lips, kissing her for a long, tender moment, showing her, then finally telling her, "Never wonder again."

"I won't."

"The residency director says they'll have a place for me here beginning in July."

"Bobbi and I want to move to Boston."

"This is something we have to talk about."

"Yes." Winter smiled. "Will you call me the second you get to Boston?"

"Of course." Mark kissed her again, a good-bye kiss; he had a plane to catch. "You'll know it's me because the first words you hear will be I love you."

"Oh, Mark, I love you, too."

Winter was discharged from UCLA after eight days. She and Bobbi returned to the mansion; Roberta Stephens returned to San Francisco; and Winter and Mark made forever plans in soft whispers three thousand miles apart.

Three days after Winter returned home, she and Allison sat in the kitchen of the mansion on Bellagio.

"What's wrong with you and Peter, Allison?" Winter asked. "Don't say 'nothing,' because you look like death and Peter sounds like death."

"You've talked to him?"

"Not about what's wrong. Peter won't talk about it. He has called several times to see how I am. He won't talk about what's wrong, Allison, but he asks about you all the time."

"What do you tell him?"

"The truth. That you look terrible. Lost. Sad." Winter paused, then asked gently, "Allison, can't you tell me? Can't you let me help you?"

"No, Winter, I can't talk about it."

"Another famous momentous and unchallengable decision?"

"Winter —"

"I'm sorry," Winter whispered swiftly, softly, as she saw the sudden tears in Allison's haunted, uncertain eyes. The familiar look of serious determination — the look of a champion who made momentous, solid gold decisions — was gone. Allision looked bewildered, the way she had after the accident when she realized she had lost her dream. "Allison, I just can't imagine what could have happened between you and Peter. You two were — *are* — so much in love. I know it isn't someone else, because you both are suffering. Can't you tell me? Maybe, if you talk about it, it won't seem quite as bad."

"Winter, I can't," Allison whispered. *I can't tell you, because it is unimaginable.*

Unimaginable, except that now Allison could force her mind to imagine it. She could recall the vivid memory of the nightmare of the evil Harlequin, a memory that was new and fresh, renewed every night, tormenting, driving her to gasping wakefulness in the rare exhausted moments when she finally fell asleep.

Allison could imagine it — a surreal fantasy — but her defiant heart refused to *believe* it.

And yet, there it was, a huge, sinister wall, built with rock-solid incriminating bricks of facts . . .

Peter hid his marriage until he was forced to tell her because of Love.

Peter hid his relationship with Rob, even though he knew Rob and Allison were friends.

Peter promised no more secrets, and that had been a lie.

From the very beginning, Peter Dalton had kept dark secrets, hiding the truth, revealing little bits only when he was forced to.

Why? Allison demanded of the massive wall of incriminating facts.

Why else? the answer bounced back again and again, *Because he is guilty, because he is the evil Harlequin.*

Allison knew how champions flew over jumps that seemed impossibly high and impossibly dangerous: *You make the place beyond the jump a place you want to be.* And she knew how she had landed safely every time except one: *You send your dreams over first, then simply follow after them.*

Allison didn't know what lay beyond the monstrous wall. Was it where she wanted to be? Did her dream—her love with Peter—exist there?

Allison couldn't find the answers by herself, and she knew that Winter couldn't help her find them, either.

Only Peter could answer the unanswerable questions.

Allison needed to hear Peter's answers. She *would* hear them. She would go to New York, look into his dark eyes, and hear what he had to say. That was the only momentous decision Allison could make, and it wasn't even a decision because her heart gave her no choice. It wasn't a *decision,* Allison realized, but it was *momentous,* because . . .

Was she planning a rendezvous with a murderer?

Or a rendezvous with the man she loved?

As they walked, fingers entwined, beneath the lighted marquee of the Via Condetti Cinema in Rome, Emily slowed. *Love* was playing.

"Who did you see *Love* with, Rob?" Emily asked with a gentle tease. It didn't matter; Emily was so sure of Rob's wonderful love.

Emily expected a handsome, sheepish grin, but she saw something else, an unfamiliar expression, unfamiliar and uninterpretable.

"Rob?"

"I haven't seen *Love*."

"Really? Then let's see it together. Now." Emily tugged gently on his hand, but Rob didn't move and his eyes became stormy.

"No, Emily. I won't ever see *Love*."

"Rob? What's the matter? Please tell me."

Rob took her hand, and as they walked around Rome, retracing the steps he and Sara had taken the February before she died, he told Emily everything. He had already told Emily about his beloved sister who had died of diabetes, but it had been the story of Sara, of her life and of her loveliness, not of her death. That she had died so young was sad, tragic, enough. Emily didn't need to hear the tormenting truths of how, why Sara had died.

But now Rob told her everything.

"I don't believe Peter would have harmed her," Emily said when Rob finished. Emily surprised herself with the confidence of her voice, and she surprised and worried Rob with the words.

"*Peter?*" Rob asked. "You *know* him?"

"Peter and Allison—"

"Oh my God."

"I don't know him, Rob, not really. I just have one memory of him. Peter drove me to the airport the day I moved to Paris. I was very frightened. I think Peter sensed my fear and wanted to help. He *did* help. He was very kind." Emily smiled lovingly. "Peter Dalton reminded me of you, Rob, and it gave me such hope."

Rob's mind swirled. Sara had told him how alike he and Peter were, but his sister had been horribly, *fatally* wrong! No two men on earth could have been more different.

"When I was in the embassy," Emily began quietly, "I had to find ways to convince myself to stay alive. I could have died so easily, Rob. I could have gotten them to turn their

435

weapons on me. I thought about it."

"Emily . . ."

"But," Emily continued softly, "three days before I was taken hostage, I saw *Love.* I kept myself alive in the embassy by replaying *Love,* over and over in my mind, imagining that *we* were the lovers, Rob, you and I. Doing that, thinking about *Love* and about us, saved me. *Love* is Peter's movie, Peter's vision, Peter's gift. I just can't believe—"

"Peter Dalton is evil, Emily," Rob interjected flatly. He added gently, "You of all people should know about evil men."

"You really believe Peter murdered Sara?"

Rob considered Emily's question for several moments before answering.

"Just after Sara died, when I was so emotional and so angry, and my mother was so convinced, I did believe it," Rob answered finally. "As time passed, as rationality replaced emotion, I decided it hadn't been *intentional,* just negligent, the carelessness of a self-absorbed man. I *blamed* Peter for Sara's death, but I didn't believe he killed her. But now . . ."

"Because of me—" Emily whispered softly, "because of me you have learned new things about cruelty."

It was true. Knowing Emily—what had been done to Emily—had taught Rob about ugliness of the soul he had never imagined existed. But he had learned even more from his beloved Emily. . . .

"Because of you, darling Emily, I have learned new things about love."

Rob and Emily sat in silence, surrounded by the noises of Rome at twilight, the harsh blare of horns in rush-hour traffic and the soft, peaceful splash of fountains where wishes made are destined to come true.

"Rob," Emily spoke finally, "I know about evil men. I don't believe Peter Dalton is one of them."

436

"He's very clever, very devious."

Emily thought for a long time before speaking again, and when she did, she spoke from a deep corner of her soul.

"Do you trust me, Rob?"

"Of course I do."

"I have trusted you with my life," Emily whispered. "Every part of me, nothing hidden."

"I know, darling."

Emily met his ocean-blue eyes.

"Come see *Love* with me, Rob."

"Emily . . ."

"Trust me, Rob." Trust *me*.

After seeing *Love,* Rob and Emily wandered the streets of Rome in wordless silence, she afraid, he tormented. On a January night not too long ago, Rob had followed Emily around Paris, feeling so helpless yet wanting so desperately to protect her from her demons.

And tonight, Emily had loosed Rob's demons, the years of hatred that gnawed destructively at his heart.

I'm sorry, Rob, Emily thought as she watched eyes that didn't seem to see her, tormented, confused, stormy eyes. *I thought it might help.*

When Rob spoke, finally, as dawn yellowed the autumn sky, his voice was soft and bewildered.

"Is it possible that Peter really did love her?" Rob had seen what Emily had only guessed. *Love* was intensely personal, and the lovely, loving, *loved* Julia was really Sara.

"Why isn't that possible, Rob?"

"Because, if Peter loved Sara so much, he would never have let her become pregnant."

"Maybe Sara wanted to be pregnant. Maybe it was *her* decision."

"Emily, you're saying Sara had a death wish."

"No, my darling," Emily answered softly. *She knew about the wish to live and the wish to die.* "Not a death wish, Rob, a *life* wish; a wish to be just like everybody else."

Chapter Thirty-one

It was raining when Allison arrived in New York. The rain reminded Allison of happier times . . . a joyous, loving champagne brunch on a soggy gray day . . . rain-soaked curls tenderly dried . . . wet silk and lace gently removed by strong hands trembling with desire.

The rain reminded Allison of love.

But it was cold tonight, and dark, and the love was lost somewhere in darkness.

Allison hadn't told Peter she was coming. When she arrived at his apartment in Chelsea at nine P.M., Allison saw no ribbon of light beneath the door. Where was he? At the theater, perhaps, although his role in Shakespeare on Broadway was virtually over. This was the week—the wonderful, happy week—when Peter should have been packing, tying up loose ends, and, in two days, moving to LA to be with her *forever.*

Allison knocked on the apartment door, not expecting an answer, wondering if she would let herself in if Peter weren't there.

But Peter was there, in the darkness.

"Allison. Come in."

Allison gazed into the darkness before entering. She saw shapes—partially packed boxes that would already have been shipped, if only . . . And she saw a small shadow—Muffin. But Muffin didn't wiggle with excitement or bound gleefully to Allison as usual. Muffin sensed the sadness. For the past eleven days, she had lived again in the once-familiar, long-forgotten silence of death.

As Allison walked inside, Peter turned on a small lamp, took her rain-wet coat, and looked at her damp red-gold curls.

"Would you like a towel for your hair?" he asked gently, sadly, remembering, as she did, the other time her rain-damp curls had needed to be dried and how those moments had flowed into wonderful loving and joyous love.

"No, thank you." Allison walked into the tiny living room and sat on the couch. She hadn't looked into Peter's dark eyes — she couldn't — but as he had taken her coat, Allison had seen the anguish on his strained, handsome face. Anguish, sleeplessness, pain. "Peter, please tell me what happened to Sara."

Peter sat in a chair across from her, staring at jade eyes that wouldn't meet his, and started the story from the very beginning.

"Did you have a forest-green Volkswagen bug?" Allison asked, interrupting him as he told her about the spring he and Sara met and fell in love while they created a rose garden.

"Yes. How did you know that, Allison?"

"I knew Sara, Peter. I was at Greenwich Academy that year, Sara's senior year. She used to watch me ride every day at noon, until spring." *Until she fell in love with you.* Allison remembered the joy on Sara's face, the soft pink radiance, the ocean-blue glow as Sara got into the battered VW with the man she loved.

"You knew Sara," Peter whispered with disbelief. Then, remembering too, he added quietly, "You were the girl with the flame-colored hair, the champion rider. Sara loved watching you ride. She said you looked so free, so happy as you floated over the jumps. It was because of you, Allison, that Sara and I took riding lessons in Central Park."

"Peter, please tell me what happened," Allison whispered after a moment. She heard such love in Peter's voice, a loving memory of Sara *and* love for the girl with the flame-colored hair. *Tell me, Peter, please. If there is a way to make this right* . . .

Allison listened in silence as quietly, softly, Peter told her *everything.* His deep, gentle voice took Allison on an emotional journey back in time, to a time when there had been great love and great joy . . . and then great sadness.

Peter told Allison of Sara's wish to be free, to have what little control she could have over the disease that would kill her; and of his promise to Sara to let her be free; and of his own fear and his own battles, as he kept that promise by fighting his own desperate desire to protect her and keep her safe, always.

Peter whispered, so softly, that he had almost believed Sara's diabetes was *cured.* But then, beginning in the last year of her life, Sara had looked very ill, as if she were dying. And then, two months before she went to Rome, as if by a miracle, it all changed again. Sara looked wonderful, radiant, healthy, happy. Her pregnancy—the pregnancy she had planned and wanted—gave her such energy and such hope.

Peter paused, then quietly he told Allison how Sara had died, quickly, peacefully, smiling as she lovingly asked him to make even *more* promises.

Peter stopped speaking, because Sara had died and his story was over.

"Sara *was* dying, Peter," Allison whispered finally, lost in the memories, vaguely aware that she knew parts of the story that Peter didn't. Hadn't Peter even known Sara was dying? Did he believe Sara might still be alive if only he had *protected* her? Did that add even more torment to the guilt he already felt?

Guilt. Allison heard the guilt and self-recrimination in his quiet voice. But now she knew the truth. And she

441

knew that Peter Dalton was guilty of only one thing.

And it was not a crime.

"You loved Sara too much," Allison whispered. *You are only guilty of a generous, unselfish, limitless love.* Her jade eyes found his at last.

Peter's tired, anguished mind searched for words that would admit *that* crime—his only crime—and allow his love with Allison to survive and flourish still.

Peter's search was interrupted, the silence shattered, by the ringing of the telephone.

Allison was closest to the harsh intrusion. She answered it—Peter's apartment used to be a place where the phone rang for her, too—by reflex, and also to stop the ringing.

"Hello?"

"Allison? This is Rob."

"*Rob.*"

"Allison, I need to speak to Peter. It's a personal matter."

"I know about Sara, Rob. I knew her. I was at Greenwich Academy. I should have told you."

"You were at Greenwich?"

"Yes, for a year, Sara's senior year. Sara used to—"

"—watch you ride, at noon, in the stable," Rob whispered. *You are the lovely young girl who was so nice to my sister!*

"Yes. Rob, I know everything. I know what your family, and maybe you, believes happened. But Peter didn't harm Sara. He never would have harmed her." Allison's eyes filled with tears and her voice trembled. "Rob, Peter loved Sara very, very much."

"Is Peter there, Allison? May I speak with him?"

Allison placed her hand over the receiver and looked questioningly at Peter.

"He wants to speak with you, Peter."

Peter didn't want to talk to Rob. Peter wanted, *needed,* to talk to Allison, only to Allison. Her soft words to Rob echoed in his mind—*Peter didn't harm Sara. Peter never would have harmed her*—and gave him such hope.

Peter didn't want to talk to Rob, but he had made a promise, and now Rob was calling him, and maybe lovely Allison had made a way for them to speak, to *talk*, at last.

Once, Allison had planned to proudly, happily, *joyfully* introduce her dear friend Rob to her beloved Peter. Now wasn't a time of great joy, but this was an introduction of sorts, a beginning, and Allison was the link, the connection, between these two strong men. Rob was her dear friend and Peter was her beloved, and she believed in them both.

Peter took the phone from Allison's hand and breathed without emotion, "Rob."

"Thank you for taking my call, Peter," Rob began, realizing it was more than *he* had been willing to do. And, when Rob finally had agreed to speak to Peter, he hadn't listened. He had only delivered a promise of a forever hatred. "I will understand if you don't tell me. Perhaps I have no right to ask."

"Sara told me about her pregnancy after she returned from Rome, Rob," Peter quietly answered the question he knew Rob was going to ask. "She was thrilled about it. It was what she wanted, what she planned. I know you blame me, Rob. I blame myself."

"Sara wanted us to be friends, Peter," Rob's voice was shaky with emotion.

"Yes, she did."

In the long silence that followed, both men had the same thought: *I don't know if it is possible for us to be friends.* And both had the same remarkable feeling, the exhilarating feeling of hope as the deep strangling roots of hatred in their hearts began to die.

Two houses, both alike in dignity . . .

Maybe it was impossible for these two proud, strong men to ever be friends—and maybe not; time would tell. But, at least, they would no longer be bitter enemies. It was a start, a beginning of the promise each had made to

Sara.

"Sometime, Peter," Rob spoke finally, "Perhaps you and Allison would have dinner with us?"

"Yes . . . perhaps . . . sometime."

The call ended without specific plans, but for the first time, it ended without hatred and rage.

After he hung up, Peter stared at the phone for several moments, calming himself, recovering, feeling the immense unburdening as hatred retreated from his heart. Then he heard a soft sound and looked up.

Allison was getting her soggy raincoat from the closet. *Allison was leaving.*

When Allison reached the door, about to leave, about to return to the rain and cold and darkness, Peter's voice broke the stillness.

Peter's voice . . . a bewildered whisper of despair.

"Allison, you don't believe me!"

Allison spun, startled. Her jade eyes gazed at him with confusion and surprise.

"What, Peter?"

"You told Rob that you believed I loved Sara and that I would never have harmed her. But you don't believe it." Peter whispered hoarsely, "You believe I murdered Sara."

"Peter, *no.* I don't believe that." *I believe you loved Sara so much . . . too much . . . forever.*

"Then why are you leaving, Allison?"

Because I don't belong here. Allison's thought came swiftly, confidently, filling her eyes with bewildered sadness.

Peter saw the sadness and the lost, bewildered look, and he realized what was happening.

Allison was leaving him so that he could be with Sara. Peter had taken Allison on the voyage into his past and she was still there, lost in *his* memories of love.

Make new memories with me, Allison!

Peter moved to her and took her hands in his. Then, so gently, he carefully began another journey with Allison, *their* journey, a journey into the present and the future. Peter spoke softly, lovingly, about *their* joyous forever love.

"Do you remember when I called you that night, Allison? Eleven nights ago? I told you I had a wonderful surprise. Would you like to hear about it now?"

"What? Oh. Yes."

"I bought Bellemeade. I bought Bellemeade for us, darling, so we can live and love in that enchanted romantic place forever. I'm moving to Los Angeles, to Bel Air, to be with you always. I will write screenplays—only happy ones if that's what you want. And I think I will begin a theater company—Shakespeare in Westwood, something like that. Muffin will get to be the California girl she really is."

Peter paused. Was Allison listening? Was she hearing his soft words of love? Muffin was listening. Muffin heard her name and Peter's gentle tone, and her blond head cocked, a small tilt of hope.

"Allison?"

Peter gazed into Allison's lovely jade eyes. She still wasn't completely with him; she was still a little lost in distant memories, but less lost, less bewildered. Allison was finding her way back to him, to their love, guided unerringly by his loving voice and by the fiery beacons of her own heart.

"Allison? Darling?" *Come with me, Allison. Be with me in our wonderful love.*

"Yes?" Allison's eyes began to focus. "Yes, Peter?"

"Do you know why I told you I wouldn't watch you jump the green and white railed jump?"

"No, Peter. Why?"

"Because I love you too much, Allison. Because I couldn't stand the thought of losing you. It's a selfish reason." Peter whispered quietly. "If you really want to jump again, I'll be there with you."

"I don't want to jump anymore, Peter. It isn't important," Allison answered swiftly. She smiled then, and the magnificent jade was suddenly clear and bright and sparkling with love. She asked softly, "Do you want to know why?"

"Yes, darling. Tell me."

"Because I love you too much, too."

WATCH FOR THESE ZEBRA REGENCIES